Her Enemy With Benefits

NICOLA MARSH
NIKKI LOGAN
NINA HARRINGTON

MILLS

First Published in Great Britain 2016
By Mills & Boon, an imprint of HarperCollins*Publishers*
1 London Bridge Street, London, SE1 9GF

HER ENEMY WITH BENEFITS © 2016 Harlequin Books S. A.

Her Deal With The Devil, *My Boyfriend and Other Enemies* and *Blind Date Rivals* were first published in Great Britain by Harlequin (UK) Limited.

Her Deal With The Devil © 2013 Nicola Marsh
My Boyfriend and Other Enemies © 2013 Nikki Logan
Blind Date Rivals © 2011 Nina Harrington

ISBN: 978-0-263-92076-5

05-0816

Our policy is to use papers that are natural, renewable and recyclable products and made from wood grown in sustainable forests.The logging and manufacturing processes conform to the legal environmental regulations of the country of origin.

Printed and bound in Spain
by CPI, Barcelona

HER DEAL WITH THE DEVIL

BY
NICOLA MARSH

Nicola Marsh has always had a passion for writing and reading. As a youngster she devoured books when she should have been sleeping and later kept a diary whose contents could be an epic in itself!

These days, when she's not enjoying life with her husband and sons in her home city of Melbourne, she's at her computer, creating the romances she loves in her dream job.

Visit Nicola's website at www.nicolamarsh.com for the latest news of her books.

For my nan, who I miss more than words can say.
Your support for my writing meant so much.
You'll live in my heart for ever.

CHAPTER ONE

SAPPHIRE INTERLOCKED HER fingers and stretched overhead, savouring the slight twinge between her shoulder blades. The twinge was good. It meant her muscles were functioning, which was more than she'd been able to say a few months ago.

But she wouldn't go there. Not today.

Today was all about relaxation and easing back into work. Minimal stress. Positive thoughts. Focus.

She tilted her face to the Melbourne summer sun, enjoying the rays' warm caress.

She should have done this more often. Then maybe she wouldn't have ended up at the brink of collapse and almost losing her cherished family business.

If it hadn't been for her younger sister Ruby… Her shoulder muscles spasmed and she lowered her arms, shook them out, using the relaxation techniques she'd learned during her enforced three month R&R at Tenang, the retreat that had nursed her weary body back to health.

She couldn't afford to get uptight. Not with so much at stake. Not when she had so much to prove in facing her nemesis tomorrow.

With hands on hips she twisted from the waist, deliberately loosening her spine. Some of the tension eased and she closed her eyes, breathed deep. In. Out.

Calm thoughts. Zen. Centred. Relaxed.

'Never thought I'd see the day when the great Sapphire Seaborn connected with her inner yoga chick.'

That voice. No way.

Her eyes snapped open and her Zen evaporated just like that.

Patrick Fourde. Here. In the tiny backyard behind the Seaborn showroom. Seeing her in daggy pink yoga pants, purple crop top and hair snagged in the morning mail's elastic band; not in the fabulous designer outfit she'd planned to wow him with tomorrow.

Freaking hell.

She could feel the blood rush to her face. A virtual red flag to her mortification. Considering their past, she'd be damned if she let him know how truly flustered she was.

The guy had made her last year of high school a living hell and she'd rather grind coal to diamonds with her teeth than work with him now. But she had no choice. She had to reaffirm her leadership of the company. Had to prove she could handle the job physically. Had to ensure she never came that close to losing it again.

She strolled towards him, stopping about a foot away. Close enough to see tiny flecks of cobalt in a sea of grey. His eyes reminded her of a mood stone: bright and electric when he was revved, cool and murky when he had his game face on. Like now.

Lucky for him she'd wised up since high school and could outplay him. Never again would the cocky rebel get the jump on her.

'Was there a problem with our meeting time?'

He grinned—the same wicked quirk of his lips that had driven her batty during Year 12 Biology—and leaned against the doorjamb.

'No problem. I happened to be in the area. Thought I'd drop by for old times' sake.'

This wasn't how she'd envisaged their first meeting after ten years. Not at all.

She didn't like being on the back foot. Not around him. Not when she needed to convince him Fourde Fashion couldn't live without Seaborns' fabulous gems for the upcoming Melbourne Fashion Week.

'Or maybe I couldn't wait 'til tomorrow to see you?'

There it was: the legendary charm. What had it taken? All of five seconds for him to revert to type?

Pity her opinion of the silver-spooned, recalcitrant playboy hadn't changed over the years.

Indulged. Spoiled. Never worked a day in his life. Everything she'd despised in the rich guys she'd grown up with at the private school she'd attended. The type of guys who thought they could snap their fingers and have a harem falling at their feet.

Not her. She'd save her seven veils for strangling him if he didn't agree to her business proposition.

'Still trying to get by on lame flirting?'

'Still the uptight, stuck-up prude?'

Ouch. That hurt. Especially as she wasn't the same person—not any more. Working her butt off to learn the family business, losing her mum and having a bruising brush with chronic fatigue syndrome had seen to that.

Besides, she'd never been stuck up or a prude. Uptight? Maybe. But he'd always brought out the worst in her. Riling her with his practised charm, swanning through high school with an entourage of popular kids, teasing her whenever he got a chance.

For some unfathomable reason he'd taken great delight in annoying the hell out of her during their study sessions, succeeding to the point where she'd been flustered and irritable.

The more she'd ignored him, or feigned indifference, the more he'd pushed, niggling until she snapped. Sadly, her cutting remarks would only spur him on, so she'd learned to curb her annoyance and focus on their assignments in the hope he'd get the message.

He hadn't.

She'd become an expert in patience, honing a cool tolerance in an effort to fight back her way.

Until the day she'd had no comeback.

The day he'd kissed her.

'Why are you really here, Patrick?'

'Honestly?'

She rolled her eyes. Did he even know the meaning of the word, with his glib lines and smooth charisma?

'I heard the rumours and wanted to see for myself.'

Uh-oh, this was worse than she'd thought.

She could handle him seeing her without make-up and in workout clothes. She couldn't handle him knowing about Seaborns' reputed financial woes. It would undermine everything and scuttle her entire plan before she'd had a chance to present it.

'You of all people should know better than to listen to a bunch of rumours.'

She attempted to brush past him but he snagged her arm. The zap of *something* was beyond annoying.

Ten years and he still had that effect on her? *Grow up.*

'The reports of my life in the media are highly exaggerated. How about you?'

She could try and outbluff him but, considering she had to meet him at his office tomorrow for the pitch of her life, it wouldn't be the smartest move.

'What have you heard?'

'That Seaborns has been doing it tough.'

'No tougher than most during an economic decline.'

A blatant lie. Not that she'd let him know. If her sister hadn't married mining magnate Jax Maroney the jewellery business that had been in their family for generations would have gone under.

And it would have been entirely Sapphie's fault. She'd been too busy playing superwoman, trying to juggle everything on her own, to let anyone close enough to help. Her stubborn independence had almost cost her the company and her health.

The bone-deep fatigue and aching muscles had scared her, but not as much as the thought that she'd almost failed in making good on her promise to her mum.

No way would she take the business so close to the edge again. She'd do whatever it took—including play nice with this guy.

'Really? Because the grapevine was abuzz with news of Ruby shacking up with Maroney to save Seaborns.'

Bunch of old busybodies— socialites who had nothing better to do than spend their lives sipping lattes, having mani/pedi combos at the latest exclusive day spa and maligning people.

She'd spent a lifetime cultivating friendships in the moneyed circles she'd grown up in, had made an effort out of respect for her mum with Seaborns' bottom line firmly in sight. Rich folk liked to be pandered to, and with the 'old school' mentality at work they stuck to their own. Which equated to them spending a small fortune on Seaborns jewellery.

But it was at times like this, when gossip spread faster than news of a designer sale, that she hated their group mentality.

'You heard wrong.'

She hated having to justify anything to him, but she knew how hard Ruby had fought for Seaborns and she'd do anything for her amazing sister and their company.

The fact that Patrick was partially right—Ruby *had* initially married Jax for convenience to save Seaborns—rankled. If they hadn't fallen head over heels Sapphie would have personally throttled her self-sacrificing sister for going to such lengths for their business.

'Ruby and Jax are madly in love. They can't keep their hands off each other.'

'Lucky them.'

His gaze dipped to her lips and she could have sworn they tingled in remembrance of how commanding his kiss had been for an eighteen-year-old…how he'd made her weak-kneed and dizzy with one touch of his tongue…how he'd made her lose control.

Her lips compressed at the memory. Damn hormones. Just because it had been over a year since she'd been with a guy it didn't mean she had to go all crazy remembering stuff from the past.

Or noticing the way his dark brown hair curled around his collar, too long for conventionality. Or the way stubble highlighted his strong jaw. Or how he never wore his top button done up, making the tanned V of skin a temptation to be touched.

Yep, damned hormones.

'You're flustered.' He took a step closer and it took all her willpower not to step back. 'Anything I can do to help?'

Oh, yeah. But she wasn't going there, and especially not with him.

Once she sealed this deal she needed a date. A hot guy with nothing on his mind but drizzled chocolate and a sleepless night.

As if she'd ever find a guy to live up to her fantasies. The guys she dated were staid, executive types on tight timelines who demanded little. Guys like her.

'Yeah, there is something you can do.' She met his gaze, determinedly ignoring the quiver in her belly that signalled Patrick Fourde would be the kind of guy to make all a girl's fantasies come true. 'Be prepared to be wowed by the best designs Seaborns has ever produced.'

He inclined his head, the sunlight picking up spun gold streaks. 'I'll keep an open mind.'

'That's all I'm asking for.'

'Pity.'

How one word could hold so much promise, so much sizzle, she'd never know. The guy had *suave* down to an art. He'd had that elusive something as a teen and it had evolved into a raw, potent sex appeal that disconcerted her.

Not that she couldn't handle him…it…whatever.

'Did that practised schmooze work for you in Europe?'

Those cobalt flecks flared and an answering lick of heat made her squirm. He didn't speak, and his silence unnerved her as much as the banked heat in his steady stare.

'Because personally it doesn't do much for me.'

'What does?'

'Pardon?'

'What *does* do it for you?' He leaned in deliciously, temptingly close and she held her breath. 'Because I'd *really* like to know.'

His breath fanned her ear, setting up a ripple effect as every nerve ending from her head to her toes zinged.

She could feel the heat radiating off him, could smell a delectable combination of crisp designer wool and French aftershave with a spicy undertone.

Heady. Tempting. Overwhelming.

Powerless to resist, she tilted her head a fraction, the tip of her nose within grazing distance of his neck.

And she breathed. Infusing her senses with him. Closed her eyes. Imagined for one infinitesimal moment what it would be like to close the gap between them and nuzzle his neck.

She had no idea how long they hovered a hair's breadth apart, the inch between their bodies vibrating with an undeniable energy.

'Hey, Saph, you out the back?'

She jumped, snagged her sneaker on a rock and stumbled. His hands shot out to grab her, anchoring her.

She should have been grateful. Instead, with his burning gaze fixed on her, a host of unasked questions she had no hope of answering flickering in the grey depths, she felt embarrassment burn her cheeks.

Patrick Fourde was the master of seduction. Always had been. It came as naturally to him as waking up in the morning. So why the heck was she responding to him on a level that defied explanation?

She couldn't be attracted to him.

Her business depended on it.

Besides, she didn't like him. She'd never liked him. He'd been a major pain in the ass during high school and by the way he'd breezed in here, determined to rile her, it looked as if nothing had changed.

For there was nothing surer—his turning up here today, twenty-four hours before their scheduled meeting, was nothing better than a ploy to unnerve her.

She might need his business, but working alongside him wouldn't be easy.

'Thanks,' she muttered, brushing off his hold in time to see Ruby propped in the doorway, a delighted grin matching the astute glint in her eyes.

'I didn't know you had company.' Ruby winked at Patrick. 'And such fine company at that.'

Debatable.

'Looking good, Rubes.' Patrick saluted her sister. 'Marriage suits you.'

'Thanks.' Ruby's assessing gaze swept over Patrick, and by her growing grin she approved of what she saw. 'Could say the same about you and Europe.'

'Paris is okay, but Melbourne can hold its own.' For some inexplicable reason he glanced her way. 'This city is filled with beauty.'

To her annoyance, Sapphie's blush intensified as Ruby stifled a guffaw.

'You're full of it,' Sapphie muttered under her breath. In

response, he snatched her hand and lifted it to his lips before she could react.

'Maybe so, but you missed me anyway.'

He kissed the back of her hand—a soft, butterfly brush of his lips that almost made her sigh. Almost.

'In your dreams.'

'Count on it,' he whispered, squeezing her hand before releasing it. 'See you tomorrow.'

Damn the man for doing it to her again. Deliberately taunting, trying to make her flustered—and succeeding. Her stupid hand still tingled where he'd kissed it. That whole in-her-face practised French charm…? Yet another of his tricks to tease her. What she couldn't understand was why. Was he trying to get her off-guard before their meeting tomorrow? Trying to disarm her and make her stuff up?

Whatever the answer, she mulled over it while watching one very fine ass as he farewelled Ruby and disappeared into Seaborns on his way out.

Ideally, she would have returned to her relaxation stretches to banish the disturbing sensations Patrick had elicited.

How many times had she done her best to ignore him in Biology, when her recalcitrant lab partner doodled rather than rote-learn the nerves in the human body, would deliberately distract her with stupid jokes, poke fun at everything from her ruled margins to her neat handwriting.

It made what had happened on graduation night all the more annoying, because it had been *him* she'd let her guard down around, *him* who'd been there to offer comfort, *him* who'd made her tingle all over just like the stupid buzz still zapping the skin on the back of her hand.

To add to her discomfort she now had to face a rampantly curious Ruby, who waited until he'd left before bounding towards her.

'Jeez. How seriously hot is Patrick now?'

Sapphie refrained from answering on the grounds that she might incriminate herself.

'I mean he was always hot, with that whole bad boy thing he had going on at school, but now?' Ruby fanned her face. 'He's a babe and he's totally into you.'

Sapphie shook her head and stuffed her hand into her pocket. 'You know better than that. The guy flirts all the time. It's his thing.'

Ruby shifted her weight from side to side, bouncing on the balls of her feet. 'Well, his thing is making you glow.'

'Bull.'

Ruby grabbed her arm and dragged her to a window. 'Go ahead. Look.'

Blowing out an exasperated breath, Sapphie glanced at the glass. Even through a film of dust and rain spots she could see pink cheeks and wide eyes. But it was the expression in those eyes, the glazed confusion of a thoroughly bamboozled woman, that sent her hopes of forgetting the past spiralling on a downward trajectory.

She might despise Patrick and all he stood for, but he appealed to her on some visceral level she had no hope of explaining.

It hadn't made sense back then and it sure as hell didn't make sense a decade later that the guy she could quite happily have strangled had *something* that made her want to explore beneath his flaky surface.

'Been a while since I've seen you look like this. A long while.' Ruby slung an arm across her shoulders and led her inside. 'Suits you.'

'I was doing a few yoga poses outside. That glow…? Must've caught too much sun.'

Ruby laughed and hugged her. 'You're cute when you're in denial.'

'Nothing to deny. Patrick and I will soon be colleagues, hopefully.'

If she hadn't botched it. First impressions counted in her business and considering he was CEO of Fourde Fashion's new Aussie branch, she'd hazard a guess they counted with him too.

Having him discover her in the tree pose, followed by the verbal sparring they'd always been unable to resist, didn't bode well.

At least she hadn't called him any nasty names—something she vaguely recalled doing just before their final exams, when he'd particularly annoyed her with his goofing off.

'Just colleagues, huh?' Ruby bustled into the tiny make-shift kitchen at the back of the showroom and flicked on the kettle. 'Wonder if he'll greet you with a kiss on the hand every day you work together?'

Sapphie's heart splatted at the thought. 'It's a French thing. Means nothing.'

'Hmm…' Ruby popped peppermint teabags into two mugs and propped herself against the bench as she waited for the kettle to boil. 'Wonder if that "thing" extends to French kissing?'

The nibble of a double-coated Tim Tam stuck in Sapphie's throat and she choked, coughing and spluttering, while Ruby poured boiling water into the mugs and grinned.

After a few thumps on her chest, which cleared her throat but did little for her pounding heart and the thought of getting anywhere near Patrick's lips again, Sapphie gratefully took the proffered tea.

'Considering I need to wow him with the presentation tomorrow, you're not helping.'

Ruby's smile waned. 'You're not getting too wound up about this, are you? Because Seaborns is doing okay since the auction and there's plenty of time for you to get back into the swing of things.'

Sapphie cradled her mug, savouring the warmth infusing her palms, and inhaled the fresh minty steam. A sixespressos-a-day gal, she'd never thought it possible she could become hooked on herbal alternatives. But her time out at Tenang had taught her many things—the importance of self-worth being one of the biggies.

She needed to do this, needed to secure Seaborns' future once and for all. Not from any warped sense of obligation to protect her little sister from the hardships of the family business. Not because of the promise she made to her mum on her deathbed.

For *her*. For Sapphire Seaborn, who loved this jewellery company and all it stood for, who secretly wanted her kids to run proudly along these polished floorboards one day, who wanted to prove to herself she didn't have to be a stress-head to be the best in this business and could physically handle the pressures of the only job she'd ever known—the job she valued above all else.

Her brush with chronic fatigue syndrome had left her weak and debilitated. She never wanted to feel that frail again. Ever.

Resuming her position as leader of Seaborns and doing a damn good job was more about proving to herself that she was past her vulnerabilities than anything else.

She had to test her physical capabilities, had to prove she could handle whatever the future held.

'You and Jax pulled off a coup with the auction. Proceeds are still coming in.'

Ruby shrugged, her bashful smirk not fooling Sapphie for a second. Her creative genius sister loved accolades, and the fact that every one of her signature Seaborn pieces had been snapped up at a recent gala auction had ensured orders flooded in. And kept Seaborns viable.

Something she now intended to do. Her way.

'We did okay.' A coy smile curved Ruby's lips. 'For two people who couldn't see what was right in front of their noses 'til it was almost too late.'

Even now Sapphie could hardly believe Ruby and Jax had

fallen in love and made their marriage real in every way that counted. The two were worlds apart yet they connected on a deep emotional level she sometimes envied.

What would it be like to be so into another person you were willing to tie yourself to them to life?

The way she was practically married to Seaborns, she'd probably never know.

'I'm so happy for you.' Sapphie's eyes misted over and she blamed it on the steam from her peppermint tea.

'Thanks, sis.' Ruby sipped at her tea before lowering it to pin her with a probing stare. 'So what are you going to do?'

'About?'

'Patrick Fourde.'

Damn, even hearing the guy's name made her belly knot with trepidation.

'I'm going to make him an offer he can't refuse.'

'Not about work.' Ruby rolled her eyes. 'About what I saw out the back.'

Sapphie didn't want to think about what had happened out the back. She didn't want to give credence to a single thing the flirtatious charmer had said or done.

She surreptitiously rubbed the back of her hand where the imprint from his lips lingered to prove it.

He'd been goading her like in the bad old days, nothing more. The fact she'd let him get to her—not good.

She was older and wiser now. Time to prove she could work with him without letting his deliberate barbs affect her.

'He could be good for you.' Ruby wound the end of her ponytail around her fingertip in the same absentminded way she did while pondering her next creation. 'Bit of fun. Nothing serious. Clear out the cobwebs, metaphorically speaking.'

Sapphie grabbed the nearest teatowel and chucked it at Ruby's head. Her sister ducked, laughing.

'You're right about me needing to date again but I wouldn't touch Patrick Fourde if he was the last guy on earth.'

Ruby smirked. 'Six-month supply of Tim Tams says you can't last a fortnight without getting up close and personal with the dishy Patrick.'

'Too easy.' Sapphie held out her hand to shake on the bet, looking forward to Ruby stocking her pantry with the irresistible rectangles of decadent chocolate. 'You're on.'

Patrick headed for the nearest café. He needed a caffeine shot. Fast. Maybe the jolt to his system would snap him out of his weird funk. A funk that had started around the time he'd laid eyes on Sapphire Seaborn again.

He shouldn't have come, he knew that, but he'd been unable to stay away.

The cool blonde had always had that effect on him. There'd been something about her in high school that had made him want to ruffle her poised, pristine exterior.

Rather than hating the way she'd turned up her pert nose, as if she had better things to do than hang out with him to study, he'd made it his personal mission to see how far he could push before she'd crack.

She never had, and seeing her name on his meeting manifesto was the reason he'd shown up today.

Curiosity. Was she still the same uptight prig? Would he be able to work with her? Seaborns were the best in Melbourne, and that was what he needed for his venture. But being stuck alongside Miss Prissy for the duration of the Fashion Week campaign wasn't his idea of fun.

Until he'd fired his first barb. She'd parried it and had unexpectedly catapulted him back in time. For some unknown, masochistic reason he'd wanted to annoy her all over again for the fun of it.

That kiss on the hand had done it too. He'd seen the initial flash of antagonism in her icy blue stare, the tiny frown between her perfectly plucked brows.

But he'd also glimpsed an uncharacteristic softening, a

thawing of ice to fire, when he'd lingered over her hand, and that had shocked him. Almost as much as his physical reaction.

Hand-kissing a turn on? Who would've thought?

It reminded him of the other time they'd kissed, when he'd managed to delve beneath her frosty veneer and prove she wasn't as immune as she'd like to think.

That was what he had to do if he were to work with her. Keep her off-guard. Maintain control. And show he wouldn't tolerate her coolly disdainful treatment.

This time he had something she wanted and she must want it real bad. For Sapphire to approach *him* for business… Well, Seaborns must be in a worse place than the rumours he'd heard.

Seaborns. He glanced at the elegant art deco cream façade, at the gleaming honey floorboards beneath discreet downlights, at the shimmer and sparkle of exquisite gems behind glass.

And he remembered. Remembered the night he'd brought her home from the graduation dance because her lousy date had been too drunk to drive. Remembered standing in this very spot outside the showroom, reverting to his usual taunts to cheer her up, hating the way the first time he'd seen her vulnerable, seen beneath her outer shell, had made him feel sad rather than victorious.

He remembered the sounds of soft laughter from nearby restaurants, the distinct clang of a tram bell, the faintest wistful sigh a moment before he'd ignored his misgivings and kissed her.

It had been a crazy spur-of-the-moment thing to stop her lower lip wobbling. He'd liked teasing the Ice Princess. He would have hated seeing her cry.

So he'd had no option but to distract her.

He'd expected a kiss to do that and then some.

The part where she'd combusted and he'd lost control a little... Not supposed to happen.

Who would have thought beneath Sapphire's glacial surface lay a bubbling hotbed of hormones?

He'd kissed a lot of women in his time, in the endless whirl of parties and fashion events throughout Europe, and dated some of the hottest women in the world, but that kiss with Sapphire Seaborn...

Something else.

Not that he deliberately remembered it, but every now and then, when a blue eyed-blonde gave him a haughty glare, he'd remember her and that brief moment when he'd glimpsed a tantalising sliver of more.

Back then she'd shoved him away and fled. Wanting to ease her mortification—and maybe rub her nose in it a little, because old habits died hard—he'd tried calling once, e-mailed and texted a couple of times.

Predictably, she'd raised her frosty walls and he'd backed off. It hadn't bothered him. He'd left for Paris a week later.

Now he was back, ready to take the Melbourne fashion scene by its bejewelled lapels and give it a damn good shake-up on his way to achieving his ultimate goal. And if he ended up working with Sapphire he'd rattle her too.

As he took a seat at an outdoor table at the café next door and ordered a double-shot espresso he remembered her horrified expression when she'd first caught sight of him.

Shell-shocked didn't come close to describing it.

Only fair, considering he'd felt the same. When he'd first seen her, arms stretched overhead, revealing a flat, tanned stomach that extended to her bikini line courtesy of ragged, low-riding yoga pants, he'd felt like he had that crazy time he'd leapt into the Seine on a dare: breathless, shivery, out of his depth.

He'd never seen her so casual or without make-up and it

suited her—as did the layered pixie cut that framed her heart shaped face and made her blue eyes impossibly large.

Usually lithe and elegant, she'd appeared more vulnerable, more human than he'd even seen her, and it added to her appeal.

She'd been hugely confident as a kid. Cutting through a crowd or cutting him down to size. When Sapphire spoke people listened, and he'd been secretly impressed by her unswerving goal to help run the family business.

Not many teens knew what they wanted to do, let alone actually did it, but Sapphire had been driven and determined. And she hadn't had time for a guy who plied his charm like a trade, getting what he wanted with a smile or his quick wit.

So he'd tried harder to rile her, needling and cajoling and charming, buoyed by her reluctant smiles and verbal flayings.

Sapphire Seaborn gave good putdowns.

If it hadn't been for Biology during their final year of high school he would have thought she really didn't like him. But being her lab partner, being forced to work with her, had shown him a different side to Sapphire—one that had almost made him like her.

Because beneath the tough exterior was a diligent, devoted girl who hated to let anyone down. Including him. Probably the only reason she'd put up with him during their assignments.

He admired her unswerving loyalty to her family, her dream to expand Seaborns. Especially when he'd had no aspirations to join Fourde Fashion and all it entailed.

Ironic how, ten years later, he was back in his home city, making Melbourne sit up and take notice of the newly opened Fourde Fashion his priority.

He had a lot to prove to a lot of people—mainly himself—and he'd take Fourde Fashion to the top if he had to wear shot silk and stilettos to do it.

The waitress deposited his espresso on the table and he

thanked her—a second before he caught sight of Sapphire leaving Seaborns.

His gut tightened as she glanced his way, her gaze soft and unfocused, almost lost.

Her vulnerability hit him again. He'd never seen her anything less than über-confident and he wondered what—or who—had put the haunted look in her eyes.

She hadn't caught sight of him so he stood and waved her over.

A slight frown creased her brows as she worried her bottom lip, obviously contemplating how to flee. He took the decision out of her hands by ordering a tall, skinny, extra hot cappuccino with a side of pistachio *macaron*, loud enough for her to hear.

Her eyes narrowed as she stalked towards him, the yoga pants clinging to her lean legs like a second skin, a pink hoodie hiding the delectable top half he'd already checked out.

Sapphire might be petite, but the way she held herself, the way she strode, made her appear taller. In heels, she was formidable.

He liked the grass-stained purple sneakers with diamante studs better.

'Care to join me?' He pulled out a wrought iron chair. 'I ordered your favourites.'

'So I heard.' She frowned, indecisive, as she darted a glance inside. Probably contemplating how to cancel the order without offending. 'Rather presumptuous.'

He pointed to his espresso. 'I hate drinking alone.'

'I'm busy—'

'Please?'

He tried his best mega-smile—the one she'd never failed to roll her eyes at.

She didn't disappoint, adding an exasperated huff as she slid onto the seat. 'Tell me you're not still using that smile to twist people around your little finger.'

He shrugged. 'Fine. I won't tell you.'

'Does it still work?'

'You tell me.' He crooked a finger, beckoning her closer. 'You're here, aren't you?'

'That's because I haven't had my cappa fix this morning.'

'And you can't resist anything sweet and French.'

She snorted. 'Surely you're not referring to yourself?'

'I've lived in Paris for ten years.' He leaned towards her, close enough to smell the faint cinnamon peach fragrance of her shampoo—the same one that had clung to his tux jacket after their kiss. 'And you used to find me irresistibly sweet.'

She pretended to gag and he laughed.

'Let me guess. You're trying to impress me by remembering my favourites after all these years?'

'Not really.' He pushed around the sugar sachets in the stainless steel container with his fingertip. 'Hard for a guy to forget when you had the same boring order every time we studied for those stupid Biology spot tests.'

She ignored his 'boring' barb. Pity.

'Remember the plant collection assignment?' She winced. 'Just thinking about poison ivy makes me itchy.'

'Though it wasn't all bad.' He edged closer and lowered his voice. 'As I recall, the human body component in last semester proved highly entertaining.'

Her withering glare radiated disapproval. The arrival of her coffee and *macaron* saved her from responding.

He let her off the hook. Plenty of time to stroll down memory lane if she wowed him with her presentation, as he expected, and they ended up working together.

It would be interesting, seeing if the old bait and switch that had underpinned their relationship in high school would apply now. If her responses to him so far were any indication, not much had changed. He relished the challenge of making her loosen up. She thrived on proving that anything he said annoyed the crap out of her.

She'd change her attitude if Fourde Fashion brought Seaborns on board for this campaign. And if that happened he should change his attitude too.

He needed this business venture to thrive, and he needed to be on top of his game to do it. Invincible. And he knew Sapphire could help him do it.

There might not have been so much at stake in high school, bar a pass or fail grade, but he hadn't forgotten her ability to command and conquer. If she brought half that chutzpah to her presentation tomorrow he had a feeling Fourde Fashion working with Seaborns for Fashion Week couldn't fail.

And that, in turn, would launch his plans—the ones ensuring the entire fashion world, including his folks, would finally forgive the mistakes of his past and recognise there was more to him than his family name.

'Fill me in on what you've been up to.'

An eyebrow inverted as she stared at him over the rim of her cappuccino glass. 'In the last decade?'

'Give me the abbreviated version.'

'The usual. Taking over the business. Working my butt off to make it thrive.' Shadows darkened her blue eyes to midnight before she glanced away.

Damn. How dumb could he be? He'd forgotten all about passing on his condolences. 'Sorry about your mum.'

'I am too.' She cradled her coffee glass, determinedly staring into its contents.

'You must miss her?'

'Every day.'

With a suddenness that surprised him she placed her glass on the table and jabbed a finger in his direction. 'Her drive and vivacity and tenaciousness were legendary. And that's exactly what you'll get a taste of in my presentation tomorrow.'

'I don't doubt it.'

He was surprised by her mood swings: pensive one moment, wary the next. The old Sapphire would never let any-one get under her guard—least of all him.

Which begged the question: what had happened to make her so...*edgy*?

'No significant others?'

A faint pink stained her cheeks again, highlighting the incredible blueness of her eyes—the same shade as the pre-cious stone she was named after.

'Haven't had time.' She picked up her glass again, using it as a security measure. 'Work keeps me busy.'

'Will you fling that *macaron* at me if I quote you the old "all work and no play" angle?'

'No, because I've heard it all before.' Her fingers clutched the glass so tightly her knuckles stood out. 'Besides, I play.'

Defensive and nervous. Yep, definitely not the woman he remembered.

'How?'

She frowned. 'How what?'

'How do you play? What do you do for kicks?'

The fact that she screwed up her nose to think and took for ever to answer spoke volumes.

'You're a workaholic.'

She puffed up with indignation. 'I do other stuff.'

'Like?'

'Yoga. Pilates. Meditation.'

He laughed, unable to mesh a vision of the long-striding, book-wielding girl going places with an image of Sapphire sitting still long enough to contemplate anything beyond Sea-borns' profit margins.

'What's so funny?'

He shrugged and stirred his espresso. 'You're different than how I remember.'

Tension pinched the corners of her mouth. 'I was a kid back then.'

'No, you were a young woman on the verge of greatness.

And I'm having a hard time reconciling my memory of you then with who you are now.'

He willed her to look at him, and when she did the fear in her gaze made him want to bundle her into his arms.

Closely followed by a mental *what the hell?* He'd learned the last time that Sapphire didn't value his comfort and he'd be an idiot to be taken in by her vulnerability again. For all he knew she could be using it as a ploy to soften him up before the presentation tomorrow.

'I'm still the same person in here,' she murmured, pressing her hand to her chest. But the slight wobble of her bottom lip told him otherwise.

She wasn't the same, not by a long shot, and it irked that deep down, in a metrosexual place he rarely acknowledged, he actually cared. Crazy when he didn't really know her, had never known her beyond being someone to tease unmercifully for the simple fact she'd made it easy.

He could have probed and prodded and grilled her some more, but she seemed so defenceless, so *broken*, he didn't have the heart to do it.

So he reverted to type.

'Maybe it's the casual exercise gear that threw me?' He winked. 'I much prefer you in a school uniform.'

'You're a sick man,' she said, the glint of amusement in her eyes vindication that he'd done the right thing in not pushing her.

'Well, then, maybe you should don a nurse's uniform instead and—'

'Unbelievable.' She pursed lips in disapproval and his chest tightened inexplicably. 'You haven't changed a bit.'

'You have.' On impulse he touched the back of her hand and she eased it away, grabbing a teaspoon to scoop milk froth off the top of her cappuccino.

'Ten years is a long time—what did you expect? To find me dissecting frogs and acing element quizzes?'

He couldn't figure why she vacillated all over the place but there was something wrong here, some part of the bigger picture he wasn't seeing, and if he were relying on her to help push Fourde Fashion into the stratosphere he needed to know what he was dealing with.

It was good business sense. It was an excuse for his concern and he was sticking to it.

'Did you stop to consider my kiss may have ruined you for other men?'

Her eyes widened in shock at his deliberately outrageous taunt a second before she picked up several sugar sachets and flung them. He caught the lot in one hand.

He'd wanted a reaction and he'd got it. It was a start.

'Newsflash: that kiss meant nothing. You caught me at a bad time and it ended up being two hormonal teens making out in a moment of madness.' She crossed her arms and glared, outraged and defiant. 'And I think it's poor form, you bringing it up a decade later when we're potentially on the verge of working together.'

'Another thing that's changed. You used to be brutally honest. Saying that kiss meant nothing?' He tsk-tsked. 'Never thought I'd see the day when you told a fib.'

He baited her again, wondering how far she'd go before he got a glimpse at the truth. He moved the sugar out of her reach just in case.

'I'm not playing this game with you.' She slammed her palms on the table and leaned forward, blue eyes flashing fire. 'No reminiscing or teasing. No pretending to be buddies. And definitely no talk of kissing.'

She waved a hand between them.

'You and me? Potential work colleagues. Our aim? To make our businesses a lot of money. So quit pretending to be my best buddy, because I don't need a friend—I need a guarantee.'

Ouch. This brutal honesty he remembered.

'Of what?'

'That you'll give me a fair hearing tomorrow and you'll judge my presentation on merit and not on our past rel—friendship.'

'You can say it, you know.' He cupped his hands around his mouth to amplify his exaggerated whisper. *'Rel-a-tion-ship.'*

When she swore, he almost fist-pumped the air. This was more like it. Sapphire riled and feisty. He could handle her this way, firing quips and barbs to get a rise. The withdrawn, almost melancholic woman she'd been a few minutes ago confused the hell out of him.

'This is important to me,' she said, her tone low and ominous. 'You may have it easy, being given a subsidiary of your folks' company to play with while you're in Melbourne for however long you care to stick around. Me? Seaborns is everything, and I'll do whatever it takes, including aligning our jewellery with your fashion, to ensure my company is never threatened again.'

Not much made Patrick quick to anger—bar anyone casting aspersions on how hard he worked.

He'd had a gutful of people doubting him. Doubting his capabilities, doubting his creativity, doubting his business brain.

It was why he'd leapt at the chance to head up this new branch. It was why his main goal was to show the world what he was made of. He intended to prove all the doubters wrong—including his parents.

Patrick Fourde had left the mistakes of his past behind and he had what it took to be a success beyond the family name and all it stood for.

'Are you done?'

Something in his tone must have alerted her to his inner frustration, for she slumped back into her chair and held up her hands in surrender.

'Sorry.'

'No, you're not. You believe all that crap.'

Just as his folks believed Jacques had single-handedly come up with the concept for the spring collection that had set the couture gowns sales in Paris soaring.

It had been the first time in ten years they'd given him another chance to work on a primary showing, collaborating on the spring collection alongside Jacques. Maybe they expected him to be eternally grateful, maybe they expected him to stuff up again, but never had they considered for one second *he'd* been the creative genius behind it.

He'd waited for their acknowledgment that he'd made amends for his monumental stuff-up when he'd first started with the company, waited for an encouraging word.

All he'd got was begrudging thanks for being part of a successful team.

Pride had kept him from confessing his true role and he'd realised something. Until he proved he'd put the past behind him *on his own* no one would believe him.

Least of all himself.

And it was at that moment he'd made his decision.

Making a success of the Australian branch of Fourde Fashion wasn't debatable. It was imperative.

He needed to do this.

For him.

He'd accept nothing less than being the highest-grossing branch in the company—and that included topping their long-established French connection. Closely followed by putting his secret plan into action.

And he was looking at the one woman who could help make that happen.

'You think I'm some lazy, indulged, rich playboy who gets by on his charm and little else.'

She couldn't look him in the eye—vindication that he was spot-on in her assessment of him.

'You never did give me any credit.'

Her mouth opened and closed, as if she'd wanted to respond and thought better of it. But her eyes didn't lie, and their shameful regret made him want to thump something at the injustice of being judged so harshly.

'Irrelevant, because my work will speak for itself.'

He expected to see scepticism.

He saw admiration and it went some way to soothing his inner wildness.

'Okay, then, I guess we both have something to prove.' She nodded, tapped her bottom lip, pondered. 'From here on in a clean slate.'

'No preconceptions?'

'None whatsoever.'

For the first time since he'd sought her out today a coy smile curved her mouth, making him wish she'd do it more often.

'Though you *do* rely heavily on charm.'

'Pity it never worked on you,' he muttered under his breath, surprised by her sharp intake of breath, as if she'd heard him.

She downed the rest of her cappuccino in record time and scooped the pistachio *macaron* into her palm. 'Gotta dash. I'll see you tomorrow afternoon.' She cocked her finger and thumb at him. 'Prepare to be wowed.'

As he watched her stroll away, the Lycra clinging to lean legs and shapely butt, he wondered what she'd think if she knew she'd already achieved her first goal.

CHAPTER TWO

'YOU'D THINK AFTER three months at a freaking health spa I'd be more relaxed than this.'

Sapphie glared at Karma, the goldfish she'd purchased after checking out of Tenang as part of her new calm approach to life.

Right now rainforest sounds spilling from her iPod dock, lavender fumes from her oil burner and talking to Karma weren't working.

She'd never felt so tense in all her life and she had Patrick Fourde to blame.

The guy was infuriating.

The guy was annoying.

The guy was seriously hot.

And that was what had her flustered deep down on a visceral level she didn't want to acknowledge.

Despite his inherent ability to consistently rub her up the wrong way, even after a decade, she found him attractive.

That ruffled, casual, bad-boy aura he had going on? Big turn-on. *Huge.*

It was why she'd deliberately held him at arm's length during high school.

Patrick Fourde, in all his slick, laid-back glory, had encapsulated everything she'd yearned to be and couldn't. She'd had major responsibilities, being groomed to take over Seaborns, and while she'd relished every challenge her mum had thrown her way she'd always secretly wanted what Patrick had.

Freedom.

Freedom to be whomever she wanted, whenever she wanted. Freedom away from maternal expectation. Freedom from being Sapphire—the eldest, responsible one. The confident, competent one. The driven, dependable one.

She'd envied Ruby for the same reason, loving her carefree, creative sister but wishing she could be like her.

It was why she hadn't burdened Ruby with the promise she'd made to their mum on her deathbed, why she'd kept Seaborns' economic situation a secret until it had been too late.

She'd learned the hard way how foolish it was to do it alone, to hide her stress beneath a brittle veneer, and if she hadn't almost collapsed with fatigue she might have jeopardised the company altogether.

The fact she'd ignored the signs of her ailing body, pushing herself to the limit with the help of caffeine drinks and energy bars, foolish behaviour she'd never accept with anyone, least of all herself. But she'd done it—driven her body into the ground because of her stubborn independence.

Thankfully she'd wised up, vowed to take better care of her body.

She never, ever wanted to experience the soul-sapping fatigue that had plagued her for weeks when she'd first checked into Tenang. The nebulous chronic fatigue syndrome—something she'd heard bandied around on current affairs programmes but knew little about—had become a scary reality and she'd fought it for all she was worth.

When she'd left Tenang she'd promised to take time out, to achieve a better balance between her business and social lives.

Karma gaped at her, opening and closing his fishy lips, and she could imagine him saying, *So how's that working out for you?*

She'd been back on the job a week, easing into the business by scouring accounts, re-establishing contact with clients and making projections for the next financial year. It had been going well, coming to work in casual workout clothes and sneakers, wearing no make-up, not having to put on her 'company face' for clients and the cameras.

Being CEO and spokesperson for Seaborns had always given her a thrill, but the stress of possible financial disaster had ruined her enjoyment of the job.

While Seaborns had recovered, courtesy of Ruby and Jax, she'd never let the situation get out of hand again. Which was why she'd latched onto the idea of working alongside Fourde Fashion for the upcoming Melbourne Fashion Week.

A mega seven days in the fashion world, it would secure Seaborns' future for ever if their exquisite jewellery designs were seen with designer clothes from Fourde's.

Despite their past, she hadn't hesitated in contacting Patrick's PA for an appointment when she'd heard the CEO of Melbourne's newest fashion house was courting jewellers for a runway partnership.

Patrick's terse, impersonal response had surprised her but she hadn't cared. She had her chance.

So why had he shown up at Seaborns yesterday, seemingly hell-bent on rattling her?

If his wicked smile and smouldering eyes hadn't undermined her, his ability to hone in on how much she'd changed would have.

How had he done that?

The guy she'd known had never pushed for answers, had never bothered to be insightful or concerned. He'd teased and annoyed and badgered his way through their year as lab partners in Biology, never probing beneath the surface.

She'd pretended to tolerate him back then, when in fact— she could finally admit it—she'd looked forward to their prac sessions with a perverse sense of excitement. Biology had been the relief of her senior year. Through the heavy slog of

Maths and Economics and Politics—subjects recommended by her mum and careers adviser, she'd craved the tantalising fun she'd have with Patrick.

It had been a game with him back then. A challenge for him to rile her into responding. She hadn't given him the satisfaction most of the time, choosing to ignore him as a way of dealing with his constant outrageous annoyances. But she'd seen his respect on the odd occasion she'd snapped back, and for some bizarre reason she'd valued it.

He'd made her rigid life bearable. Not that she'd ever let him know. The more he teased and taunted the harder she'd pushed him away.

Until graduation night. The night she'd let down her guard and he'd swooped, making a mockery of her stance to ignore him.

She'd never had a boyfriend in high school, had never been kissed before that night. And the fact Patrick had been her first had really peed her off at the time.

She'd blamed him. *He'd taken advantage of the situation. He'd seen her at her worst and had kissed her as part of his usual taunts. He'd probably laughed at her afterwards.*

But none of that had been true. In reality he'd been gallant in bringing her home after her date ended up drunk. And his kiss had been one of comfort, not cruelty.

It wasn't his fault she'd gone a little nuts.

That was why she'd ignored his overtures to meet after that night. Pure mortification. And a small part of her knew she would have hated having him belittle something as special as that spectacular first kiss.

He would have too, to lighten the mood between them—would probably have been as embarrassed as her and covered it by taunting her.

Thankfully he'd given up after a week, headed to Paris, and she'd forgotten about it.

Until now.

Beyond annoying.

She glanced at the alarm clock next to the bed and winced. Less than an hour until her pitch.

Yesterday had been an aberration. The feeling that she'd connected with him on some deeper level that went way beyond their banter in high school hadn't happened. It had been a figment of her imagination—the same imagination that insisted she go out and find the hottest guy in Melbourne to have some fun with.

That was what their tenuous bond had been about: her need for some male company and his inherent ability to flirt with anything that moved.

Harsh? Yeah. But it was the only way she'd cope with the riot of uncertainty making her doubt her choice of outfit, accessories, and the wisdom of meeting up with him—albeit for work.

'This is business.' She squared her shoulders. 'I can do this.'

Karma's affirmation consisted of a gill twitch as he ducked behind his treasure chest.

At least she looked the part. Knee-length, A-line sleeveless dress with a fitted bodice and cinched waist in the deepest mulberry, towering stilettos in black patent, and an exquisite amethyst pendant on a simple white gold necklace with matching earrings.

Throw in the dramatic make-up, designed to accentuate her eyes and lips, a hairspray-reinforced slicked-back coif that could withstand the stiffest breeze, and she was ready to face him.

This was how she'd envisaged their first meeting after a decade: with her power-dressed, strutting into his office, demonstrating her control and confidence and *savoir-faire*.

Considering he'd seen her in her oldest yoga pants and a crop top yesterday she'd kinda lost her advantage.

Then she remembered the look in his eyes when he'd first

seen her, as if he'd wanted to gobble her up and come back for main and dessert… Maybe she still held the upper hand after all.

Not that she'd stoop so low as to use her sexuality to seal a business deal, but knowing the great and powerful Patrick found her attractive made her walk that little bit taller.

'Wish me luck,' she said, snatching up her bag and smoothing her hair one last time.

Karma gave a lazy swish of his tail. No problem. When she stalked into Patrick's office shortly armed with a presentation to wow him, she'd have all the good karma she needed.

She'd make this Fashion Week deal happen.

Let him try to stop her.

'The pieces are good. Really good.'

The fact that Sapphire sat close to Patrick on his office sofa, her stockinged leg within tantalising touching distance, was not so good.

How was a guy supposed to concentrate?

The moment Sapphire had strolled into his office, looking as if she'd stepped off the pages of a fashion mag, he'd been befuddled.

There was nothing revealing in her outfit but the cut of the fabric and the way she wore it made him think of the screen sirens of old. Beautiful, curvaceous women who were proud of their bodies and weren't afraid to flaunt them in understated elegance.

And stockings… He loved them—the sheerer the better. None of those thick opaques for him. The way they added a sheen to Sapphire's legs, highlighting their shape…and the possibility that she might be wearing suspenders to hold them up…

Another thing he'd discovered since she'd arrived: hardons were distracting and guaranteed to scuttle a business meeting.

His plans to take the Melbourne fashion scene by storm would be derailed before he'd begun if he started thinking with the wrong head.

'These pieces are some of Ruby's best work, but she's willing to design whatever you want—depending on the concept you come up with.'

Her eyes sparkled with enthusiasm and he wondered if they darkened when she was aroused.

Hell. Still thinking with the wrong head.

'The show's next month. Sure you can deliver?'

He hated how abrupt he sounded, but he needed to refocus and stifle the urge to readjust his pants.

'Definitely. We'll work nights, do whatever it takes.'

'You want to be on the runway alongside Fourde that badly?'

A flicker of fear shimmered in her defiant gaze before she blinked, leaving him wondering if he'd imagined it.

'Yeah, I want Seaborns to be featured with your designs. I'm a savvy businesswoman and, as you know from the suitors bashing down your door, any jeweller in this city would give their last diamond tennis bracelet to accessorise your clothes.'

He admired her honesty. But she was right. He'd had back-to-back meetings all day in which he'd been systematically wooed and impressed by the calibre of jewellers in Melbourne.

The city might not have the same *joie-de-vivre* as Paris but it had certainly come a long way since he'd lived here.

The fashion scene thrived, with worldwide designers setting up shop, which was the only reason his folks had deemed it prudent to launch a branch of Fourde Fashion here.

With Jerome, his older brother, heading Milan, and his younger sister Phoebe heading New York, he'd been the only one left to thrust into a makeshift CEO position.

Not that he was complaining. He'd been desperate to prove

he could do this. The disaster of his first campaign had seen to that.

He knew they thought he was only a figurehead, a puppet whose strings they could yank at will. They'd even installed Serge, the manager of Fourde's flagship store near the Champs-Élysées, alongside him.

Apparently Serge *'had the expertise'* and was *'worth his weight in gold'* despite the fact he and Serge, his best mate, had cut a path through Paris, Monte Carlo, Nice, Barcelona and most of the other cities in Europe together, living the high life, partying their way through each country.

He'd done it in an attempt to shrug off the taint of his first showing, wanting to be known for something other than his notorious failure.

It had worked too. His socialising antics had been diligently reported and the press had soon forgotten the savaging he'd received at their hands following a mistake that had cost Fourde Fashion megabucks.

He'd eventually returned to the company in different roles, learning what he could without being given any real responsibility.

It had suited him. Given him time to re-evaluate personally what had gone wrong. But no matter how many times he tried to analyse it, no matter how many angles he considered, it all came back to one thing: he'd tried to take an established brand and create something new that wouldn't fit.

His parents had given him free rein for his first showing, wanting to see what he came up with, and he'd been determined to show them what he could do.

Correction: he'd wanted to wow them. He hadn't had their attention in years—they'd moved to France for their precious business when he was still a teenager, had barely acknowledged their late-life 'mistake' for years before that—and he'd wanted to make a major impression.

He'd done that all right. For all the wrong reasons.

He'd swapped the Forde designs for ones he'd planned as part of a small group of designers. A catastrophic move that had cost the company a small fortune and pretty much sealed his career where his parents were concerned.

He'd been a fool to think Fourde Fashion was ready for cutting edge contemporary, and the fact his folks had distanced themselves from him—*'to protect the company,'* apparently—still burned after all this time.

It shouldn't have come as any great surprise. They'd been emotionally distant for as long as he could remember. Not from any deliberate cruelty but for the simple fact that their business came first. Always.

Birthdays and Christmases were spent having snatched lunches and the obligatory presents before they headed back to the office. Phoebe and Jerome were used to fending for themselves and his parents had expected him to do the same despite their fourteen-year age-gap.

He'd been the baby they'd never expected to have in their mid-forties. He got it. He'd grown used to their absence early on.

But when he'd finally joined the fold and wanted them to sit up and take notice of his talents, of *him*, it had been a flop.

Their continued lack of appreciation of his efforts, their distrust of his talents, all stemmed from his first failure, and despite how hard he'd worked since they couldn't forget it.

Well, the success of Melbourne Fashion Week would make them forget.

He'd make sure of it.

'What can you offer me that the other jewellers can't?'

Her eyes widened imperceptibly before her gaze dipped momentarily to his lips, and for one crazy, irrational second he wished she'd make an offer that had nothing to do with business.

'One hundred percent commitment.' She tilted her chin

up and eyeballed him. 'I'm willing to do whatever it takes to
have our designs accessorising yours.'

'Anything?'

Until now he'd been the epitome of a corporate businessman, with his mind on the job. But with a hard-on that
wouldn't quit, her body enticingly close, and her tempting
cinnamon-peach fragrance wrapping him in an erotic fog,
he couldn't help but flirt.

Besides, that was what she thought he was—an idle playboy who'd never worked for anything in his life. He'd gladly
disillusion her. Later.

Now, he wanted to play a little.

'Within reason.' A tiny frown slashed her brows and she
held up hand between them.

Yeah, like *that* would stop him.

'Hmm…' He drummed his fingers against his thigh, pretending to ponder. 'I could get you to privately model a few
designs.'

Her frown deepened and her lips thinned.

'Or you could help me with the lingerie line.'

She didn't speak, but the daggers she shot him with her
narrow-eyed glare spoke volumes.

'Or we could get together in my penthouse suite and do
some serious—'

'Stop toying with me.' She jabbed at his chest. 'You want
the best? Seaborns is it and you know it.'

She snatched her hand away when he glanced at it, still
lingering on his chest.

'Quit stalling. Do we have a deal or not?'

With her eyes flashing indigo fire, her chest heaving from
deep breaths and her designer-shoe-clad foot tapping impatiently an inch from his, she was utterly magnificent.

Once again she brought to mind starlets of old: glamorous,
powerful women who knew what they wanted and weren't
afraid to go after it.

That was when it hit him.

The idea that had been playing around the edges of his mind, taunting him to grab it and run with it.

'You're a frigging genius!' He grabbed her arms so suddenly she was startled, and his maniacal laughter sounded crazy even to his ears.

'You're out of your mind.' She brushed him off with a slick move that suggested martial arts training. 'Just tell me already.'

He leapt from the sofa and started pacing, riotous ideas peppering his imagination. He needed to sit, jot them down, make some sense of the brainstorm happening in his head.

This was what had happened in Paris, when he'd nailed the spring showing.

He'd done it. *His* ideas. *His* campaign. Not that upstart smarmy Jacques with his stupid berets and fast talking.

This creative freefall had also occurred for his first showing too—*the one that must not be named*, as he'd labelled it in his head following the shemozzle.

The spring collection might have gone some way to restoring his confidence, but it was this show that would prove beyond a doubt that he had what it took to make it in the fashion world.

With Sapphire Seaborn along for the ride every step of the way.

He stopped in front of her, itching to get started. 'You know we'd be working on this project twenty-four-seven, right?'

'Of course,' she said, and the vein in her temple pulsed.

It had been her 'give' when she'd been younger—a telltale sign that she was rattled—and he didn't know whether to be flattered or annoyed that spending time with him disconcerted her.

'And that doesn't bother you?'

She stood, cool and confident and lithe. 'This is business. Why should it?'

That vein beat to a rap rhythm. Yeah, she was rattled. Big time.

'Okay, then, let's do it.'

'Fantastic. You won't regret this.' Her lush mouth eased into a wide grin. 'We're going to be great together.'

'Absolutely.'

And he kissed her to prove it.

CHAPTER THREE

SAPPHIE'S FIRST INSTINCT was to knee Patrick in the groin. But he'd probably enjoy the contact too much.

She settled for placing both palms on his chest and shoving—hard.

'Can't blame a guy for wanting to celebrate the most significant moment of his career.'

The fact he was still using that boyish grin to try and disarm her a decade later made her want to knee him again.

As for the flutter low in her belly? It was a reminder that she hadn't eaten lunch and nothing to do with the insistent tug of attraction between them.

An attraction torched to life by his kiss.

Why did the most annoying guy on the planet also have to be the best kisser?

It didn't make any sense. She'd barely given him a second thought all these years—discounting the first few months after he'd left—yet all it took was one smooch—okay, one pretty scorching smooch—to resurrect how amazing he'd made her feel with his first kiss.

She could kill him.

Willing her pulse to stop pounding, she glared at him through narrowed eyes. 'You do that once more and I'll take Seaborns jewellery and walk.'

He merely raised an eyebrow, not in the least intimidated by her bluff. 'You need me as much as I need you, sweetheart.' She gaped at his insolence and he laughed. 'Come on, you know better than to con a con. I'm blunt. I say it as it is. You and me?' He waved a hand between them. 'We're going to take Fashion Week by storm, so don't let your predictable outrage over a little spur-of-the-moment celebratory kiss get in the way of a beautiful friendship.'

Predictable outrage? She shook her head, unsure whether to applaud his honesty or reconsider that knee to the balls.

She had to regain control of this situation—fast—and the way to do that was to focus on business.

Not the naughty twinkle in his grey eyes.

Not the smug smirk quirking his lips.

Not the way he continued to stare at her mouth as if he was primed for a repeat performance.

'What's with the *"most significant moment of your career"* big talk?'

For the first time since she'd entered his ultra-modern office he appeared a tad uncertain, tugging at the cuffs of his shirt.

'I've been looking for an angle for Fashion Week—something to play to the company's strengths.'

'And?'

His gaze raked over her but there was nothing overtly sexual about it. Maybe she'd imagined his hungry stare a moment ago. In fact he seemed to be sizing up her outfit and accessories in a purely professional manner.

'When you first walked in here you made a statement.' He tilted his head to one side, evaluating. 'Class. Elegance. Timeless. Made me think of screen legends in the past.'

A compliment from a guy who threw them out there like confetti. Who would have thought it?

'Should I be flattered or concerned you just called me old?'

The corners of his mouth quirked. 'You don't need to fish for compliments. You're stunning and you know it.'

Actually, she didn't. The designer clothes, the jewellery,

the make-up and hair were all part of her duties as spokesperson for Seaborns. Take away the fancy outer dressing and she was Sapphire Seaborn—the responsible one, the devoted one, the sensible one. She didn't do outrageous things. She dated *suitable* men and socialised with a *suitable* crowd.

Spending more than five minutes in the company of Patrick Fourde was decidedly *un*suitable. Or, more to the point, it elicited decidedly unsuitable thoughts.

He'd always had that effect on her. Been able to confuse and bamboozle and intrigue her with the barest hint of that lazy half-smile he had down pat.

She might have been immune in the past, but having him in her face again— bolder, brazen, still bamboozling—unnerved her far more now than he ever had.

'Get to the point.'

He stalked around his desk and fired up his laptop, swivelling the screen to face her.

'Bear with me a sec.'

His fingers flew over the keyboard and, increasingly curious, she propped herself on the edge of his desk.

The tip of his tongue protruded slightly as he concentrated on typing and her chest tightened in remembrance.

He'd used to do the same thing when they studied together. She'd known when he'd stopped goofing off—which had been rarely, admittedly—and started taking their studying seriously by that tell, and it was as endearing now as back then.

At the time, she'd done her best to give him the impression she couldn't stand the sight of him. Had berated him constantly about slacking off and sketching instead of studying. Her chastisement had only served to stir him up further and he'd deliberately make fun of her work or call time out for a coffee.

Interesting how his doodling had probably been a prelude to his career in fashion, an outlet for his creativity. And to see him now, CEO of a branch of a world-renowned fashion house, made her feel ashamed she'd given him such a hard time.

Then again, considering the amount of time he'd spent poking fun at her study timetables and subject spreadsheets, her guilt quickly faded.

Whatever he was doing now, it had captured his attention and given her an opportunity to study him. In his flawlessly fitted charcoal suit and open-necked black shirt, perched behind a glass-topped desk large enough to fit an entire classroom, with the skyline of Melbourne surrounding him with three hundred and sixty degrees of floor to ceiling windows fifty storeys high, he looked like the consummate businessman.

A guy on top of the world, in total control and loving it. Who would have guessed the laid-back charmer had ambition?

He'd never shared any of his plans with her—had never showed any interest in business beyond teasing her about taking such a manic interest in Seaborns.

She'd been surprised when he'd absconded to Paris—had assumed it had been to live the high life on his family money.

After that first kiss she'd reluctantly kept an eye on him, had followed him on the internet for six months, surprised by mentions of him doing an internship at Fourde Fashion headquarters.

Pity those internet hits had also shown her the type of life she envied: parties and nightclub openings and theatre galas. The type of life she'd secretly craved but had been too focused on work, on proving herself, on seeking approval, to do anything about.

How different would her life have been if she'd let go just a little? Had hung out with Patrick for fun, not study? Responded to his teasing with smiles, not frowns? Allowed herself to indulge in a few wild teenage stunts without thought for the consequences?

Maybe she wouldn't have ended up stressed, repressed and almost losing the company.

'Here. Take a look.' He pointed at the screen, filled with images of stunning screen sirens.

Grace Kelly. Eva Marie Saint. Ingrid Bergman. Audrey Hepburn. Marilyn.

She knew them all, had shared her mum's love of old films, but had no clue why he was showing her these pictures.

He must have read the unasked question in her eyes for he grabbed a pen and notepad and started scribbling.

'Tell me the first words that pop into your head when you look at those women.'

It would be a lot more fun brainstorming if she knew what he was getting at but she'd play along for now.

'Stylish. Chic. Classy.'

'Exactly.'

He continued jotting, muttering under his breath. The tip of his tongue was back and she couldn't help but smile. If he was this enthused now, she had full confidence their joint collaboration would steal the show.

'This is my significant moment.' He twirled the pad so she wasn't reading upside down. 'Hollywood glamour of old.'

She squinted at his illegible notes as he flung the pen down and stood.

'We go all out. Elegant clothes. Curvy models. Bold colours and designs. Dramatic make-up.'

He started pacing and she'd never seen him so focussed.

'A theme to make people wish they'd lived decades ago. We play on the fashion frenzy *Mad Men* has recreated but take it a step further back in time. When women were proud to be sensual and lush and weren't afraid to hide the fact.'

For some reason heat crept into her cheeks at the way he said *sensual*. Jeez, what would it be like to have a guy like him go all sensual on her?

Yeah, *that* was helping her blush.

'Rich fabrics. Satin. Lace. Hugging curves. Fitted pencil skirts. Long elbow gloves. Hourglass silhouettes.'

He fired the words out at random, his eyes sparking with passion, and the heat in her cheeks spread to the rest of her body.

She literally tingled with the urge to touch him, to see if the powerful vibe emanating from him would zap her.

If he were this passionate about work, how worked up did he get in the bedroom?

She swallowed. It did little to ease the sudden dryness in her mouth. The exact opposite in other areas of her body.

She really needed a date desperately if she were having illicit fantasies about the guy who drove her mad.

'You like the idea.' He grabbed her hand and twirled her, and she couldn't help but laugh. His enthusiasm was infectious.

'What gave it away?'

'This.' He trailed a fingertip from the outer corner of her eye, down her cheek and around her lips, tracing their shape with exquisite precision. 'When you're relaxed your face lights up.'

'Probably a reflection of yours,' she muttered, knowing she should step back and put some much needed distance between them, but captivated by the incredible longing she glimpsed in the depths of his gaze.

He had to be longing for success, not her, right? The guy who'd squired starlets to gallery openings and models to movie premieres. The guy who'd cut a path through Europe with his legendary parties. The guy who'd teased her incessantly at high school.

They couldn't be attracted; it wouldn't be prudent.

But the longer they stood like this, invisible energy crackling between them, his fingertip lingering at the corner of her mouth, which he now stared at as if he wanted to devour it, the more she knew she was kidding herself.

Working with Patrick was going to be a living nightmare.

She stepped back and forced a smile. 'You're right. This idea is fabulous.'

'Great.'

He picked up his notepad, but not before she'd glimpsed confusion creasing his brow. Join the club.

She'd always labelled their relationship as volatile. He'd taunt her, she'd fake aloofness, until they reached an *impasse* fraught with unresolved tension. At least on her behalf. For being around him back then had made her tense in a way she couldn't describe. It had gone beyond exasperation at his deliberate teasing, had left her feeling... *frustrated*.

She'd put it down to being a hormone-ridden teen with a secret passion for romance novels and no time to date. And she was beyond grateful he'd never seemed clued in to her dissatisfaction.

He'd never given any hint he liked her as more than a friend, and she'd been deluded enough to believe her self-talk that she didn't like him *that* way.

But she had.

It was why that kiss on graduation night had meant so much. And why she'd freaked out because of it.

Because a momentous kiss like that had the power to change dreams and hers had already been set in stone.

She would be the next CEO of Seaborns.

Nothing—no one—could change that.

So why the relentless *yearning* now? The feeling that she'd missed out on something and regretted it?

It annoyed her, this uncertainty. Usually she knew what she wanted and made it happen. Yesterday.

She didn't like doubting herself. Or him, for that matter. And she did. A small part of her wondered how the larrikin teen could morph into this determined businessman and pull off something this big.

Having an inkling he was in this position purely because

he'd got the job handed on a silver platter from his folks and having her suspicions confirmed by asking him was mutually exclusive. She couldn't ask without alienating him or emasculating his pride and potentially stuffing this collaboration up before they'd really begun.

But she had to voice some of her doubts, couched in business terms.

'While I think something like this could cause a sensation at Fashion Week, and make the world sit up and take notice of our companies, do you think it's too ambitious?'

He glanced up from his notepad and stared at her as if she'd suggested he don one of the dresses.

'One thing I've learned in this biz is to dream big. Go all out. Make an impact.'

He knew. Knew she doubted him. She saw it in the slightly narrowed eyes, the disappointment pinching the corners of his mouth.

'If you're questioning my credentials, why did you come here in the first place?'

Yep, he was mad. She'd never heard his voice like this: hard, flat monotone with a hint of ice.

'I'm not questioning—'

'Yeah, you are.'

He flung the pen he'd been holding onto his desk and raked a hand through his hair, ruffling the too-long-to-conform whorls.

'Here's a newsflash. Don't believe everything you read in the press, because sometimes it's what goes on behind the scenes that counts.'

Oo-kay, so that was cryptic. What did his social antics have to do with work?

'Besides, you know me—always the risk-taker.' He stabbed a finger at the scrawl-covered notepad. 'Thinking big is what's going to have every person in this city and beyond talking about Fourde Fashion, and that's my number one goal.

To go places.' He eyeballed her with a steely determination she hadn't known he had in him. 'And if you're smart you'll be along for the ride.'

Sapphie didn't know how smart it was being tied so closely to Patrick for the next month but she did know business, and every cell in her body was screaming that this deal was the opportunity of a lifetime.

'The new me is in favour of risks.' She held out her hand to shake on it. 'Let's make this happen.'

As Sapphire chatted with Ruby on the phone, outlining the basics and the timeframes involved to ensure their proposal hit the ground running, Patrick surreptitiously studied her.

What had she meant, *'the new me'*?

Apart from a shorter layered haircut and a few more blonde streaks she looked as if she hadn't aged a day since he'd last seen her.

Though the curves were new. And that look in her eyes…

He couldn't put his finger on it but, while she looked the same on the outside, he had a feeling she'd gone through some major stuff to put that bordering-on-haunted gleam in those big blue eyes.

Not that she'd tell him. She seemed determined to keep him in the same box she'd constructed for him back in high school. The one labelled 'Lazy Lout Happy to Coast on his Family's Fortune'.

He'd pretended it hadn't bothered him back then, had gone out of his way to tease her for being the opposite—'Little Miss Prissy Being Groomed to Follow in Mama's Footsteps'.

But now? Yeah, it bothered him. He'd had a gutful of being labelled and misjudged by everyone from the paparazzi to his folks. Especially his folks.

Ironic that growing up he'd craved their attention, and yet when they'd finally given it, it had been for all the wrong reasons.

To have Sapphire echo their doubts felt as if someone had slugged him in the guts.

For some unfathomable reason her opinion mattered after all this time. It shouldn't. They were now business colleagues.

The irrefutable, irrational urge to rip her clothes off and devour her didn't come into it at all.

Sex without complications. That was what he wanted, and for one insane moment earlier, from the way she'd been looking at him, he'd almost say she wanted it too.

For Sapphire wouldn't have room in her well-ordered life for complications. He respected that about her—her focus on her job. He'd met women like her around the world—highfliers who took no prisoners, who didn't have time for emotional entanglements, who were happy being independent and forceful and in control.

Not every female needed a wedding ring and kids to feel validated, and by Sapphire's go-get-'em attitude, she'd chosen to marry her career instead.

She glanced at him and rolled her eyes, imitating Ruby's garrulousness with her hand. He mimed hitting the disconnect button and she smiled—a genuine, dazzling display that left him slightly winded.

Sex without complications, remember?

Sleeping with Sapphire wasn't wise. That was one giant complication just waiting to happen.

She *had* changed. The Sapphire he'd known would never have taken time out to do yoga, let alone be seen dead in leisure clothes. When she hadn't been in school uniform she'd worn tailored pants and button-down shirts, appearing way older than her years but making it work regardless.

She hadn't cared what other kids thought of her, and while their rich, indulged classmates at the exclusive school they'd attended had been boozing and partying their way through high school she'd been friendly yet aloof, happy in her own skin, proud of her choices.

He'd envied her that—her certainty in knowing what she was going to do with her life. He hadn't had a clue, and had taken the Fourde internship by default, accepting it when a PR job at a Paris magazine had fallen through.

And look how that had turned out.

Maybe he would have been better staying well away from the family business but despite what had happened he didn't regret the years he'd spent at Fourde.

He wouldn't have discovered his talent for taking conceptual ideas and seeing them through to fruition. He wouldn't have discovered his passion for brainstorming and elaborating and collaborating. And he wouldn't have known he had the creative spark passed down in his genes if he hadn't been surrounded by the passion of Fourde Fashion on a daily basis.

A huge part of him was grateful for the opportunities he'd been given, but another part wished he'd been brave enough to put his plans in motion earlier.

Seeing his folks in action had gone some way to soothing his resentment. If they'd been time-poor with him when he was growing up, they were frenetic now. They never stopped. Working eighteen hour days. Rarely taking time to eat. Grabbing coffee and croissants on their way between meetings.

Their dedication to Fourde explained why they'd missed his first footy game—missed the whole season—why they'd never shown up at his school presentations, why he'd thought eating dinner alone was the norm until one of his school buddies had invited him around to his place one night.

It had sucked at the time, fending for himself, and their neglect had fed his antipathy. But working alongside them in Paris had shown him it wasn't personal. They didn't have time for anyone unless it involved Fourde's.

Were they selfish and self-absorbed? Hell, yeah.

Malicious? No.

And his tense relationship with his folks had more to do

with people co-existing but not really knowing each other than any residual bitterness on his behalf.

That didn't stop him wanting to prove how damn good he was, and that was exactly what he'd do with Sapphire's help.

'Done.' She slid her phone back into her handbag. 'Ruby's hyped. She's on the Net as we speak, researching the general feel of old Hollywood glamour, and she'll start doing some virtual mock-ups for you to take a look at by tomorrow.'

'Wow, no grass growing under her feet.'

He watched her walk towards him, gorgeous in designer mulberry and high heels, and all that self talk about not going there was gone in the few seconds it took for a hard-on of mammoth proportions to return.

Gritting his teeth against his apparent lack of self-control, he turned away to look out of the window.

He had to hand it to his folks. Nothing but the best for Fourde Fashion, with this sky-high office on the top floor of one of Melbourne's newest developments. Though he knew his fancy office had more to do with maintaining the image behind the Fourde name than any caring for him on their part.

Fourde Fashion needed a presence in Australia. He was it. They didn't expect soaring profit margins or breakout collections. They'd be happy with same-old, same-old and a steady cashflow from a market they deemed insignificant at best.

Lucky for them he never settled for anything but the best. Ever. He would never accept failure again, and he intended on proving that to everyone—including the woman now standing by his side.

Her subtle cinnamon fragrance teased his senses and he curled his fingers into his palms to stop himself reaching for her.

Maybe he should sleep with her and be done with it?

'Some view.'

He grunted in response, surprised when she laid a tentative hand on his arm. Yeah, *that* was helping.

'What's wrong?'

'You really want to know?'

'Wouldn't have asked if I didn't.'

He dragged in a breath, another, staring at the iconic city landmarks so many floors down. Flinders Street Station, Federation Square, St Patrick's Cathedral—buildings he'd explored as a kid on school excursions, usually with this woman by his side.

What the hell was he doing, contemplating telling her the truth? It wouldn't end well.

But he knew one thing for sure. He couldn't go on like this.

It had been two measly days since he'd marched back into her life, and this relentless, driving urge to have her wasn't going away any time soon. In fact it would probably intensify the more time they spent together working.

Probably best to get it out of his system? Then focus one hundred percent on blowing the competitors away?

But how did he tell her without sounding like an ass?

Hey, Saph, the reason I keep kissing you—can't keep my hands off you. Want into your pants. Now.

Yeah, that would go down a treat.

'Not like you to be at a loss for words.' She removed her hand and he instantly wished he'd grabbed it and held on. 'Maybe working with you is going to be tolerable after all?'

A reluctant chuckle spilled from his lips and he turned to face her.

And that was when he knew he couldn't tell her about his driving need to ravish every inch of her body.

Staring into her guileless eyes, seeing concern clouding their perfect blue, he couldn't do it.

Ten years had passed, but how well did he really know her? If she'd freaked out back then, what was to say she wouldn't do it now and jeopardise the entire showing?

He needed this Hollywood glamour idea to fly. He needed to wow audiences and critics and guarantee that orders flooded in. He needed to show everyone he wasn't the wealthy flake they wrongly assumed.

And that meant focussing on the goal and not on his rampant libido.

'We have to make this work. It's important to me.'

Her eyes widened in surprise, as if she'd doubted his sincerity before but didn't now.

'Me too,' she said, her nod brisk and businesslike. 'You meet with your designers, I'll put the PR machine in motion, and we'll reconvene later today.'

'Sounds like a plan.'

He liked plans. Plans were orderly and well thought out and logical. The opposite of the uncertainty rioting through him.

'We should do dinner.'

It was a vast improvement on what he really wanted to say: *We should do each other.*

A tiny crease reappeared between her brows. 'A working dinner, you mean?'

He'd prefer something along the lines of cosy and candlelit, with the two of them naked, but he'd settle for working. It was the one thing to keep him focussed away from wanting her, right?

'We'll be working long into the evening—stands to reason we need to eat.'

'Okay, then.'

She'd reverted to brusque and he mentally kicked himself for wanting what he couldn't have.

'Meet back here at five?'

He glanced around the room, at the contemporary sterility, and made a rash decision he'd probably live to regret.

'How about we meet at Seaborns? That way you can show me what Ruby has in mind for some of the major pieces?'

'Sure, that's doable.'

There he went again. One word—*doable*—and he could see the two of them *doing* each other.

'Better get cracking.'

He mentally cringed at how abrupt he sounded, not surprised when she shot him a sideways glance.

But in true Sapphire form she didn't push the issue or demand answers. She picked up her portfolio, hoisted her handbag onto her shoulder, and headed towards the door.

With her hand on the doorknob, she paused. 'Want to hear something crazy?'

Crazier than how badly he wanted her?

'Yeah?'

'I'm actually looking forward to this.'

Her impish grin as she eased through the door made him want to stride across the office and haul her back in.

She wasn't the only one looking forward to the month ahead.

Who said he couldn't mix a little pleasure with business?

CHAPTER FOUR

RUBY AND OPAL had a plate of double-coated Tim Tams waiting for Sapphie when she got back.

They'd closed the showroom and were lounging around the makeshift living room near Ruby's studio. It was a new addition in her absence and, while she liked Ruby having a place to chill between inspiration hits, it reminded her of her failure.

She should have been here.

Instead she'd been recuperating after being an ass, not trusting Ruby enough to share the responsibilities of running Seaborns, and driving herself into the ground because of it.

If she hadn't wound up chronically tired, her body aching all over, barely able to lift her head off the pillow because of the headaches... No, she wouldn't think about the possible consequences of her controlling behaviour. Not today, when hopefully she'd ensured that Seaborns would never face the threat of closure ever again.

She'd been so stupid, thinking she could control everything. Lucky for her, her body had sent out some pretty powerful warning signals, and she'd listened before the chronic fatigue syndrome had really taken hold.

For weeks before she'd finally admitted defeat she'd existed on caffeine energy drinks and liquid vitamins, trying to push through the tiredness, taking on a bigger workload.

It wasn't as if she'd never been tired before. Running a

business took its toll, and she'd been used to functioning on minimal sleep and snatched meals.

Until her body had other ideas.

She'd pulled yet another all-nighter after a long week of meetings with accountants and suppliers, had been in the process of downing her second energy drink for the morning, when she'd fainted, clipping her head on the corner of her desk on the way down.

Ruby had heard the noise, panicked when she'd found her unconscious and called an ambulance.

She'd come to before the paramedics arrived, but by the hard glint in Ruby's eyes Sapphie had known her number was up and she couldn't fool anyone any longer.

The paramedics might have pronounced her vital signs to be sound, but that hadn't stopped Ruby badgering her into a doctor's visit and a thorough physical.

Sapphie had barely got through the preliminaries before admitting defeat. Her body simply hadn't been holding up under the pressure she was placing on it.

If Ruby's scathing scolding hadn't convinced her to take three months off and check into a health spa the doc would have.

The moment she'd heard the long-term repercussions of CFS she'd booked a place at Tenang ASAP. Ongoing joint pain, visual disturbances, recurring sore throats, chronic cough, chest pain, allergies, depression… She'd asked the doc to stop around then, wishing she hadn't been so stubborn in shouldering Seaborns without real help.

She'd had a lucky escape, had listened to her body's symptoms in time, but every morning when she woke she experienced a moment of fleeting panic that maybe she wasn't as strong as she thought she was.

She went through the same daily routine now: deep breaths, ten in total, pushing her abdomen out, filling her lungs. Followed by pointing her toes towards the end of the bed five times, contracting her leg muscles. Bicycling in the air, loosening up her back. A few gentle reps of abdominal curls, finished with a hands-overhead stretch from top to bottom.

It had become a ritual, a way of ensuring her muscles woke slowly before she actually got out of bed, a way of caring for them when she hadn't before.

The regular meditation and yoga sessions had helped her reconnect with her body too, and she actually looked forward to the muscle-twanging stretches and peaceful interludes within a busy day.

As for her diet, she'd ditched the caffeine, always managed to scrounge three small protein-rich meals a day and drank her weight in filtered water.

She needed her body in tip-top working order, and making Seaborns successful now had more to do with proving that her physical strength hadn't diminished as keeping a promise to her mum before she'd died.

Ruby patted the sofa next to her. 'Take a seat and tell us everything.'

Where should Sapphie start? The part where Patrick had kissed her again and she'd let him? Or the part where they almost needed a force field to keep them from ripping each other's clothes off whenever they got within two feet?

That meeting in his office had been horrendous—much worse than she'd anticipated. Not on any professional level, he'd seriously impressed her there, but for the simple fact she couldn't explain where the heady sexual tension had sprung from.

If she'd had to deal with that during Year 12 she would've failed Biology for sure.

He wasn't helping matters either, playing up to it. Not that she should be surprised. It was what he did.

But her reaction... The flushed skin, the sweaty palms, the buzz thrumming her body... Inexplicable.

She couldn't afford to be attracted to Patrick—not when they'd be working on this campaign together.

Try telling that to her body.

And that was what bugged her the most. She'd been going to great lengths to take care of her body yet in one hour he'd managed to make her feel alive in a way she hadn't for a long time.

She could put it down to endorphins, the euphoria associated with nailing her presentation, but what was the point in lying?

Her body had hummed because it strained to be naked with Patrick's, endorphins or not.

'There's not much to tell,' Sapphie said, hoping her cheeks wouldn't show a betraying blush.

'Yeah, and I'm about to abseil down the Eureka Towers wearing nothing but a tiara,' Ruby said, shaking her head. 'You know we'll make it up if you don't tell us.'

Sapphie settled for the abridged version.

'Patrick came up with the idea of old Hollywood glamour as the lynchpin of his Fashion Week show.' She cradled her tea, the warmth a welcome infusion for her icy hands. They matched her cold feet after spending too many hours one-on-one with the guy who made her body hum just by being near him. 'I think it's fantastic.'

'Sure is.'

Opal slid the plate of Tim Tams across to her and Sapphie took two, demolishing the first before the chocolate oozed onto her fingers.

'This is going to gain recognition for Seaborns overseas. I just know it.'

'Great going.' Ruby nudged her with an elbow. 'Now tell us the rest.'

Opal stifled a giggle and Sapphie glared at her sister. 'What have you been saying?'

'Nothing.'

Ruby's deliberately wide eyes and *faux* innocent smile wouldn't have fooled anyone. 'When our lovely cuz was helping me do inventory I happened to mention the way Patrick looked at you yesterday.' Ruby pointed at Opal. 'Not *my* fault if she jumps to conclusions.'

Opal snorted. 'If memory serves correctly, you were the one waxing lyrical about Saph *"needing to get some"* and Patrick being *"just the guy to give it to her".*'

Sapphie glared at Ruby. 'Tell me you didn't say that.'

'Okay, then, I won't tell you.' Ruby winked and crammed another Tim Tam into her mouth while Sapphie resisted the urge to bury her face in the nearest cushion to hide any incriminating blushes.

Opal studied her over her skinny latte before placing the coffee glass on the table. 'We looked him up Saph, and I have to say he's incredibly hot. If he's half as good in person as he is on screen…'

Great. Just what she needed. Her cousin and her sister joining forces in trying to get her laid.

'I used to dissect frogs with the guy. It kinda takes the shine away.'

'Bull—' Ruby covered the rest of her declaration with a fake sneeze. 'I saw the way you looked yesterday after he'd dropped around.'

'Tired and frazzled?'

Ruby made a buzzing sound. 'Incorrect. Try perky and glowing.'

'You're full of it,' Sapphie said, glancing at Opal for support.

She shrugged and picked up her coffee to hide a burgeoning grin.

'Okay, then, let's look at this rationally.' Ruby elbowed her. 'You've been recuperating for months, and for half a year before that you were steadily driving yourself into the ground—

which is why you almost ended up with severe chronic fatigue syndrome.'

Sapphie opened her mouth to respond but Ruby held up her hand.

'During that time you didn't date. You didn't eat either. But that's another lecture you've already had.' Ruby tapped her bottom lip, pretending to ponder. 'And, as I recall, one of the things you said when I picked you up from Tenang two weeks ago was, "I really need a date—bad."'

'You said it. *Date* being the operative word. *Date*—not business colleague.'

'That's beside the point and you know it.' Ruby dunked a Tim Tam in her espresso. Pushy and sacrilegious. 'It's not like you guys are strangers. You hung out all through senior year—'

'Once again, that was for *work*. We were Biology lab partners, that's all.'

Ruby waved the Tim Tam around; it would serve her right if it softened, and the dunked bit fell off and landed on the floor.

'I'm not that much younger than you, Saph, and I remember the way you'd be after *studying* with him.'

Sapphie clamped her lips shut. Of course she'd looked different after studying with Patrick. The guy had driven her insane with his lack of concentration and constant distractions.

'You'd look the same way you did yesterday. *Glowing.*'

Sapphie waited until Ruby had stuffed the Tim Tam into her mouth so she couldn't respond.

'I was a serious student and Patrick's mission in life was to make our study sessions as hard as humanly possible. He was a pain in the ass. Who may have made cramming for exams bearable with his bickering. So that glow was probably relief that for a few hours a week I could forget about everything else and just be a kid, maybe even laugh a little.'

Ruby's hand paused halfway to her mouth as Opal darted confused glances between them.

'As for yesterday? Already told you. I probably caught too much sun while doing yoga out the back.'

Opal smirked at that one, while Ruby shook her head. 'You know how I feel about you shouldering the load and the unrealistic expectations Mum put on you. Not fair. Not by a long shot. So the fact Patrick made you laugh…don't you want to recapture that feeling again?'

Ruby didn't have to say it but the rest of her sentence hung in the air, unsaid… *After all you've been through?*

She knew Ruby wouldn't let this go until she gave her a snippet of truth. ''Course I want to feel carefree, but that's just it, Rubes. All the meditation and yoga and Pilates in the world aren't going to change facts. Sure, I've learned to chill, but I am who I am, and the best way for me to start feeling good again is to do what I do best. Work. Run Seaborns. Contribute.'

Ensure she could cope physically with the demands of a job she loved.

That was what had scared her most during recovery—hoping her body could keep up with her mind.

She had so many plans she wanted to instigate, so many ways to ensure Seaborns stayed on top in the jewellery business, but she wouldn't be able to do a darn thing if her body let her down.

Hopefully, with a little TLC, her battered body would be back to its invincible best soon.

'Crazy workaholic,' Opal muttered, pretending she didn't see the death glare Sapphie shot her.

'You can still do all those things and have fun,' Ruby said, slinging an arm across her shoulders. 'The thing is, if you're so busy working and getting this showing together, how will you have time to find a date? Bonking Patrick kills two birds with one stone—'

'How about killing two family members with one stone?' Sapphie jabbed a finger at the octagonal lapis lazuli pendant hanging around her sister's neck. 'That's big enough to do the trick.'

Opal laughed and pointed at Ruby. 'She started it.'

Ruby chuckled and squeezed her shoulders. 'Think about it, okay? You're busy but you need to have a little fun. Patrick seems like the perfect solution.'

Unfortunately Sapphie happened to agree.

She could protest all she liked but Ruby made sense. She'd be working on this showing with him twenty-four-seven. She wouldn't have time to socialise let alone date.

Would it be so bad to give in to a little harmless flirtation?

Only one problem. Considering how her body came to life around him, how harmless would the flirtation be?

Several hours later Patrick questioned the wisdom of meeting Sapphire at her place to work.

Keeping his hands off her in the sterility of his office had been difficult enough without this…this…cosiness.

Meeting at the Seaborns showroom should have been entirely business-focussed. Instead they'd reported their day's progress in an hour and made an agenda for tomorrow in the following thirty minutes. Leaving him pacing the tiny apartment over the showroom while she *slipped into something more comfortable.'*

Yeah, she'd actually said those words, completely ingenuous—until he'd snorted. Only then had recognition dawned.

She'd rolled her eyes at him, accused him of having a filthy mind and strolled into the bedroom, slipping off her towering ebony patent leather pumps along the way.

The black seam of her stockings, starting at her heel and running all the way up her legs and underneath her knee-length crimson skirt had not helped the filthy mind situation.

If any other woman had uttered those words he would have

been prepped for a bout of wild sex. Coming from Sapphire, after ninety minutes of work focus, he acknowledged it for what it was. The simple statement of a tired workaholic who wanted to change out of her business suit.

He knew the feeling. Following her example, he unknotted his tie and stuffed it into his jacket, hanging on the back of a chair. He unbuttoned his cuffs and rolled them up to his elbows but stopped short of slipping off his pants. Time enough for her to see his boxers.

Chuckling under his breath at what she'd think of that cocky declaration, he wandered around the apartment. The place wasn't like Sapphire at all, with its ethnic cushions in bright colours, mismatched multi-coloured bottles serving as vases and a stack of chick-flicks in towering disarray next to an ancient DVD player.

She'd told him Ruby used to live here, before she'd moved out recently to be with her husband, and that Sapphire found it convenient while she eased back into the business.

When he'd asked why she had to ease back she'd clammed up and made a big deal of going over their itineraries for the next week.

Discomfort had made her babble so he'd let her off the hook. For now. Day two of the frantic month's work ahead wasn't the best time to be interrogating his colleague. He'd bide his time. Maybe a fine bottle of Grange wouldn't go astray?

Great, not only was he assuming he'd get her naked, he wanted to get her drunk too.

Way to go with his reformation.

Those days of carousing were long behind him. He'd grown tired of the paparazzi's constant scandalmongering in Paris, had found their scrutiny of his social life tiresome. Sure, his lifestyle had served its purpose, getting them to focus on his wild ways rather than that botched first showing, but it had reached a stage where he hadn't been able to travel through

Europe without some journo assuming it involved a woman, a secret assignation, or both.

And when there was nothing they simple invented it. Funny how one mistake in his past had long-term ramifications. Despite him towing the company line for many years now, he'd never shaken the feeling the paparazzi were one step away from reviving the disaster of his early show.

So he'd played up to the party animal image, hung around Serge despite the two of them growing apart in the maturity stakes, because it had been way easier being seen as a playboy than as a disillusioned guy out to prove himself.

His parents had written him off a long time ago, so nothing he'd done socially mattered. As long as he stuck to the rules where Fourde Fashion was concerned they were happy.

Those rules were mighty restricting, and not conducive to creativity, but he'd done what he had to do the last few years to regain respectability in a cut throat industry that didn't give too many second chances.

It had been part of his long-term goal to become a valued member of Fourde Fashion, because no way could he pull off his plans unless he had an established name in the biz.

After the *'flamboyant, avant garde, cutting edge'* show that had cost the company thousands when he'd first started, he'd learned to bide his time.

He'd known the fashion world would be ready for a contemporary transformation eventually. It was just a matter of when. Lucky for him, that time was now.

He'd watched the tide turn in Europe with increasing excitement. Sure, there would always be a place for classic couture houses like Dior, Chanel and Fourde Fashion, but an influx of young designers had seen a few indie collections that made his blood fizz with anticipation.

The modern wave wasn't taking over the catwalks yet, but give it time. And he intended on cresting that wave with contemporary designs the fashion world had never seen.

Opening a branch of Fourde Fashion in Melbourne couldn't have come at a more opportune time. It gave him time to prove he could launch a successful solo show and lend kudos to his upcoming venture.

The one driving force behind everything he did these days.

He picked up a photo of Sapphire and Ruby, with their arms slung across each other's shoulders outside the gigantic laughing mouth of Luna Park, and rubbed the dust off the glass with his thumb. It must have been taken a few years after he'd left. Ruby looked in her late teens, Sapphire early twenties, but the age difference was more pronounced by the worldly expression on Sapphire's face.

She didn't look like a young, carefree woman having a fun day hanging out with her sister at a St Kilda amusement park. The slight crease between her brows, the rigid posture, the half-smile screamed too much responsibility.

He should know. His siblings had worn the same expression since the time they'd graduated from high school and gone straight into the fashion business, taking night courses to stock up on their theoretical knowledge while working alongside their folks during the day. Before they'd all moved to Paris, leaving him behind.

He'd thought it pretty cool at the time, being trusted enough to live with a dotty aunt who didn't care what time he got home from school or who he brought with him. At least that was what he'd told himself in order to handle the seething emotions he'd hidden deep down.

Though what had he expected? Considering his folks' focus on Fourde Fashion, it shouldn't have come as any great surprise that they'd left him behind.

His family were virtual strangers. Living in the same house, barely conversing. Jerome had sat him down when he'd turned twelve and told him the cold, hard facts. With two teenagers, their folks hadn't banked on having a third child—a 'mistake'. They had goals to achieve and glass ceilings to shatter.

Jerome's advice had been simple: if he didn't expect anything he wouldn't be let down.

He'd remembered that when they'd left him behind, but it hadn't made the pain any easier.

They'd cited a logical reason, of course: wanting him to finish his education at the prestigious private school so he had a *'good grounding in order to enter the family business'* when he joined them.

No choice. An order. One that he'd been determined to ignore until he'd got lousy grades for his final exams and realised he'd rather be doing something creative than bumming off his folks.

When he'd joined them in Paris and the PR magazine job had fallen through he'd been determined to prove his worth. He'd been given free rein to demonstrate what he could do and ended up costing the company and losing his parents' respect because of it.

In not following protocol, being cocky and over-confident, he'd let his family down. And it seemed as if nothing since had been able to convince them of his seriousness when it came to work.

The long hours he put in, the extra duties he assumed, the collaborations he worked on—all had garnered the barest of recognition from his folks. Sure, they'd given him an end-of-year-bonus like the rest of their workers but the acknowledgement he secretly craved, where they'd recognise his creativity as being ahead of its time, had never come.

Until he'd realised something. He could never be who he truly wanted to be while under the Fourde Fashion brand.

For that was all his parents cared about: living up to their name, producing the same kinds of clothes with a different twist according to season and year. They wanted to deliver on the promise of sameness, while he longed to be different.

It made good business sense, and their long-standing reputation in the fashion industry was testament to it but he was tired of being part of a crowd.

He wanted to stand out—wanted his designs to stand out.

But first he had to ensure Fourde Fashion in Melbourne produced the best show Fashion Week had ever seen.

His swansong for Fourde's and a launching pad for him.

Doubts plagued him—had he read the fashion scene correctly or was the timing all wrong again—but he'd never know unless he tried.

He'd mentioned leaving the company to his folks and they'd hardly blinked. No begging him to stay. No heaping praise on him as a valued worker. They'd given him the customary brush-off with *'we'll discuss this later'* and assigned him to head up the Melbourne office.

If they thought the token CEO role would make him stay with the company, they were mistaken.

He appreciated the opportunity, but that was all it was. An opportunity for bigger and better things. Done his way.

And then he'd put his other plans into action.

'Don't know about you but I'm starving.' Sapphire padded silently into the room, barefoot, hair down, clad in worn denim and a teal tee, and he took extra care replacing the photo on the table, so he wouldn't give away the slight tremor of his hands. Hands that wanted to be all over her.

She frowned when she noticed he'd been checking out old photos. 'I'm ordering take-out. You're welcome to stay.'

He should go.

He should grab his stuff, head for the office, and bury himself in work all night in an effort to forget how sweet and tousled and *available* she looked right at this very minute.

He should remind himself how important this showing was, and how getting involved with Sapphire Seaborn on any level other than business was a monumentally daft idea.

'Sounds good,' he said, silently cursing his weakness when it came to this intriguing woman.

'Fancy anything in particular?' She rifled through a stack of restaurant flyers next to the phone, glancing up when he didn't answer.

She had Indian in one hand, Thai in the other, and all he could think was how he'd like to devour *her*.

His hungry gaze started at her feet, the high arches and long toes, moved up legs encased in denim that could have been poured on, skirted around the area that had driven his decision to stick around, lingered on her small, firm breasts before eventually meeting her eyes.

He'd expected censure and condemnation for his blatant perving. He hadn't expected an answering heat that had him hard in a second.

If she gave him a sign—any sign—that she wanted this as much as he did he'd vault the sofa and take her up against the wall.

He willed her to say something, to be brave enough to articulate what was zapping between them.

For the decision had to come from her. He knew what he wanted—hot, wild sex—but would she view it the same way?

Sapphire was so intense, so focussed, would she read too much into a quickie to take the edge off?

He'd never mixed business with pleasure before, had turned down numerous models, campaign managers and even rival CEOs. It never did to complicate matters. But this time with Sapphire he'd compartmentalise.

But would she be able to do the same?

His fingers curled into his palms and he clenched his hands into fists, holding himself perfectly still. He couldn't afford movement, for when he did move it would be in a beeline straight for her.

Their gazes locked for an eternity—his taunting her to accept his unspoken dare, hers surprisingly bold.

He waited, unaware he'd been holding his breath until she broke the deadlock and his lungs emptied in a rush.

'I fancy Thai.'

Not quite the *I fancy you* he'd been hoping to hear and not half as satisfying he'd hazard a guess.

As she studied the menu with intense fascination he came to a lightning quick decision—the kind of impulse he'd been famous for in his wilder partying years, the kind of decision that had made Paris sit up and take notice of his first dramatic show. Not in a good way.

But this was different. He was a decade older, a decade wiser. And going after Sapphire because he wanted her was a purely primal drive he needed to slake before it became an obsession and screwed with his concentration completely.

Ignoring this attraction was growing old fast. He couldn't do it. Couldn't spend the next thirty days working alongside her without going insane and taking enough cold showers to contribute to Melbourne's water shortage.

There was only so much curtailing a guy could take.

'Sapphire?'

She took an eternity to glance up, and when she did she was worrying her bottom lip with her top teeth. 'Yeah?'

'I think I should go.'

Schmuck that he was, he gave her one last out. If she agreed, he'd bolt—make that hobble—out of here. It was his final concession to the reformed him. One last attempt to do the right thing before he went frigging insane with wanting her and took whatever he could get.

He'd leave if she asked and make sure all their future meetings took place within office hours in an office environment. There was only so much temptation a guy could take.

He had no idea how long they stood there, the silence taut and expectant.

He could hear a clock ticking somewhere behind him, the

dripping of a faulty tap, and eventually the soft, wistful sigh of a woman as confused as him.

'Why?'

One word. That was all she uttered. It was enough.

He stalked towards her, even now expecting her to back-track, to make some flimsy excuse and turf him out on his ass.

Instead she stood ramrod straight, head tilted, unwavering stare defiant.

Lord, he wanted her. Wanted her with the kind of consuming lust that could make a man forget his name.

This thing between them went beyond a teenage fantasy, went beyond the basic craving for sensational sex. He saw something in her that called to him on some base level that defied logic. He couldn't label it—didn't want to. What he did want was her. Naked. Hot. Wet.

He stopped a foot in front of her, close enough to hear her sharp intake of breath, too damn far away when he wanted her body plastered against his.

'If I stay, it won't be for food.'

'Food can be overrated.' Her lips curved into a smug smile, sexy as hell. The kind of smile to give a guy depraved thoughts. 'So why *are* you staying?'

'You need me to spell it out?'

'I'd rather you show me—'

He claimed her mouth in a brutal kiss. No thought for sweet seduction or taking it slow. No thought beyond the incessant pounding in his head urging him to be inside her *now*.

She matched him, grabbing his shirt lapels, yanking him closer so that their bodies melded in a fusion of heat.

And it still wasn't enough.

He changed the pressure, his mouth sliding over hers in slow, tantalising sweeps, and she moaned, straining towards him.

With a tenuous hold on his self-control he grabbed her butt and hoisted her onto the breakfast bar—his turn to groan when his hard-on settled between her open legs. Her heat penetrated the clothing barriers between them and he wanted in.

She closed her eyes and arched into him, her abandonment so at odds with her usual reserve. He would come way too soon.

When her hips involuntarily moved, rubbing against him, he bit back an expletive. One that described what they were about to do.

If they had protection.

'Do you have condoms?'

Her eyes snapped open, incredibly blue amid the pink blush stealing into her cheeks. 'No. Don't you?'

He shook his head and cursed again. Cursed his stupidity in starting something he couldn't finish. Cursed his new lifestyle choices. Cursed the same impulses of the past that had got him here—frustrated as hell.

'You think Ruby would have any stocked in the bathroom?'

Sapphire frowned. 'Nope. She cleaned all her stuff out.'

For the first time in a long time he was at a loss for words. This was awkward. Rampaging lust was fine in the heat of the moment, but now...

'Though I guess we could double check?'

Her tone held a hint of devilry. He liked it. It meant she hadn't retreated or gone brusque on him. It also meant she might be up for other stuff if latex couldn't be found.

She snagged his hand and tugged him into the bathroom— surprisingly large compared with the rest of the apartment.

It had a glass-enclosed shower, a marble tub big enough for two and a floor-to-ceiling mirror with distinct possibilities.

She released his hand long enough to rummage through three drawers and a cabinet under the sink. He would have laughed at her frantic search if he weren't practically crippled from wanting her so badly.

When she straightened the disappointment in her eyes vindicated what he was about to do.

'Doesn't matter.'

Her mouth down-turned. 'Yeah, it does. I don't do unprotected sex.'

'Neither do I.' He reached out and touched her collarbone, then let his fingertip trail downward, around one breast, then the other, in slow concentric circles, until she sagged against the vanity. 'But there's loads we can do without the grand finale.'

Her eyes lit up as she registered the meaning behind his words and before he could say anything she'd whipped off her tee-shirt, giving him an eyeful of demi-cup black satin and pushed-up cleavage.

'Well, I guess that answers my next question—whether you'd be up for it or not.'

In response she reached for his zipper, tugged it down and slid her hand inside.

He gritted his teeth as she stroked him through the cotton of his boxers, until she reached the tip and he damn near exploded.

'Turn around.'

Her hand stilled at his command and her eyes widened, but he didn't see fear. He saw excitement and heat and yearning. Major turn on.

He missed her touch when she eased her hand out of his pants and swivelled towards the mirror but this would be worth the wait.

He wanted to watch her come.

He wanted to watch her watch him.

With surprisingly steady hands he popped the snap on her jeans, unzipped her and slid the denim down to mid-thigh-level.

Man, she was wearing a thong. Black satin. Same as the bra. He liked black. Some would say it matched his soul, but he didn't agree.

Right about now his soul was red. Fire-engine red. Crimson. The colour of passion and sin and debauchery. Maybe he'd buy her red lingerie for next time.

Her gaze was riveted to his hands as he hooked his thumbs into the elastic riding low on her hips and tugged, revealing her to him.

That expletive spilled from his lips again as he pressed against her—a gentle pressure that had her head falling back to rest on his shoulder.

But she didn't stop staring at his hand as he slid a finger between her slick folds, circling her, her wet heat driving him slowly but surely insane.

'Do you trust me?'

'I'm watching you pleasure me. What do you think?'

He grinned. Even now she was feisty. He liked it.

'Okay, then.'

He made quick work of tugging down his pants and boxers, biting back another curse when his hard-on made contact with her butt.

'Spread your legs a fraction,' he said, and slid between them when she did. The exquisite contact of his shaft with her moist heat almost undid him.

Amazingly, she didn't stop him or ask questions. She trusted him not to enter her and that knowledge, after all he'd been through over the last year, turned him on more than anything she could have said or done.

'Watch.'

He pushed forward, his erection fully between her legs, and she gasped as she saw him appear just beneath his hand.

'Keep watching.'

And she did, as he slid in and out between her legs, mimicking what he'd give anything to be doing deep inside her now.

As his finger picked up the tempo she started moving, her hips pushing back against him, urging him to go faster.

So he did. The torturous friction was building. Peaking. Crescendoing.

She arched a second before she screamed, riding his hand as he'd have liked to be riding her.

He eased away, shocked by the intensity of her orgasm, and even more suprised when she dropped to her knees.

'What are you doing—?'

'If you have to ask, you're not as good at all this as I thought.'

He would have laughed if she hadn't taken him into her mouth. All the way.

It was his turn to watch, but he didn't know where to look. At his fantasy come to life or in the mirror, where what she was doing was reflected back to him in eye-popping erotic detail.

He settled for watching her—the golden sheen of her hair beneath the bathroom lights, her lips surrounding him.

Then she started using her tongue and he lost it. He'd been close when she came, and all it took was three sweeps of her tongue around the tip.

His orgasm ripped through him with the force of an explosion and he swore loudly.

As residual shudders of pleasure rippled through him he held out his hands to help her stand.

She ignored them, pulling up her jeans as she ducked down to the sink.

Uh-oh.

He made himself decent, waiting for her to finish and look at him. The tap eased to a drip, she used a handtowel, still didn't glance up.

'Look at me.'

After a few moments her reluctant gaze met his.

'Don't go having second thoughts now.' He snagged her hands, grateful she didn't pull away this time. 'What we just did blew my mind.'

Relief eased her drawn-together brows. 'You're inventive. I'll say that for you.'

He laughed, and thankfully she joined in. He liked that she hadn't clammed up on him or gone distant. He would have hated that.

'But for the record—next time I'm bringing a box.'

'To stand on?'

'Of condoms.' Buoyed by her sense of humour, he pulled her close, enveloping her in his arms with his chin resting on her head. 'Guess I should be grateful you didn't say there won't be a next time.'

She nuzzled his neck in response, and if it wasn't the damndest thing he was ready to go again. 'There'll be a next time. Count on it.'

He was. What he wasn't counting on was the dazed anticipation in his eyes as he stared at his reflection.

For a guy used to being in total control, a guy who liked his sex without commitment, a guy wary of anything more, he looked like a guy in way over his head.

CHAPTER FIVE

SAPPHIE SHOWERED AND brushed her teeth the next morning without looking in the mirror.

She couldn't. Not unless she wanted to go into meltdown.

The stupid thing was, she'd expected not to sleep last night—to be so wound up with analysing and second-guessing she couldn't—but the oddest thing had happened.

She'd had her first full night's sleep for months. Heck, for years.

And she owed it to Patrick.

Great, even thinking his name made her flush in remembrance.

What they'd done in this bathroom... Who would have thought having pseudo-sex could be so steamy?

She might not be super-experienced in that department—being a workaholic meant she could count the number of guys she'd thought hot enough to sleep with on one hand—but what she'd done with Patrick...

Wow. Simply *wow*.

And she still wanted him as badly this morning.

Her theory last night—that an orgasm might take the edge off her craziness and let her concentrate on working alongside him without the desperation to tear his clothes off—hadn't worked. It had backfired in a big way.

Now she wanted more. So much more. Both of them naked and sweaty. Going the whole way.

Stupid theories.

She should have ordered the take-out, made small talk, and let him walk out of here.

But the way he'd been looking at her… There was only so much willpower a girl could draw on.

Thankfully, it had been okay afterwards. They'd glossed over potential awkwardness, and he'd left after she'd pleaded tiredness and a need to prep for work tomorrow. Today. When she'd be seeing him again in less than an hour. Which meant she needed to apply make-up. Now.

With a groan she dragged herself back into the bathroom, took a deep breath and stared at her reflection.

Still the same tired old face, but there was a new glint in her eyes. A glint she didn't like. A glint that signalled a little bit of lust and a lot of crazy.

She blinked, hoping it would vanish.

Nope, still there. Lord only knew what Patrick would make of that glint.

She tried to concentrate on applying foundation, mascara, eyeshadow and lip gloss, she really did, but every time she focussed on the mirror a snippet of last night would flash into her head.

Courtesy of her shaky hands she'd gone through two applicators and a mascara wand already, and she resembled a clown.

Muttering a few choice curses under her breath, she gathered up her make-up and stalked towards the bedroom. The light might be crappy in there, and her clown face could worsen, but she'd take the risk. She'd rather apply make-up in the tiny oval mirror tacked onto the wardrobe door than use the bathroom one.

Maybe she could call a glazier today and have him remove it?

Then again, Patrick had promised to bring a box of condoms next time, and her newly discovered inner vixen really had had a lot of fun watching…

Realistically, she shouldn't want a repeat. Sex with Patrick would be phenomenal but wrong. A giant complication just waiting to happen.

But she'd felt so good last night—*alive* in a way she hadn't in a long time.

The chronic fatigue syndrome symptoms had drained her mentally, emotionally and physically, particularly the latter, and it was her need to reassert her fitness that was driving her to follow through with Patrick.

Nothing like a sex-a-thon to give a girl a workout.

Okay, so she was making light of the situation, probably making excuses to go through with it too, but Patrick had made her feel sensational last night and she wanted to feel that good again.

The post-orgasmic endorphins had lasted a long time after he'd left, and for the first time in ages she'd had the energy to unpack the rest of her cases, clean the kitchen and rearrange her DVDs and books.

She'd bounced around the apartment, humming eighties tunes and shimmying between cleaning, feeling so good she could have run a marathon.

How long since she'd felt that invincible?

Logically, sex with Patrick might be a disaster. Physically? She'd help him haul that box of condoms over pronto.

Patrick needed neutral. A neutral playing field where he could work alongside Sapphire without the constant urge to rip her clothes off.

Last night had only worsened his lust for her. A small part of him had hoped it would ease. *Yeah, right.*

He should have known better than to believe his delusional self-talk that a quickie with Sapphire would soothe him.

A guy didn't do what he had done with Sapphire last night

and *get it out of his system*. Not to mention the added tension of knowing she was up for more. A whole box-worth more.

He didn't get it. It wasn't as if he'd been hung up on her in the past. He'd enjoyed baiting her at school, made it his mission to get a rise out of her because he'd wanted to ruffle her uptight exterior. Sure, he'd had the odd fantasy about her— what teenage guy hadn't?

Sapphire was an attractive woman now. It figured that he'd want to have sex with her. The part he hadn't figured out was why it was pounding through his brain until it was all he could think about.

He couldn't afford distractions—not with so much at stake. But the thought of using a box-worth of condoms pleasuring Sapphire Seaborn couldn't be denied, and he'd damn well better get control of his libido before he botched this business opportunity before it had begun.

'Hey, Rick, the models are ready.'

Patrick glanced up at his right-hand man and best bud, Serge. Though they'd ripped a path through Europe's party scene together when Patrick had needed the distraction, while Serge continued to live the high life Patrick now opted for more sedate pursuits: like making his fashion house dreams come true.

They'd grown apart over the years but Serge was still a good manager, and it helped having someone he could trust on his side. He couldn't say that about many people.

'Thanks, but Sapphire's not here yet. Give us five.'

'No worries.' Serge spoke into a bluetooth clipped near his right ear before slipping onto the chair next to him. 'What's up?'

Great. Just what he needed. Serge's legendary interrogation. He had no intention of telling anyone about Sapphire— not when they'd be working together. But he and Serge had told tall tales over beers too many times to count, and the guy could read him like the latest bestseller.

'Not much.' Patrick pointed towards the stack of documents in front of him. 'This is taking up all my time.'

'Bull.'

Patrick sat back, folded his arms and feigned ignorance. He only succeeded in making Serge laugh.

'Work never fazes you. You took on that spring showing in Paris and hit it out of the ballpark.' Serge tilted his head to one side, studying him. 'Nah, this isn't about work. This is about a chick.'

Patrick didn't want to discuss Sapphire with Serge but he hated dishonesty.

'That Paris gig? What we're doing here has to nail that a hundred times over and you know it.'

Serge smirked. 'I also know whoever this chick is, she must be special for you to be this rattled.'

Thankfully Sapphire's arrival put paid to any further ribbing from Serge but it disconcerted him in a whole other way.

She'd gone for masculine chic today: crisp white shirt, fitted ebony pinstripe pants suit, designer loafers, hair slicked back, dramatic make-up. It didn't detract from her femininity. He'd seen exactly how womanly she could be last night.

What her mouth had done to him…

His gaze found its way to her lips—their sheen, their fullness—and he instantly hardened.

He heard Serge's hissed breath of surprise as she strode towards them and he knew the feeling. When Sapphire Seaborn walked towards a man he wanted to meet her halfway.

'She's a stunner,' Serge muttered under his breath, earning a glare from Patrick that probably increased his friend's speculation.

Let Serge think what he liked. He wasn't getting one snippet of information about Patrick's private life here in Melbourne. Patrick had moved on from the carousing of the past and intended focussing on things that mattered. Namely:

wowing Fashion Week. And bedding Sapphire. Not necessarily in that order.

She barely glanced at him when she reached them, focussing a dazzling smile on Serge instead. 'Hi. Sapphire Seaborn.'

Serge grinned like the predatory male he was and snagged her hand, raising it to his lips. 'The pleasure's all mine, *mademoiselle*.'

When Serge kissed her hand, Patrick had to clench his to stop from slugging him.

'You're French?'

Serge nodded and, luckily for him, released her hand. *'Oui.'*

'He's as Anglicised as you and I,' Patrick said, shooting him a frown. 'Only uses the accent to win friends and influence women.'

'It's charming.'

Figured. What was it with females and European accents?

'Serge was just leaving to organise the models for a quick demo if you're ready?'

Sapphire finally looked at him, her gaze imperious, the tilt of her head snooty. 'Sure, let's get started.'

She made it sound as if he'd chastised her unnecessarily, when in fact he'd wanted to get rid of his leery friend pronto.

'Au revoir, Sapphire.' Serge gave a formal little bow and Patrick gritted his teeth. 'We will meet again.'

'No doubt.'

If her smile had been dazzling before, she notched it up a level now. What red-blooded guy stood a chance?

Patrick mentally counted to ten, slowly, waiting until Serge had left the room.

'Don't flirt with Serge. It only encourages him,' he said, trying to sound casual and failing miserably if her inverted eyebrow and smirk were any indication.

'I was being polite, not flirting, but thanks for the advice.'

She slid onto a seat and patted the one next to him. 'Now, why don't you sit so we can talk business?'

Fan-frigging-tastic. He'd been mulling over how to approach this first meeting post-bathroom and she'd waltzed in here as if nothing had happened, gaining the upper hand and commandeering the conversation.

Patrick didn't like losing control. Bad things happened. Things he'd never risk happening again.

'Talking business is fine,' he said, sitting next to her and deliberately leaning into her personal space. 'For now.'

The faintest stain of pink on her cheeks was the only indication that he'd scored a hit. She didn't respond, taking her sweet time slipping a slimline laptop out of her satchel and setting it up, laying a blank notepad and pen next to it.

Only then did she swivel in her seat to face him, her imperious mask firmly in place. 'Don't you think it's a tad unprofessional, bringing up our social activities in the workplace?'

Her directness impressed him. But the resumption of her haughtiness, not so much. Hadn't she learned by now that the snootier she acted, the harder he worked to rile her?

'Social activities?' He lowered his voice to barely above a whisper, his lips almost brushing her ear. 'Why don't we call it what it is? Good old-fashioned f—'

'Keep that up and there won't be any *socialising* of any kind,' she said, shoving him away, her tone frosty.

'You haven't changed a bit,' he said, chuckling at her rigid shoulders and ramrod spine as she determinedly stared at her laptop screen. 'You always needed to have the last word during our Biology assignments too.'

'I did not.' She shot him a death glare.

'Yeah, you did. And it's just as cute now.' He smiled, waiting for her to glance his way.

He didn't have to wait long. She blew out an exasperated breath before angling her chair towards him.

'Okay, the thing is this: I'm confident in the business arena.

Invincible. But what happened last night threw me, and focussing on work is the only way I can handle this without…'

'What?'

'Without losing it,' she said softly, her wide-eyed baby-blues imploring him to listen. 'Aren't you just the tiniest bit uncomfortable?'

He shrugged. 'Sure, but honestly? That ice princess act you had down pat in Biology only made me want to taunt you more. And when I first rocked up in Melbourne it looked like nothing had changed. Then last night…' He shook his head, still blown away by the erotic memories that had filtered across his consciousness ever since. 'I got a glimpse of how hot you are beneath the ice and it's a major turn-on. Last night was great. Stupendous, in fact. And a great prelude to going the whole way. So I'm not going to make excuses for it or apologise or act recalcitrant.' He pinned her with a direct stare. 'For the fact is I'd do it again right now, right here.'

Her frosty façade melted a little as her mouth curved at the corners. 'I've always wanted to do it on a desk.'

'Duly noted.' He trailed a fingertip across the back of her hand where it rested on her lap. 'For the record, mine's padded.'

'No, it's not. It's bevelled glass.'

He winked. 'I'll make sure to bring a blanket next time we meet in my office.'

She waggled her finger at him. 'Didn't I just say we should keep business and social stuff separate?'

'Yeah, but that doesn't mean I agree with it.'

She huffed out an exasperated breath—something she'd done often when they'd been studying. 'You know we have to talk about what happened last night, right?'

They did? From where he was sitting, he'd rather be doing much more than talking. Like finishing what they'd started last night, with him deep within her this time around.

'Talk is overrated.'

'Spoken like a true male,' she said drily, jabbing him in the chest. 'We need boundaries, that sort of thing.'

'We need a desk with our name written all over it,' he said, *sotto voce*, earning a delightfully unassuming, tempting pout for his trouble.

'You're the same infuriating, annoying, over-confident—'

'And you're the same subtly sexy, smart, amazing woman,' he said, meaning it.

He'd met some incredible women around the world, had enjoyed every moment of his bachelor life, but it hadn't been until he'd arrived back in Melbourne and strutted into Seaborns that he'd remembered Sapphire had a certain something that elevated her among other females.

He couldn't explain what it was, but the hint of vulnerability underlying her usual toughness appealed on a deeper level he rarely acknowledged.

And that meant he had to focus on one thing only. Sex. No time or inclination to discover where her newfound softness had come from or to delve beyond the obvious: they were two people with a serious sexual attraction that would combust if last night's prelude was any indication.

And he couldn't wait for the main event.

Her mouth opened, closed. Her loss of words was cute. A rarity. He took full advantage.

'I meant what I said.' He snagged her hand beneath the table and she let him. 'I had no idea you were so hot in high school—' She pursed her lips in disapproval and he rushed on '—which is probably a good thing, as I would've made you fail Biology. But seeing how into it you were last night, us hooking up, major turn-on. Fantasy stuff.'

He must have said the right thing, because she turned her hand over and intertwined her fingers with his. 'You drove me nuts in high school, teasing me and mucking around with your slackass attitude.'

'Surely that kiss on graduation night redeemed me slightly?

She winced. 'Another thing I'd rather not talk about.'

'Yeah, I kinda got that impression when you didn't return my calls.'

Her fingers convulsed for a second. 'I was mortified.'

'Why? Because your date was a drunken dumbass?'

She shook her head, dislodging a few strands from her slicked back do. Mussing the severity of that product-drenched hair added to her vulnerability.

'No, I was embarrassed because I'd treated you badly yet you didn't hesitate in stepping in to help me out of a rough spot.'

He saw genuine regret in the reluctant gaze that met his, and he didn't like his answering zap of emotion.

Who cared what her motivations had been back then? He wanted her in his bed now. That was all that mattered. No room for emotions whatsoever.

'Hey, I liked the putdowns and the cutting remarks. It spurred me on to tease you harder.'

'That's what the kiss was about, wasn't it?'

She'd lost him.

'Huh?'

'I thought you kissed me out of pity.'

She said it so softly he strained forward to hear it.

'What the—?'

'I thought you felt sorry for me after Mick ditched me at the dance,' she said, bolder this time, daring him to disagree. 'You teased me during the drive about my lousy taste in dates, said maybe it was my dress or my hair or my corsage that drove him away, then we got home and you kissed me and I thought it was a big joke—you taking your usual taunts that one step further.'

He swore.

'You thought I was that shallow?'

'That's the only side of you I ever saw,' she said, as if that made it better.

It didn't. There was a reason he'd acted that way, why he'd only shown the world a certain side, but he couldn't tell her. He'd divulged enough truths for one day.

'Well, sweetheart, here's a tip. When a guy kisses a girl it isn't out of pity. It's usually driven by hormones.'

He shrugged, trying to make light of the situation before he blabbed about why he'd really kissed her that night. It wouldn't help to admit he had felt sorry for her, that he'd kissed her as a distraction to prevent tears. She'd slug him for sure. Or worse, not follow through on the promise of sensational sex.

So he was a guy? Sue him.

'And here's a heads up. My motivation for kissing you back then is irrelevant. Because all that matters now is I sure as hell want you. *Right now,* if I had my way.' He tugged on her hand and she leaned in close. 'I'd clear this table, hoist you onto it, and have you out of those pants in two seconds flat.'

Her eyes widened, locked on his. Thankfully she'd lost the injured lamb look. He could handle her cool and controlled. He didn't do her insecure side well. It unnerved him, seeing the woman who'd verbally fended off his barbs and then some all soft and susceptible.

It made him *feel* stuff he didn't want to, so he regained control the only way he knew how.

'I'd spread your legs, start at your right knee and kiss my way upward. Nipping your inner thigh…gentle bites.'

Her sharp intake of breath spurred him on.

'I'd tease my way along your hip, across your belly to the other side, where I'd kiss you all the way down. Hot, open-mouthed kisses, until you were squirming for me.' He locked gazes with her. 'Begging for it.'

She groaned.

He knew the feeling.

'Keep going,' she said, squirming in her seat.

'Then I'd lick my way up your thigh until I could hardly

control myself. But I'd taste you, circling you with my tongue, sucking you into my mouth until you came—'

'Patrick, please…'

He released her hand in her lap and edged over, cupping her mound. She cursed, the word spilling from her lips as much of a turn-on as her reaction to him here in the boardroom.

The fact she was letting him do this to her here, with the risk of anyone walking in, heightened the pleasure.

'Yeah, I'd love to be doing that to you right now, but this will have to suffice.'

He pushed the heel of his hand into her and she ground against it. It took several small, circular undulations of for her to come, her fingers digging into his thigh while she lifted off the chair slightly.

They never broke eye contact the entire time, so he saw everything. Her need, her passion, her release.

And it humbled him in a way he'd never dreamed possible.

If he'd thought he was in over his head last night, her response to him now made him feel like a drowning man without a chance of being saved.

The door creaked open and they sprang apart. She muttered underneath her breath: he tried to act as if wanting to tear this woman's clothes off every time he saw her wasn't all that unusual.

Sex…nothing more, nothing less. Maybe if he mentally recited it often enough he'd believe it.

He shot her a glance but she stared straight ahead, fixed on the models strutting through the room in preliminary designs, the pinkness of her cheeks the only giveaway sign that she wasn't the same über-cool princess he remembered.

Fine, let them concentrate on business for now, but when they'd wrapped up here they needed to sort out where and when they were going to get this *thing* out of their system— for he had a feeling he wouldn't be functioning on any useful level until he did.

* * *

Sapphie had learned from a young age to shield her real feelings.

The expectations associated with being the eldest child, the one with highest grades, the responsible one, had pretty much ensured she was under scrutiny as heir apparent to run Seaborns from the time she hit high school.

Maybe even before, considering her mum had spent every Saturday afternoon poring over the company's finances and making Sapphie sit next to her.

When kids her age had been riding their scooters or playing netball on the weekend, she'd been tagging along on buying expeditions, or scouting the opposition, or hanging around at fancy tea parties, listening to her mum talk shop.

Sure, she'd learned to love Seaborns, and had strived to gain great grades to enter her chosen Economics and Management degree, but over the years it had become ingrained to maintain a calm outer persona. To pretend everything was right with the world. When in fact she'd had bad hair days and hated the school bully and crushed on the football captain.

That persona would serve her well now, when she had to sit next to Patrick during a preview and pretend he hadn't just rocked her world again.

What he'd done... What she'd let him do...

Her fingers convulsed, digging into her thighs. She'd never been wild or wanton. Maybe that was her problem. When an experienced playboy like Patrick glanced sideways at her she was ready to jump him.

She blamed Ruby and all that talk of getting laid. Sure, it had been a while since she'd been with a guy, but she hadn't really been interested, what with the fatigue.

Ironic that coming back to work and throwing herself into this campaign was all about physically proving she could handle leading Seaborns, but what if there was a better way to test her endurance? Or at least a more fun way?

For she had little doubt sex with Patrick would involve an aerobic capacity workout to push her to the limit.

As if sensing her wicked, wayward thoughts he cast her a glance, which she deftly deflected by pretending to concentrate on the models strutting into the room.

Thankfully he returned to muttering into his smartphone, dictating changes and minor adjustments on the gowns to follow up later: hem too low here, stray seam there. He was so focussed, so tuned in to his work, she couldn't help but stare a little.

He'd surprised her. She'd wondered if he could pull off his mega idea for old-world Hollywood glamour, and by the looks of the early designs he'd come through in a big way.

It pained her to admit, even to herself, that she'd doubted him. But she had, and now she was going to have to eat her words.

How could the guy who'd laughed his way through school before absconding to Paris be responsible for these exquisite designs?

She glanced at the models, poised in a holding pattern on a makeshift runway, stunned anew by the colours and gowns before her eyes.

A riot of rich hues: deep crimson, emerald, peacock-blue. Lush satins, shimmering silks. Strapless evening gowns. Timeless cocktail frocks. Curves and class. Absolutely stunning.

Patrick might not have personally drawn the designs, but he'd come up with the concept, had supervised the designers night and day to get them to this point.

Not only did the guy have a sound business head, he had creativity to burn.

And not just for this fashion show.

She resisted the urge to squirm in her seat—and tried to ignore the occasional brush of his shoulder against hers or the touch of his thigh pressing close as he leaned over to point out a minor detail. Perfectly innocuous actions that shouldn't have made her burn but she did. For him. With an unrelenting heat that sparked every time he touched her and shot off at tangents throughout her body, zapping and scalding and corroding her resistance slowly but surely.

This wasn't good.

Their bathroom interlude should have taken the edge off her sudden interest in seeing him naked.

Instead it had put her on some heightened awareness where having him near sent her pheromones into overdrive.

The preview concluded way too quickly. Serge departed and the models filed out after him, leaving her rueing the approaching time where she'd have to do some fast thinking, fast talking, or both.

She'd had an orgasm.

In Fourde Fashion's boardroom.

With an unlocked door.

Seconds before people had come traipsing in.

It had been phenomenal, but the fact she was becoming like him—reckless, live in the moment—was not good.

That might have been one of her goals after leaving Tenang—to make the most of every second and not dwell on things she couldn't change—but now she had Patrick urging her, how far would she go to test her newfound strength?

Pushing it physically was one thing, but seeing how far she could push with Patrick…

Danger with a capital D.

For sex with a guy like him could become addictive, and she had no intention of getting hooked.

'Thoughts?'

He really didn't want to know.

By the amused glint in his eyes, maybe he did.

She took a deep breath and pushed her notepad towards him. 'On what you've done? Amazing. Here are a few things I jotted down to capitalise on the theme you're going for.'

He sped read her dot-point list, nodding thoughtfully, pen tapping against the pad, so absorbed in business that she wondered if she'd dreamt the whole dirty-talk orgasm incident.

'Great pick-ups. I'll get onto Serge right away to get the designers to incorporate.'

He glanced up and her heart leapt.

'Sure Ruby's the only creative genius in your family?' He pointed at the list. 'These are insightful suggestions.'

Chuffed by his praise, she shrugged. 'This coming from the guy who has single-handedly come up with an amazing concept and is seeing it through to the most glorious designs I've ever seen.'

He winked. 'Flattery will get you everywhere.'

That was what she was afraid of.

Now was the time she had to lay down the law about mixing business with pleasure, about setting boundaries. But with her body still humming and her mind still reeling at how sexual he made her feel, maybe now wasn't the best time.

He touched her arm, the barest brush of his fingertips against her skin, and she jumped.

'Your reaction just answered my next question.'

'What's that?'

'That until we get this thing out of our systems are we going to be useless working together?'

She should disagree. Should give him a spiel about her ability to remain professional and focussed at all times.

Totally hypocritical, considering she'd almost screamed his name less than thirty minutes ago.

'What do you suggest?'

'Damned if I know.' He pinched the bridge of his nose. It did little to clear the frown above it. 'We have three weeks left 'til Fashion Week, so the next seven days are crucial in finalising the designs and incorporating changes.'

No argument there.

'That means we both need to work our butts off without interruptions.' He sent her a pointed glare. 'Or distractions.'

'Hey, I'm not the one going around…' She trailed off, unwilling to articulate exactly what he'd been doing to her. 'So you're saying we work apart?'

Was that even feasible with the workload they had?

He nodded, and while her head said this was the perfect solution, her body wailed a loud, resounding *nooooo!*

'We talk on the phone, e-mail, Skype. But this?' He gestured to the limited space between them. 'Too distracting when I can't keep my hands off you.'

His declaration soothed her wailing body somewhat.

'But some time in the future, when the campaign is done…' He snagged a tendril curling around her ear and wound it slowly around his finger, caressing the top of her ear, tracing its shape, sending a shiver of longing vibrating downwards. 'We play.'

How two words could hold so much promise she'd never know.

'Define play.'

His mouth eased into a breath-stealing grin. 'You and me. "Do not Disturb" sign. And that box I promised you. Maybe two.'

Her body gave a betraying howl of longing.

'Your stamina's that good?'

'You bet.' He leaned close, his lips grazing her cheek, and she clamped down on the urge to turn her head a fraction and ram her mouth against his. 'And I can't wait to prove it.'

Oh, boy.

'Sound doable?'

She—it—was extremely doable.

'Sure.' She nodded, her insides trembling with need, as she gathered up her work paraphernalia.

'Sapphire?'

She couldn't stop, for if she did she'd never make it out of here without flinging herself at him.

'Yeah?' she mumbled, trying to stuff her laptop into her bag with limited success—until she realised she was trying to force it into her handbag.

'You know time apart will feed my hunger for you?'

She gulped.

If they were this turned on now, imagine what time apart would do?

'And while we focus on business this next week it doesn't rule out phone sex.'

A ripple of pleasure spread through her at the thought.

'I've never done phone sex,' she said, sounding like an inexperienced neophyte but not caring. She had a feeling this guy would be teaching her a plethora of unspoken delights.

'Then this is going to be fun.'

He brushed a kiss across her lips and she let him, lingering a few seconds longer than necessary, aware it would be their last physical contact for a long seven days.

When the need to linger became a driving need to straddle him, she yanked away and grabbed her stuff.

She strode for the door, desperate to put some distance between them. With her hand on the handle and a safe space between them, she said, 'Patrick?'

'Yeah?'

Her only consolation was that he looked half as dazed as she was.

'Better make that three boxes.'

CHAPTER SIX

SAPPHIE LASTED A whole three days without succumbing to the temptation of seeing Patrick's face.

Then he sent her a text, citing an urgent Skype meeting, and she caved.

Purely business, of course. And the fact she spent ten minutes primping in front of a mirror? It was the usual routine she'd do before any work meeting.

The part where her palms grew clammy as she swiped on mascara and scrubbed off her lippy twice before settling on the perfect shade was pure feminine preening.

She had four more days before he made good on his promise. Just the two of them and a decadent weekend. With boxes.

She'd been a smart-ass, taunting him at the conclusion of their last face-to-face meeting, but deep down she was a quivering mess of confusion and nerves and lust. The kind of lust she'd never experienced. The kind of lust guaranteed to turn her into a fool.

She didn't suffer fools lightly, and respected hard work and dedication in comparison with deceitful women who faked helplessness in order to score points with men. The type of women Patrick usually hung out with if the internet was anything to go by.

It had been a stupid, spur-of-the moment decision to check out his more recent past, spurred by two glasses of Chardonnay and a rampant curiosity.

It had been the end of a long eighteen-hour day—the day after she'd seen him; a day in which she'd determinedly buried herself in work to erase the lingering memory of his touch, and her response.

The wine had helped her wind down but it hadn't taken the edge off her curiosity and she'd succumbed to temptation.

The internet had been enlightening, to say the least, and had provided her with a plethora of images and articles. Usually depicting Patrick with a stunning supermodel on his arm, laughing into the camera, with a different country landscape in the background. From Santorini to Monte Carlo, Nice to Barcelona, Patrick was there, partying his way through Europe.

She'd given up after the tenth page. The endless hits had been rather depressing.

He'd lived such an exciting life amid glamorous people while she'd spent the last ten years devoting hers to Seaborns.

She didn't regret a single moment—discounting the last year when she'd been an idiot in shouldering the burden alone—and still experienced a thrill when she walked into their amazing showroom. But seeing pictorial evidence of Patrick's lifestyle reinforced what she'd always felt around him: gauche, prim, floundering a little.

And envious. She'd always been a tad envious of his ability to charm people, his ease to cruise through life without a care in the world, his natural exuberance that made everyone around him smile.

If anything, those images had reinforced what she already knew deep down: that Patrick was way different and always had been. Back in high school he'd annoyed her, so what had changed now? He was still brash and cocky and charming, and had waltzed into this new Fourde Fashion with the ease of a practised CEO.

As far as she could tell from her research he'd been a minion in Paris, so this position was a massive boost up the corporate ladder for him. From what she'd been able to find of his professional life, that was. There'd been a glut of social stuff and pics, and *nada* on his work. She'd found it odd but had been too depressed by the gorgeous glamazons on his arm in every photo to worry about it.

And that exacerbated her annoyance—the fact he'd probably been handed this job on a silver platter and would rock it because he had the backing of his family name.

The irony wasn't lost on her: people would say the same about her and Seaborns. But there was a difference. She'd been groomed from a young age to take over, had acted in accordance because of it. Had made sacrifices, had never lost sight of the end goal, had strived to be the best leader this jewellery company had ever seen.

Could Patrick say the same? Doubtful.

For a guy who'd spent his final year doodling and folding origami figures with his study notes he'd come a long way.

And judging by this current show he was nailing it too.

Admiration tempered her annoyance at his glib, charmed life. The guy might have skived off during that final year at high school but he was putting in the hard yards now.

And she admired hard work. She understood it. What she didn't understand was her undeniable, clamouring attraction to him.

She felt *good* around him, in a way she hadn't in a long time. Her skin tingled, her blood pounded and she felt *alive*.

Proving she could physically handle her role as Seaborns' boss was one thing, but handling whatever Patrick dished out took her recovery to a whole other level.

Matching him sexually would push her out of her comfort zone, and it would take the edge off this insane lust she had for him.

Most importantly, it would prove to herself she was whole again.

That had been the worst part of her enforced rest at Tenang—the insidious self-doubts that would creep up on her at inopportune moments and make her wonder if she had what it took to continue leading Seaborns.

For someone who'd loved being the face of the company, who'd attended posh soirées and glamorous events and talked up Seaborn's fabulous jewellery every chance she got, during her recovery she'd wondered if she'd ever find that kind of energy again.

Sure, she'd improved, but every time she yawned or had a twinge in her muscles or a minor headache from spending too long at the computer, she experienced a fleeting panic that she could suffer a relapse.

Being with Patrick, having him desire her, made her feel physically thriving, and that, more than anything, silenced her doubts in getting sexually involved with him.

Anything, or any*one*, that could make her feel on this constant high, as if she was invincible, was worth pursuing.

She remembered the way he'd looked at her those times he'd pleasured her, the way he'd been turned on, the way he devoured her with his eyes every time he thought she wasn't looking—and her body buzzed.

The endorphin release from Patrick's touch was much better than any workout.

But craving him this much…how had she morphed from a successful, confident businesswoman to this muddle of need?

His fault for being so darn appealing. Which raised the question: if she did throw herself into a dirty little fling with him, would her sensibilities return or would this crazy, out of control feeling intensify?

She couldn't afford the latter—needed to ensure Seaborns presented their best work at the Fashion Week show. A real quandary: indulge in a no-holds-barred fling with Patrick, feel utterly amazing and the best she had in ages. Or walk away from any further physical involvement and run the risk of going completely batty wanting him regardless.

She stuck her tongue out at her reflection. How had she ended up in this situation?

She didn't lust after guys—especially ones who'd driven her nuts in high school. She worked hard and worked out. That was the extent of her life.

Maybe that was half the problem?

Probably. Which was why a decadent weekend of raunchy sex could be just what the doctor ordered.

She chuckled, wondering what the physicians at Tenang would think about that as a treatment for CFS.

Though could she do it? Shuck off her business suit and become a sex-starved goddess for a weekend with Patrick?

As she settled in front of her PC and waited for Patrick's Skype call one thought reverberated through her head: *first time for everything.*

Patrick had worked his ass off the last three days. Pulled an all-nighter. Done the work of ten men. Supervised and brain-stormed and delegated.

Usually this manic pace gave him a buzz. In the past it had come from partying; these days it was from ensuring Fourde Fashion stayed ahead of competing European designers.

This time working like a maniac hadn't taken the edge off. Only one woman could do that and he couldn't wait to see her—even if it was only via a screen.

He didn't like how she'd got under his skin. Didn't like the anticipation making his palms clammy. She was a distraction he could ill afford but somehow, despite working his butt off, he couldn't stop thinking about her.

At least Skype was safe. A visual without the temptation of touching. And he'd been doing a lot of that, fantasising about touching her...

He'd half expected Sapphire not to respond to his call, but in a few seconds she appeared, her eyes wide and luminous, her cheeks pink, her lips glossed, and his gut tightened.

'Hey, gorgeous.'

'Hey.' A smile played around her lips but it didn't quite reach her eyes. 'What did you want to discuss tonight?'

'Business, of course.'

He had to stay focussed on business before he ignored his vow to stay away from her and drove like a maniac to her apartment.

Seeing her, even through a screen, wasn't such a smart idea after all. He should have stuck to e-mails.

'Good.' She nodded, as if his answer had allayed her fears of getting too personal. 'What did you think of those shots I e-mailed this morning?'

'Ruby's incredibly talented.' He held up a sketch. 'The embedded sapphire choker will look amazing with this evening gown. And the emerald dog collar will accentuate the showstopper perfectly.'

'Great.' Her shoulders relaxed a little but her studiously polite smile didn't slip. 'What about the yellow diamond set? Could it be used with the saffron sheath or the alabaster A-line?'

'Think we'll make that decision when the models wear the final pieces.'

'Timelines still on track?'

He nodded. 'Absolutely.'

'Good, because we've been working like maniacs over here.'

'Same here.' He slipped a finger between his tie and collar. 'I'm in danger of becoming a very dull boy.'

Her lips quirked into a coy smile. 'I doubt that.'

'I miss playing,' he said, knowing he shouldn't flirt but unable to stop.

'I never have time to.'

He heard the wistful undertone, well aware that if she were anything like she'd been in high school Sapphire would never take time out to play.

'Everyone should make time to play. It's healthy.'

'So I've been told,' she said, glancing away from the screen, fiddling with the neckline of her dress.

In that moment he knew exactly how to make her come out to play.

He locked fingers, stretched and settled them behind his head. 'Tell me what you're wearing.'

A cute little crease appeared between her brows. 'Pretty obvious, I would've thought. Ochre shift dress.'

'I meant what you're wearing beneath it.'

Her lips parted in a delightful O of surprise before she clamped them shut. 'We are *so* not having Skype sex.'

'Why not?'

'Because.' She darted a glance away from the screen. Probably trying to find something to cover the inbuilt camera. 'I don't see the point.'

'The point being it's fun to play. And if you're half as horny as me it might take the edge off.' He unlocked his hands and leaned towards the camera. 'Plus I love seeing you get off.'

A deep crimson flushed her cheeks.

'Come on, give a guy a little something to tide him over while he's working all-nighters.'

The tip of her tongue darted out to moisten her bottom lip before she said, 'I—I—haven't done this before. I'm not sure—'

'It's all about the fantasy, sweetheart.' He lowered his voice, knowing he needed to say the right thing or he'd lose her. 'There's no right or wrong way. Just do what feels good.'

She paused, worrying her bottom lip for a few indecisive seconds, before her chin tilted and he knew he had her.

'You tell anyone about this and you're a dead man.'

Victorious, he leaned back in his chair. 'Consider this a prelude to the real thing.'

She nodded, and a sweep of hair the colour of gold silk swished across one eye before she pushed it back impatiently.

'Let's try this again. Tell me what you're wearing.'

She inhaled and blew out a breath. 'Pale pink lace.'

'Bra and panties?'

'Thong,' she corrected, and his hard-on twitched.

'Sheer?'

'Yep.'

He cursed.

'Take off your thong.'

Her eyes widened. 'Patrick—'

'Do it,' he said, his voice thick with lust. 'And I want to see proof.'

'I'm not doing that—'

'Relax, just seeing the thong will do.' He grinned. 'For now.'

She huffed out a breath but he saw her wiggling, and in a few moments she waved the flimsiest excuse for underwear he'd ever seen in front of the camera.

'Satisfied?'

'Not by a long shot, babe, but we're getting there.'

He wondered how far he could push her and decided to go all the way.

'Now touch yourself.' He throbbed, and shifted in his chair. 'You're turned on, wet, and as you touch yourself I want you to imagine it's my tongue.'

She moaned, and it was the sweetest sound he'd ever heard via electronic medium.

'I'll do it,' she said, 'but only if you do it too.'

Kudos to his sexy Sapphire. She was a quick learner.

'Okay, but only because you asked so nicely.'

He unzipped and sprang free of his boxers, rigid and straining. As he wrapped his fingers around himself he closed his eyes, visualising the encounter he'd had with Sapphire in her bathroom. How her breasts had bounced as he'd thrust between her legs, how slick she'd been, how her face had looked as she came.

'Can you feel my mouth on you?' she said, and it was his turn to groan. 'Because I'm taking you in all the way as I'm touching myself.'

He wanted to open his eyes, to watch her face, but he knew if he did this would be over all too quickly.

'Tell me what you feel like,' he said, moving his hand, wishing it were hers.

'I'm so wet for you,' she murmured, giving a little pant of surprise. 'I think I'm going to come pretty soon.'

'That's good, because I was ready to blow the second I imagined your mouth around me.'

'Let's do this together, okay?'

He heard the vulnerability in her voice and his eyes snapped open. And, yeah, he immediately wished he'd kept them closed.

She had an incredibly rapt expression, filled with wonderment and excitement and awe, and it made him want to fling himself through the screen and cyberspace to sweep her into his arms.

Her wondrous gaze never left his. 'Patrick, I'm so close...'

'Come for me,' he said, his hand quickening as his muscles tightened in pre-release.

'Patrick...this feels...*oooh*...'

She came on a drawn-out keen and it was enough to push him over the edge.

His mind blanked as he blasted to outer space and back, despite the fact this had been a poor substitute for where he'd like to be.

'Patrick?'

'Hmm?'

'I have a newfound respect for Skype.'

'Good, because we're having another *business* meeting tomorrow night.'

* * *

Patrick was a glutton for punishment.

It was the only explanation for why he'd agreed to personally drop off the fabric swatches to Ruby at Seaborns.

Though it wasn't Ruby he was hoping to see and he knew it.

It had been two nights since his Skype session with Sapphire and while he hadn't contacted her since he couldn't stop thinking about her.

She invaded his every waking moment, and most sleeping ones too.

His vow not to be distracted by her during preparations for this show was not working out so great.

He didn't like feeling this…*confused*. Women always held some fascination, but in the past he'd been able to relegate them to his downtime without a problem. But Sapphire? Whether he was working, or at the gym burning off his frustration, she was there, in his mind, the echo of her pleasure reverberating in his ears until he couldn't think straight.

Turning up at Seaborns today was about proving to himself he wasn't enthralled. That he had a grip on this thing between them. That he wasn't such a schmuck he couldn't control his libido.

Then Sapphire opened the door and his blasé self-talk faded into oblivion.

'Thanks for dropping the swatches by,' she said, holding open the door and beckoning him in. 'Ruby's dying to match them to the latest batch of gems.'

'No worries,' he said, taking great care not to brush her as he entered.

One touch and he'd take her up against the nearest glass display case.

'Want a drink?'

He swallowed his first response, a resounding *no*, and nodded out of politeness. 'Sure, coffee would be great.'

'Through here.'

He followed her into a tiny kitchenette at the back of the showroom and immediately regretted his decision to stay, manners be damned. The room was no bigger than a box. A very tiny box that resulted in her light cinnamon peach perfume mingling with the coffee bean aroma and wrapping around him in a sweet, tempting blend.

While the percolator did its thing, she propped herself against the bench and he struggled not to stare at the teal silk wraparound dress that did incredible things to her body and highlighted the sparkle in her eyes.

'Can I see the swatches?'

He wanted to fling the fabric samples at her and make a run for it while he still could. For he knew without a doubt that if she took a step towards him he wouldn't be able to keep his hands off her.

'Yeah.'

He fished them out of his pocket and held the swatches at arm's length, earning an amused smile.

'For someone who was mighty forward the other night, I find your sudden reticence intriguing.'

'Just take the swatches,' he said, gritting his teeth against the urge to say more.

Such as what he'd like to do to her right here, right now, up against the tiny kitchen bench.

'You? Shy?' She reached out and rubbed a piece of crimson satin between thumb and forefinger. 'Rather cute.'

He watched her feel the satin, how the soft material slid between her fingers, and counted to ten. Slowly.

It didn't work.

He snagged her fingers and hauled her towards him, their bodies slamming into one another with enough force to leave them winded.

He didn't give her a chance to catch her breath, ravishing

her mouth with the desperation of a man who'd been pushed to his limits.

This idea of his to keep his distance, to keep distractions to a minimum—*so* not working.

Her hands tangled in his hair, finding purchase, as he shoved her against the nearest wall and pressed into her.

She groaned and he deepened the kiss, yearning to be inside her with a hunger that left him reeling.

How could he be this out of control over a woman? One who could never be more than a fling, considering his long-term plans?

Crazy.

The percolator made a god-awful noise as it clicked off, the sound penetrating the sensual cocoon enveloping them.

Sapphire broke the kiss, her chest heaving, her eyes flashing. 'One sugar or two?'

He laughed, easing the tension between them. 'Two. With a double shot of brandy if you have it.'

'Sorry, you'll have to make do with sugar,' she said, busying herself with organising the coffee but unable to hide the betraying tremble in her hands.

He knew the feeling—this relentless, all-consuming craving that had him off-kilter.

Maybe he was going about this all wrong? If an enforced absence wasn't working, maybe he should try the opposite? Getting her out of his system?

It couldn't be any worse than the agonising torture he was going through now.

'Come away with me for the weekend.'

Her hand stilled, holding the kettle in mid-air as she poured boiling water into her mug.

'I thought we were going to not see each other during the campaign—'

'Screw it.' He dragged his hand through his hair and took two steps, which constituted pacing in the tiny kitchenette.

'We need to get this thing out of our systems, and staying apart isn't helping, so let's go for it.'

'Well, when you put it like that, how can a girl refuse?' She topped off her mug and placed the kettle on its stand.

He winced. 'Sorry, that didn't come out right.'

'I get it.' She handed him his coffee. 'We're going a little stir crazy. I guess a weekend away can't hurt.'

'Great. I'll set it up—e-mail you the details.'

She nodded, cradling her mug, staring at him with wide eyes over the top of it.

He couldn't read the expression in those rich blue depths, but if she was half as shell-shocked as him he couldn't blame her.

Hopefully this impulsive weekend away would ease this clamouring attraction between them once and for all. And then he could concentrate on more important things—like putting his plans into action.

'What's got you in a tizz?' Ruby held out an arm, effectively blocking Sapphie's exit from her workshop.

'Nothing,' she said, wishing she hadn't snapped at her sister. It was a sure-fire sign something was going on, considering she'd been nothing but the epitome of calm since Tenang.

Before Patrick showed up, that was.

Ruby pointed to a spare stool next to her workbench. 'Sit. Spill.'

Sapphie shrugged, pretending she didn't have a care in the world, when all she could think about was getting naked with Patrick face to face. Or other bits to other bits, more precisely.

'I'm getting angsty about the show.'

Ruby frowned. 'I thought you weren't allowed to get angsty? Part of your new relaxation routine?'

'There's only so far yoga can take you, Rubes.'

Her sister's astute gaze swept over her. 'This isn't about work, is it?'

''Course it is—'

'Why don't you just bonk him and get it out of your system, already? You'll feel a lot better for it. Trust me.'

Sapphie screwed up her nose. '*Euw!* Please don't elaborate on how you and Jax managed to brainstorm that auction.'

Her sister's smug grin reeked of sin. *Half her luck.*

Ruby laid down her pliers, pushed her loupe out of the way and crossed her arms.

'You've been working like a maniac this last week. Why don't you take the weekend off? Call Patrick? Get together—'

'He's taking me away for the weekend,' she blurted, unable to keep it a secret any longer.

She'd had no intention of telling Ruby anything, expecting to be teased, interrogated or both for the next millennium, but with her departure to destination unknown creeping ever closer Sapphie had to say something for no other reason than articulating made it real.

Ruby clapped. 'Way to go, Saph.' She wiggled her eyebrows. 'Dirty weekend away, huh?'

Sapphie's first instinct was to say *It's not like that*, but after withholding the promise she'd made to their mum on her deathbed and the resultant fallout she'd vowed never to keep the truth from her sister again.

Which meant full disclosure. Within reason.

'I haven't been out with anyone in a while, he seems keen, so it's a bit of harmless fun.'

'Uh-huh.' Ruby nodded, her sly grin particularly worrying. 'So it's just a fling, right? Nothing serious?'

'Yeah.'

'Then why are you so flustered?'

'I'm not,' Sapphie said, making a mockery of her declaration by edging backwards and tripping over a crate.

Ruby chuckled. 'I've never seen you this worked up over a guy before. It's cute.'

'Cute is puppies and newborns. Cute is not the relationship I have with Patrick.'

'Oh? Then what would you call it?'

Raunchy. Decadent. Naughty.

Very, very naughty.

Images of what they'd done in her bathroom and the boardroom and via Skype in her bedroom earlier this week flashed across her memory and heat touched her cheeks.

Ruby held up her hands. 'Never mind. Spare me the details. I can see how good it is written all over your face.' She slugged her on the arm. 'Proud of you.'

At least that made one of them. Sapphie wasn't entirely proud of using Patrick—for that was exactly what she was doing. He wasn't her type, and she had no intention of continuing this dalliance once their work together on Fashion Week ended, so using him didn't sit well.

The fact he seemed more than happy to use her back was a moot point.

'Stop thinking so hard. You'll get frown lines.' Ruby swiped a finger between her brows. 'There's nothing to over-analyse here, sis. Mutual gratification. Fling. Whatever you want to call it— just enjoy.'

She fully intended to. As for what happened after? She'd cross that mannequin when she came to it.

'Where are you taking her?' Serge propped himself on the end of Patrick's desk, the epitome of male chic in one of Fourde's five-grand-a-pop suits.

'What's it to you?' Patrick practically snarled, and instantly regretted it. It wasn't Serge's fault a week's worth of cold showers and iceberg documentaries hadn't taken the edge off. Throw in the lack of sleep from working all hours to distract himself, and he was a grouch.

'Come on, mate, we've always discussed our women in the past.'

He'd deliberately shut the door on his past. And Sapphire was no ordinary woman.

He didn't want to discuss her with Serge, didn't want to hear the usual ribald jokes and innuendo. Sapphire deserved better than that, and the last thing he needed as Fashion Week crept closer was to lose his right-hand man because he'd punched him in the mouth.

Which led to the question: why did he feel so strongly about this? About *her*? He had a job to do in Melbourne: make Australia and the world sit up and take notice of Fourde Fashion's latest branch before he moved on to bigger and better things. That was his primary goal.

Sapphire was great as a temporary distraction but that was all she could ever be. Temporary.

For he had monumental dreams. Ones that involved taking on his folks head-on back in Europe.

Yeah, he'd do well to keep the endgame in sight. Despite the extremely attractive distraction.

Serge slid off his desk and stalked towards a side table, pointing at the basketball-size globe. 'Let me see.' He spun the globe with a finger, jabbing at it to stop it when the map of Australia came around. 'Well, look-ee here.'

Patrick didn't like where this was going. He'd played Serge's stupid flag game in the past, when bedding women had gone in conjunction with partying. Not that he'd ever kept tally of the nationalities of the women he'd slept with, so he could stab a pin into a country as some kind of warped bedpost-notch equivalent, but he'd laughed when Serge had presented him with his round-the-world dalliances.

Later, he'd kept the globe as proof of the life he'd left behind—a life deliberately shunned because it had left him feeling shallow and worthless. Two feelings he'd had a gutful of after his major screw-up.

It served as a visual reminder of how far he'd come and a place he'd never return.

Serge let out a low wolf-whistle. 'Just as I suspected. No flag on Melbourne.'

He hated Serge's sly smirk.

'I'm guessing that's about to change come Monday.'

'I haven't got time for childish games.' Patrick lowered his voice with effort. 'And neither do you. Showtime in two weeks and we're nowhere near ready.'

'Chillax. We'll get there. We always do.'

Patrick wished he had half Serge's confidence. He might be taking charge with Sapphire when it came to sex, but no amount of planning or executing could guarantee a fault-less show.

So many variables could go wrong—from a broken sti-letto to a thread unravelling, from a model's hissy fit to a competitor sabotaging.

Patrick didn't like the unknown. He intended on planning for every contingency and if that meant working night and day for the next fortnight so be it. After this weekend, that was.

This weekend was all his. And maybe, just maybe, sex with Sapphire would ease his stress levels and make concen-trating on work easier.

'If I can't talk about your dirty weekend, can I ask if you've had any feedback from Hardy and Joyce on the Fashion Week presentation?'

Yeah, Patrick had heard from his folks. A vague, general go-ahead while they focussed on more important matters, like booking the Louvre for an innovative Fourde Fashion show or gearing up for Milan.

As if they'd deem the Aussie office worthy of more than a cursory glance.

Well, he had news for them. He'd make them sit up and take notice of Fourde in Melbourne. Then he'd confront them with his plans to take them on in Europe.

They'd probably ignore him again, as they had the first

time he'd mentioned it. When they realised he was for real they wouldn't like it. Worse, they'd probably laugh at him.

But he was sick of being patronised. It seemed nothing he did could make up for the mistakes of the past but this time he intended on making his mark. He'd make them—and the world—pay attention to Patrick Fourde for all the right reasons.

'I don't need their approval,' he said, unclenching his fists beneath the desk.

'Man, you better get laid this weekend because you're wound tight.' Serge shook his head. 'I asked if you'd had feedback, not their approval.'

Sadly, Patrick had a feeling even sex with Sapphire wouldn't alleviate his long-standing stress levels when it came to his folks.

'They're busy as usual. We'll gain their attention soon enough.'

Serge nodded. 'The old Hollywood glamour concept is brilliant. And the designs...' He kissed his fingertips in a flamboyant European gesture. *'Magnifique.'*

Patrick had no doubt his idea would wow the fashion world. What he doubted was gaining the recognition from the two people who mattered the most.

'So you'll be ready for a preview showing first thing Monday morning?'

'Yeah, we'll be ready.' Serge smirked and spun the globe with his finger, hovering over Melbourne again. 'The question is, will you?'

'I'll be here.' He stood, glanced at his watch, making a grand show of having somewhere else to be when in fact he needed to get rid of Serge so he could get on with his plans. 'I've never mixed business with pleasure before and you know it.'

'There's always a first time for everything,' Serge said,

giving the globe a final spin before lumbering towards the door. 'And come Monday there'll be a pin there to prove it.'

Patrick frowned, not liking Serge's immature ribbing, and liking the fact he was probably already mixing business with pleasure less.

CHAPTER SEVEN

'THERE ARE RULES for the weekend.'

Sapphie wriggled in the soft leather seat as Patrick slowed his Ferrari to enter the Southbank precinct. She didn't care what his rules were, as long as they involved the two of them naked. 'Such as?'

'No work talk. No checking e-mails. No leaving the hotel room.'

'But what if I get hungry?'

'You'll get plenty to eat.' He stopped at a red traffic light and shot her a loaded glance packed with sizzle that implied food wouldn't be the only thing on the menu.

Her body pinged in anticipation. 'Any other hoops you want me to jump through?'

'No, but there will be acrobatics involved.'

She laughed at his exaggerated wink as the lights changed and he concentrated on steering through the heavy Friday night traffic.

Banter was good. Banter kept her nerves at bay. And it detracted from the constant doubts whirring through her head as she overanalysed this situation from every angle.

She wanted him. There was no question. But the aftermath? A thousand scenarios, none of them pleasant, plagued her.

Despite his reassurances to keep business and pleasure separate, what if sex screwed things up—literally?

They were both mature, consenting adults with a major attraction going on, but deep down she couldn't quite subdue the tiny voice that kept chanting, *This is Patrick you're going to sleep with.*

The same Patrick who'd tracked down her favourite cola flavoured lollipops when they'd crammed for an exam one week during the school holidays.

The same Patrick who'd collated her assignments and e-mailed the lot when she'd missed a few days with the flu.

The same Patrick who'd rescued her on the night of the grad dance and proved with one scintillating, unforgettable kiss that he wasn't solely the annoying rebel she'd branded him.

And that was what scared her the most. That on some intrinsic level she still craved this guy like a wistful teenager. If those old yearnings were resurrected…

Nope. This was physical all the way. Come Monday they'd revert to work, with a side-serve of flirting.

'We're here.'

Sapphie had been so busy battling with her doubts she'd lost concentration and missed the moment when he steered his boy-toy through the driveway of the Langham Hotel and cut the engine.

'Ready?' His hand sneaked across the console and found hers, his gentle squeeze reassuring.

'Hell, yeah,' she said, earning a wicked grin that made her belly go into freefall.

The next five minutes passed in a blur of bags and valet parking and checking in as Patrick took charge. She liked that about him—how the laid-back guy he'd once been had developed into a go-getter who hadn't lost his ability to have fun.

Decadent weekends away in posh hotels reeked of fun and something she'd never done. She'd stayed in luxurious hotels for work, but never checked in to one with the intention of wallowing in the room.

The new her approved. Spending the weekend holed away was on par with a few hours' meditation or yoga or Pilates.

The old her? Too scared to put in an appearance for fear a stray incense stick would clobber her.

As Patrick handed over his credit card—he'd bristled when she'd insisted on paying half, so she'd let it go for the sake of his manly pride—she glanced around at the exquisite swirled cream marble floors, the sweeping staircase, the fountain cascading water to the ground floor, the stunning floral arrangements.

Combined with the hint of ginger and lemongrass in the air, the Langham exuded a quiet elegance that appealed to her battered soul.

Maybe if she'd taken time out to appreciate places like this over the years she wouldn't have ended up almost losing Seaborns and driving a wedge between her and Ruby in the process?

She'd devoted her life to the company—so many hours she could never take back. At the time she hadn't wanted to, had been content to bury herself in work, but her enforced absence had readjusted her priorities.

When Patrick headed back to Europe she'd make time to do stuff like this, even if it meant checking into a swank hotel for a weekend on her own.

A few spa treatments, a stack of chick-lit novels on her e-reader and Room Service would be the perfect antidote to her frenetic schedule.

And if she'd probably remember this time with one of the sexiest guys she'd ever met and maybe crave him a tad? She'd better make sure they created some pretty unforgettable memories this weekend to resurrect when needed.

'Let's go.'

His breath fanned her ear as he placed a hand in the small of her back. The simple touch sent a shiver of longing through her.

He must have felt the faintest tremor, for his fingers

strummed her spine on the way to her neck, where he caressed the exposed skin. 'The faster we hit room 2227, the faster we get to unpack those boxes.'

She almost corrected him and said suitcases—until she realised what he meant. While her body couldn't wait to hit that room, her rationale couldn't be ignored completely.

Her hands cupped his face, leaving him no option but to look into her eyes. 'We're really doing this? I mean, we still have to work together, and what if—?'

He kissed her—a soft, tender sweep across her lips that had her melting into him.

'I picked a hotel because I wanted this to be special. Not a quickie in your apartment or on my desk.' He raised an eyebrow. 'Though that's not entirely out of the question later.'

Okay, so he wanted a 'later'? Before she could ponder or question what that meant, he continued.

'We've known each other a long time so there's no pretences, no awkwardness later. We indulge ourselves, have a memorable weekend without regrets.' His arms slid around her waist, anchoring her. 'You with me?'

With her heart still questioning the validity of what she was about to do, she nodded. 'All the way.'

All the way echoed through her head as the elevator whisked them to the twenty-second floor and their exclusive Club suite.

It continued to plague her as he deftly swiped the key card and held open the door for her.

Then she stepped into the room and her fears faded.

Sapphie had a keen eye for beauty. It came with the territory of being groomed by a society mother who'd prided herself on appearance and showing the world grace and elegance at all costs. Growing up surrounded by exquisite jewels, being the spokesperson for Seaborns, had developed that keen eye. So stepping into the gorgeous Club room should have sent her observatory radar onto high alert.

Instead, the floral embossed carpet, the deep green drapes, the luxurious Old Worlde furnishings and the amazing view of Melbourne's Flinders St Station, Federation Square and surrounds faded into oblivion the moment Patrick closed the door and backed her up against the nearest wall.

'I've been going frigging nuts with wanting you,' he said, kissing her before she could respond.

That tender kiss in the lobby had been nothing like this. Desperation. Hunger. Insanity. All combined to make her press against him as if she'd never get enough.

Sex in the past had been okay. Probably more her fault than the guys she'd dated, because her mind would always wander to business and she'd be mentally making lists instead of making whoopee.

But Patrick's passionate kiss and the way his hands were tearing at her clothes... Her mind delightfully blanked.

She ripped at his shirt. Buttons flew.

He tugged at her skirt. The zip stuck.

They swore in unison, laughed, and their fingers became more dextrous as pants, tops and underwear were stripped in haste and protection donned.

'Finally,' he said, his gaze hot and potent as he started at her chest and swept downwards. 'You're as beautiful as I imagined.'

Sapphie's first instinct was to squirm, but she forced herself to stand still beneath his scrutiny. People had stared at her over the years when she'd been modelling Seaborns' jewels but that was different.

No one had ever made her feel so thoroughly exposed as Patrick did at that moment.

'You have no idea how long I've been fantasising about this.' He reached out, tracing a nipple with his fingertip. 'And it's way better in reality.'

'Good to hear,' she breathed on a sigh as he stepped closer, his erection brushing her abdomen. 'Because I haven't been thinking about you at all.'

He laughed and pressed harder against her. 'Well, then, I'll have to change all that.'

His hands cupped her butt, hoisted her up, and she instinctively wrapped her legs around him. 'What I plan on doing to you this weekend will be unforgettable.'

Sapphie didn't doubt it. That was the plan anyway: store up amazing memories for the long nights ahead when she mulled over how to make Seaborns bigger and better.

The Fashion Week campaign might keep the company in the black for years to come but she'd never stop striving. It had been her mum's dream, was too ingrained, and while she intended on taking more time out in the future it didn't mean she'd ever stop taking Seaborns to the top.

'You're that confident?'

'Want me to prove it to you?'

He nuzzled her neck and she moaned. 'Please do.'

He eased back a tad and tried to slide a hand between their bodies but she stopped him.

'You've pleasured me enough. This time's all about you.'

His eyes darkened to slate as he remembered the times in the bathroom, the boardroom.

'I want you inside me. Now.'

'I like it when you're bossy,' he said, sliding into her with one long thrust. 'A woman who knows what she wants is such a turn-on.'

He eased out and she could have sworn she whimpered— a needy sound so out of character her she froze in surprise.

'In that case, I want you to…' She whispered exactly how hard and fast she wanted him in his ear, her cheeks burning the entire time.

But knowing how much Patrick wanted her, feeling him fill her, was incredibly empowering.

When her last command faded on a whisper Patrick took over. Hoisting her higher. Driving into her harder. Gripping her tighter as every thrust drove her closer to release.

She'd never achieved release by internal stimulation alone, but as Patrick talked dirty and demonstrated how he could follow through the tension in her muscles built and coiled in a delicious combination of pleasure bordering on pain.

'Patrick, jeez…' She shattered, spasms making her shudder a moment before he joined her on a drawn out groan.

They didn't move for several long seconds as Sapphie tried to comprehend the enormity of what had just happened.

She'd just had her first cataclysmic, fabled internal climax. And while it had been monumentally stupendous, with her body still trembling in aftershocks, she couldn't ignore the niggle of concern—the one that insisted the connection she'd just experienced with Patrick was one in a million.

Closely followed by a thought: what the hell would she do when he left?

Patrick's grand plans to keep Sapphire locked away in their hotel room for the entire weekend hit a hurdle on Saturday.

He had to get out.

If he didn't he was in dire danger of doing something he'd sworn he'd never do.

Committing to a woman.

The sex was phenomenal, but it was more than that. It was the shared laughter and confidences in bed last night, the common cravings for buttered popcorn and orange soda while watching an action flick, the crazy, scary feeling of total 'rightness' being with her induced.

He'd dated a lot of women the world over, but not one had managed to get under his skin as quickly as Sapphire.

How had the prissy, uptight kid from school turned into this temptress?

He'd expected his raging hunger for her to abate after last

night. It hadn't. If anything he had serious concerns he'd never be able to get her out of his head again.

Not good, considering their goals were worlds apart.

She had a high-end Melbourne jewellery institution to run, he had grand plans to take on his folks head-on in Europe.

Yep, worlds apart.

Where did that leave him? He'd gone into this with few expectations: short-term fling, move on.

So why, after spending one incredible night in her arms, had that thought become unpalatable?

'Good to know you're a rule-breaker.' Sapphire raised her G&T in his direction. 'Mighty generous of you, letting me leave the room.'

He gestured around the exclusive Club lounge on the twenty-fourth floor. 'Didn't want to push my luck with you getting bored of me. Thought you might appreciate a change of scenery.'

'No chance of that.' She sipped at her drink. It did little to cool the telltale blush staining her cheeks. 'For much as I love the incredible city views and drinks and amazing seared scallops, I think you have plenty to offer by way of entertainment.'

He grinned as her blush deepened. 'You think I'm entertaining, huh?' He beckoned her closer and murmured in her ear. 'Would that be when I'm going down on you or taking you from behind in the shower?'

'Shh,' she said, and shoved him away—but not before he'd glimpsed the hint of a smug smile. The smile of a satisfied, multiple-pleasured woman who hadn't been reticent about letting him know.

Another thing that had surprised him—her absolute joyful abandonment when it came to sex. Sure, she'd been responsive in her bathroom and his boardroom, but he hadn't expected her to be so utterly horny.

There was something infinitely appealing about a woman

who enjoyed sex and wasn't afraid to show it, and he loved that beneath her cool, businesswoman façade she was a sex-pot vixen.

And she was all his.

At least for the weekend.

'You're really enjoying this, aren't you?'

Her eyes lit up with pleasure and she nodded. 'Not dismissing the last twenty-four hours in our suite, I'm having a ball being here.' She beckoned him closer with a crook of her finger. 'I never do stuff like this. Feels like I'm playing hooky and I love it.'

'Don't you go away for girls' weekends with Ruby?'

Shadows blanketed the light in her eyes and the corners of her mouth drooped. 'We've been pretty busy keeping Seaborns afloat since Mum died, so most of our weekends have been spent working.'

Her response surprised him. Sure, he'd heard the rumours about Seaborns being in financial trouble but that had only been recently. As far as he knew the jeweller was a Melbourne institution and supplied pieces to the stars.

It looked as if a lot had happened in his absence.

'I thought Mathilda was an astute businesswoman?'

Sapphire gnawed on her bottom lip, her G&T forgotten. 'She was, but the shoddy economy hit us hard. Even rich folk stopped spending big on frivolities like new bracelets or necklaces and our profit margins tightened.' She shook her head. 'I made a promise to Mum to do whatever it took to keep Seaborns lucrative.'

'You're doing a great job—'

'I almost lost the company,' she said, her tone soft and plaintive. 'Pushed myself too hard, didn't enlist Ruby's help— would've collapsed with a healthy dose of chronic fatigue syndrome if I hadn't taken an enforced leave of absence.'

'I didn't know.'

'Not many people do. Rubes did a great job keeping us viable while I recuperated at a health spa near Daylesford.'

'How long?'

'Three months.'

He couldn't imagine this successful, driven woman taking a week off, let alone twelve weeks, and that fact rammed home how bad it must've been.

'How do you feel now?'

'Invigorated.' She raised her glass in his direction, her smile self-deprecating. 'Thanks to you.'

She'd given him an opportunity to dismiss the heavy stuff she'd revealed and move onto familiar teasing territory.

He wanted to—didn't want to delve into personal territory that might strengthen the bonds between them. But the shadows in her eyes remained and he'd be damned if he'd let her down now she'd opened up. He might not want to complicate what they shared by taking it further, but the least he could do was hear her out if she wanted to offload.

'When did you return to work?'

A slight frown creased her forehead. 'The week before you walked in on me.'

He swore. 'So you take months off and then jump straight back into the fray by pitching for the Fourde show?'

She glared at him, sass and defiance, and he'd never wanted to hold a woman more than he did at that moment.

'I'd done my time. Rested, chilled, unburdened my soul to a bunch of self-help groups. Meditated, stretched—you name it, I probably tried it. But in the end…' She made a circular motion with her finger at her temple. 'I was going a little stir-crazy with all that wholesome goodness.'

'Understandable. But we've been working manic hours on this show. How are you holding up?'

'You tell me.' She actually winked, obliterating the seriousness of their conversation. 'At the risk of your ego getting any bigger than it already is, hanging out with you has been good for me.'

'Care to clarify "hanging out"?'

'At work.' Her coy glance from beneath lowered lashes was adorable. 'Out of work.'

'In clothes.' He ran a fingertip down her bare forearm, savoured her involuntary reaction as he raised goosebumps. 'Out of clothes.'

She smiled, the tension of the last few minutes gone.

'If I'd known you'd be better for me than months' worth of yoga and meditation I'd have considered flying to Europe.'

She'd meant it as a light-hearted quip, a continuation of their word-play. But hot on the heels of his realisation that their fragile relationship could never go further it stung.

In a hypothetical world, if she were free from responsibilities, would they have a future?

Fruitless, irrelevant musings. But for a moment, with the thought of her joining him in Europe, it had been nice to dream.

He raised his Scotch and clinked it against her glass. 'Well, lucky you don't have to travel to Europe for my exclusive services. You can have as much as you want of me right here.'

'I'll drink to that.'

She took a sip, lowered her glass and pinned him with a curious stare. 'What's it like working in Paris? Must be ultra glam.'

Unease tightened his throat. He didn't want to talk about his life in Paris. Didn't want to run the risk of saying stuff he shouldn't. But she'd opened up to him with surprising honesty. The least he could do was give her a snippet.

'It's competitive. All the best fashion houses in the world vie for attention there.'

'Yet Fourde Fashion continues to thrive? Your folks must be proud.'

Her steady stare never wavered, and along with the lies

he'd now have to tell came the wish he'd changed the subject when he'd had the chance.

'The business is their baby. As long as Fourde flourishes all is right with the world.'

He tried to keep the bitterness out of his voice but Sapphire was smart, and by the slight frown crinkling her brows he knew she must have picked up on the hint of hostility in his tone.

'Can be tough, working for your folks.' She swirled her drink absentmindedly, took a sip. 'I adored Mum but she was a ruthless boss. And being family muddied the boundaries sometimes.'

If she only knew. His familial boundaries weren't muddied—they were clearly obliterated.

'Yeah, can make for interesting employee evaluations.'

Not that he'd been subjected to any from his folks. They preferred to let their silent disapproval do the talking.

'I used to envy you.' She snuggled into her seat and cupped her hands around her glass. 'Not having parents looking over your shoulder all the time.'

'They would've had to care to do that,' he blurted, instantly regretting his blunt response when her eyes widened in surprise.

'You didn't get along?'

He shrugged, wishing he'd kept his big mouth shut, trying to play down his obvious resentment after that clanger.

'I was a late arrival—a mid-life mistake. They had a burgeoning business and self-sufficient teenagers when I arrived. The rest is self-explanatory.'

Her pity was palpable. 'So you didn't spend much time together as a family?'

'Try none.' This time he managed to keep the acrimony out of his voice. 'But, hey, as you said, I got to spend my last years of school parent-free. Lucky me.'

Then why did he feel so unlucky?

'Bet they're glad you're all making up for lost time now.'

He grunted in response. Enough with discussing families, already. 'Another drink?'

Thankfully she let him change the subject.

'I haven't finished this one yet.' She glanced at the half-empty glass in her hand and raised an eyebrow. 'Are you trying to get me drunk so you can take advantage of me?'

He winked. 'Newsflash, sweetheart. I don't need you tipsy to do that.'

'Good point.' Her eyes darkened to midnight as the tip of her tongue swept along her bottom lip, eliciting an instant tightening in the vicinity of his groin.

'I need a refill,' he said, also needing to get this evening back onto light-hearted ground. 'Maybe you can take advantage of me?'

She laughed. 'Keep wishing.'

As they continued their banter while feasting on delicious dips and breads, flirting outrageously, Patrick couldn't dismiss the niggling feeling he'd be missing out on something great when he followed his dream in Europe.

And for the first time ever he wondered if it was worth it.

CHAPTER EIGHT

SAPPHIE WASN'T IMAGINING the deep freeze.

Patrick had been distracted during breakfast this morning, cool at check-out, and more distant the closer they got to Armidale.

When he parked outside Seaborns she could have created ice carvings—the chill in the car was that palpable.

She knew what he was doing. Deliberately establishing distance between them after the intimacy of the weekend. Understandable, considering the manic fortnight ahead of them before Fashion Week. She'd pretty much planned on doing the same thing—withdrawing on a subtle level to concentrate on work.

What she hadn't planned on was feeling this…this…*bereft*. As if she'd had something wonderful, lost it, and was now grieving.

Crazy, as she'd known what this was going in: a short-term fling and some much needed fun after a disastrous twelve months. A rotten two years, in fact.

Since her mum had died, when was the last time she'd had fun? Had a weekend off for that matter?

She hadn't, and it made the last forty-eight hours all the more precious. Physically, she'd wanted to prove something to herself, and the weekend with Patrick had done that and more.

Withdrawing was one thing, but feeling this crappy because of it was not good.

She hadn't expected to feel like this—didn't want to feel like this for the next two weeks—so she had no option but to draw attention to the obvious: iciness didn't foster good working relations.

'You're coming in to check out the latest designs?'

Patrick glanced at his watch, reluctance radiating off him. 'Yeah, but just for a few minutes. I'm heading to the office for the afternoon.'

'I thought I was the only workaholic who'd forgo a gorgeous Sunday arvo for the office?'

He shrugged. 'It's how success is bred.'

'Wow,' she said, wishing he'd smile or wink or give some semblance of the laid-back charmer she loved. *Liked*. 'This from the guy who had to be bribed to show up for study weekends?'

Finally a flicker of light in his eyes. 'Those Dairy Bell milkshakes were so worth it.'

'Not my scintillating company?'

He snorted. 'You were an acid-tongued killjoy when it came to hitting the books.'

'How do you think you're successful now?'

'Good looks and charm?'

She rolled her eyes, secretly thrilled he was thawing. 'Throw in modesty.'

At last the corners of his mouth eased into the lazy grin that never failed to make her heart skip a beat.

'Did you ever think we'd end up here?'

She had no idea if he meant professionally or personally.

He gestured towards Seaborns' shopfront. 'I guess you always knew you'd be running this one day. It's all you ever focussed on—getting good grades, working here part-time.' He blew out a long breath, his expression pensive. 'Me? I didn't have a clue.'

Interestingly, they hadn't discussed how he'd ended up working in fashion. She'd assumed he'd entered the family business like her, by living up to familial expectations. But, considering his revelations regarding his folks over the weekend, she found it surprising he'd choose to work with them. It sounded as if they'd been rotten parents and he still bore the emotional scars, so how had he ended up fronting their fashion house in Australia?

'You had grand plans to travel during a gap year. What made you enter fashion?'

What little headway she'd made in re-establishing warmth vanished as the shutters descended, effectively wiping the warmth from his eyes.

'I fell into it,' he said, staring out through the windscreen at nothing in particular. 'Did an internship, studied part-time, then needed time away. Got bored with travelling after a while. Had a Marketing degree under my belt. Dropped by the Paris office more regularly on my return.'

There was more to it—a lot more, judging by the rigid shoulders and compressed lips—but now wasn't the time to push.

'Well, I for one am glad you did, because together with Seaborns you're going to take Fashion Week by storm.'

'Hope so,' he muttered, tearing his gaze away from a tram trundling by to turn towards her. 'You know how busy we're going to be the next few weeks, right?'

Ah, here it comes. The brush-off.

She could make it easy for him, but what they'd shared wasn't two strangers hooking up for a dirty weekend and then going their separate ways.

They shared a past—albeit a platonic high school friendship. And they shared a professional bond that would single-handedly take Seaborns into a new stratosphere.

She—they—deserved more.

'Agreed,' she said. 'I'm assuming a busy work schedule precludes us from having sex?'

Her bluntness surprised him. An eyebrow twitched.

'I'm trying to make this easier on both of us—'

'Don't.' She shook her head. 'Don't give me some lame spiel you've probably used on a million women before.'

This time his jaw dropped a tad.

'We're both professionals, with a clear goal in sight, and we're going to get there. But if what's happened over the last few weeks is any indication, that spark we share can't be turned off because we've pulled an all-nighter or have spreadsheets to prepare. So let's not waste time doing this.'

She waved a hand between the two of them. 'You and me? Phenomenal sex. So why don't we see how it goes over the next few weeks? If we have a spare moment and our schedules coincide we hook up.'

'You're something else,' he said, staring at her with undisguised admiration. 'And for the record? Thousands of women, not millions.'

She punched him on the arm.

'And the reason why I've cooled off today is because spending the weekend with you has solidified what I already knew.' His hand snaked across, captured hers. 'The reality of being with you far surpassed the fantasy and it's doing my head in.'

Okay, she hadn't expected that.

'I really like you, but I don't have room in my life right now for complications.'

'Jeez, thanks. Way to go with the flattery.'

His sheepish smile made her want to hug him. 'I need to make this show work before…'

He squeezed her hand, released it, his look away not inspiring her with confidence.

'Before…?' she prompted, her rampant curiosity filling in the blanks.

Before he absconded to the Pacific with a Bond girl?

Before he revealed his secret harem?

Or, the most likely, before he headed back to Paris?

'Everything's up in the air at the moment, so I can't really talk about it.' He swiped a hand over his face. It did little to ease the tension lines bracketing his mouth. 'I don't want to lead you on or build false hopes. I can't be any clearer than that.'

'So what was the weekend about?'

'Selfishness.' He drummed his fingers against the steering wheel, as if he couldn't wait to escape. 'Ever want something so badly when you finally get it you can't quite believe it's real?'

Yeah, that was how she'd initially felt about assuming control of Seaborns. Until she'd realised she was more enamoured of the idea of being in charge than the reality. Her mum had built up the place, had constructed her dreams around it, and she'd happily gone along with it.

But poring over sales figures at midnight and haggling with diamond mines over undercutting prices wasn't quite as glamorous as she'd been led to believe, and while walking through the showroom still gave her a buzz it wasn't quite the same buzz being with Patrick over the weekend had given her.

'I want you even more now, if that's possible, but I won't jerk you around.' He eyeballed her. 'I may be gone in three weeks and I don't want you hurt.'

Having him articulate the inevitable should have allayed her fears and reinforced her decision to view this as purely a fling. So why did his last words echo through her head like a mournful warning?

A warning she should heed if she knew what was good for her. But that was just the point. Patrick was good for her. She'd felt more alive, more buzzed over the weekend than she had in years.

She liked the feeling. Liked the uncharacteristic feeling of invincibility it gave her. For someone who'd been on the brink of not being able to get out of bed because her muscles wouldn't co-operate, it was a heady high and a powerful aphrodisiac.

She wanted more.

Even if her potent medicine had an end-date stamped all over it.

'We can squeeze a lot of fun into three weeks,' she said, proud her voice didn't give a hint of her inner turmoil.

She wanted him.

She didn't want him to leave.

She didn't want to get too attached.

It was a confusing jumble, making her want to shake him or kiss him. She hadn't decided which yet.

'How can a guy say no to that?'

'You can't.'

She opened the car door, grabbed her bag and headed for Seaborns with Patrick not far behind.

He'd finally fallen in with her plans but he might need a little convincing.

And she knew just the way to do it.

Patrick checked out the dazzling display of jewellery Ruby had created for Fashion Week, snagged a yellow diamond choker on his finger and held it out to Sapphire.

'Model it for me.'

'Sure,' she said, reaching for it.

He raised his arm, waved the necklace just out of reach. 'Naked.'

She elbowed him. 'If you want to see me wear it—fine. But the clothes stay on.' In a slick move involving an armpit tickle and a semi-jump, she recovered the choker. 'For now.'

'I'll hold you to that,' he said, meaning it. He'd hold her all night long if he had his way, but he had to leave. If he didn't get out of here soon who knew what he'd divulge?

He'd been close to blurting the truth—all of it—in the car. She'd been so open, not pulling any punches like most women he knew. Guileless and honest, stating what she wanted in clear terms. No room for misunderstandings. No unrealistic expectations.

She knew he'd be leaving.

And it didn't matter.

He should be high-fiving.

A short-term sexual dalliance without complications.

Instead it had made him think. Why didn't she want more? They were good together. She'd admitted it. So why didn't she want to consider continuing this relationship beyond a month?

Not that he wanted to do long distance, or anything remotely like it, but to have her dismiss anything beyond a fling as a possibility kinda stung. Stupid guy pride.

He'd thought he'd stuffed up, revealing all that stuff about his folks and their neglect. Emotional baggage usually had women wanting to delve and analyse and grow closer.

Not Sapphire. She'd done the opposite—proposing they continue with the sex with an end-date in sight.

He couldn't fathom it.

The gentlemanly thing to do would be not to take advantage of the situation. To say, *Thanks, Saph, I've had a great time but sleeping together will ensure we grow closer over the next few weeks and neither one of us wants that...* Ah, hell. Maybe the gentleman in him should shut up.

This was why he didn't do relationships. They confused the hell out of him.

He'd deliberately pushed her away, terrified of the closeness they'd established over the weekend. He'd never told any woman about his folks—least of all a woman he had feelings for.

Feelings?

Uh-uh. No way. He needed to amend that to a woman he was *at risk of developing feelings for.* Yeah, much better.

Jeez, he could be an idiot. All the amendments in the world wouldn't change facts: he might have agreed to take advantage of Sapphire's offer and continue the sex for as long as he was around, but pretending he didn't feel more for her would be tough.

He should have stuck to his guns and ended it in the car as he'd intended. It would have been easier than this floundering, out-of-control feeling that made him contemplate crazy things—*long distance things*—he had no intention of following up on.

'Sure you don't want to see the pieces with the gowns?'

Her voice drifted out from the bedroom, soft and alluring, and it took every ounce of his limited willpower not to barge in there and say *Screw the jewellery.*

'Designers' meeting is first thing in the morning, so it would be great to get a sneak peek at them now,' he said, managing to sound businesslike when all he could think about was her strutting back into the room wearing a diamond necklace and towering stilettos only. Totally making a mockery of his moral dilemma a few moments ago.

He'd never been a gentleman. No point starting now.

'Okay, you asked for it.'

She strutted into the room wearing a sheer black lace teddy, suspenders, stockings and stilettos. Oh, and the necklace was somewhere in the vicinity of her neck, but he was too busy checking out the rest to notice.

Yep, that inner gentleman was long gone now.

'Are you trying to give me a heart attack?' He clutched at his chest and pretended to stagger.

'Nothing wrong with your heart if that workout over the weekend was any indication.'

She struck a provocative pose, mischief lighting her eyes. 'You've seen this piece. Shall I try on the next?'

'No.'

He strode towards her with one thing on his mind—and it wasn't the carats of diamonds draping her neck.

'But what about the designers' meeting in the morning and needing to see them before then?'

'Screw the meeting,' he muttered, sweeping the small desk behind her clean and pinning her against it. 'I have more important things on my mind.'

She wriggled against his hard-on. 'Like?'

'You. Me. Naked.'

'You're fixated on the naked thing.'

'I'm fixated on you.'

The teddy looked hot, but it was a pain in the ass to undo so he did the only logical thing. Ripped it.

'Caveman,' she said, her smile saucy.

'Wait 'til you see my club.'

She groaned at his pun—or it might have been due to his tongue working its way down to her breast.

He sucked her nipple into his mouth, laved it while easing a finger inside her at the same time.

She was so eager, so responsive, so hot.

'Patrick…'

She grabbed his head and practically dragged him up to meet her mouth, demanding and ravenous.

He loved how she matched him, clamorous and unrelenting, striving for satisfaction.

Her tongue taunted him as he unzipped and sheathed himself in record time.

Her hands grabbed his butt and hauled him closer as he propped her on the desk.

Her body arched and her head fell back as he thrust into her with one stroke.

She gripped the edge of the desk. He gripped her hips.

She watched him drive into her, eyes wide and dazed. He watched her and had never been so turned on in all his life.

She came hard and fast, clenching around him, sighing his name. He came a second later, exploding into her with a force that made his head snap back.

'Thanks for making my desk fantasy come true,' she said, flushed and sated and utterly ravishing.

'My pleasure,' he said, when in fact he wanted to thank her for being his fantasy come true.

His hopes to focus solely on work these next few weeks were royally screwed. Like him.

For, come the end of this Fashion Week campaign, he knew he didn't have a hope in hell of walking away from this.

Sapphie ran a face-washer over her skin, aware they had a ton of work to do despite it being Sunday afternoon.

However, the speedy scrub with the small towel didn't invigorate her skin half as much as the sensual encounter with Patrick a few moments ago.

It had been a test.

Ironically, she wasn't sure if she'd passed or failed.

She might have just proved she could physically continue this relationship without any future, but her insistent voice of reason, the one nagging nonstop that she was being foolish, wouldn't shut up.

The smart thing to have done when he'd given her the brush off earlier in the car would have been to end this *thing* between them. They'd had a great time, worked the attraction out of their systems, and now could focus on work.

Well, from his spiel maybe *he* could, but no way would she be able to work closely with him over the next three weeks and pretend she hadn't seen him naked, hadn't kissed him all over, hadn't touched him, held him…

She scrubbed her face again. It did little for her flaming cheeks.

She could justify her decision to prolong their sexual relationship as the best kind of therapy for her body. She hadn't felt this good in years…blah, blah, blah.

While that might be true—and she revelled in feeling physically empowered for the first time in yonks—she knew continuing their relationship had more to do with the emotional connection they'd reluctantly established over the weekend than anything else.

And she didn't want an emotional connection. Had deliberately seduced him fifteen minutes ago because of it. Determined to prove to herself she could handle the sex and little else.

Instead all she'd proved was what she'd known all along: the sex was incredible. And maybe they could be too, given half a chance.

She flung away the face-washer in disgust, poked her tongue out at her reflection, and shimmied into the nearest clothes handy: a faded rock band T-shirt—one of Ruby's remnants—and a denim skirt.

She didn't have time for a relationship even if she wanted one, and it looked like Patrick felt the same way.

She needed to prove she could be the best leader Seaborns had ever had, and by the sounds of it Patrick had a lot to prove to his folks even if he didn't know it yet.

When he'd opened up about his upbringing it had been pretty obvious where his bitterness sprang from. They'd neglected him as a kid so he'd probably go all out as an adult to show them what he was capable of. Gain the attention he'd never had.

And she hoped he'd succeed. For while Mathilda had been a tough taskmaster, her mum had always been there for her and she couldn't imagine it otherwise.

Yeah, best for her to strive to be the best and for Patrick to chase his dreams. She should be thankful they'd both been perfectly clear in the car. No expectations. No regrets.

So why did her heart give a little lurch as she exited the bathroom and caught sight of him waiting for her?

As Sapphire walked Patrick out a flash of white gold caught his eye.

He'd strolled through this showroom several times now,

was almost immune to the precious gems and stunning creations cradled lovingly on midnight-blue velvet behind glass-enclosed cases highlighted by muted light.

What captured his attention about this piece was where it was situated—tucked into a corner, almost invisible behind the more dazzling displays up front.

'What's wrong?'

'Nothing,' he said, holding onto Sapphire's hand as he detoured towards the cabinet. 'Why's this piece hidden away?'

'Poor seller.' Sapphire shrugged. 'Ruby loves creating modern stuff for fun—has a whole storeroom full of it—but no one wants to buy it.'

As Patrick stared at the lightning bolt white gold and jade pendant edged in pinpoint diamonds a buzz of creative excitement zapped his gut.

This was the kind of piece that would have accessorised his first show perfectly—the kind of edgy, contemporary vibe he loved. But the traditional fashionistas in Europe didn't.

Staring at Ruby's exquisite piece of modern art, he felt a long-suppressed urge stir to life. He had grand plans to instigate when he returned to Paris shortly, but why not give the fashion world a little pre-emptive taste?

'How adventurous are you?'

A faint pink stained Sapphire's cheeks. 'Considering what we just did on the desk upstairs, you tell me.'

He tugged her in for a quick kiss on the lips, determinedly ignoring the urge to deepen it.

'I'm thinking of running a little adjunct to our fashion show. Something edgy. Funky. Contemporary.' He pointed at the lightning bolt. 'Showcasing modern fashion with pieces like that.'

Sapphire gaped. 'But the timeline… It's impossible—'

'You said Ruby has a storeroom full of modern pieces like this?'

'Yeah, but co-ordinating the fashion on top of our current workload...how do you expect to pull this off?'

He wanted to blurt the entire truth, wanted to trust her. But she'd doubted him at the start—doubted he could co-ordinate something as big as the old Hollywood glamour campaign—how would she feel if she knew the extent of his plans for his modern series?

'I've had designers do some mock-ups for a contemporary show I'm planning in Paris. Wouldn't take long for Ruby to have a look, match the jewellery.'

She stared at him with an ego-boosting mix of awe and admiration. 'You're serious about this?'

'Absolutely.' He gently tapped the glass cabinet. 'Wouldn't it be great if Seaborns started selling more of this stuff too?'

'Rubes would love you for ever,' she said, peering closer at the pendant. And it would be so good to give something back to her. 'Given a choice, she'd rather create contemporary stuff like this every day of the week. If she had a chance to show some of it at Fashion Week she'd freak out.'

'Good. That's settled.'

He squeezed her hand and released it. 'I'll get the designs couriered over later and let you get to work co-ordinating the pieces.'

'Okay.' Sapphire stared at him as if she still couldn't quite believe they were doing this. 'Have to say I'm surprised.'

'By?'

'Fourde Fashion's signature couture is all about timeless elegance.' Her quick doubtful glance at Ruby's lightning bolt spoke volumes. 'Isn't this confusing the brand a tad?'

That was putting it mildly. It wouldn't just confuse the Fourde brand, it would give his folks a coronary.

Which was why he had no intention of launching this event under the Fourde Fashion label.

He'd planned on doing it when he returned to Paris shortly. But this could be a perfect opportunity. How this short collection was received would be a fair indication if the European market were ready for him or not.

It hadn't been a decade earlier, but a lot had changed in ten years. *He'd* changed in ten years, and no longer would he be quashed into thinking his ideas were wrong or unsuitable.

His mistake back then had been trying to fit a bright, shiny new idea under the guise of a long-established vintage company.

This time he'd be using his name all the way.

The buck stopped with him.

'I'm thinking of producing this independent of the Fourde label.'

She paused, a tiny frown creasing her brow, and he half expected her to renege. Hitching Seaborns to the successful Fourde Fashion wasn't a problem, but would she be up for the risk associated with an unknown brand?

The astute businesswoman he knew her to be wouldn't go for it. And the fact she'd asked the question signalled her doubts. Doubts in him.

And he hated it. Hated that no matter how far they'd come, both personally and professionally, she didn't deem him capable enough.

'You have a problem with that?'

His tone sounded way too harsh and her frown deepened.

'Actually, I'm thinking it's better this way. Break away from the established mould.' She tapped her lower lip, deep in thought. 'Fashion peeps will have expectations of anything that launches under the Fourde Fashion label, and you don't want something new and innovative to be unfairly judged because it's not the norm.'

Some of his anger faded at her insight. She'd pretty much honed in on the number one reason he'd failed the first time around. And why he wouldn't make the same mistake again.

'Exactly. Modern and edgy isn't what Fourde is renowned for.'

She hadn't lost the frown. 'You're up against your employer. In direct competition with your folks.'

'They know I'm keen to branch out.'

True enough. He'd mentioned it on several occasions—not that they'd given his aspirations much credit.

As long as he kept performing for Fourde they weren't terribly concerned about where he expended his creative energy.

They'd assumed the failure of his first showing would maim his desire to break into contemporary fashion. No great surprise. They didn't know him well, didn't know he used the bitter rejection of that first show as the spur that drove him every day.

'If you say so.'

By the dubious twist to her mouth he hadn't allayed all her doubts. No matter. He'd add her to the list of people he had to prove something to.

'I'll call you,' he said, dropping a kiss on her cheek. 'We'll chat after you've seen the designs later today.'

'No worries,' she said, but as he eased out through the door and glanced over his shoulder that groove slashing her forehead said she had worries indeed.

Irrelevant. Patrick would prove he had something to offer the fashion world.

Today Melbourne. Tomorrow the world.

'Can't believe we pulled this together in five days,' Sapphie said, shaking her head as the last model took to the catwalk, wearing a leopard print mini-jumpsuit and a funky rose-gold topaz necklace and earring combo, to another round of rapturous applause from the audience.

'The Fashion Week organisers were happy to squeeze me in.' Patrick rubbed his thumb and forefinger together. 'Guess the fact Fourde Fashion is sponsoring the main event helped them see the wisdom of supporting the launch of this indie collection.'

'I think the designs have helped sell the collection more.' She laid a hand on his arm, relishing the innocuous touch. Working on this contemporary show had been a blast, but the fact they hadn't had a spare second to play had her jumpy. 'They're seriously good. Cutting edge stuff.'

'Thanks,' he said, not taking his eyes off the model as she did her final pose at the end of the catwalk before strutting back towards them. 'Let's hope the critics agree with you.'

'They will.' She gestured towards the other models, waiting in the wings for the finale when all the designs would be on the catwalk at once. 'Bold colours. Textured fabrics. Short diagonal hems. Asymmetrical necklines. A pretty eye-catching combination.'

'Don't forget the jewellery,' he said, some of the tension in his rigid shoulders easing. 'We're a package deal.'

'And doesn't Ruby know it?' Sapphie jerked a thumb over her shoulder in the direction of her sister, who flitted between the models ensuring clasps were fastened tight and earrings clipped and bracelets snug.

She'd seen Ruby animated backstage before, but the fact her sister had an extra pep in her step was obvious. Ruby had freaked when she'd heard about the chance to showcase her contemporary designs, and had worked two all-nighters to ensure Patrick's outfits were perfectly paired with the right jewellery.

Sapphie had to admit she'd been wary at first of taking a risk with designs not backed by the Fourde Fashion name. But then she'd seen the clothes, and there had been no denying this was a golden opportunity to promote Seaborns in a whole new light.

Moving into a contemporary market would be a dream come true for Ruby, and anything that put a permanent smile on her sis's face was fine by her. Ruby deserved it after all she'd done for her and the company over the last year.

Ruby and Jax had singlehandedly wiped out the mortgage

she'd taken out on the showroom and her place, and had cemented Seaborns as a force to be reckoned with again.

They'd given her a chance to resume leadership duties on her terms and she'd always be grateful. Proving she could physically handle the job would have been ten times harder if she'd had to deal with financial woes too.

She wanted these designs to rock—wanted the public to love Ruby's creative genius as much as she did.

By the rousing applause from the crowd, they were well on their way.

'Let the finale begin,' Patrick muttered as the models took to the catwalk *en masse*.

The noise from the crowd crescendoed amid myriad camera flashes, and the hoots, stomping and wolf whistles were vindication that she'd done the right thing in taking a chance on Patrick.

Which begged the question: How far was she willing to go to really take a chance on him with what mattered? Her heart…

'Can you hear that?' He stared at her in wide-eyed wonder before letting out an exultant whoop and hoisting her high, spinning her around until she was dizzy. 'They love us.'

She laughed as he lowered her back to her feet. 'Get ready for the orders to flood in.'

Some of his joy dimmed. 'Yeah—going to be an interesting few months ahead.'

She couldn't fathom his shift in mood—not when he'd just launched both their companies into a new market. Unless he was concerned about his parents' reaction… But he'd said they were fine with him branching out.

Whatever the reason, she wished he trusted her as much as she trusted him.

'Are you going to expand on the collection?'

'Probably,' he said, his reticence complete as he took out his smartphone and scrolled down his to-do list. 'But for now we've got a final run through for the Hollywood glamour campaign scheduled.'

She could accept his reluctance to talk, could pretend it was okay he'd given her the brush-off without consequences. But they'd come too far to fake that all they shared was a meaningless fling. She might have no idea how to label what they had, but him demeaning it with his lack of trust was unacceptable.

'You've just nailed a preview show that could take your contemporary designs worldwide. So what's the problem?'

'No problem. I just can't afford to rest on this success when we have a major show coming up.'

Perfectly logical explanation. But his evasiveness was palpable. And it disappointed her more than she'd expected. Which could only mean one thing. She was in way over her head.

She didn't want to push him, didn't want to make a big deal out of this, but she'd vowed to live every moment to the max—and that meant confronting issues head-on, not skirting around them in the hope they'd vanish.

'Why won't you let me in?'

His thumb stilled over the smartphone and he finally raised his gaze after an eternity.

'What do you mean?'

'You need me to spell it out?'

With a typically male sigh of exasperation he thrust his phone back into his pocket and folded his arms.

'I care about you, Sapphire, but I've got too much on my mind to get into this now.'

If his posture didn't scream *back off*, the deep frown slashing his brows did. She guessed he expected her to be happy he'd admitted he cared. How magnanimous.

Though she had to agree with him. This probably wasn't the best place to discuss anything beyond work. Not if she wanted honest answers.

There'd be time for confrontation later, but the longer this went on she knew one thing. Patrick had grown on her, and having him walk away without giving him some indication of how she felt would be a travesty.

Letting him leave without the truth would be something she'd regret, and she was done living with regrets.

'Fair enough.' She shrugged as if it didn't matter, when in fact it mattered a great deal. 'You did good, by the way,' she said, standing on tiptoes to kiss his cheek. 'You should be proud.'

His stricken expression bamboozled her before he forced a smile. 'Thanks, I'll see you at Fourde later?'

'Count on it,' she said, wondering what had undermined this confident man to the point where he found praise uncomfortable, and knowing she'd never find out if he didn't trust her enough.

Mesmerised, Sapphie watched the Fourde Fashion show from a front row seat.

She'd envisaged the possibilities when Patrick had first had the Old Hollywood Glamour idea for the show, but never in her wildest dreams had she anticipated something so…so… *stupendous*.

Vibrant satin evening gowns in magenta, sapphire, crimson and gold, bias cut and strapless, highlighted by Ruby's exquisite creations and elbow-length ebony satin gloves.

Dramatic red lipstick, finger-waved hair and kitten heels.

Crisp white shirts tucked into high-waisted pants, hair parted on the side, lashings of mascara.

Models channelling Katharine Hepburn and Marlene Deitrich, classic elegance, bold statements.

Sapphie didn't know where to look first.

If she'd thought his contemporary show had been amazing, this one would shoot his reputation into the stratosphere.

And hers. Having the runway hit of Fashion Week would solidify Seaborns' success for years to come.

And she owed it all to Patrick.

He'd given her this opportunity, had believed in Seaborns despite the rumours and she couldn't thank him enough.

Maybe she could show her gratitude later, when they finally caught up outside of work for the first time in seven days. The snatched smooches and illicit touches beneath the boardroom table didn't cut it and she'd been clamouring for him all week.

How she'd survive—*physically*, she had to focus on physically—when he returned to Paris was beyond her.

No way would a gym workout hold half the appeal of a night in Patrick's arms.

Those arms... Never had she felt so secure than the times he'd wrapped her close, content to hold her. For an independent gal with no plans for marriage, let alone a relationship beyond dinner and fun nights, their closeness seriously shook her.

They'd developed a bond no matter how much they wanted to deny it.

So what now?

Back to business as usual for her—running Seaborns and trying not to run herself into the ground again. And back to Paris for Patrick.

What she wouldn't give to swap places with him...

In that moment the catwalk, the applause, the audience faded as an idea so shocking, so far out of left field, blew away every logical reason insisting they could never be together.

Go to Paris.

She shook her head, trying to dislodge the ludicrous idea. It didn't work. Instead the idea morphed, expanded, and presented a host of unwelcome possibilities she shouldn't acknowledge but couldn't ignore no matter how much she wanted to.

Logically, it wasn't possible. Even if she were to visit for a while, see how a potential relationship developed, would it ultimately change anything?

Old workaholic Sapphie insisted *not a chance.*

New revived Sapphie said '*you won't know unless you give it a go.*'

Confused, and a little shaken by an irrational surge of hope, she tried to mentally recite every reason why she couldn't do this.

Who would run Seaborns?

Well, Rubes had done a good job of it during those three months she'd had off.

Would there be a future in it?

She'd never know if she didn't try.

How would Patrick feel?

She'd have to ask him to find out.

And that was what had her angsty. She'd have to confront the guy she loved and see how he felt about her spending some time with him in Paris.

The guy she loved...

Uh-oh.

Somewhere between him barging into Seaborns, catching her in grungy workout clothes, and romancing her in style at the Langham she'd stupidly fallen in love with the guy.

A guy based in Europe.

A guy who'd gone out of his way to spell out the unlikelihood of a future.

Sheesh, he hadn't wanted to continue their fling for the two weeks after the hotel. What chance did she have of convincing him to give anything longer a go?

Logistically it would be a nightmare doing the long distance thing. And realistically how long could something like that last? A few months tops, before they moved on, caught up in their careers.

It might be nice to dream about, but on a practical level it couldn't happen.

Could it?

Sapphie glanced at the stage and caught sight of Patrick applauding the excited models as they passed him, the laugh lines around his eyes as familiar as the permanent wicked tilt to his lips.

Her motto after she'd left Tenang was to live in the moment more, to take calculated risks rather than playing the safe option all the time.

But there were risks and there were *risks*, and following Patrick to Paris on a whim in the hope he'd love her back...

That wasn't risky. That was downright certifiable.

CHAPTER NINE

PATRICK WOULDN'T ADMIT it to anyone but the backstage buzz at a fashion show really got him going. He couldn't thank his folks for much, but for unwittingly instilling a love of fashion into him? Yeah, he could be magnanimously grateful for that.

As Fourde Fashion's showstopper, a daffodil-yellow shimmering silk sheath that cascaded in layers from the waist to the floor, took to the stage a roar from the crowd filled the room.

Thunderous applause, standing ovation, photographers' flashes for the second time this week as Fourde Fashion wrapped up Fashion Week with a requested encore show reinforced what he'd known: this collection would be going places.

And so would he.

He'd done it. Put his past behind him once and for all. Vindicated the trust his folks had placed in him this time around. Proved he could take an untried entity and turn it into a winner. Which meant it was time. Time to confront his parents with his plans. Big plans.

Never in the history of Fashion Week had a house been asked to repeat their show, but that was exactly what had happened when the audience and media had gone wild for his Old Hollywood Glamour campaign earlier in the week.

His phone hadn't stopped ringing with congratulations and orders—so many orders for the gowns *his* idea had inspired.

This was the beginning. Next stop Paris, and he wouldn't stop until he'd gone all the way to the top.

Pity the only congrats he'd received from his folks consisted of a brief e-mail citing revenue projections if initial orders continued and a terse 'good show'.

It should have stung but it didn't. He'd done this for himself, to prove he had what it took to launch solo.

As much as he hated to admit it, albeit to himself, the failure of his first show all those years ago had left a lasting legacy.

Logic explained away that initial disaster as being a combination of factors—wrong show at the wrong time, too innovative, breaking out of an established mould, not delivering on a tried and true brand—but he'd be lying if he didn't admit to a sliver of doubt undermining his big plans for the future.

He wondered if his folks even remembered him mentioning his plans to leave the company and set up on his own. Doubtful, as unless anything he had to say involved Fourde Fashion they weren't interested.

No matter. They'd hear it soon enough when he confronted them shortly, for he had every intention of capitalising on the buzz surrounding his indie show to open his own label.

'We did it.' Sapphire sidled up to him, touched his arm, and he immediately wanted to bundle her into his.

'Never any doubt.'

Her eyes shone with pride.

'I wondered if we could pull this off.' When he raised an eyebrow she hurried on. 'I mean, your idea was amazing, but to squeeze in the contemporary show, then co-ordinate the clothes and the accessories for Fourde in a month, and make it look like that—' she gestured towards the models tittering in a huddle backstage '—nothing short of a miracle.'

'We're a good team,' he said, meaning it. She'd inspired him, both in and out of work, and for the hundredth time this week he wondered how he could walk away from her.

'This could be the first of many successful Fourde/Sea-borns collaborations?'

'About that…' He intertwined his fingers with hers and tugged her towards a quiet corner, away from sound and lighting technicians, models, dressers and neurotic designers.

There'd be no easy time to tell her and he'd rather she heard it from him.

'I'm leaving for Paris in two days.'

Shock widened her eyes. 'So soon?'

'Yeah—have to capitalise on this success while the entire fashion world is still talking about it.'

'Makes sense.'

He'd been worried how she'd take the news. Sure, they'd agreed on a no-strings-attached fling, but they'd grown closer than he'd expected. And the way she'd bailed him up after the indie show, asking why he wouldn't let her in…

Yeah, there were emotions at play here and this could get messy.

'My time in Melbourne has been great—'

'Maybe I could visit you in Paris?'

His heart leapt in exaltation, before logic slapped it down. Her making a trip to Paris to continue their fling wouldn't ul-timately change anything. Their relationship had an end date and prolonging it would only make it more difficult.

He needed to focus on work for what was to come. The confrontation with his folks and the resultant fallout wouldn't be pretty. The paparazzi would have a field-day, plastering his proposed defection to start up his own fashion house to rival Fourde all over the media.

Then there were the actual set-up logistics: finding offices, showroom space, hiring staff, marketing plans… Yeah, he needed to be one hundred percent focussed, and having Sap-phire alongside him in Paris would guarantee a major dis-traction he didn't need.

'For a holiday?'

He hated seeing her tentative joy at joining him in Paris crumple in the face of his deliberately cool response.

'For a few weeks. To see if…if we—'

'We've had a great time, but I'm going to be pretty busy in Paris for the next few months, so maybe you should postpone your holiday?'

The words tumbled out of him in a rush, harsh and confronting. He willed her to understand, to be grateful for the time they'd had together.

Pain lanced his chest as she yanked her hand out of his and stepped back, her accusatory glare filled with retribution.

'You don't want me to come,' she said.

The eerie monotone was as scary as her expressionless pallor. But he saw the shattered pain in her eyes, mirroring his.

'It's not that—'

'Then what is it?' Her metamorphosis from cool to furious happened in an instant. 'This thing between us moved beyond a fling ages ago, so for you to stand there and pretend what happened between us was just a convenient side benefit while we worked together—' She shook her head, her hair tangling like spun gold around her face. 'I'm such a moron.'

'Listen to me—'

'No!'

She lowered her voice when several people glanced their way. 'I'll drop by your office later to tie up loose ends but I don't want to hear another word about you and me. Got it?'

Damn it, he'd made a frigging mess of this. He needed to give her some snippet of truth because he couldn't leave her hurting—not like this.

'You're wrong. You mean everything to me—'

She bolted, her red-soled stilettos clacking against the floorboards, echoing the furious beating of his heart.

He could have sworn it pounded out a repetitive rhythm: *idiot…schmuck…jerk…*

* * *

Sapphie's first instinct to flee might have been a foolish one business-wise as she brushed off countless congratulations, but she had to get out of here. Had to find somewhere she could breathe without feeling as if she'd faint.

He didn't want her.

Tears burned the backs of her eyes as she exited the Melbourne Exhibition Centre, slipped off her heels, and joined the crowds strolling along the Yarra River's Southbank.

Anonymity was good. No one would give her a second glance on a busy Saturday night, when black-clad women dangling shoes off their fingertips wasn't all that unusual. Though they might stare if she bawled, so she swallowed her tears and walked. And walked.

Past the Crown Towers and casino, past the upscale Southbank restaurants, past the Langham Hotel. She practically ran past that landmark, her throat clogged with grief. For she *was* grieving. Grieving over the loss of Patrick, the guy she'd trusted enough to love, the guy who'd flung the lot back in her face.

Okay, she hadn't exactly told him she loved him but didn't the guy have half a brain? He knew how much Seaborns meant to her. She'd told him she'd almost ended up a basket case because of it. So the fact she'd wanted to follow him to Paris should have clued him in to how she felt.

Idiot. Him. Not her.

Actually, her too. For thinking for one second a guy like Patrick could change.

Just because he'd become a whiz-bang businessman didn't mean all those internet reports were behind him. For all she knew he'd schmoozed her as part of his business plan, adding her to the long list of women he'd bedded.

Harsh? Maybe. But it was a pretty good explanation for the way he'd thrown her away now their business association had come to an end.

However, as she reached St Kilda Road and turned left, crossing the bridge and ending up outside Flinders Street Station, she managed to calm down enough to view this rationally.

Patrick had never made any promises. In fact he'd gone out of his way to explain the short-term nature of their assignation. She'd known it, had acknowledged it, yet had gone ahead and fallen in love regardless.

Her bad, not his.

He'd done nothing wrong. They'd worked incredible magic together professionally and managed to combust a little personally.

She felt whole again, physically capable of taking on anything, and she had him to thank. Rather than berate him she should be thanking him.

All very logical, but it did nothing for the ache in her heart. Acknowledging the truth and accepting it were miles apart.

As she waited in a taxi rank, watching partygoers bustling around Federation Square opposite, she knew what she had to do.

Head home, meditate, get a little space and perspective, then drop by his office as planned and show Patrick Fourde how accomplished she was at moving on.

Easy.

If she could just get past the fact that after tonight she probably wouldn't see him again.

Patrick paced his office, blind to the lights of Melbourne spread out like diamonds on a cape many storeys below.

He should be on top of the world right now. Out with the team, celebrating their success. Solidifying his plans to expand. Maybe even rehearsing the spiel he'd need to give his folks to avoid them having coronaries.

Yet all he could think about was Sapphire.

The devastation in her eyes when he'd told her not to follow him to Paris. The pain twisting the lips he craved. Her disbelieving pallor.

They'd moved past a fling after that Langham weekend, yet he'd relegated what they'd shared to just that by dismissing her offer.

He knew how much it must have cost her to tell him, knew how much she prized Seaborns. For her to contemplate coming to Paris with him...

He cursed out loud.

It looked as if her feelings mirrored his.

Which meant...

He slammed a fist against the sideboard, watching Serge's globe and the stupid pins he'd stabbed into various countries jump.

How far he'd come from those days when he'd travelled the world schmoozing and partying, playing up to the reputation he'd deliberately courted after his first failure.

The opinion of so many had burned in his gut, never doused no matter how much alcohol he poured down his throat, never easing no matter how many beds he lay in.

But judging from the reception his indie collection had received at Melbourne Fashion Week it was time to have another go at entering a market he knew he had a lot to offer to.

Interestingly, his folks had ignored the e-mail he'd sent them with links to press accolades for the indie collection.

Not that they could ignore it for too much longer, considering he had their meeting all planned out. Present the latest sales figures and projections, introduce his plans for a breakaway company, thank them and hand in his resignation.

It wouldn't be easy—far from it. Fourde Fashion was one of the oldest establishments in Europe. For the youngest son to go head to head with his parents...yeah, it would be tough. He could handle it—had handled being a focus of the media for years.

This time, though, he intended on being front and centre in the media for all the right reasons.

'Security let me up.'

Patrick turned, unprepared for the slash of sadness to his gut, which intensified as he caught sight of Sapphire striding across his office, head held high.

She'd changed into a pale blue leisure suit and let her hair down, managing to look coolly elegant and comfortable at the same time. Soft and approachable, at odds with the mutinous twist to her lips.

He'd expected her to be tentative and shaken when she showed up—not defiant with a battle gleam in her eyes.

'Let's get to work,' she said, flopping into the chair opposite his desk and flicking on her iPad. 'I assume I'll be liaising with Serge from now on?'

'Yeah,' he said, sitting opposite her, his hands curling into fists at the thought of Sapphire liaising with anyone but him. 'He's in charge in the interim.'

'Interim?' She typed, pretending his answer didn't mean anything, but he saw her shoulders tense.

''Til we figure out who's heading up the Melbourne branch permanently.'

It wasn't going to be him, once he'd vocalised his plans to his folks.

'That's it? You breeze in for a month, hit a major home run, and leave?' She continued typing, not looking up. 'Seems like a funny way to run a business. Especially when Fourde is trying to get a foothold in the Aussie market.'

'I know what I'm doing,' he said, wishing he could tell her all of it.

But he couldn't afford a leak. Not with so much at stake. This time he would do it right.

'Do you?' She finally glanced up, fixing him with a piercing glare that eviscerated. 'Because from where I'm sitting, it looks like you haven't changed a bit. Still flitting from one thing to another, searching for the next shiniest toy to play with, unable to settle.'

She'd nailed his past persona to a tee. *Past.* And the fact she thought him so shallow irked.

'There's a lot you don't know.'

'Enlighten me.'

She carefully placed her iPad on the desk and leaned forward, tapping the bulging manila folder containing their brainstorming. 'We did good with this. Real good. We're in every major fashion magazine around the world this week, not to mention the online forums and websites.'

She leaned back, folded her arms, so sure appealing to his business side would get him to change his mind.

'This could be the start of something great, so why are you running away?'

'You're not just talking about work here,' he said, knowing they needed to have this conversation but not prepared for it.

What could he say? That he had to launch his own company in Paris as vindication for the failures of the past? That he wanted his folks to sit up and finally take notice of him for once? That everything he'd done the past few years, working his butt off for Fourde, had been leading towards this moment?

He couldn't give it up—even for the only woman who had ever made him feel.

'You've made yourself perfectly clear but I don't get it.'

She spoke so softly he had to strain to hear the rest.

'We've connected on an emotional level and you have no intention of seeing it through.' She tapped her chest. 'I'm the one willing to travel to Paris to be with you, to see if there's any chance at a future, but you're not interested. And I guess my ego is demanding to know why not.'

He shook his head, frustrated with the situation, frustrated with *her*. If they'd connected, how come she thought so little of him?

The thought of them together in Paris appealed on so many levels. Except the one that mattered most—the one that said he couldn't afford to lose sight of the end goal, not now.

'Not everything's about you,' he said, hating the flash of pain in her bold gaze but needing to establish emotional distance before he caved. 'I'm heading back to Paris for business and you need to accept it.'

'We don't stay in touch? We pretend like we never happened?'

Her quiet stoicism slugged him hard. Classy to the end, she wouldn't rant or swear or blame. It would have been better if she had. He could have coped with histrionics. This quiet acceptance, as if she'd expected him to let her down all along, sucked big-time.

'I can't give you any promises. I have important stuff to do in Paris and that's my priority for now.'

'*Stuff?*' She made it sound as if he'd be dancing the cancan rather than launching a new business.

In that moment, despite his obsession with secrecy until his company went live, he knew he'd have to tell her to get her to back off. To understand. He wasn't toying with her. He just didn't want to make any promises he couldn't keep.

He'd been working too long and too hard to sacrifice his dream now.

'I'm launching my own fashion house.'

Her eyes widened in surprise and she stared at him as if he'd announced he'd be constructing the next Louvre by hand.

'It's confidential for now. You can probably appreciate the delicacy with being Fourde's rival.'

'Of course.' She nodded. 'Congratulations.'

Her voice sounded strangled and she couldn't meet his eye.

Great. He'd finally told her the truth and *this* was the reaction he got? Then again, he'd vetoed any possibility of a future between them so what did he expect? For her to throw a party?

'Well, then, I guess you go do your *stuff* and I'll do mine.'
She stood so quickly his head snapped back.

'Hand over to Serge tonight and I'll meet with him to-morrow.'

'But I thought—'

'What?'

She whirled on him with so much fury he wouldn't have been surprised if the air between them had crackled.

'You thought I'd sit here meek and mild tonight, being the good little business associate?'

She towered over him, hands on hips, brows drawn, eyes narrowed, magnificent.

'Newsflash. I've finally got your message loud and clear.'

For the second time that evening he found himself yelling, 'Wait...' to her retreating back as she ran from his office.

He swore, long and hard, a string of French and English curses that did little to ease the frustration pounding through his body.

Of course Serge chose that moment to saunter into his office, an aged double malt Scotch in one hand, ice bucket in the other.

'Looks like you could use one of these,' he said, laying both on the sideboard. 'Was that Sapphire I saw heading towards the elevators?'

'Shut the hell up,' Patrick said, stalking across the office to grab one of the glasses Serge had filled in record time.

'Hmm... I'm guessing you won't be liking this so much, then.' Serge grappled in his pocket for a moment, before pulling out a pin and sticking it in Melbourne on the globe. 'Look at this this way—she's another flag in your world domination.'

Patrick had never been a violent man, despite being pushed to the limits by his dad on numerous occasions, but at that moment, with Serge's smug grin taunting, he'd never felt like hitting anyone more.

'Leave. Now.'

Serge held up his hands. 'Thought you needed to lighten up. It's harmless fun—'

'Get out.'

Serge reached for the Scotch, took one look at his face and thought better of it, backing away instead.

'We can go over the latest orders in the morning.'

Patrick grunted in response, willing the fury making his hand shake to subside.

He wasn't angry with Serge so much as the situation. He hated feeling helpless, and watching Sapphire walk out had rendered him more powerless than he'd ever been.

He needed time and space to calm down. The bottle of Scotch wouldn't go astray either.

'Take it easy, *mon ami*,' Serge said, backing through the door with a final concerned frown.

Alone. Finally.

He downed the Scotch in three gulps and had poured another when the door flung open again.

'Dammit—'

'What did he mean, "she's another flag"'

Sapphire's voice was quiet, deadly, at odds with the shattered agony in her eyes.

The alcohol burned in his empty gut. His sudden nausea was more to do with explaining to Sapphire what that stupid globe meant than drinking on an empty stomach.

She jabbed a finger at him. 'I came back because I didn't want us to end like we did first time around, with me not saying what I should've.'

She toyed with the string on her hoodie and he hated that he was the cause of her stricken pallor.

'Back then I acted like an immature child. I should've taken your call and thanked you for seeing me home on graduation night, should've told you I appreciated you caring enough to bother after the way I treated you during our final year.' She shook her head. 'So that's why I'm here. I'd like to think I'm more mature these days and I should've congratulated you properly before. Shouldn't have let my feelings cloud your success. For that's what you'll be with your own company. I have no doubt.'

She shrugged. 'But after what I overheard maybe I should've left well enough alone, like in high school.'

He didn't speak and she hovered in the doorway, vulnerable in a way he'd never imagined.

'Tell me what Serge meant.'

He glanced at the inanimate object encapsulating the stupidity of his past and wondered why he'd kept it. He didn't need a reminder of how far he'd come. He stared at the reality in the mirror every morning while shaving. He wasn't the same person he'd once been. He'd become so much more through hard work and dedication.

'I'm not leaving 'til you tell me,' she said, her voice quivering. Something inside him broke.

In a pique of rage he swept the globe off the sideboard, sending it spinning onto the floor, surrounded by countless pins dotting the carpet.

She gaped, but didn't move, and he clenched and unclenched his fists several times before being able to speak.

'Sometimes any form of attention is better than none.' He kicked the globe. 'Serge and I were young. He came up with the stupid idea to…uh…catalogue our conquests according to location.'

Her sharp intake of breath killed him, but not half as much as the devastation crumpling her mouth.

'I never did, but Serge hung onto this, and after a while I used it as something to spur me on—a reminder of a past I didn't want to go back to. I channelled my energies into my work, hoping to gain recognition that way.'

'Did it work?'

'Still trying.'

As the words popped out he wondered if he'd ever feel truly vindicated. He'd taken Fashion Week by storm. Had provided a good launch-pad for his contemporary fashion house. Had garnered attention from around the world.

So why the emptiness deep down, in a place he'd expected to be filled once he'd done what he'd set out to do?

'You keep trying.' The shimmer of tears hit him hard. 'In the meantime, why don't you admit all I ever meant to you was another flag on your globe.'

He crossed the room in four strides and reached for her. 'You know that's bull. What we shared was really special.'

She shrugged out of his grasp. 'Yeah, so special you won't give us a chance.'

He wanted to explain but couldn't find the words. No other woman made him feel as perplexed, as out of his depth, as Sapphire Seaborn.

Confusion churned his gut as he struggled to articulate, and his true feelings hit at the same moment as she ran.

This time for good.

CHAPTER TEN

SAPPHIE DIDN'T WANT to meet with Serge. She didn't want to set foot in the Fourde Fashion offices ever again. But her wishes didn't come into this.

She was doing it for Seaborns. She'd do anything for Seaborns. The one constant in her topsy-turvy life.

Managing the family business might have almost driven her into the ground, mentally, physically and emotionally, but it was still standing, resolute and dependable, while the rest of her life crumbled around her diamond-clad ears.

Continuing a business relationship with Fourde Fashion was a smart move. Thanks to the Fashion Week success Seaborns had enough orders to fill for the next decade. Only a fool would walk away from something so lucrative.

Besides, Ruby would be at this meeting too, and she had to act as if everything was fine. The last thing she needed was Rubes freaking out if she thought Sapphie was stressing over losing Patrick.

As she strode into the boardroom her business focus stalled. Memories did that to a girl. Memories she'd have to forget if she expected to get through this meeting without falling apart.

'*Bonjour*,' Serge said, bowing over her hand in the flamboyant way she'd come to expect whenever their paths crossed. 'How are you?'

'Fine.'

She made a mockery of the monosyllabic response by slamming her portfolio down a little too hard on the table.

Ignoring his questioning glance, she busied herself with setting up the data on her iPad and finding the figures they needed to go over for future projections.

His silence unnerved her but she kept busy. As long as she stayed busy everything would be okay. She could ignore the permanent ache in her chest and the sick emptiness in her belly.

According to Serge, Patrick had left. A day early. Caught a flight late last night. Could he have got away any faster?

She'd been up all night, wishing she hadn't run out on him. He'd been sincere about that stupid globe, had said she'd meant more to him than any other woman and she believed him.

So why was he hell bent on pushing her away?

She'd hoped to confront him today, without the heat of last night's emotions clouding the issue. Instead he'd brought forward his departure, pretty much telling her he'd meant it when he'd said they were over.

'Your sister is joining us?'

Sapphie nodded. 'Far as I know.'

'She's very talented.' Serge tapped the latest industry magazine cover, featuring Patrick's showstopper and Ruby's choker.

'Someone mention my name?' Ruby breezed into the room, the only person Sapphie knew who could pull off a pink poncho, purple velvet mini, black and white striped leggings and maroon ankle boots. 'Because I've got talent in spades, you know.'

'Modesty too,' Sapphie muttered as Serge laughed.

'Can you ladies give me a few minutes while I grab some stuff for our meeting?'

'Sure.' Ruby waved him away, her astute gaze zeroing

in on her, making Sapphie wish she'd cancelled this meeting after all.

Ruby dumped her portfolio on the table and plopped onto the chair next to her, waiting until Serge had left before elbowing her.

'What's going on?'

Sapphie took a deep breath. Convincing Rubes she was fine would take a monumental effort.

'What do you mean?'

Ruby rolled her eyes. 'I spoke to Serge a few hours ago. He said Patrick left.'

'No great surprise there.'

Ruby frowned. 'But I thought...'

'What?'

'That you two were in it for the long haul.' Ruby slung an arm around her shoulders and hugged. 'You okay?'

'Fine.' Her clipped tone suggested otherwise and Ruby sighed.

'What happened?'

'Nothing. He's going solo in Paris, launching a new company.'

Ruby's eyebrows rose as she sat back. 'He's a talented guy. The European scene won't know what's hit it.'

'Absolutely.'

And he hadn't told her about it—any of it—until she'd practically dragged it out of him.

Ultimately that was what had made her walk away last night. His lack of trust in her, his inability to confide in her after all they'd shared.

It had hurt more than she could have imagined.

Apparently short-term flings weren't privy to long term plans.

Ironic. She'd been hell-bent on confronting him this morning and demanding answers—she could thank her mum for her dogged determination too—but it had been too late.

She'd taken it as a sign. They were over. For good.

'You two were great together,' Ruby said, patting her hand. 'Professionally and personally.'

Sapphie *sooo* didn't want to have this conversation.

'Can we focus on work today—?'

'Serge said he's never seen Patrick like this—totally obsessed with a woman.'

Yeah, gaining that extra 'flag' would be enough to fuel any obsession.

'Rubes—'

'He hasn't dated for a year. Has focussed on making it big in this biz.' She frowned. 'Not that his parents care. He got shafted in Paris.'

Despite her wanting to put Patrick behind her, Ruby had piqued her curiosity.

'What happened?'

Ruby rubbed her forehead. 'Apparently his first show years ago was too cutting edge. Buyers rebelled. Cost Fourde megabucks. His parents distanced themselves and the company, treated him like a second-class citizen. So he's worked his ass off since—was the sole inspiration behind the Fourde spring collection, coming up with that unique twist on the Eighties. Fashion world went wild for it.'

'Like they did for Old Hollywood Glamour?'

'Exactly.' Ruby picked up a pen and doodled diamonds. 'Another employee took the credit. Patrick didn't tell his folks the truth.'

'No way?'

'Serge said they've got this screwy relationship.'

'I figured from what he told me.'

Ruby smirked. 'So you guys *did* manage to talk between other activities?'

Sapphie punched her in the arm.

'Explains why he's so determined on heading back to Paris.' Ruby tilted her head to one side, studying her. 'Don't you think this start-up company has a lot to do with proving his success to his folks?'

'Don't know. Don't care.'

'Liar,' Ruby said, swivelling to face her. 'Are you going after him?'

Sapphie stared at Ruby as if she'd suggested Sapphie steal the Crown jewels alone. 'Even if I were remotely interested any more, which I'm not, remember that business I run? Seaborns? Ring any bells?'

'I've run it before. I can do it again.' Ruby shrugged. 'You're obviously in love with the guy. Why don't you give a relationship a chance?'

'Because I don't—I can't—ah, hell…'

'Deep breaths, sis. It's not that hard, really.'

Sapphie sighed. 'I already told him I was willing to head to Paris for a while. See how things developed between us.'

Ruby squealed and clapped her hands.

'He said no.'

Ruby grabbed her hand. 'What the—?'

'Looks like launching his precious company is more important than what we shared.'

Ruby squeezed her hand, released it. 'You're both as bad as each other.'

Sapphie pointed at her ear. 'Did you hear a word I said? I was willing to follow him—'

'So why didn't you?'

'Because he doesn't bloody want me.'

Ruby shook her head. 'At some point in time both of you will need to stop hiding behind business and lay your hearts on the line.'

'That's not what I'm doing—'

'Isn't it?' Ruby gestured to the stack of work on the table in front of them. 'It's what you've always done, Saph. Put the business ahead of your own needs. Don't let it ruin what you could have with Patrick.'

When Sapphie opened her mouth to reiterate that Patrick didn't want her, Ruby held up her hand. 'And don't give me that bull about him not being interested. He's ga-ga over you.' She paused only long enough to draw breath before continuing, 'The guy's probably terrified. He's spent his life searching for approval he's never got from his folks. Maybe he's scared he won't measure up to your expectations? Maybe he's scared of failure? He failed workwise once. Maybe he doesn't want to stuff up with his new company? Or maybe he's scared of failing at a relationship with you—?'

'Stop.' Sapphie held up her hand. 'That's a heck of a lot of maybes.'

Ruby grinned. 'Here's another one. Maybe you should give over that six-month supply of Tim Tams you owe me.'

'What for?'

'That bet we made when he first arrived on the scene.' Ruby smirked. 'That you wouldn't last two weeks without getting up close and personal with the delicious Patrick.'

'You've got a memory like an elephant,' Sapphie muttered, relieved to be joking rather than contemplating her sister's outlandish encouragement to follow him to Paris.

Ruby rubbed her hands together. 'Now we've got my chocolate bikkie situation sorted, when are you leaving?'

So much for a reprieve.

'Rubes, drop it—'

'Jax is in South Africa for the next six weeks so I can hold the fort 'til then. You should go,' Ruby said, slipping Sapphire her mobile—to book a ticket, presumably. 'I've done this before, remember? It'll be a cinch.'

Handing over the reins of Seaborns to Ruby again wasn't the problem. Potentially having her heart broken by Patrick Fourde was one big problem waiting to happen.

But what if Ruby was right?

What if Patrick did love her?

What if he'd pushed her away deliberately for some warped rationale she had no hope of figuring out?

And, the doozy, what if she headed to Paris to lay her heart on the line once and for all?

As Patrick waited for his folks to wrap up a conference call with a buyer in New York he lounged in a Louis XIV chair next to his favourite window.

How many times had he sat here, waiting for his folks to give him a few seconds of their precious time? Hardy and Joyce, the toast of Paris and beyond, willing to do anything in the name of Fourde Fashion.

He'd always wondered how far they'd go for their company...and he'd found out the hard way. Interestingly, after his first disastrous show and the fallout, they hadn't spoken of it. Had swept it under their priceless antique rug as if it had never happened.

They'd never trusted him to run a show again until Melbourne, and that was probably only because of the distance from Paris and their low expectations. If he stuffed up in Australia who would care?

He'd shown them. Not only had he hit a home run, he'd landed on the front page of every fashion mag in Europe and beyond.

Old Hollywood glamour was the new catch cry and he knew knock-off designs would be in shows and shops worldwide in the upcoming season.

It pleased him, leaving the company on a high, having given something back to his parents, ensuring he'd made his mark at Fourde—a positive mark this time.

As he stared out over Paris and the exquisite view of the Montmartre district he couldn't wait to get this meeting underway.

It would be predictable. He'd tell them his plans, they'd

nod absentmindedly, ask a few questions out of politeness and leave him to it. Classic Fourde parenting.

It wouldn't matter if he strutted into their office wearing a satin sheath and stilettos. They wouldn't notice.

Who knew? Maybe his new company, in opposition to theirs—and grabbing consumer dollars—would finally make them sit up and take notice of their youngest son?

He'd make his fashion house succeed if it killed him. And that included accessorising with the right jewellery. Jewellery he'd scoured Paris for but had come up with nothing that matched the stunning creations by Seaborns.

If he wanted to succeed he needed the best, which meant he needed to talk to Sapphire. But he hadn't figured out how to do it in business terms without letting emotions cloud the issue.

'Patrick? You wanted something?'

Joyce's cultured accent sounded the same as ever: cool, clipped, closed. He'd never heard his mother sound warm or happy and it saddened him. Amazingly glamorous at sixty, one of the most envied women in the fashion world, but with an aloofness that underscored her timeless beauty.

He stood and headed towards the door that had opened on silent hinges. 'Hey, Mum.'

He kissed her cheek, not surprised when she bustled him through the door as if she had more important matters to attend to.

'Dad.' He nodded a greeting at his father, who glanced up from the spreadsheets scattered across his desk long enough for a reciprocal nod.

Joyce sat on a chaise and gestured him to a seat opposite. 'Do you have more projection figures from Fashion Week?'

Not *How are you? How was your flight? Congratulations on doing an amazing job in Melbourne.* Nope, straight to the point: how their number one baby, Fourde Fashion, was doing.

'I haven't come here to discuss that,' he said, picking imaginary lint off his trousers before realising how nervous he looked. 'I've got something to tell you.'

He'd finally captured his father's attention. Hardy pushed back from the desk, rounded it in three strides and took a seat next to Joyce.

'What's going on? Did that order from the mega department store fall through? Thought it was too good to be true—'

'I'm leaving Fourde's to start up my own fashion house.'

The rhythmic tick-tock of a grandfather clock filled the silence as his stony-faced folks stared at him as if he'd proposed they scale the Eiffel Tower in couture.

'I've already mentioned this before, and the time is right now.' He tapped his smartphone and pulled up the spread on his indie show. 'I had a test run at Fashion Week in Melbourne. The contemporary, edgy stuff I want to focus on. It was a hit.'

'Interesting concept.' His father studied the phone screen through narrowed eyes. 'Is it sustainable?'

Surprised by his father's apparent interest, Patrick nodded. 'From the positive feedback so far, I think so.'

Hardy swiped his finger across the screen, a frown denting his brow. 'These are good, but it takes more than modern concepts to build a company.'

Patrick had expected censure, not praise—however begrudging—and he eased into a smile. 'I'd like to think I've learned from the best.'

Hardy's bushy eyebrows bristled before he cleared his throat. 'Fourde has dedicated workers, that's for sure. If you put in the hard yards, who knows what can happen?'

Patrick knew. He'd be sitting across from his folks at the next premier fashion show, sharing top billing.

'Thanks, Dad. I'm grateful for the experience but I'm looking forward to the challenge.'

Concern bracketed Joyce's pursed lips as she glanced at

the phone screen. 'These designs are stunning, Patrick, but have you forgotten the disaster of your first show?'

'No, Mum, I haven't.' He refrained from adding, *It's what drove me every day.* 'Paris wasn't ready for funky and contemporary back then. It is now.'

His father nodded, thoughtful. And with this meeting working out better than he'd expected, Patrick ventured into uncharted territory. Having a real family conversation.

'Why did you leave me to take the fallout back then?'

There—he'd asked the million-dollar question. He'd bet their answer would be priceless too.

Joyce had the grace to blush as she fiddled with a ruffled lace cuff and Hardy looked plain embarrassed. 'You were new to the business. Any adverse publicity wouldn't affect you as much as it would the company. We chose to protect the company.'

How noble. At the expense of their son.

His mum piped up. 'And we were right. Everything blew over. You returned to work, the company absorbed the financial losses and we moved on.'

They made it sound so simple, compartmentalising everything into a neat box. The disaster might have *blown over* for them, but he'd spent years trying to outrun the laughing stock he'd been made out to be in the press—had portrayed himself as a slick playboy to prove he wasn't the worst in the business. Gaining attention from all the wrong sources when he should have captured the attention of the two people standing before him now.

'I guess we've all moved on,' he said, sliding his phone back into his pocket. 'I'd like to resign—effective immediately.'

Joyce's perfectly plucked brows arched. 'That soon?'

He nodded. 'I want to capitalise on the buzz surrounding my Melbourne indie show.'

A loaded glance he had no hope of interpreting passed

between his parents before his father sagged onto the nearest surface—his desk.

'Before you go, there's something we need to discuss.'

Here it came. A counter-offer? A buy-out before he'd begun?

'We recently learned *you* came up with the spring collection concept.' Hardy shook his head. 'Why didn't you say something?'

How could he explain that pride had kept him silent? That he'd hoped his parents would recognise his signature talent? That even though his first collection had tanked for being innovative before its time, some of the same flair had been evident in those spring gowns? That even when he did voice his ideas they rarely deemed him worth listening to?

He could have said so much, but after a lifetime of their not being interested in what he had to say what would be the point now?

'Because ultimately it wouldn't have changed anything.' He thrust his hands in his pockets and took a few steps, pacing, before he stopped. He had nothing to be uncertain about. 'My plan was always to leave. I wanted to do the best job I could before that happened.'

'Then why did you take on the CEO role in Melbourne?' His mother laid a cerise-taloned hand on his forearm.

'Same reason.'

Not entirely true, but his folks didn't need to know his number one reason for nailing that show in Melbourne: proving to himself he could do it.

'The Hollywood glamour campaign was a perfect fit for Fourde Fashion, and if I hadn't worked here all these years, surrounded by the elegance this label stands for, I never would've been inspired to come up with something like that. So thank you.'

Joyce patted his forearm and Hardy straightened in what Patrick could only label as pride.

'You've given me an amazing start in this business, and I'll always be grateful, but my vision for the future isn't a good match for the Fourde brand—as we discovered the hard way. So it's time we part ways.' As he said the words he realised that they were true. They *had* given him an amazing start to the business. And perhaps even a start in changing the future of his relationship with them.

'There's nothing we can say to change your mind?'

Patrick shook his head. 'That's flattering, but no.'

That was when he saw the first real sign of emotion from his mother ever. Tears glistening and pooling in her artfully made-up eyes. Her vulnerability was shocking and frightening at the same time.

'I wish you luck, son,' she said, her voice quivering but her posture ramrod-straight.

Hardy held out his hand. 'Me too, son. You've done us proud.'

Ironic that it took him leaving the company for his father to articulate what he'd wanted to hear all along. What he'd wanted since he was a kid. A little attention.

'Just so you know, I'm going to put a positive spin on this in the media. Talk up Fourde, make this a personal decision so we don't face too much fallout.'

'Thanks.' Joyce's slight nod reminded him of a queen acknowledging a recalcitrant subordinate.

He'd done it.

He was on his own.

Time to instigate proceedings—starting with securing the best in the jewellery business.

He needed to talk to Sapphire.

His parents might have given their approval and finally acknowledged he had talent, but Sapphire had supported him all along. Had taken a risk on him. Even after he'd made her life impossible in high school and they hadn't spoken in ten years she'd taken a chance on his indie collection when she didn't have to.

And she'd still been willing to support him—to the extent she would have followed him to Paris.

What had he done? Deliberately pushed her away.

He'd been so wrapped up in proving he could do this on his own he'd lost sight of the bigger picture. A picture that had an amazing woman who complemented him right by his side.

Not wanting to be distracted from achieving success and the ultimate vindication in going it alone was one thing.

But not taking a chance on letting Sapphire get close because he half expected her to let him down eventually too was foolish.

She'd stood by him after he'd barged into her life just over a month ago when she really hadn't had any reason to.

He could rationalise away her loyalty as being for the Fourde Fashion name, but that didn't explain her devotion to making his contemporary collection succeed.

That had been about him, all about him, and she'd backed him regardless.

The kind of devotion she'd displayed was beyond rare.

Confronting his folks, vocalising his plans, had ensured one thing.

He was about to make his dreams come true.

The question was could he convince Sapphire to join him for the ride?

Sapphie rushed into the elaborate foyer of Fourde Fashion, slowing when her heels struck marble. Ruby had told her to break a leg during her Paris trip. Her sister hadn't meant literally.

She'd completed her third lap of the foyer when Patrick emerged from the wrought-iron elevator, striding for the glass front doors as if he had a million demons on his tail.

He had the long strides of a guy with places to be, but gone was the half-smirk, half-grin—the kind of daredevil smile women found infinitely appealing and that he'd used to great effect over the last month.

The way he looked now… Pensive. Driven. Tense. It sent her already thriving nerves into overdrive.

'Patrick?'

He stopped and swivelled as she stepped out from behind a marble column, his expression incredulous.

'What are you doing here?'

'We needed to talk so here I am.'

He stared at her as if he couldn't quite believe she was real and his mouth relaxed into that sexy smile. 'Guess I should've expected it.'

Sapphie didn't know if that was a good or bad thing. The fact he seemed pleased to see her was a plus. The fact he hadn't touched her yet? Big fat minus.

'Can we go somewhere private?'

He winked. 'So that's why you really came to Paris?'

She rolled her eyes. 'You're such a guy.'

'Sue me.' He gestured for her to step out through the door first. 'Come on, there's a little café around the corner.'

So far so good. At least he hadn't run screaming. Now to make him listen and hope to hell he'd tell her the truth.

They didn't speak, but she caught him sneaking glances at her and she self-consciously tugged at her leopard-print trench, winding her black cashmere scarf tighter.

She'd headed for Fourde straight from the airport, desperate to see him before she lost her nerve, so she hadn't seen much of Paris beyond the frame of a taxi window.

Now, as he ushered her towards an outdoor table at a cosy café tucked between an art supplies store and a shoe shop, she registered the fact she was in *Paris*. With a gorgeous guy.

It had been a secret fantasy when Patrick had first absconded all those years ago: imagining herself here, having fun, no responsibilities.

She'd resented him as time passed, envisaging him whooping it up while she threw herself into university studies and assisting her mum in her limited 'free' time.

After a while she'd deliberately forgotten him, wiping him from her mind, but every time she'd heard a mention of France, or had an illicit chocolate croissant treat or celebrated another Seaborns success with the finest French champagne, she'd remember him.

And wonder what might have been if he hadn't run.

'I want to know the real reason you didn't want me to come here.'

She fired the question before he'd sat down and he stared at her in disbelief.

'Can't a guy order an espresso before the inquisition starts?'

'Make it a cappuccino, throw in a *macaron*, and I'll give you a few seconds to compose some believable excuses.'

He chuckled, and it gave her hope that maybe this trip hadn't been a massive waste of time after all.

She waited until he'd placed their order and sat before leaning her forearms on the table and eyeballing him.

'Care to enlighten me?'

'Actually, I was planning on contacting you so we could talk—'

'Sure you were.' She took a deep breath and plunged on. 'Look, I didn't come all this way to stuff around. I want us to have an honest, adult conversation about why you pushed me away. And I'm not leaving Paris 'til you tell me the truth.'

His eyes narrowed. 'I don't do ultimatums all that well.'

'Yet you were quite happy to do me.'

Shock tightened his mouth. 'Crassness doesn't do you justice.'

'Oh, come on,' she said, throwing her hands in the air in exasperation. 'Can't you see I'm trying to snap you out of this stupor you seem to be in?' She slammed her palms on the table, not caring when several people glanced their way.

'How did your folks take the news of your impending departure from the family bosom?'

The tension pinching his lips eased. 'Surprisingly well.'

'That's great.' Seeing his softening had her hand snaking across the table, her fingers touching his. 'In case you haven't figured it out, dummy, I wouldn't have flown all this way unless I was in love with you, and I'll do whatever it takes to give us a fighting chance to see if we can make this work.'

Her chest heaved with the effort of blurting all that in one go and she inhaled deeply, willing him to say something—anything—rather than stare at her with a disheartening mix of wariness and shock.

'You love me?'

She would have laughed at his stunned expression if her heart hadn't been in her mouth. 'That's the general gist.'

'I was coming to see you… I didn't think… I mean, it's all so complicated…'

So complicated. But he'd been coming to see her. That had to be a good thing, right? Especially when he'd effectively ended it in Melbourne.

'What's complicated?'

He dragged a hand through his hair, tugged on his collar, loosened his tie—anything to out off answering.

'You being with me right now.'

'Isn't that my choice to make?'

A camera flash went off at a nearby table and he jumped. 'See that? Just the beginning. I've lived through media scrutiny before. It's tough—really tough. I wouldn't be willing to put you through the stress of it.'

Okay, so he was looking out for her. That meant he cared. Cared enough to give her up rather than put her through whatever he thought she couldn't handle. But she still didn't understand what it was.

'Thanks, but I'm a big girl. I can take care of myself.'

'Wasn't that the problem before, when you wound up at

that health spa? You tried to take care of everything and ended up getting ill?'

She frowned, more embarrassed by her foolishness in letting the situation get that out of hand than how fragile she'd been.

'That was physical exhaustion from pushing my body too hard. I learned from it. Changed. That's what people do—learn from their mistakes.'

Look at you, she wanted to say. This power-driven, determined entrepreneur was far removed from the laid-back goof-off he'd once been.

But now wasn't the time to bring up high school. She wanted answers to the here and now.

'I'm not the same person I was twelve months ago, and I'm guessing you're not either.'

He folded his arms and leaned back. 'Let me guess. Dear old Serge blabbed about the spring collection.'

'He might've mentioned it to Ruby, who told me.' She wrinkled her nose. 'I'm sorry that your parents had such a problem with you. They should have your name up in lights after scoring two major coups in a year.'

'It's no big deal.'

But it was. She could see it in the slight slump of his shoulders, the downturned corners of his mouth.

And it broke her heart to see an amazingly gifted guy like Patrick not being recognised for his talents.

'Then I think you've made a stellar decision in branching out on your own. The fashion world's going to love you.'

'Like you do?'

He spoke so softly she had to strain forward to listen.

'I never thought...' He shook his head and looked away.

'Thought what?'

He dragged his gaze back to hers, the hint of vulnerability buoying her hope. 'That someone like you could love someone like me.'

In that moment it all clicked into place—his reasons for pushing her away.

Thanks to his parents' chronic neglect over the years he didn't think he was good enough.

The thought that they'd bruised his self-esteem to such an extent made her want to march back to Fourde Fashion and tell them a few harsh home truths.

'Listen to me. You're the most amazing man I've ever known. You're smart and funny and gorgeous. And you have more creative flair in your little finger than half the people in this business. Surely you know that?'

He shrugged. 'The fallout from my first show was nasty. I got savaged in the press, shunned by aficionados for a while—'til I started playing their game. Attending their parties. Living their lifestyle. Going it alone I'll risk alienating a lot of people again. Sure you want to be part of that?'

Swallowing the rising lump in her throat because he cared that much, she flexed her biceps. 'Thanks to you, I'm stronger now than I've been in years. You've made me more energised and more alive than I could've hoped for. So whatever you face—count me in.'

'What about Seaborns? It's your life.'

'My life is wherever you are.'

'Careful, I see a violin quartet heading our way,' he said.

His dry humour was one of the many things she loved about him.

Sapphire Seaborn loved Patrick Fourde.

Who would've thought it?

'That's why you ran, isn't it? You expected the *merde* to hit the fan once you'd broken away from the family business and you didn't want me exposed to it?'

'Actually, it's also to do with the fact I needed to do this on my own.' He sighed. 'Last time my folks had to handle the fallout. This time I didn't want anyone else to take the flak but me.'

'Want to know something? Going it alone can be incredibly exhilarating. When you're successful, you're flying. It's an incredible rush. But then there are other times when it's nice to have people along for the ride.' She tapped her chest. 'How do I feel in here? Invincible, with you by my side.'

A hint of wariness still hovered. 'That's a hell of a responsibility for a guy to handle.'

She blew out an exasperated breath. 'I meant I'm stronger than I've ever been. How you make me feel empowers me.' Her hand gestured at the space on her right. 'I don't need you here all the time to feel good, but it's a lot more fun when you are.'

A glimmer of a smile eased the tension lines bracketing his mouth. 'You're a lot ballsier now than you were in high school. I like it.'

'Don't you mean love?'

He took an eternity to answer, literally leaving her on the edge of her seat.

'Walking away from you proved that,' he said, pinching the bridge of his nose before pinning her with a stare that snatched her breath. 'Only a dumb guy in love could rationalise himself into walking away from the best thing to ever happen to him.'

She sank back into her chair, sporting a goofy grin. 'You love me, huh?'

'Oh, yeah.' He grinned right back at her, but it faded too soon. 'This could get tough. Launching a new fashion house in Europe is highly competitive, and throw in the angle that I'm going up against family? Paparazzi will have a field-day.'

'So? All publicity is good publicity, right?' Sapphire waved away his concern. 'Know what I say? Bring it on—because Patrick Fourde is headed for the stars and nothing can stop him.'

He stared at her, wide-eyed. 'You have that much faith in me?'

She nodded and snagged his hand across the table. 'Absolutely. I made the mistake of not believing in you once. Never again.'

He squeezed her hand. 'You thought I was a no-good lout in high school.'

'No, I thought you were the hottest rebel I'd ever seen and I envied you beyond belief.'

'Why?'

'Because I wanted to be like you. Carefree. Cool. No responsibilities. I hated the fact you were so popular and didn't seem to work at it, while I was this rich nerd girl who had her whole life mapped out.' She giggled nervously. 'I developed a crush, and that only added to my angst. Because no way could I risk you finding out—'

'So you pushed me away instead?'

Sheepish, she shrugged. 'I had no choice in Biology, because we had to work together, but the rest of the time? Yeah, being around you was tough.'

The cocky grin spreading across his face was familiar and welcome. 'Must've been…pretending you didn't like me while wanting to jump me.'

'It wasn't like that.' She blushed. ''Til that kiss…'

'Lucky we made up for lost time in Melbourne recently,' he said, lifting her hand to his mouth to brush kisses across her knuckles, setting her latent desire for him alight.

'You know, I've heard Paris is the most romantic city in the world.' She glanced around, taking in the centuries-old buildings, the paved paths, the lovers strolling arm-in-arm. 'We should put it to the test.'

'You sure about this? Putting Seaborns on hold? Trialling a relationship among the frenetic pace of launching a new business?'

She should be glad he was putting her first. Instead all she could think about was holing away with him in some tiny, cosy garret with wine and pastries and boxes of condoms.

'Ruby is running Seaborns for the next six weeks 'til we figure out where this is going. And I'm hoping you'll want our jewellery for all your upcoming designs. As for the rest? I'm with you all the way.'

He let out a whoop that had passers-by glancing at them with indulgent smiles. Romance was commonplace in Paris after all.

'How about we take the coffee and *macarons* to go?'

'*Oui*,' she said, standing before he'd barely finished the question.

He pulled her into his arms, holding her as if he'd never let go.

Fine by her.

'You know my new venture will need the best accessorising money can buy?' he murmured in her ear, nibbling the lobe and shooting sparks through her body. 'How would you feel about taking Seaborns global? Or at least to France?'

'You're full of brilliant ideas,' she said, thrilled he'd arrived at the same solution she had on the long flight over here. 'And here's one for you.'

She stood on tiptoes and whispered in his ear what she'd do to him in the privacy of wherever they were staying.

They never did get to have their coffee and *macarons*.

EPILOGUE

PATRICK WASN'T A fan of long distance relationships. There was only so far Skype and a phone could go, despite his girlfriend being the most inventive woman he'd ever met.

He'd always known Sapphire had hidden depths, and he was eternally grateful he was the guy she'd chosen to plumb them.

Though there *was* an upside to long distance. The reunions. Over the last twelve months they'd snatched time together in Melbourne, Paris and once halfway in Singapore for a long weekend.

Their individual schedules had been manic but they'd survived. And tonight he'd repay her trust in him.

True to her word, she'd stood by him. Her faith in his capabilities was rock-solid.

His company had swept the buyers off their feet during the spring, summer and autumn collections. He'd graced the cover of every glossy magazine worldwide, and his company's designs had been seen on the red carpet from Cannes to Hollywood.

Accolades had ranged from *'Ahead of his time'* to *'Pure design genius'*. *'Bold.' 'Innovative.' 'Hip.'*

Supermodels clamoured to wear his clothes. Actresses proudly strutted to awards ceremonies in his contemporary designs.

The same magazines that had so harshly labelled him over a decade earlier now ran features on his clothes.

The entire world now knew who Patrick Fourde was—an entity in his own right.

He'd made it. Achieved his goal.

Now for the next challenge.

'Where are we?' Sapphire snuggled into his side, content to stare at him more than their surroundings.

'Home.'

One word that filled him with pride and warmth.

He'd never really had a home—not a place where he felt he belonged.

That would all change with this incredible woman, starting now.

A cute little frown creased her brow. 'This is your new place?'

'*Our* new place,' he said, keeping a firm hold on her with one arm while sliding a box out of his other pocket. 'This comes with it.'

Her mouth made a cute little O of surprise as she stared at the box.

'A wise woman once told me at my first solo fashion show in Paris that accessories make anything special,' he said, flipping open the box with great deliberation.

His choice in engagement ring, secretly designed by his future sister-in-law, was vindicated by Sapphire's sharp intake of breath.

'So a house like this needs a good proposal.'

And there, in front of an eighteenth-century apartment just off the Rue du Monde, he knelt in front of the woman he adored.

'Will you marry me, Sapphire Seaborn? Live in our home? Accessorise our marriage with a bunch of kids?'

'Kids aren't accessories,' she said in mock outrage while

her eyes glistened with tears. 'I can see I'll have to accept your proposal and set you straight.'

'Is that a—?'

'Of course it's a yes,' she said, dragging him to his feet and flinging herself into his arms. 'Yes, yes, *yes!*'

They kissed as if there was no tomorrow—wild and passionate and unhinged.

When they eventually disengaged he slid the diamond-encrusted sapphire onto her ring finger. 'You're the love of my life.'

'And I have the ring to prove it,' she said with a jubilant yell, holding her hand at arm's length to admire it. 'Best. Accessory. Ever.'

'Considering my future wife owns a jewellery store, there'll be plenty more where that came from,' he said, sliding his arms around her waist. 'Complimentary, of course.'

'Sure—as long as my future husband keeps me in a lifetime of exclusive couture,' she said, straight-faced.

'We make a great team, sweetheart.'

She kissed him in absolute agreement.

* * * * *

MY BOYFRIEND AND OTHER ENEMIES

BY
NIKKI LOGAN

Nikki Logan lives next to a string of protected wetlands in Western Australia with her long-suffering partner and a menagerie of furred, feathered and scaly mates. She studied film and theatre at university and worked for years in advertising and film distribution before finally settling down in the wildlife industry. Her romance with nature goes way back and she considers her life charmed, given she works with wildlife by day and writes fiction by night—the perfect way to combine her two loves. Nikki believes that the passion and risk of falling in love are perfectly mirrored in the danger and beauty of wild places. Every romance she writes contains an element of nature and if readers catch a waft of rich earth or the spray of wild ocean between the pages she knows her job is done.

To Jo—for your support, your friendship and your unfailingly good judgement over the past ten books.

CHAPTER ONE

TASH SINCLAIR STARED at the handsome, salt-and-pepper-haired man across the bustling coastal café as he exchanged casual conversation with a younger companion seated across from him. The electric blue of Fremantle harbour stretched out behind them. She should have been all eyes for the older man—Nathaniel Moore was the reason she was here, monitoring from across the café like a seasoned stalker—but she caught her focus repeatedly drifting to the modestly dressed man next to him.

Not as chiselled as his older friend, and closer to Tash's thirty than Moore's fifty-odd, but there was something compelling about him. Something that held her attention when she could least afford it.

She forced it back onto the older man where it belonged.

Nathaniel Moore looked relaxed, almost carefree, and, for a moment, Tash reconsidered. She was about to launch a rocket grenade into all that serenity. Was it the right thing to do? It felt right. And she'd promised her mother…kind of.

The younger man reached up to signal the waiter for another round of coffee and his moss-green sweater tightened over serious shoulders. Tash felt the pull, resisted it and forced her eyes to stay on Nathaniel Moore.

It wasn't hard to see what first attracted her mother to the executive thirty years ago. He had a whole Marlon Brando thing going on, and if she couldn't guess it for herself, Tash had dozens of diaries, decades of memories and reflections captured in ink, to spell out the attraction. Adele Porter—she'd abandoned the name Sinclair right after Eric Sinclair had abandoned her—might have had trouble living her feelings, but she had no difficulty at all writing them down in the privacy of her diaries once her divorce had come through.

Tash studied him again. Her mother had died loving this man, and he—from what she could tell from the diaries and family gossip only now coming to light—had loved Adele back.

Yet they'd been apart most of their lives.

She might never have thought to look at those diaries—to look for him—if not for the message she'd received from him on her mother's phone. A fiftieth birthday message for a woman who would never get it made about as much sense as Tash maintaining her mother's exorbitant mobile phone service just so she could ring and hear her voice message when she wanted to. When she needed to.

Because it was *her* voice. And apparently that was what they both needed.

Tash's eyes returned to the man across the café.

Nathaniel's head came up and he swept the diners vaguely with his glance, brushing past her table, past the nameless woman in dark sunglasses disguising her surveillance. That was when she saw it: the bruising beneath his eyes, the dark shadows in his gaze. The same expression Tash had worn for weeks.

Nathaniel Moore was still grieving, and she would bet all of her best art pieces that he was doing it completely alone.

His colleague pushed his chair back and stood, sliding the empty espresso cups to the side for collection by the passing staff. A small kindness that would make someone's job that tiny bit easier. He excused himself to Nathaniel and headed towards the restrooms, crossing within feet of her table. As he passed, his eyes brushed over her in the way that most men's did. Appreciative but almost absent, as though he were checking out produce. A way that told her she'd never be going home to meet his family. That said she might get to wear his lingerie at Christmas but never his ring.

The story of her life. Ordinarily she would steadfastly ignore such a lazy appraisal, but today…the chance to see what colour his eyes were was too good to resist. She turned her head up fractionally as he passed and crashed headlong into his regard. Her breath caught.

How had she, even for a moment, thought he was the lesser of the two men? Not classically handsome but his lips were even and set, his jaw artistically angled. And those eyes… bottomless and as blue as the rarest of the priceless cobalt glass she'd worked with…. They transformed his face. Literally breathtaking.

She ripped her stare away, chest heaving.

He kept walking as if nothing had happened.

Her heart tugged against her ribs like a nagging child and she took a deep, slow breath. She wasn't used to noticing men beyond their mannerisms, their social tells, the things that told her who they really were. With him, she'd been so busy studying the shape of his mouth and the extraordinary colour of his irises she'd failed to notice anything else. She'd failed to think of anything else.

Like the reason she was here.

Her focus dragged back to the water's edge and the man sitting there alone, staring out.

Do it.

The voice came immediately. Not her mother's and not her own. A weird kind of hybrid of both. But it was the reason she was here today and the reason she'd paid particular attention to a newspaper article in which Nathaniel Moore was captioned in the photograph. The reason she was able to find out where he worked and, then, how to contact him. The voice that was just…planting seeds. Inspiring particular actions. Pushing when she needed a nudge. Kind of like a guardian angel with an agenda, prompting from off-stage.

Do it now.

Tash's hand reached for the call button on her mobile even as her eyes stayed glued on the greying man across the alfresco area. He reached into his suit pocket casually, tugging his tie a little looser, winding down a notch further. She was about to dash all of that against the rocks of the harbour side they sat on. Tash very nearly pressed the 'end' button but he flipped his phone open as she watched.

'Nathaniel Moore.' Deep and soft.

Tash's heart squeezed so hard she couldn't speak and a frown formed between elegant eyebrows.

He lowered the phone to check the caller ID. 'Hello?'

Speak! Her mouth opened but the tiny sound she uttered was lost in the café noises. He shook his head and started to close his phone. That was the shove she needed.

'Mr Moore!'

He paused and lifted his eyebrows, speaking again into the phone. 'Yes?'

She took a deep breath. 'Mr Moore, I'm sorry to interrupt your lunch—' *Damn!* She wasn't supposed to know where he was. But he seemed to miss the significance. She narrowed her eyes and looked closer. In fact, he seemed to have paled just slightly. His hand tightened noticeably around the phone.

'Mr Moore, my name is Natasha Sinclair. I believe you knew my mother.'

Nothing.

Tash watched expressions come and go in his face like the changing facets of good glass. Horror. Disbelief. Grief. Hope.

Mostly grief.

His free hand trembled as he fidgeted with a napkin. He didn't speak for an age. Tash watched his panicked glance in the direction of his lunch partner and she twisted slightly away as his gaze dragged back past her table.

Eventually he spoke, half whispering, 'You sound just like her.'

It sickened her to be doing this to a man her mother had loved. 'I know. I'm sorry. Are you all right?'

He reached for the water pitcher and poured a glass. She heard him take a sip even as she watched him raise a wobbly glass to his lips. 'I'm…yes. I'm fine. Just shocked. Surprised,' he added, as though realising he'd been rude.

Tash laughed. 'Shocked, I think.' She took a breath. 'I wanted to call you, to touch base. To make sure you knew…' Yes, he already did know; his expression spoke volumes.

Silence fell as Nathaniel Moore collected his emotions. He glanced towards the restrooms again. 'I did hear. I'm sorry I couldn't come to the funeral. It was…not possible.'

Tash knew all about the fall-out between their two families; she'd seen the after-effects repeatedly in her mother's diaries. 'You didn't get to say goodbye.'

He looked desperately around the café and then turned his face away, out to the harbour. His voice grew thick. 'Natasha. I'm so sorry for your loss. She was…an amazing woman.'

Tash took a deep breath and smelled a heavenly mix of spices and earth. She knew, without looking, who was passing her table again. Broad, moss-green shoulders walked away from her towards Nathaniel Moore. He spared a momentary, peripheral glance for her. It was the least casual look she'd ever intercepted.

Her heart hammered and not just because her time was running out.

'Mr Moore,' she urged into the phone, 'I wanted you to know that regardless of how your family and mine feel about each other, my door is always open to you. If you want to talk or ask any questions…'

The younger man reached his seat, recognising immediately from the expression on the older man's face that something was up. Nathaniel Moore stood abruptly.

'Uh…one moment, please…will you excuse me?'

Was that for her or for his colleague?

Nathaniel moved unsteadily from the table, indicating the phone call with the wave of a hand. Concerned blue eyes followed him and then looked around the café suspiciously. Tash threw her head back and mimed a laugh into her mobile phone as the stare sliced past her. Not that he'd have a clue who was on the other end of Nathaniel's call but she absolutely didn't want to make difficulties for the man her mother had died loving.

Not for the first time since finding the diaries, Tash imagined how it would feel to be loved—to love—to the depths described in such heart-breaking detail on the handwritten pages. Her eyes drifted back to the younger man now sitting alone at the waterside table.

'Are you there?'

'I'm sorry, yes.' She found Nathaniel where he stood, back to her, half concealed in giant potted palms. She groaned. 'Mr Moore, I just wanted you to know that…my mother never stopped loving you.' The Armani shoulders slumped. 'I'm sorry to speak so plainly but I feel like we don't have time. Her diaries are full of you. Her memories of you. Particularly at…the end.'

Her heart thumped out the silence. His posture slumped further.

'You've lost so much.' His voice was choked. 'Endured so much.'

She glanced back to the table. Hard blue eyes watched Nathaniel from across the café, narrowing further.

Tash shook her head. 'No, Mr Moore, I *had* so much.' *More than you ever did. More than just one extraordinary night together.* She sucked in a breath. 'As hard as it has been to lose her, at least I had her for my whole life. Thirty years. She was a gift.'

The greying head across the alfresco area bowed and he whispered down the phone. 'She was that.'

Silence fell and Tash knew he was struggling to hold it together. 'You should go. I've called at a bad time.'

'No!' He cleared his throat and then glanced back towards his table, sighing. Blue-eyes stared back at him with open speculation. The hairs on Tash's neck prickled. 'Yes, I'm sorry. This isn't a good time. I'm here with my son—'

Tash's focus snapped back to the younger man. *This* was Aiden Moore? Entrepreneurial young gun, scourge of the social scene? Suddenly her physical response to his presence seemed tawdry, extremely *un*-special, given that half the town's socialites had apparently shared it.

'I have your number in my phone now.' Nathaniel drew back to him the threads of the trademark composure she'd read about in business magazines. 'May I call you back later, when I'm free to speak?'

She barely heard the last moments of the call, although she knew she was agreeing. Her eyes stayed locked on the younger Moore, realisation thumping her hard and low. He couldn't be compelling. He couldn't smell as tantalising as an Arabian souk. She couldn't drown in those blue, blue eyes.

Not if he was Nathaniel Moore's son.

The Moores hated the Porters; and the Sinclairs, by association. Everyone knew it, apparently. Why should the heir be any different?

It took Tash a moment to realise two things. First, she'd let down her guard and let her eyes linger on him for too long.

Second, his ice-blue gaze was now locked on her, open and speculative.

She gathered up her handcrafted purse, slid some money onto the table and fled on wobbly legs, keeping her phone glued to her ear as though she were still on it even after Nathaniel had returned to the table.

She felt the bite of Aiden Moore's stare until she stumbled out into the Fremantle sunshine.

CHAPTER TWO

THE WOMAN IN front of him was barely recognisable from the one he'd seen in the café, but Aiden Moore had learned a long time ago not to judge a book by its cover. She may have looked fragile enough to shatter last time, but watching her wield the lance with the molten ball of glass glowing on its tip, watching the control with which she twisted it and lifted it closer into the burning furnace, and he was suddenly having doubts about the likelihood of her caving to a bit of his trademark ruthlessness. That strong spine flashing in and out of the light coming off the blazing magma ball didn't look as though it lacked fortitude.

His plan changed on the spot.

This woman wouldn't respond to one of his calculated corporate stares. She wouldn't sell out or be chased off. Waiting her out might not work either. The focused way she persuaded the smelted glass into the shape she wanted with turn-after-agonising-turn of the rod spoke of a patience he knew he didn't have. And a determination he hadn't expected her to.

She lifted the glowing mass—whatever the hell it was going to be when finished—and balanced the long tool on an old fashioned vice, then reached forward with something resembling tin-snips and started picking away at the edges of the eye-burning mass of barely solid glass.

She was tiny. She'd peeled down her working overalls in

the heat and tied the arms around her waist, leaving just a
Lara Croft vest top to protect her against anything that might
splash or flare up at her from her dangerous craft. Incredibly confident or incredibly stupid. Given how hard she'd
worked to catch his father's attention, he had to assume the
former. He'd bet his latest bonus that her eyes would hold an
intelligence as keen as the rapidly cooling shards she sliced
away from her design—if they weren't disguised behind in-
dustrial-strength welding goggles. In the café, it had been
oversized sunglasses. She'd used them well to disguise her
surveillance, but he'd finally twigged to how much attention
the stranger across the restaurant was paying to his father.
And how hard she was working to hide it. The moment she
realised her game was up she took off, but not before he got
a good look at the line of her face, the shape of her lips, the
elfin shag of her short hair. Enough to memorise. Enough to
recognise a week later when she turned up in the park across
from MooreCo's headquarters.

And met his father there.

She plunged the entire burning arrangement into a nearby
bucket of water and promptly disappeared in a belching surge
of steam. It finally dissipated and Aiden realised that her
body was still oriented towards her open kiln, but her face
had turned to where he stood in the doorway, those infuriating goggles giving her the advantage. Tiny droplets of steam
clung to every one of the light hairs on her body, making her
look as if she were made from the same stuff she was forging.

But this woman was a mile from fragile glass.

'Mr Moore. What can I do for you?'

It took him a moment to recover from the brazen way she
immediately admitted to knowing who he was. She didn't
even bother faking innocence. More than that, the soft,
strained lilt of her voice; nervous but hiding it well. He found
it hard not to give her points for both.

How to play this? *'You can end your affair with my father,'* was hardly going to effect change. Except maybe to set those tanned shoulders back even further.

He cleared his throat. 'I was hoping to purchase a few pieces for our lobby. Something unique. Something natural. Got anything like that?'

She could hardly say no, he knew; everything she had was like that. He'd taken the trouble to search the web before coming here. Tash Sinclair had quite the reputation in art circles.

She pushed the enormous tinted goggles up into pale, sweat-damp hair. 'That's not why you're here.'

Aiden sucked in a slow, silent breath. The goggles left red pressure marks around the sockets of her eyes but all he could look at were the enormous chocolate-brown gems shining back at him, as glorious as any of her glass pieces. And full of suspicion.

Immediately, a ridiculous thought slipped into his mind. That they had each other's eyes. He had his mother's dark, European colouring and her blue, blue eyes. Whereas Tash Sinclair was practically Nordic but with brown eyes that belonged in his face. The combination was captivating.

'It may not be why I came, specifically, but I do mean it. Your work is amazing.' He wandered permission-less into her studio and examined the pieces lining the shelves. An array of tall, intricate vases; turtles and manatees and leafy sea-dragons, extraordinary jellyfish detailed in fine glass. This wasn't where she displayed her works but it was where they were born. The genesis of her expensive pieces.

Only her eyes followed as he moved around her space. In his periphery, he saw her lift trembling fingers to her messy hair, then curl them quickly and shove them out of sight behind her back. His eyes narrowed. Despite working on his father, she could still find time to be concerned about whether she looked okay for him.

Charming.

But it gave him an idea. If Little Miss Artisan here was hell-bent on hooking up with his father, perhaps the most effective weapon in his arsenal wasn't from his corporate collection of steely glares. Or his chequebook. Perhaps it was something more personal.

Him.

If she was after the Moore name or Moore money, he had both. Maybe she'd allow herself to be diverted from his father—his married-thirty-years father—in favour of the younger, single model. Long enough for him to do some good.

If she cared what he thought when he looked at her, then he had something to work with.

Mind you, if she knew what he *really* thought when he looked at her she'd probably run a mile. She might work with fire every day but she didn't look as if she regularly played with it. Not the way he had. He liked it rough and he liked it short and blazing with volatile, brilliant, ambitious women. About as far from a tiny, tomboyish artsy type with big, make-up-less eyes as you could possibly get.

Which would make it all the easier to remember not to blur the lines. He was the toreador and she was the bull. His goal was to keep her eyes on him long enough that she'd forget her obsession with his father. To keep dancing around her in big flamboyant circles drawing her farther and farther from the family he was so desperately trying to protect.

His mother had sacrificed her life raising him. The least he could do was repay the favour and help keep her husband faithful.

If it wasn't too late.

'Make yourself at home,' she mocked, one eyebrow raised, stripping off protective wrist covers and tossing them on her workbench.

He swallowed a smile and glanced at the still-steaming bucket. 'What are you working on?'

'It was a practice piece for an ornamental vase. I wasn't happy with it.' She pulled the rod and the inadequate creation on the end out of the nearly evaporated water. The glass had completely shattered. She nodded to a series of coloured glass sticks laid side by side on the workbench. 'Those will be lorikeets mounted around its mouth.'

'I'll take it.'

'It's not for sale until I'm happy with it.' She laughed as she tossed the waste glass into a recycling bin off to one side. The two sounds melded perfectly. 'Besides, you don't strike me as someone who would appreciate a pink lorikeet vase.'

'I appreciate quality. In all its forms.' He lifted his eyes intentionally and locked onto hers. Classic Moore move.

Doubt-lines appeared between her brows, drawing them down into a fine V. But where he'd expected a blush, she only looked irritated. 'If you still like it when it's done, I'll make you a pair for your reception desk. At a price.'

'I'm not expecting mates' rates.'

'That's good, because we're not mates. I don't even know you.' Her dark eyes shone. 'But you know me, it seems. What really brought you here?'

Aiden used silence to best advantage in boardrooms. The speed with which an opponent rushed in to fill a thick silence said a lot about them. But the one he unleashed now ticked on for tens of seconds and the diminutive woman before him simply blinked slowly and waited him out, serenity a shimmering halo around her.

Well, damn...

He broke his own rule. 'You were watching us at the café.'

Those eyes widened just a hint. She took a careful breath, shrugged. 'Two good-looking men...I'm sure I wasn't the only one looking.'

The blank way she said it made it feel like the opposite of a compliment. 'You met my father last week.'

She took a careful breath. 'Across the street from your offices. Hardly clandestine. Does your father know he's being monitored?'

'I was passing by.' *Liar!*

'Does he know I'm being monitored, then?'

Aiden blinked. The woman was wasted in an art studio. Why wasn't she working her way rapidly up one of Moore-Co's subsidiaries? For the first time he got a nervous inkling that his father's interest in the pretty blonde might not just be connected to those full lips and innocent eyes. Natasha Sinclair had a brain and wasn't afraid to use it.

'Have dinner with me.'

Her instant laugh was insulting. 'No.'

'Then teach me to blow glass.'

The shocked look on her face told him he'd just asked her for something intensely personal. 'Absolutely not.'

'Make some custom pieces for MooreCo.' That was work; she was a professional artist. She couldn't refuse.

He hoped.

Those dark eyes calculated. 'Would I be required to go to your offices?'

It was a risk, putting her so close to his father, but he'd be there to run interference. Moreover, it would allow him to keep her close; where all enemies belonged. Win her over. And gather more information on what this thing between her and his father was all about. 'For consultation, design and installation.'

She wavered. His own brilliance amazed him, sometimes.

Her eyes narrowed. 'Will you be there?'

Oh, that was just plain unkind. 'Naturally. I'm the commissioning partner.'

If a *humph* could be feminine, hers was. 'When do you want me there?'

He mentally scanned through the appointments he knew his father had, and picked the most non-negotiable one. One taking his father halfway across the city. He named the date and time.

Nothing wrong with stacking the deck in his favour. It was what he did for a living. Find opportunities—make them—and turn them into advantage.

She reached up for her goggles. 'Okay. I'll see you then.' Without waiting for his answer, she re-screened her soul from his view, pressed her steel-caps onto a pedal on the floor and turned towards a brace-mounted blowtorch that burst into blue-flamed life.

Aiden let his surprise show since she was no longer looking. He'd never been so effectively dismissed from his own conversation. Firm yet not definably rude. Had he even had control of their discussion for a moment or was that just a desperate illusion?

Still, at least he'd walked away with what he'd set out for, albeit via a circuitous route. Whatever Natasha Sinclair and his father had going on was thoroughly outed. And he was now firmly wedged in between any opportunity for her to engage with his father.

Couldn't have worked out better, really.

If not for his already monumental ego, Tash would have kissed Aiden Moore.

He'd handed her the perfect excuse, the other day, to get closer to her mother's lost love with his transparent commission. She'd been hit on enough times to know the signs. And the likely outcome. Every guy she'd ever dated had started out by buying something of hers. Or expressing interest in it. She'd lost interest in those kinds of sales—those kinds of men—no matter how lucrative.

She knew from firsthand experience that men with Aiden Moore's charisma and social standing didn't plan lifetimes with women like her. Women like her made terrific mistresses or fascinating show-and-tell at boring dinners or boosted your standing in local government in an arts district.

She'd met—and dated—them all.

Not that she cared. Aiden was a Moore and she was a Porter-by-proxy and if he hadn't already joined the dots he soon would and that would be that. Their families' feud would only add to the antagonism he so clearly felt towards her.

Because that had to be what was zinging around the room when he was in it.

Nathaniel had told her to put their family differences out of her mind. But it was easy to be dismissive of a family feud when you were the cause of it. She had simply inherited it. So had Aiden.

She jogged up the railway-station steps into daylight and wandered towards the Terrace, her trusty sketchpad under her arm. The excitement of a new commission bubbled away just beneath the surface, hand in hand with some anxiety about seeing Nathaniel again. So publicly. He'd changed an important meeting when he'd heard she was coming in, embracing the opportunity to get to meet her in a work capacity. To legitimise all the sneaking around they'd been doing.

She was sure they both considered it worth it. They spent hours chatting about her mother, about their families, their lives. Nathaniel Moore wasn't a man to regret his choices but he was human enough to need to set some ghosts to rest. And she was motherless enough to want to hang onto Adele Porter-Sinclair no matter how vicariously.

'Natasha. Welcome.'

The silken tones drifted towards her from the kerbside taxi

in front of the MooreCo building just as she approached it.
Aiden leaned in to pay the driver, then turned and escorted
her into his building with a gentle hand at her back. She ignored it steadfastly.

The first time she'd been here, she'd been too nervous to
appreciate her surroundings. Now the enormity of this opportunity struck her. MooreCo's lobby was high, modern and
downright celestial with the amount of West Australian light
streaming in the glass frontages. Tiny dust particles danced
like sea-monkeys in the light-beams. The best possible setting for glasswork.

'You'll just need to sign in.' Aiden directed her to the security desk.

Once she was done, the security guard slipped her an ID
tag and smiled. 'Thank you, Ms Sinclair. I'll let Mr Moore
know you're on your way up.'

The deep voice beside her chuckled. 'He knows.'

'I'm sorry, Mr Moore, I meant the senior Mr Moore. He's
waiting for Ms Sinclair's arrival.'

The masculine body to her left stiffened noticeably.
Couldn't be helped. Nathaniel was an adult and could socialise
with whomever he chose. Whether his son liked it or not.

Aiden's jaw clamped tight. 'Up we go, then.'

The elevator ride was blessedly short and horribly tense.
Aiden's dark brows remained low even as he stole sideways
glimpses of her in the mirrored wall panels. Tash did her best
to remain bright and carefree even though she was sure it was
infuriating him further. The elevator climbed and climbed
in silence and, just as Aiden opened his mouth to speak, it
lurched to a stop and a happy *ding* ricocheted around the
small space.

Saved by the bell. Literally.

The elegant doors parted and Tash all but fell out, eager
to be moving again. A familiar face waited at the landing.

She stepped forward and extended her cheek for Nathaniel's waiting lips.

'Natasha. Such a delight to have you here. An unexpected delight.' He directed a look to his stony-faced son. 'I was not aware that the two of you knew each other.'

'I might say the same, Father.'

He ignored that. 'I believe you are to create some wonders for our entry lobby, Natasha? I look forward to seeing the designs.'

'I look forward to working with you—' common courtesy demanded she say it '—both. Shall we get started?'

They turned down a long hall. 'Your meeting with Larhills?' Aiden murmured towards his father.

'Conveniently delayed.'

'Ah.'

Tash saw the older man slip his hand onto his son's shoulder. 'A change of fortune. I wouldn't have appreciated missing Natasha's visit.'

Aiden held the boardroom door respectfully. 'How do you know each other?'

'I knew her mother.'

I loved her mother. Tash heard the meaning behind the words ringing as clear as the elevator bell. Even Aiden narrowed his gaze as he followed them into the generously appointed boardroom overlooking the wide blue river to the leafy riverside suburb beyond it.

'But I didn't know of her stunning artistic talents until very recently,' Nathaniel went on. 'Let's see what she can do for our shabby foyer, eh?'

She could practically smell Aiden's frustration and confusion, and a small part of her pitied him. If not for the predatory way he'd tracked her down and tried to ask her out. If not for the likelihood that he'd toss her out on the street when he found out she was a Porter in disguise. Commission or no commission.

But the anxious furrow that he hid from his father wheedled its way into her subconscious and brought an echoing one to her brow, and she felt, for the first time, guilt for barging into their perfectly harmonious lives with her bag of secrets.

She placed her hands serenely on the polished jarrah table. Timber was too clunky and dense to have ever interested her much but she recognised the craftsman and knew his price tag. Just a pity she wasn't planning to charge Nathaniel for this commission. No, this would be a gift from her mother to the man she'd loved.

'Your foyer light is perfect for glasswork,' she opened, speaking to Nathaniel. 'Well oriented for winter light and high enough for something cascading. Something substantial.'

Aiden's left brow peaked. 'We've gone from a pair of vases to "something substantial" very quickly.'

She turned her eyes to him. 'The space determines the piece.'

'I would have thought I'd determine the piece,' he pointed out, 'being the commissioner.'

She flicked her chin up. 'Commissioners always think that.'

Nathaniel laughed. 'It may be your commission, Aiden, and your creative offspring, Natasha, but it's my building. So it seems we're equal stakeholders.'

She turned her head back to him, quite liking the idea of being partners in something with Nathaniel Moore. Even if it also meant tolerating his son. 'You own the whole building?'

She hadn't realised quite how wealthy the Moores were. Entire buildings in the heart of the central business district didn't come cheap.

'Did your price just go up?' Aiden asked.

'Aiden—' Disapproving brown eyes snapped his way.

'I'm interested because that means you don't need to get the buy-in of the other tenants. That will save a lot of time and hassle.'

Nathaniel nodded. Satisfied and even pleased with her answer. 'So, shall we talk design?'

In Tash's experience, the number of times a man glanced at his watch during a business meeting was directly proportional to how important he believed he was. A man like Aiden should have been flicking his eyes down to his wrist on the minute.

But he never did. Or if he did, she never caught him at it. He gave her one hundred and ten per cent of his attention.

Nathaniel was similarly absorbed and entirely uncaring about the passing of time, it seemed. But at the back of her mind, she knew what ninety minutes of a company's two top personnel must be worth.

'I think I have enough to get started with,' she said. 'I can email you some early designs next week.'

'Bring them in,' Nathaniel volunteered and Aiden's eyes narrowed. 'We can have lunch next time. It's a bit late to have it now.'

Not if you asked her gurgling stomach. She'd been too nervous to eat beforehand. Still, there were more than a dozen cafés between here and the railway station. Hopefully, their kitchens would still be open. 'Okay. That sounds lovely.'

Aiden frowned again. If he kept that up, he was going to mar that spectacular forehead perpetually.

Their goodbyes were brief; she could hardly give Nathaniel the open-armed hug she wanted to in an office full of eyes— even if his all-seeing son weren't standing right there—and so she left him standing as she'd found him, on the landing to MooreCo's floor. Aiden summoned the elevator for her and then held the door as it opened. As if to make sure she actually got in it. When she did, he stepped in as well.

'You must have somewhere better to be,' she hinted. Somewhere other than stalking her.

'I'll call you a cab,' he murmured.

'I'm taking the train.'

He stayed on her heels as she stepped out into the foyer. 'I'll walk you to the station.'

'I'm stopping for something to eat.'

'Great. I'm starving.'

She slid her glance sideways at him. *Subtle.* Most men at least feigned some reason to hang around her long enough to hit her up. Aiden Moore didn't even bother with excuses. She slammed the brakes on his galloping moves.

'I'm not going to go out with you, Aiden.'

He turned. 'I don't recall offering.'

'No. You just assumed. Our relationship is professional.'

Speaking of excuses…

His pale eyes narrowed. 'It's just lunch, Natasha. I'm hardly going to proposition you over a toasted sandwich.'

She straightened her shoulders. 'In my experience that's exactly how it goes.'

The assumption. The entitlement.

His head tipped. Something flickered across his expression. 'Then you've had the wrong experiences.'

She laughed. 'Hard to disagree.'

She spent the last four years of high school disappointing the raging hormones of boys who thought her hippy clothing reflected her values. Being disappointed by them in turn. Waiting for the one that was different. The one who liked her for who she was, not for what they thought she might do for them. To them.

And then, after graduation, the men who wanted an unconventional arty sort on their trophy wall. And then Kyle…

'Lunch. That's it.' He peered down on her, a twist to his lips. 'Until you tell me otherwise.'

Ugh. Such a delicate line between confidence and conceit. One she couldn't help being drawn to, the other sent her running. She'd had her fill of supercilious men. She fired him her most withering stare and turned for the exit. In the polished glass of the building's front, she saw the reflection of his smile. Easy. Genuine.

And her gut twisted just a hint.

Nice smile for a schmuck.

They stopped outside a café called Reveille two blocks down, probably better for breakfast but beggars couldn't be choosers. Aiden chose a table at the back.

'So how do my father and your mother know each other?'

The question took her aback. She'd not expected him to ask outright.

'Did.' She cleared her throat. 'She died last year.'

He frowned. 'I'm sorry. I didn't realise.'

'No reason you should.'

'How did they originally know each other?'

'They went to the same university.'

True. And yet not complete. The whole truth wasn't something she could share if he hadn't already done the maths. It wasn't her place.

'That means your mother and mine may have known each other, too. That's where my parents met. Although she dropped out before graduating so perhaps not.'

Tash held her breath and grabbed the subject change. 'She didn't finish?'

He smiled at the waiter who brought their coffees. 'My fault, I'm afraid. Universities weren't quite so family friendly back then. My grandparents pulled her out of school when she got pregnant.'

'She never went back? Finished?'

'I think child-rearing and being the wife of an up-and-coming executive rather took over her life.' His eyes dimmed. 'She sacrificed a lot for me.'

'You're her son.'

'I'm still grateful.'

She didn't want to give him points for being a decent human being. Or respond to his openness. She wanted to keep on loathing him as a handsome narcissist. 'Do you tell her that?'

He glanced up at her and she found herself drawn to the innate curiosity in his bottomless eyes. Opening up in a way she normally wouldn't have risked. 'The first thing I regretted when I lost Mum was not telling her all the obvious things. Not thanking her.'

For life. For opportunity. For all the love. Every day.

His eyes softened. 'She knows.'

Was he talking about his mother or hers? Either way, it was hard not to believe all that solid confidence. He didn't understand. How could he? Plus, Aiden Moore's business was none of hers, and vice versa.

She handed him a menu. 'So were you serious about a toasted—?'

'Are you a natural blonde?' he asked at the same time. The menu froze in her fingers. But he hurried on, as if realising how badly she was about to take that question. 'It's your eyes…I thought blonde hair and brown eyes was genetically impossible. Like all ginger cats being male.'

Her frost eased just a little and she finished delivering the menu to his side of the table.

His eyes grazed over the part of her visible above the table before settling back on hers. 'Unless they're contacts?'

'I've had both since birth. And I've met a female ginger cat, too. It happens.'

Kyle's old ginge was a female. One of the things that let her get so close to him was how loving he was of that cat. Turned out how people treated animals *wasn't* automatically a sign of how they'd treat people. Just another relationship myth.

Like the one about love being unconditional.

Or equal.

She opened the menu and studied the columns.

Aiden took his cue from Natasha, but he knew what was on the menu and he didn't really care what he had. The meeting before theirs had been a luncheon so he wasn't hungry. At least not for food.

Information he was greedy for.

Her mother was dead. That explained why the woman wasn't hovering on the scene discouraging her daughter from dating a man twice her age. Maybe it explained the vulnerability in her gaze, too. But one personal fact wasn't nearly enough.

He'd work his way slowly to what he really wanted to know.

'Have you been a glass-blower all your life?'

She didn't look old enough to have had time to become a master at her craft. With her sunglasses holding her shaggy hair back from her lightly made-up face, she looked early twenties. Fresh. Almost innocent.

But looks could be deceiving. She was old enough to have a reputation for excellence in art circles and old enough to have worked out that there were faster ways to make money than selling vases when you looked as good as she did.

'Twelve years. We went to a glassworks when I was in school and I grew fascinated. I started as a hobby then took it up professionally when I left school.'

'No tertiary study?'

Her chin came up. 'Nothing formal. I was too busy getting my studio up and running.'

'It's a good space,' he hinted. 'Arts grants must be pretty decent these days.'

Her lips thinned. 'I wouldn't know. I haven't had one for years.'

He studied her closely. 'You're fully self-sustainable just on your sales?'

'I traded pieces for studio space until I was established enough to sell commercially.'

'So somewhere there's a crazy Tash Sinclair collector with a house full of glass seahorses?'

She shrugged. 'He had empty commercial space and I had investment potential. Our boats rose together.'

'Ah, a patron.' Of course.

Her eyes darkened for a heartbeat, then flicked away. 'At the time. Now he's the mayor.'

Kyle Jardine. He knew the man. Big fish, small pond. Always a little bit too pleased with himself given what little he'd actually achieved in life—mid-level public office. Exactly the sort of man to be suckered by a hot, intriguing gold-digger.

'A *notable* patron.'

Her lips twisted. 'Notable enough to drop his support the moment he had candidacy.'

Ironic that an opportunist should find herself so treated. And now she was working up his father to fill the vacancy for sucker?

She flicked back her hair. 'Except him cutting me free made me discover that I could stand on my own. So, yes, I've been self-sufficient for two years now. I own my studio thanks to him, I own my house, thanks to Mum, and I make my rates and put something better than fast-boil noodles on the table at night thanks to my seven-day-a-week glass habit.'

'And thanks to your reputation. Your pieces don't come cheap.'

She shifted in her seat but held his eyes. 'As you're about to find out.'

He chuckled and then asked something off-script. Something just because he was curious. 'It doesn't bother you that Jardine got rich on your talent? Then cut you loose?'

She looked as if she wanted to say a whole lot more on the subject but thought better of it. 'He can only sell them once. I can make a new one every week. Besides—' she smiled at the woman who came to take her order '—when you're an artist, every single piece you sell is going to make someone else more money than it made you. Nature of the beast. It doesn't pay to get attached.'

Did that go for people as well? Was that a survival tactic in her world?

She turned to order. All-day breakfast. Totally unapologetic that it was nearly four o'clock. He ordered something small and a second coffee. This was going to be an interesting meal.

'So why the fascination with nature?' All those sea creatures and birds and stormy colours.

She considered him and then shrugged. 'I make what the glass tells me to. Usually it's something natural.'

'"The glass made me do it." Really? That's not a bit… hippy?'

She smiled. 'I am a hippy. Unashamedly so.'

If she was, she'd reined it in today. Dark crop top with an ornate bodice over the top, and a full skirt. Feminine and flowing. He couldn't see her feet but he itched to know whether she'd have sandals or painted nails or—something deep inside him twisted sharply—a toe ring. Maybe tiny little bells on her ankle. Some ink?

Get a grip, Moore. Fantasising about a woman's foot decoration. Pervert.

'What?' she asked, a breadstick halfway to her mouth.

He composed his expression. What had he betrayed? He scrabbled his way to something credible. 'I have a memory,' he said. 'Of my parents. When I was young. My mother was dressed a bit like you. I think they might have been a bit… organic…in their day.'

She smiled. 'What was that, mid-eighties? The New Age movement would have been burgeoning about then. It's very possible. Or did you think your father was born in a business suit?'

The memory that his subconscious spat up when he needed the lie became manifest. He *did* remember his mother dressed loose, earthy and free. Down by a river somewhere. Laughing with his father, her arms wrapped around Aiden as a toddler. The memory even had that Technicolor tinge, the way old photos from the eighties did.

But, it was his mother's happiness that struck him as incongruous. It had been a long time since he'd had any memories at all where she'd looked at his father like that. Adoring. Engaged.

Maybe it was more figment of imagination than of memory.

Because he kind of *had* thought his father was born in a suit. And some days it felt as if he had been, too. Mergers and acquisitions did that to you after a decade or two. He couldn't imagine father or son on their back in the grass by a river. Picking shapes out of the clouds. Breathing in synch with the tumbling water.

The water feature out front of MooreCo was about as close as they got. And the last time he was on his back in the grass…?

Not a thought for a public place.

'So you don't know a lot about your parents' past, then?' she asked, her face carefully neutral. As if he wouldn't notice her poor attempts to elicit information about his father. Maybe information she could use in her seduction.

He fixed his jaw. 'Before I came on the scene? No, not really. I know they met at uni. He was doing a double-major in commerce and law and she studied arts until she withdrew at the end of second-year.' All pretty much public record. 'That's about it.'

'Aren't you curious?'

'Not especially. It's ancient history.' If they'd had any friends at university, they didn't stay in touch into adulthood. If they had, he'd have known. They'd be amongst the endless honorary aunts and uncles that visited the Moore home when he was younger.

Which made it strange that Tash's mother didn't rank amongst them, now that he thought about it.

Almost as strange as realising he now thought of her as Tash.

She lifted one brow. 'Or is it more that it doesn't involve you so it doesn't rate?'

Ouch. Had he been that much of a jerk since meeting her? Yeah, probably.

'My family are close but they've always tried to keep the kids out of the old business.' In fact, in his family the kids got knuckle-rapped for sticking their noses into anything adult.

Which was how he knew exactly how pissed his father was going to be when he realised his son was running interference with a gold-digger. But he didn't care. He was hardly going to stand around and let Natasha Sinclair lure his father's attention away from his wife of thirty years like some toe-ring-wearing siren.

His father was a handsome, rich man. Ambitious women came and went regularly. But generally they didn't make a ripple. In all the years they'd worked together, he'd never seen his father so fixated on a woman. Especially such a young woman. Though he knew there'd been at least one time…. It was infamous in his family and no one talked about it above a whisper.

So, like it or not, he was going to keep himself right up in their faces and on alert. If she wanted to mess with a wealthy Moore, she could have a crack at the heir. He was more than capable of taking her on, and—as his body tingled at the thought—more than willing.

Maybe some of her free spirit would rub off on him like a breath of fresh air.

He didn't know.

Or, if he did, he had an outstanding poker face.

Nothing about that had changed in the week since she'd first sat in this boardroom.

Tash glanced out at the suburbs across the river stretching off beyond the horizon. The MooreCo building executive floor had to have one of the best views in town.

Aiden Moore seemed entirely oblivious to their parents' shared past. Exactly as oblivious as she was before she'd opened that first diary. For a whispered-about family secret, this one was surprisingly well maintained. She was hardly in a position to enlighten him.

She glanced at both men. *By the way, did you know that my mother and your father were lovers?*

She didn't owe Aiden any loyalty just because they were offspring-in-the-dark in common. Her loyalty lay with Nathaniel—her mother's love—and outing them both to Aiden would damage more than just his relationship with his own father. They were close, she could see. Not close enough to share secrets—and she had no doubts that Aiden had his fair share, too—but they were respectful of each other where it counted and disrespectful enough to speak of a close, affectionate relationship. Much closer than she could ever imagine with her own father. Their humour was pretty much aligned with hers and she had to concentrate on not smiling as they gently ribbed each other.

She wasn't part of this family, even if she felt like it.

She was an outsider.

All this affection and father-son camaraderie wasn't for her to enjoy. No matter how she craved it. And no matter how connected she felt to them. How much she felt as if—inexplicably—she belonged here with them.

'All right,' she said, sitting forward. 'So everyone's happy with the design?'

Six little scale models in glass and a large pencil sketch decorated the table between them. Fish of various sizes, seahorses, a diving kestrel, strips of kelp, a sparkling school of krill. 'And this will be the shards of sunlight cutting down through the ocean.'

Nathaniel smiled, but he wasn't looking where her fingers pointed. 'We've never had anything like it in any of our buildings. It will be astonishing.'

'How much is it going to cost?' Aiden asked, lips pressed.

So the arctic thaw over lunch the week before was only a lull, it seemed. Just as she might have relaxed.

'Aiden,' his father barked. 'Unimportant.'

Tash moved to ease the sudden tension between the two men. 'This is a showpiece for me. I'll be doing it for material costs only.'

Aiden frowned.

Nathaniel sat up. 'No, Tash. You mustn't...'

She locked eyes on his. 'I'm not going to charge you, Nathaniel. Not for my time. But there'll be a lot of glass in this piece so if you'd cover that I'd be grateful.'

Insisting would just be awkward and she'd handed him a chivalrous out. But, of course, this was Nathaniel. 'Naturally we'll pay for materials but...' He pursed his lips and thought for a moment. 'What we really need is a public announcement. That way you get the PR benefit in lieu of payment for your time.'

'I don't require payment for my time.'

Aiden's eyes darted between the two of them.

'Well, I wish to show off this marvellous design and if I choose to do that in front of my corporate equivalents and that just happens to lead to more work for you, so much the better.'

'Nathaniel—'

'It's decided. I won't protest at you not charging MooreCo for what I'm sure will be a considerable amount of your time and artistic focus, and in return I expect you to be gracious and professional about my desire to throw a party to celebrate the acquisition of our biggest ever art piece.'

Snookered.

She glared at him. Then very *un*graciously snorted. 'Fine.'

His smile was immediate. 'Good girl.'

Aiden's left eye narrowed.

She met his gaze and held it.

'That's worked out well, hasn't it?' he asked flatly.

But she got the sense that he really wanted to add *'...for you'* to that.

CHAPTER THREE

TASH STEPPED OUT of the expensive vehicle onto the highest heels she owned. Their engineering had always seemed pointless, but she'd take the extra inches against Aiden any day.

'I'm still struggling to understand why I needed to be *invited* to a party in my own honour?' she said.

'Think of it as more of a VIP escort than an invitation,' he murmured.

Uh-huh. She would have believed that from his father, but not from Aiden. Although it was entertaining to imagine him as an escort. Upper-case E. He was slick, handsome and full of fakery enough for it…and he had the right body.

'Something amusing?'

Tash forced her lips into a more serious line. 'No. Just appreciating the architecture. I've never been inside this building.' The second part was true, at least.

'You're in for a treat. It's beautifully restored.' His hand dropped to her lower back as he guided her up the stairs and through the ornate doors. Heat from his fingertips tingled through the soft fabric of her dress. 'I thought you would have seen the glasswork, at least. That's why we chose this as a venue for the launch party. And this time of day.'

She let her eyes drift up to the stunning stained-glass windows on the western side of the building practically glowing in the rich, low afternoon light. 'I've seen them from the outside, of course.'

'Natasha. Aiden.' Nathaniel moved towards them, as dapper and handsome as ever. 'Did you arrive at the same time?'

Aiden's chin lifted the tiniest bit but it was enough to put paid to his lie about her needing an escort. But it was too entertaining watching him trip up on his own transparency to make a big deal of it. She leaned in for a kiss on each cheek from Nathaniel then glanced around the beautifully appointed venue. Up on the big screen her glass prototypes had been photographed and lit by a professional and looked about as good as the finished artwork would. The AV team flicked quickly through them in rehearsal for the speeches later.

'This is all so beautiful. Are all your parties this lavish?'

'Usually. Aiden sets a high bar.'

She turned her surprise to him. 'This is your work?'

'I didn't personally choose the flowers, if that's what you're asking, but I do know the quality planners in town and how to get the best out of them.'

I'll bet.

'Will you forgive me?' Nathaniel said. 'The inexcusably prompt are starting to arrive.'

He waved his arm in a flourish and the visuals on the big screen ended with a snap as the lights sank in a subtle crossfade with the music that grew out of the silence around them.

And just like that, it was a party.

Aiden's hand was back at her lower spine again but where before it had only tingled, now it blazed with un-ignorable heat. Either he'd developed a raging temperature in the last thirty seconds or hers had inexplicably plunged. So much so that tiny bumps prickled up all over her back.

'Would you like a drink?' he murmured, close to her ear.

How galling. That his charm and charisma should have actually had some effect. She spun away from his gentle touch.

'You don't actually *need* to escort me, Aiden. I'm quite capable of getting safely to the bar.' Or not, since she didn't drink much and certainly not at work events. 'I'm sure you'll have better things to do this evening than shadow me.'

And as the word slipped unconsciously across her lips she realised that was exactly what he was doing. Babysitting her. Controlling her arrival and departure and her movements while here.

Why?

'Tonight is very important to my father,' he simply said. 'I'm on hand to run interference should anything go...wrong.'

Interference? By sticking close to her? 'What is it you imagine I'm going to do here? Lie back on the bar and drink shots straight from the bottle?'

His blue eyes crackled. 'I would pay good money to see that.'

'I'm sure you would, given some of the other things you're famous for spending your money on—' she ignored his flare of surprise '—but I've been to many of these nights, Aiden. I know the drill. Turn up, look good and be wild enough to be interesting but not inappropriate. Intrigue but don't offend. Generate speculation but not gossip.'

It was all about appearances. And buzz.

She fronted the bar and ordered a virgin cocktail in a fast and low breath. If he noticed the virgin part, he didn't comment. The important thing was that it *looked* like something harder. But she'd be in full control of her faculties all night.

He frowned. 'Is that what you think you're here for? Entertainment?'

She turned and drew a long sip of her drink through the pretty glass straw. A clever and thoughtful touch given the focus of this evening. 'This is a little different, I'll admit. But the principle doesn't change just because the date does.' Not that he was her date... 'The important thing is that I won't be doing anything to embarrass Nathaniel in front of his associates.'

'You think I'm worried about that?'

'I don't know what to think, Aiden. All I know is you've been playing me since the day we met and running *interference*—' it felt so good to throw his own word back at him '—between myself and your father. MooreCo has already given me a massive commission. What more do you imagine I'm trying to screw him out of?'

His dark brow lifted. 'Your word, not mine.'

Realisation rushed in, tumbling and tripping over astonishment. How stupid she'd been not to see it before. The straw dropped from her gaping lips. 'You think I'm *hitting* on your father?'

For the first time, he dropped the casual veneer and that carefully neutral expression simmered with something else entirely. Something quite captivating in its passion. 'He's obsessed with you. And you shower him with your attention and your come-hither smiles and keep him dangling, helplessly, in your thrall.'

Come-hither? She wasn't sure what offended her more: the suggestion that she was consciously trying to seduce Nathaniel or the realisation that any interest that Aiden had shown in her until now was purely strategic. 'He's a grown man, Aiden. I'm sure he's managed to fend off women much more beautiful and much more skilled than I am in his fifty-five years on the planet.'

'Then why the interest?' he urged. 'Why him?'

Her chest tightened. 'He knew my mother.'

Aiden snorted and tugged her around behind a large potted arrangement, out of view of the arriving guests. 'Then go hang your neediness on one of her other friends. Leave my family out of it.'

Her breath backed up in her gridlocked chest. The term

needy cut her much deeper than it should have but something bigger than that stole focus. A clue about what this was all really about—and who this man really was.

'Family? I thought we were talking about money.'

His nostrils flared wildly. 'Because it's always about money with you?'

It was almost *never* about money with her. Even with Kyle she'd believed he had genuine feelings for her. Money was just what brought them together. That and necessity. 'I think that's just what you expect. Because it's the language you speak.'

He snorted. 'You're trying to tell me money doesn't talk.'

'It talks; I'm a realist. But it's not what makes the world turn.'

She might as well have sprouted antennae; he looked at her as if she were from another planet. 'Please don't say love,' he sneered.

'I was going to say people. People are what matter, but, yes, love is part of that. For each other. For our *families*.' She leaned on the word extra-hard.

'You'd rather be loved than wealthy?' Disbelief dripped from his handsome lips.

'You say that as if it's worse than preferring to be wealthy than loved.'

'Maybe it is.'

She stared at him. 'Is your mother like this?'

Instant granite. Eyes, face, body. 'What does my mother have to do with anything?' he gritted.

'You are so unlike your father, attitudinally. I can only assume it's your mother's influence that has made you like this.'

'Like what? *Un*like you? If you are so damned hippy about love and people and flowers and sunshine, I'd have expected you to be more accepting of the differences between us.'

That would have niggled less if not for the peace-symbol

tattooed on her ankle. 'I'm not *un*accepting of the differences. I'm just trying to understand them.'

'Why? You don't like me. You don't want to be around me. What the hell does it matter?'

Was it possible that he was wounded by her lack of interest in him—way down deep where the bluff and bluster didn't penetrate? She stared into those hard eyes and found it impossible to believe.

'I guess it doesn't matter.' Though that didn't stop her from being interested...*way down deep* where her protective veneer didn't penetrate. 'Except that you've made stalking me your personal project so I get the feeling we'll be seeing a lot of each other.'

His laugh was short. 'If I'm stalking you I'm doing a lousy job.'

'No. Not stalking. Your brand of creepiness is much more overt.'

The moments the words were out, she regretted them. Not that anything he'd said to her these past minutes was particularly polite but branding a man *creepy* was quite an indictment. Especially when he was commissioning your next work.

He reeled for just a moment, astonishment vivid on his face. 'I'm not sure I've ever been summed up quite like that before.'

But she wasn't backing down. She straightened and drained her glass. 'What did the last woman you subjugated like to call it?'

His lips twisted and his eyes darkened and, in that moment, the little corner he'd backed her into shrunk just like Wonderland around Alice. Yet he still found room to take one more half step forward.

'The last woman I subjugated begged me to do it,' he breathed. His eyes flicked down and he stretched out a finger and ran the knuckle down the laces of her arty bustier.

Instant heat rushed up into her chest and bloomed tellingly in her décolletage.

She twisted away from his cloying presence and crossed back to the bar. 'Nice try.' She laughed, one-hundred-per-cent casual and two-hundred-per-cent fake, and signalled the bartender for a repeat of her drink. 'But I'm not buying it.'

He was right behind her. 'Buying what?'

'All of it. The charming, rich bad-boy act, the overbearing son, the interfering business partner.'

'Are you saying I'm not all those things?'

'Oh, you're definitely all of them, but I don't buy that that's *all* you are. There's something else going on. I'll just have to work out what it is.'

'I'm no mystery, Tash. What you see is what you get.'

She turned to face him. 'You're in business, Aiden. What you see is never what you get.' She glanced around. 'Now if you'll excuse me, there's someone over there I'm sure I should meet.'

She spun, skirts flowing, and left him standing speechless in her wake.

Tash Sinclair worked the room like a professional. Ten days ago, he would have imagined the wrong kind of professional, but now he watched her through a different lens. A Tash-coloured lens. One not quite so tinted by what he thought he knew.

She'd summed him up so accurately earlier this evening, nailed him to the cross of his own bad behaviour and then promptly ignored him for the next two hours. She flitted from guest to guest charming the men, engaging the women and drafting them into the ranks of Team Tash. She was exactly as she promised him to be: intriguing enough to have multiple curious eyes follow her around the room, but appropriate enough to give the tabloids nothing tangible—or even intangible—to work with. She'd brushed past his father several times and the glances they exchanged were carefully neutral, blank enough to give no cause for comment whatsoever.

Unless you were looking for cause.

Or was he still digging for something that just wasn't there? Reacting to a decades-old incident that he still didn't fully understand. Something had happened twenty years ago, something that had created tension in his extended family and a wedge between his parents. Something to do with a woman. And he'd grown up with the echoes of that event and the memory of his mother sobbing in the wine cellar where she'd gone not to be heard and cursing a name he'd only ever heard whispered by his aunts and uncles thereafter.

Porter.

That was all he knew. But it was enough to teach him an early lesson about fidelity. And about how many different things a man could be at the same time. Successful businessman. Loving father. Cheating husband. He'd learned to compartmentalise the same way his mother presumably had in order to continue living with—and loving—the man that could do something like that. They'd worked their way through it and onto another twenty years of marriage and Aiden had, too.

But he'd never forgotten it. Or the lessons it taught him about trust.

His eyes tracked Tash the length of the room.

'She's something else, isn't she?' The voice came out of nowhere, low and edgy to his left. 'Have you slept with her yet?'

Aiden spun to face the question.

'Something to look forward to,' the man went on. 'She's a cracker.'

The disrespect and sheer contempt in Kyle Jardine's eyes stabbed in below Aiden's ribs. Hard and ugly. His curiosity hardened up into pure anger. 'Harsh words considering you got rich off her back, Jardine.'

The mayor's eyes narrowed. 'Or she got rich *on* hers. Though, to be fair, she was on top more often than not.'

The urgent need to defend Tash slammed headlong into the unbidden image of her, all golden and glorious reared back above him. Jardine's words should have been exactly what he wanted to hear. That she was the gold-digger he'd always suspected. That she'd slept her way to her present success.

Except, inexplicably, he didn't believe that. Not for one moment.

That just wasn't Tash.

'I didn't realise you were on the list for tonight,' Aiden muttered, knowing full well Jardine wasn't. Though it had been tempting to get him along to pick his brains about Tash. Turned out there wasn't much brain there to pick amongst.

'Admin error, I'm sure. I came with Shannon Carles.'

Right. His latest 'cracker'.

'I hadn't realised exactly who your father's ingénue was,' Jardine went on, blind to the tension pouring off Aiden. 'Should I give him a heads-up that there's not too much that's innocent about her?' He shoved his hands deep into his pockets and Aiden had never had a stronger urge to step slightly away.

His fingers curled into fists of their own accord. 'Her personal life is none of MooreCo's concern. We've simply commissioned her artistic skills.'

'I give that a week.' Jardine snorted, swigging down the last of his drink. 'She's insidious.'

If he'd said anything else…any other word…

'What do you mean?' The question bled out of him. So maybe at least one part of him was still looking for evidence.

'You won't mean to. You won't know quite how it happened. But one day you'll have her toothbrush in your cabinet and her brand of milk in your fridge.'

'That doesn't sound too sinister.' It actually sounded weirdly good. For a half a heartbeat.

'She's like one of those spiders that lures you in with the pretty exoskeleton and the seductive dance and then, once she's got you, *wham*, not so pretty and not so seductive any more.'

He couldn't really imagine either of those things. 'She doesn't strike me as the black widow type.'

'I'm talking about the tears and the neediness that start.'

Needy. Hadn't he used the exact same word himself, earlier? Aiden stared at Jardine and wondered if this was how *he* came across to strangers. Or, worse, to people he knew.

Maybe to Tash.

'Classic bait and switch, mate,' Jardine said, turning for the bar. 'That's all I'm saying.'

No. He was saying so much more, and he was probably saying it to everyone here. Suddenly those eyes following Tash around the room didn't seem so benign. He scanned the venue, found Jardine's date drinking it up at the second bar and reached for his phone.

He and Carles had at least two mutual friends. One of them was bound to owe him a favour.

Within ten minutes, Carles was shoving her mobile phone back into her purse and copping an earful from a very unhappy Jardine as they moved towards the exit. He couldn't really stay without his date and she'd just received an urgent phone call from her marketing department....

Unfortunate, but necessary, she'd gushed.

Aiden had just smiled and held the door for them both.

As he turned back to the room he caught the tail end of Tash's glance. Her relief was patent and he knew, without asking, that Jardine had likely been enjoying taunting her with his presence.

'Jerk,' he muttered.

'I hope that wasn't for me, darling,' a familiar voice said from behind him.

He turned into the warmth of a familiar smile. 'Mother.'

'Well, I'm here. I hope this will be worth it,' she announced. It had been years since Laura Moore had been to any of MooreCo's events. The ribbon-cutting for the Terrace high-rise was probably the last. Corporate parties, unlike dinner ones, just weren't his mother's forte. She didn't do well with all that pressure and no formal role to play.

'Thank you for coming,' he murmured, kissing her cheek. Though his purpose for asking wasn't quite as solid now as it had been at eight o'clock this morning. This morning he'd believed that his mother's presence might help to remind Tash that Nathaniel Moore had a loving wife to go home to. That there was a marriage about to be wrecked. And it might help his father, too, to have them in the same room at the same time. For the same reasons.

Maybe that was all he needed to be cured of this obsession he seemed to have.

Insidious. An ugly word from an ugly human being but he just couldn't shake it. Tash had certainly wheedled her way dangerously close to *out* of his bad books, which was quite an achievement given how *in them* she'd been when he first walked into her studio.

He furnished his mother with something from the bar, topped up his own glass and then turned to search out his father.

'Who's your father talking to?'

Aiden's heart shrivelled to half its size as his eyes followed the direction of his mother's enquiry, but then plumped out again as he realised it wasn't Tash. 'Margaret Osborne. The wife of—'

'Trevor Osborne, yes, I recognise her now. Goodness, the years haven't been kind.'

Every part of him cringed at the slightly too-loud tenor of her voice. Guess that was what came of being out of the scene for so long—she'd lost her social skills when it came to business matters. Though he couldn't even imagine her working a room quite as fearlessly as Tash, even at the top of her game.

He shepherded his mother across the crowded room until they caught his father's eye. It widened with alarm—as well it might....

'Laura?'

She leaned in for an air kiss—so she hadn't completely forgotten how to be Mrs Nathaniel Moore—and then smiled at her husband's surprise. 'I know. I'm as flummoxed to be here as you are seeing me. Your junior partner invited me.'

His father seemed about as discomposed as Aiden had ever seen him. 'You're always invited, Laura. You know that.' Dark eyes scanned the room and then flared even further.

'Nathaniel, should we—?' Tash appeared by Aiden's side and then jerked to a halt at the immediate tension in his father's body language. 'Oh, I'm sorry for interrupting.'

She turned her curiosity to his mother, who stood politely blank-faced.

His father quite literally couldn't speak.

'Laura Moore,' his mother finally said, introducing herself on a smile, her dark brows slightly folded in. 'And you are?'

'I'm—' Tash opened her mouth to speak but both men rushed to cut her off.

'The guest of honour,' Nathaniel said.

'Natasha's here with me,' Aiden blurted, simultaneously. The surprise Tash turned on him very neatly matched his own. Why the hell had he said that? Was it because inviting his mother here tonight suddenly seemed like the worst idea ever?

Or was it because he didn't want to be proved correct all of a sudden?

'Oh, you're the artist?' Laura covered for both her momentarily inept men. 'Nathaniel has brought home photographs of your work. Just lovely.'

Tash smiled and Aiden recognised it instantly as her *gameface* smile. The one she'd been feeding everyone here. The one she'd used with him the first few times they met. The fact that she couldn't be genuinely polite to the wife of her biggest commissioner instantly brought his suspicion screaming back to the fore.

Why not—what did she have to lose? Or hide?

But her answer gave nothing away. 'Thank you, Mrs Moore.'

'Please, call me Laura.'

That offer seemed to actually pain Tash, but she kept the fake smile glued to her face. Was he the only one who could see how it paled just slightly at the corners?

His own frown deepened until it must have matched his mother's.

'Have we met?' Laura queried. 'You seem so familiar....'

'I don't think so,' Nathaniel cut in. 'Perhaps in the newspapers?'

'Perhaps.' She pressed steepled fingers to her lips and it was the first time his mother had struck him as old. But compared to the golden, smooth skin of the woman by her side, the wrinkles on his mother's hands cried out with obviousness. 'Never mind, it will come to me.'

'A drink, Laura?' Nathaniel asked.

Everyone's eyes went instantly to the glass of wine already in his wife's hands. Okay, it was official...he'd *never* seen his father this ruffled.

'Tash has quite a rare talent,' Aiden murmured, to cover his father's gaffe. He'd wanted to throw the spectre of 'the wife' in between Tash and his father, not cause his mother any further pain, and his father's sputtering was only going to pique her curiosity and have her asking questions she might not like the answer to. 'Her work is going to make such a statement at the entrance to MooreCo.'

Tash turned her surprise to him. 'Thank you, Aiden. I think that might be the first nice thing you've said about me.'

'Your work is beautiful,' he hedged.

She laughed. Right when he expected her lips to purse up tight. 'I'll still take it. I get the feeling praise is a rare thing from you.'

His mother's eyes immediately honed in on her, and immediately jumped to the wrong conclusion. Or the right one given he'd just, stupidly, declared her to be his date. She turned positively conspiratorial. 'He's a Moore, Natasha. You could die waiting for a pleased word....'

Tash's laugh-lines immediately reconfigured into a complicated little cluster of confusion. Perhaps it was easier for her to do what she was doing if she imagined that Laura Moore was a cold, distant wife.

Far from the truth.

Certainly his father seemed unable to countenance them speaking directly to each other.

'Perhaps it's time for the speeches, Tash?'

She turned, bestowed the only genuine smile of the night on his father and then excused herself. As soon as both of them began making their way towards the small stage, his mother rounded on him. 'An artistic type, Aiden? That's very *un*-you.'

There was a reason for that. 'Perhaps I just don't meet arty types, usually.'

'She seems very sweet.'

'That *would* be very un-me. Besides, how would you know? The two of you barely spoke a word.'

'I don't need to converse with her to know. I could practically feel the electricity coming off the pair of you.'

Or perhaps she was just misreading the source of whatever she'd sensed. Maybe the sparks were the energy zinging back and forth between Tash and his father. And maybe that was what caused the apparent short fuse in his father's brain.

'Bring her for dinner.'

Into his parents' home? *Uh, no.* Not going to happen.

The lights around them dimmed, triggering a reluctant hush to fall over the liquored-up crowd. His father stepped up onto stage, drawing Tash in his wake. She stood right on the edge of the lit area of the stage, polite and demure but impossible to take your eyes off. Even doing nothing, she was intriguing. The blonde flare of her hair, the single streak of perfectly positioned, artistically oriented burgundy sweeping down across her smooth forehead. Artful smudges around her eyes and very little else on the intelligent face focused entirely on his father. And then the open expanse of creamy shoulders and chest above the patterned bustier that kept her cleavage firmly restrained behind a zip. The light fairly glowed off her unmarked skin and it was all too easy imagining lowering that convenient zip to see if the skin beneath was as pristine.

'The light favours her,' his mother whispered, her gaze correctly tracking his to its destination.

It galled him to hear her compliment the woman who was stealing her husband's focus. He pressed his lips together and forced his attention off the woman practically glowing on-stage and onto his father. 'I think she just knows how to use it,' he murmured.

'It's not like your father to be so discomposed. Perhaps it's because I'm here? Or perhaps he has some secret lover tucked away behind the scenes?'

Aiden laughed where he was supposed to—a tight, short chuckle—and focused on his father's face. The tense, formal man before them wasn't a shade of the relaxed, casual man of a few hours ago. Of just ten minutes ago. It contrasted awkwardly with the beautiful, flowing images of Tash's glass design glowing on the big screen behind him.

'…and so, without further ado, I give you the creative spirit behind MooreCo's newest acquisition—' he took a long breath in, found his wife in the darkened crowd and braved her curious stare '—Natasha Sinclair.'

The audience's burst of applause almost drowned out his mother's gasp, but Aiden felt it in the stiffening of her body where it pressed against his side in the crush. He tore his eyes from Tash long enough to look down on his mother's pale face. Her lips made a straight, devastated line in her face but her eyes were busy, flicking back and forth between her husband and his ingénue.

Tash started speaking, and her disarming cadence had the audience enraptured as she described the creative intent behind her thalassic theme, but it did nothing to lessen the tension pouring off his mother. He turned with her as her body spun away and he hurried to follow her outside.

'Mum…?'

Something major was going on. Something he was starting to wish he understood before the flawed brilliance of inviting his mother here tonight.

'I take it back,' she choked, hurrying down the steps to the old building. 'Do not bring that woman to dinner.'

That woman. He'd heard that phrase before. When no one knew he was listening. But Tash would have been a little girl when that phrase was first whispered between his mother and her siblings. She simply couldn't be *that woman.*

'What's going on, Mum?'

'Was it not bad enough twenty years ago?' she half raged.

'Now he brings her back into our lives this way through her cheap daughter. God, I *knew* I recognised her from somewhere....'

He reached out and caught his mother by the arm. 'Calm down. Stop. Tell me what the problem is.'

'I'll tell you exactly who the problem is, Aiden.' Her chest rose and fell with pained regularity. 'It's your *date*.'

She peered up at him with the kind of motherly authority and blatant agony that no son could stomach. 'Natasha?'

'Did you know who she was when you asked me along tonight?'

Guilt raged from cell to cell in his body. He *had* brought her here tonight to shake things up a bit. But he'd had no idea that he was setting his mother up for this kind of hurt. And, deep down, he didn't believe that his father and Tash had done anything wrong. Yet. Certainly not enough to be upsetting his mother to this degree.

'She's Natasha Sinclair. An artist—' he started.

The snort of derision was immediate and unfamiliar in his genteel mother and it morphed into a half-sob. 'She may be a Sinclair, but she's also a *Porter*.'

CHAPTER FOUR

'"*He knew my mother...*"' Aiden snarled, shunting Tash back into the tiny coat-filled room with his big body. He slammed the door on prying ears and locked it.

She literally recoiled from the ugly accusation in his handsome face and shrugged back a few more inches into the protection of the expensive coats all around her. 'Aiden, what—?'

'We had a fifteen-minute wait for the taxi I called because Mum was too hysterical to drive. She shared the whole sordid story. All about your mother's affair with my father. I never would have invited her if I'd known.'

'Is she all right?'

His lips flattened. 'No. You do not get to play the gracious innocent party. Her sister is en route to meet her at home and try and repair the damage you've done here tonight.'

'I've done? You invited her.'

'You hunted us down. Forced your way into my family's lives. None of this would have happened if not for that.'

'That's not what—'

But he wasn't listening. Of course he wasn't. He was a Moore. 'In my family we know her as Porter,' he barged on. 'Why?'

The he-man thing was getting old. Tash stood up taller and gained some return ground on him. 'In *your family* she was a pariah, and you lot made her life miserable!' she hissed.

'Porter was her maiden name. That's what they knew her as at uni.'

'University? But that was years before.'

'That's how they met. They were all in the same year. My mother and yours. They were friends.'

'Friends?' That took him aback. 'I guess I shouldn't be surprised at your behaviour, then, if that's the kind of treacherous stock you come from.'

She stepped up to him hard. Peered up into all that anger and ignored the cheap, ugly shot at her. 'Your father cheated, too.'

'Oh, I have a whole other conversation waiting for him, don't you worry. This is about you.'

'Why? I was seven years old when they…' She couldn't bring herself to say the word. *Affair*. Besides, did the word even apply if it was only one weekend? Although deep down she knew that their love affair had gone on for decades regardless of only being together the once.

He glared down on her. 'Guilty by association. Why are you in our lives now? Why suddenly emerge?'

'Because *she died*, Aiden. And she died still loving your father.' She swallowed back the choke. 'I just wanted to know the man that held her heart all these years.'

He struggled with that news. 'Why stir it all up?'

'I wasn't stirring anything. I only wanted to meet him, talk to him. Try to get some closure for both of them. *You* were the one that forced the issue of the commission and dragged me into your lives. *You* were the one that brought your mother here tonight and ripped the decades-old scab off it all.'

He didn't look as if her being right made the truth any easier to swallow. He practically scraped around for an out and found it in picking a fight. 'You looked at her like you didn't like her.'

'Why would I like the woman that helped make my mother's life a misery? Why would I like any of you? You Moores trashed the Porter name any chance you got. She was practically ostracised from her community because of you all.'

He glared down on her. 'Leave me out of it. I was the same age as you.'

'Right. So neither of us was responsible—we're just left picking up the pieces.'

He *so* looked as if he wanted to keep arguing but the logic of her argument was hard to refute. His nostrils flared twice before his body sagged. 'You just wanted to meet him?'

'I needed to. Her diaries were full of him. I wanted to give them both that closure.'

'That's why he's so obsessed with you?'

It hit her then. Exactly why Aiden Moore thought she was spending so much time around his father. 'Isn't it bad enough you thought I was chasing him? Now you think we were actually on together?' The thought would have been vaguely disturbing if not for the obvious truth. 'I'm a shadow of an obsession. A last chance at something he once wanted so badly.'

'You're talking about my father, Tash.'

'I know. And I'm sorry. It affects my family, too, but it doesn't change the truth. They were in love. They just could never be together.'

'Together enough to get caught.'

She had to remember this news was just minutes old for Aiden. She'd had much longer to come to terms with the whole sorry mess. 'They weren't caught. Your father confessed.'

'What do you mean?'

'The one time they acted on it. He regretted betraying his promise to your mother. So he told her what he'd done, and never saw my mother again.'

Though, in truth, he'd been betraying Laura Moore his

whole life by loving someone else secretly. And betraying himself by not acting on it.

Poor Nathaniel. Poor Laura. Her poor mother. Not one happy person in the whole sorry mess.

'Did she tell your father?'

Tash dropped her eyes. 'No. He found out through mutual friends.' Not how she would have done it herself, but then she'd never been trapped in violence the way her mother had with an angry, gutless man.

'Lack of character must run in the family.'

She shoved his chest, hard; loyalty blazing hot and live in her heart. 'You can take all the shots you want at me, but don't you dare impugn a woman who can no longer defend herself or her actions.'

He didn't respond, but his eyes darkened two shades and blazed down into hers. Her shove hadn't even budged his feet from the tips of hers. 'She must have been something, your mother,' he breathed down on her. 'To inspire such passion in her child. To inspire such treachery in my father.'

'She was an *amazing* woman. And it takes two to tango. Especially horizontally.'

His hand moved up to finger a stray lock of hair back to the safety of its fellows and her mind filled with images of her and Aiden getting horizontal. Her chest tightened instantly.

'You really believe that.'

'I really do,' she breathed. 'I'm sorry that it has caused pain for your family but I'm not sorry my mother got a single weekend of heaven in what was otherwise a pretty miserable existence.'

'She loved him that much?'

'She lived for him.' Until the day she just couldn't live any longer, even for him.

Aiden dropped his forehead and let his eyes squeeze shut.

Tash tried to remember that his world—his family—had just imploded.

'Do you want to drop the commission?' she asked after an age.

'No.' Those blue-grey eyes snapped open. It was almost as if the word had fallen off his lips without his consent. 'We have a contract. Besides, the next step is up to my father. This is his mess. If he asks you to go, will you?'

It hurt having her mother's memory summed up as a mess. 'If he asks me. Yes.'

But he wouldn't. Her mother's memory was too strong. Although, if staying led to Nathaniel getting hurt she'd definitely go regardless of what he wanted.

'You are such a paradox,' Aiden murmured, leaning his weight back onto the old counter. His expensive suit cuffs pulled up as he crossed his arms across his chest. 'Jardine called you insidious.'

'Kyle's a mean drunk.'

'But he's not wrong.'

Her heart sank. Really? *Him too*? Somehow, she'd hoped for better from the son of the man her mother had loved. Which was probably stupid.

'There's something about you....' Aiden went on. 'It's hard to put my finger on.' But he did, tracing it along the top edge of her bodice.

Her throat tightened up immediately and the *thing* between them surged and swelled as a ball of heat low in her chest. There it was again...the connection. So ready to combust. 'Two minutes ago you were angry.'

'I'm still angry. Just not at you, specifically.'

'And two minutes ago you thought I was sleeping with your father.'

He shuffled closer. 'But you're not. And my relief about that is quite...disturbing.'

'Why relieved?' She didn't dare ask *why disturbed*....

'Because it means I can do this.'

The warmth of the cumulative coats hanging at her back was nothing to the furnace pumping off Aiden as he swooped down to capture her lips with his. They took hers with a certainty that stole her breath. As if he knew exactly how well they'd fit together and how welcome he would be. And how little resistance she'd give him. He pressed hard against her and held her firm with strong arms banded around behind her.

Every sultry look, every snark, every narrow-eyed glare he'd given her had been leading to this moment. Tash wondered if he knew it as well as she did. She'd felt it back in that café, the first time he'd passed her table.

She wanted to respond to him—his size, his intensity and the sheer overwhelming maleness of him—but something told her if she gave an inch, she'd be lost. Aiden Moore was a man who knew what he wanted and how he wanted it.

And right now, the answers were *her* and *here in the coat-room of MooreCo's party*.

As if he sensed her slight withdrawal, his fingers stole up and tangled in her cropped hair, making gentle fists in the shaggy locks and then pulling on it, strong and steady until her throat was bared to the ravages of his lips. The touch of dominance sent her blood racing even faster and made her squirm against his hard body. His mouth feasted on her throat, one big hand sliding down to bunch a fistful of skirt up under her bottom.

Every part of her responded to his magnetic pull. It would be so easy just to slip her arms up around his neck and hold on as he kissed her half to death. It would be just as easy to let him lift her up onto the original timber counter in this old building and wrap her legs around him, too.

'Won't this be tough to explain to your mother?' she gasped between kisses. If she was thinking more clearly, she might also have spared a brain cell or two as to how his father might take the news.

'I don't generally get her to sign off on who I'm sleeping with.' He pressed the words against her ear.

'You assume I'll be sleeping with you,' she breathed.

'Oh, you will,' he bit against her lips. 'Besides, it's not like you'll ever be coming to a family dinner or anything.'

He meant because of their family situation. She knew that. But the stark reality was enough to pull her completely out of the sensual fog robbing her of strength. She'd promised herself she'd never be treated like that again.

He lifted his lids to reveal glazed eyes. 'What?'

She brought both hands around and pressed them into his chest with as much certainty as he'd kissed her. It opened up precious air between them. Not much, but enough. 'We can't do this.'

'You mean not here?'

'I mean not at all.'

'But you're not sleeping with my father....'

As if *his* issues were the only ones standing between them. 'I work for you, now.'

'So?'

'So it's inappropriate.' That concept clearly had never occurred to him. 'And it's too messy, politically.'

He stepped in closer. Smiled in that Cheshire cat way. 'I was counting on it being messy.'

'Aiden, stop.' She pushed him harder and he staggered back all of an inch.

But he did stop. Exactly when it mattered. 'You're serious?'

'Of course I'm serious. Did you think I was just playing hard to get?'

His brows folded in. 'Well…yeah. Is it because it's too public?'

Actually, the risk of someone knocking on that door made

the whole thing even more breathless than it might otherwise have been. It wasn't why she was stopping.

'It's because it's too…close.' She took a deep breath. 'You and I getting together never would have worked. Plus I barely know you.'

'You know my family. You know where I work. You know what I like for lunch and how I take my bourbon. And you know what happens when our pheromones start mixing. What more is there?'

And that was probably exactly how it worked in his world. The world where relationships were days long. 'Other things. Normal things.' Lord, what she wouldn't give to be treated like something to be treasured instead of conquered or leveraged. Just for once. 'But it's a moot point. This—' she gestured back and forth between them '—isn't going to happen.'

'All those reasons you just gave me for why not can be addressed by the same thing.' The fact he was helping her straighten her skirt was the only reason she wasn't shoving him away harder. 'We keep it quiet. Only meet privately. Then no problem.'

She stared at him. God, the male mind was a complex, beautiful and totally naive thing. 'It's still a problem. It's just hidden.'

And dishonest. And cheap. And she was through with feeling cheap.

His hiss reflected his expression exactly.

She sat back and regarded him. 'You don't hear "no" very often, do you?'

His laugh mocked. 'I'm not going to cry, if that's what you're thinking. Or beg.'

'I can't even begin to imagine what that would look like.'

He stared at her in silence. Refixed his tie.

'You strike me as the sort who only wants me because you can't have me,' she said, wrestling her breath under control.

'Is that right?'

'Isn't it?'

His eyes narrowed and he glared at her, failing abysmally at intimidating her. Strangely, she realised, she held all the power here.

Lord, how he must hate that.

She finally broke the silence. 'So now what?'

'Now you walk out of here well ahead of me.'

She laughed. 'Suddenly you're concerned for my reputation?'

He smiled and opened the door wide for her. Wide enough to exit but narrow enough that she had to press against him. She did so with the greatest care. But as she squeezed her body past his, his lips brushed her ear for half a heartbeat, and his warm breath caused a riot in her nerve endings.

'Not yours, Tash...'

Aiden watched Tash stride confidently out of that little room and knew she was faking it. She was as shaken as he was by what had just happened.

He could see it in her eyes.

But was she shaken by what *he'd* done, or by what *she'd* done? That was the question.

The part of his mind that should have been dealing with what he'd discovered about his family tonight was in lockdown, but, as it always had, a good physical distraction helped him to suppress the thoughts until a more appropriate time. A time when he wasn't surrounded by their colleagues. A time when he wasn't going to have to face his father, smile and be the picture-perfect son.

Or, if he got lucky, he'd suppress it enough that he wouldn't have to face it at all. Done was done, dissecting it wasn't going to change a thing.

Lord knew that was how it was done in the Moore family. If you worked hard enough at ignoring something then it just…ceased to be. The status quo eventually returned without anyone having to strip themselves raw emotionally.

You just had to wait it out.

He'd only ever seen his mother as she was tonight once before. Though that time he'd not *seen* her, only heard her through the ventilation system as she wailed her heart out down in the wine cellar while he crouched next to his child's bed with its Batman linen, his arms circling his knees, ear pressed to the air vent in his room. That was twenty-odd years ago. So he didn't know what to do tonight when the mother that he adored fell apart right in front of him, other than get her the hell out of there and then get really, really angry.

And hunt for an outlet.

And Tash's infallible logic had robbed him of the outlet he'd planned to have, so he changed tack and redirected it.

Kissing her was a much better idea all round. Firing her blood and bending her to his will was both intensely satisfying and fantastic selective anaesthesia. It simply wasn't possible for him to feel anguish and desire at the same time. It numbed all the parts that he didn't want to think about and stimulated all the parts he liked to think about most.

And it caused the deep chocolate of Tash's eyes to first spit with resistance and then melt with passion. As always, he'd loved the power implicit in the moment that happened. And he loved her capitulation even more for being such an intriguing mix of resignation and anticipation.

Until she'd turned the tables on him, of course.

'Son…'

He tacked away from his father and headed for the bar. 'Later, Dad.'

'We need to talk.'

No. They really didn't. What they needed was to be far

apart for as long as it took for the wounds to start scabbing over. Then they'd see. 'Later,' he cut back over his shoulder.

His father slowed to a stop and Aiden could feel his eyes boring into his back as he ordered the largest bourbon the barman would serve him. That was pretty good selective anaesthesia, too.

He took a healthy swig and turned to face his father, but he'd disappeared into the partying crowd.

His eyes scanned the room, searching for someone else. For a slash of Nordic blonde hair. When he found her, Tash was doing a bang-up job of ignoring him, but he sensed that she knew exactly where he was. She laughed and smiled as she spoke with some of MooreCo's less controversial clients but—even from across the room—he could see the smile was a thin veneer.

And it pleased him—bastard that he was—to know that he was responsible for its fragility. Just to know he had any kind of impact on her at all.

That was a satisfactory revenge for the fact that, while he might have set out to distract Tash from his father with faux interest, somewhere along the line the interest had grown very, very real.

CHAPTER FIVE

TASH DRAGGED HER eyes back from the crowded football stadium beyond the triple-glazed windows and focused back on Nathaniel, who was just settling back into his seat after leaping to his feet at the hard-won goal down on the field.

'So you never told him?'

Nathaniel tugged at the bottom of his jacket, and his eyes drifted across the crowded corporate box to Aiden chatting to two men over by the table laden with a luscious seafood spread. 'How could I? He's my son.'

Tash lowered her voice despite knowing Aiden would never hear them in the noisy room on the other side of the glass. 'But he found out anyway?'

'He was such a quiet child, people tended to say more than they should in front of him.'

Quiet? Aiden? That wasn't an image she could easily conjure. 'What else was he like?'

Nathaniel's eyes narrowed just slightly at the direction of her question, but then softened at the corners and refocused thirty years over her shoulder. 'He was a spectacular boy. Thoughtful and considerate. Keen to learn. Focused. His quiet nature meant he thought about things deeply, even then.'

Thoughtful and considerate? 'What happened?'

It was only as the words tumbled off her lips that Tash realised how insensitive they were.

'Don't misjudge him, Tash. Aiden feels things passionately and he has such a refined sense of right and wrong. Sometimes those things come into conflict.'

'Does that include his father now?' Nathaniel's eyes dropped. 'I know you're staying in a hotel. Are you also avoiding the office?' Or is he? They were only at this football game together because they had guests who expected to see both of them. The happy front.

He shook his head with determination. 'He's grown up with all the murmurs and none of the facts.'

See, now…this was what a father was supposed to do. Defend his child against everything. Even the hint of criticism. *This* was how it should be. Something she'd never had from Eric Sinclair. It was hard not to covet it just a little bit.

'Did you ever think about telling him once he was an adult?' she asked once the roar of the crowd for a goal well kicked settled.

'His good opinion means too much to me.'

'You had to know he'd find out…. Your wife too.' If not last week then…some time.

He nodded. 'I knew. Maybe I thought I could delay it, control it.' He stared some place over her shoulder. 'Bring things to a head at long last.'

Insight flooded into her. 'You wanted this.'

His groan drowned under the cheers of another brilliant on-field play. Tash saw it in the slump of his shoulders more than heard it. 'I wanted it revealed. Exposed.' His eyes lifted. 'Denying your mother broke something in me. She's beyond harm now. I can finally acknowledge us. I can finally acknowledge *her*.'

After thirty years of holding it in.

Sorrow-drenched eyes lifted to hers. 'I've used you, Tash. But I didn't mean for it to hurt you. I'm so sorry.'

'You haven't caused me any harm.' Unlike his son. 'But I am sorry for what it means for your marriage.'

He sighed heavily. 'That's for Laura and me to sort out. My marriage has been flawed for a very long time. Twice I failed to have the strength to do what I should have. Maybe I've finally grown up.'

She almost missed it, so casually was it uttered. Yet her mother's diaries attested to them never seeing each other again after that one time two decades ago.

'Twice?' she risked.

He smiled and patted her hand. 'No, I kept my word to Laura. I haven't seen your mother since you were young. I meant before. At university.'

She frowned. 'I don't understand.'

He matched her confusion. 'Your mother and I were an item before I was with Laura.'

'What?' Tash sat up straight. 'Why wasn't that in her diaries?'

He measured his words as he thought that through. 'Perhaps your father. He was a petty and jealous man. My mere name enraged him. Maybe she feared he would read her diaries?'

Yes. He was absolutely the sort to do that. And to take out that anger on her mother. 'But then you were together, and she wrote about that.' If she hadn't, Tash wouldn't have known about any of it.

'She'd left him by the time she wrote about it. I remember her saying, once, that she left blank pages in the diary where I would be.'

'So she went back and wrote it in?'

'I assume so. Once she was safe to.'

Safe. So he knew. Anxiety churned over in her stomach. She wanted to ask but knew it would be an accusation. 'How could you leave her with him?' she whispered. 'Knowing how violent he was?'

His skin blanched. 'I acted as soon as I knew for sure. But Adele refused to let me expose myself. The most I could do was give her the money she needed to get the two of you away from him. And arrange the trigger.'

Tash studied the awkwardness of his expression. The careful way his eyes avoided her. 'Trigger?'

Nathaniel blew out a long breath. 'I made sure that Eric found out about us. To force his hand. Your mother never knew.'

The accidental slip by her mother's sister suddenly made more sense. Not accidental at all. But her father didn't like Aunt Karen and so would totally have bought the apparent betrayal. And revelled in it. 'But then you *were* exposed.'

His eyes were so earnest. So very intent. 'I didn't care about my reputation. I just wanted her safe. And you, too.'

And maybe he'd wanted to bring things to a head even two decades ago. So he'd manufactured the trigger and funded her mother's escape and the cottage they'd moved straight into. Did Laura know that?

'So...what happened at university, then? Why didn't you stay together?' If the love was so deep.

He shrugged. 'Aiden was conceived.'

She wasn't quick enough to moderate the inward suck of her shock. 'You slept with Laura while you were seeing my mother?'

'No.' The fierceness of his denial threw her. Considering it was coming from a man who'd cheated on his wife. 'We broke up for three weeks over something stupid but in that time I...' His colour rose. 'I was a child for all I thought I knew about the world. I slept with Laura to make a statement.'

Oh, God. 'And she got pregnant.'

'She did.'

Instant karma. 'When did you find out?'

'About a month after your mother and I got back together.'

'And you stood by Laura?'

His back straightened. 'I got her pregnant. It was the eighties.'

Exactly; not the fifties. But Nathaniel Moore was old school in some ways. And maybe his honour was as twisted as his son's. 'And Mum?'

'Devastated.' As you would be. 'I don't think she ever would have become involved with Eric if I hadn't hurt her so badly.'

'You blame yourself.'

'Every day for the past thirty years.'

'But you don't blame Aiden?' Where did that come from? And why did she care what kind of relationship was between the two men?

Nathaniel studied her closely. 'Tash. I hope you're not entertaining thoughts of…Aiden and you would not be a good fit.'

The low blow got her hackles up. That kind of attitude was not something she expected from this man, so disappointment bit low and sharp. 'Not good enough for the Moore heir, Nathaniel?'

His eyes hardened. 'You know me better than that. He should be lucky to find a woman as intelligent and talented and good as you.'

The betrayal stung. For Aiden. 'He's your son.'

'That's right, he is. And so I'm in the best position to suggest that he's a bad fit for someone with your softness. I just think you can do…better,' he urged, unnaturally intent.

Awkwardness saturated the air around them for the first time. 'Well, you don't have to worry. We don't have that kind of relationship.'

'Promise me you won't get involved with him. On your mother's memory.'

Images of heady kisses amongst luxury coats skittered through her mind. But her mother's memory was not something she could take lightly. 'I promise I will never settle for less than I believe I'm worth. How's that?'

Not good enough, judging by the shadow that struck across his gaze. 'Tash—'

'Sorry to interrupt,' a thoroughly unamused voice said from behind. 'Richard was hoping to get a few moments of your attention some time today.'

Nathaniel straightened as stiffly as if he'd been caught ensconced in conversation with Adele rather than her daughter. Tash used the moment it took him to push to his feet to brush away her confusion at what had just passed.

Nathaniel warning her thoroughly off his son. Was Aiden really that damaged?

'Yes. Of course,' he said.

Nathaniel excused himself and quietly closed the glass door between the viewing room and the socialising room behind him. Neither man met the other's eyes as they passed. Aiden gifted all his concentration to the football game proceeding far below in the stadium, then turned to stare at his father, inside.

Pain reflected back at him from the glass.

Watching two men who loved each other drift so far apart was awful.

'How are you doing?' Tash risked after a tense silence.

His answer was only a nod, but at least he tossed that in her direction. 'How's the piece coming along?'

'Very well. It's shaping up to be quite something.'

More silence. *Excellent.*

But before she could break it, he turned and spoke directly to her for the first time in days. 'You know, you don't need to feign interest in things to spend time with him. He's not going anywhere now that he's found you.'

Tash sighed to discover they were still no closer to a truce than before. 'I'm not feigning anything.'

'You don't strike me as an Aussie Rules fan.'

'This is my team. I used to come with my mother. I love football.'

'Uh-huh.'

'You find that hard to believe?'

'You're more WAG territory than fan territory. And you laugh at his jokes constantly. You're telling me that's not a bit sycophantic?'

Tash frowned. What was going on? 'We share a sense of humour.'

'You've even adopted some of his mannerisms.'

'What mannerisms?'

'That one there, for starters. The single brow-lift when challenged.'

Oh, for crying out loud. 'Me and half the world.'

'You're playing up to him.'

She curled her fingers at the side where he couldn't see them. 'No. I'm not. We just have things in common.'

'Carefully engineered things.'

'Why would I do that?'

'To draw him closer. To reel him in.'

She let the insult slide. Those she was used to. 'To what end? You've already said he's not going anywhere.'

'I don't know. Maybe just shoring up your place in his life?'

Or *Aiden's* place, perhaps. Something about the turmoil behind his eyes hit her then. A trace of desperation. In a man who'd negotiated as many big deals as Aiden had, that was a careless tell. She stood and crossed to his side by the viewing window.

'Aiden, look…' He turned a baleful expression on her. 'I

can see how bad things are between your father and you and I know how that must feel—'

'Oh, you know? Really?'

Actually yes, she did. As a woman who'd spent her childhood trying to be good enough to please her father.

She tried again. 'I'm sure it's easier to target your anger on me—'

'You don't think you've earned my displeasure?'

'We were both kids, then—'

'I'm not talking about then. I'm talking about now.'

'What am I doing that's making you so mad?'

'You're flirting with him.'

Seriously? This again? 'I'm not—'

'I'm not saying it's sexual, but you're hovering, keeping him on your hook.'

'I'm—'

'What hope does he have of getting things sorted between him and my mother if you're hanging around reminding him of *her*?'

Colour flared up his neck and her heart squeezed. It was slow to fill again.

She lowered her voice. 'Is that what you want? For them to sort things out?'

He stepped dangerously closer and lowered his voice. 'I want to visit my mother and not find her with an inch of make-up over obviously swollen eyes. I want my father's attention back on MooreCo and not constantly fixated on the past while important deals wither. I want him to stop finding excuses to invite *her* shadow along to every little thing.'

It hurt being nothing more than her mother's shadow in Aiden's eyes. Tash tipped her head—would he accuse her of copying another of his father's traits?—and regarded him. 'I think you would have preferred it if your father and I *were* having an affair.'

'Bloody oath I would. At least it would only be physical.'

Her blood was simmering well and truly now. But it was an ice-cold bubbling. She stood straighter. 'And why's that?'

'Because of who you both are: the CEO and the artisan. At least then there'd be no emotional threat.'

He said 'artisan' as if he meant 'courtesan'. Old scabs of worth tore open deep down inside. 'You don't think a CEO and a glass-blower could make it work?'

His laugh was harsh. 'Do you?'

She shrugged. 'I don't see why not. You certainly seemed interested enough.'

And suddenly she realised they weren't talking about Nathaniel at all. This was about those heavenly moments in the coatroom. When nothing but the chemistry between them mattered.

'I'm not talking short-term.' His eyes raked her from the ground up. 'That's totally possible. I'm talking more permanent.'

Emotional threat, he'd said. As though long-term relationships were pure danger to him. She picked her words with precision. 'Are you saying I'm unworthy of more?'

'Not at all. You're a beautiful woman, exceptionally talented. You're worthy of much more than you've had. But we come from completely different worlds.'

Thank you, Mr Darcy. 'I'm perfectly capable of running in your world. I did it for a year.'

'Jardine's world is small fry compared to the sharks I swim with.'

How apt.

'You wouldn't last a week,' he went on.

She straightened. 'Is that so?'

'Very much so.'

'Prove it.'

His eyes narrowed. 'I don't have to prove it. I know it.'

'Come on, Moore. Put your money where your mouth is.'

'You want to bet on it?'

Why not? 'Yes.'

'On whether or not you can survive in my world?'

'Yes. Because you have some fairly unattractive ideas about life and I think you're wrong.' Suddenly, proving him wrong felt vitally important. Both for his sake and hers.

'That's ludicrous.'

'You don't want me out of circulation?' she challenged and his eyes narrowed. 'I can't be distracting your father if I'm out with you all the time, can I? Isn't that what you want?' An opportunity for him to refocus on his wife.

Her words soaked into his busy brain as she studied him closely. Because yes, that was exactly what he wanted. Which would explain why he'd said yes, but why had she suggested it?

He leaned his hip onto the balustrade of the viewing window and crossed one foot carelessly over the other. 'What are you offering?'

'Not what you're thinking.' She shut that one down quick smart. 'Let me prove to you that status has no bearing on whether two people can get along.'

'Get along? Is that what we're talking about?'

She ignored him. 'On one condition.'

'This whole thing is your condition.'

'You extend me the same courtesy.'

Blue eyes narrowed. 'How?'

'You come to a few things with me.'

'What sort of things?'

'I don't know. I haven't thought of them yet. *My* things.'

'And this will prove what, exactly?'

'That you're a decent guy. And that relationships work both ways.'

He leaned in and murmured, 'And why is that important?'

Absolutely no idea. It just was. As important as proving she was up to mingling with the beautiful people. She was desperate to get a glimpse of the Aiden his father saw. The Aiden of youth.

If that Aiden even existed any more.

His lips parted in a knowing smile. He glanced inside where some of MooreCo's biggest clients were doing a great job of draining the bar and stripping the platters of shellfish. 'If this is an example of how you handle an upper-class crowd—hiding out in the viewing room—then we're not off to a great start.'

'Forgive me for thinking I was invited to watch the football.' Tash tossed back her hair and straightened, indignation roiling through her. 'Let the games begin, then.'

With that, she strode to the door, opened it wide and marched through, a bright smile fixed on her face. 'Gentlemen…'

It took a special talent to be able to distract a group of overprivileged executives from an open bar and seafood buffet but Aiden took peculiar pleasure in watching Tash pull it off. He'd seen her work her magic at the launch party but that was a very different environment. This was the MooreCo corporate box—a much-lauded haven of excess and indulgence. A *what-happens-in-the-corporate-box-stays-in-the-corporate-box* type of place. A woman that looked like Tash was just as likely to find herself with a fifty tucked in her cleavage in this room.

But no…

She had them eating out of her hand.

Not that there wasn't an obligatory amount of speculation in all their eyes, but they weren't voicing it. And they weren't acting on it. They were being…respectful. That didn't happen all that often in here. Though a lot of business definitely got done here. Which was kind of the point.

'Are you just going to watch?'

The colour in her cheeks was high as she drifted towards him. And incredibly appealing. 'Looks like you're doing fine all by yourself,' he said, forcing away thoughts of how he could get her just as flushed. It involved kicking everyone else out of here and Tash pressing outwards against the big glass wall that separated them from the screaming fans.

He cleared his throat. 'What are you talking about with them?'

'The match. The installation. How glass-blowing works.'

'What happens when you've used all those up?'

'Then I fake interest in their business.'

A laugh barked out of him. 'Is that what you did with me? When you were asking questions about MooreCo?'

'You love talking about yourself, and your work by extension. It was the natural in.'

He couldn't help the chuckle. It was true. A robust ego was essential at his level of business.

She tipped her head in that way that was so like his father. 'No one's ever called you on that before?'

'Most people are too polite to actually comment.'

'Advantage of being an *artisan*,' she tossed back at him, popping a carrot stick between those full lips and then crunching down on it. 'Socially inappropriate is tolerated.'

He glanced at his father, deep in discussion on the far side of the room.

'Looks like he's not so distracted, after all,' she murmured.

'About time,' he muttered.

She kicked her chin up. 'Don't tell me you're not up to running things for a bit?'

'Oh, I'm up to it. I'd just like it to be on different terms.'

One brow lifted. 'Your terms?'

He stared at her. 'Different terms.'

She wasn't convinced. But she also wasn't going to press. 'So what do you think? Am I assimilating nicely?'

He couldn't help the smile. 'You're doing great.'

'Ready to eat your words, yet?'

'Not even close.'

'This room is full of ambitious executives. What more will it take to convince you?'

'A room full of their ambitious wives.' He knew the type well. Hungry for the success of their husbands and the life-style that it bought. Protective of whatever edge they had. Suspicious of beautiful young women trying too hard.

His mother in multiple guises, in other words. 'I'll review after that,' he finished.

'After what?'

'After you come with me to dinner Friday night. At Max-ima.'

Dropping the name of the city's most exclusive restaurant did little more than thud mutely on the expensive carpet in the corporate box. It certainly didn't impress Tash. At all.

Her eyes narrowed. 'A business dinner this weekend. How convenient.'

'I have one just about every weekend.' Sometimes two. And why was he defending himself?

She scrunched her nose. 'How tiresome.'

Yeah, it was sometimes. Increasingly so. 'It's business.'

She leaned closer to him. Just a hint. 'And are you always about business?'

From anyone else he'd take that as a come-on. 'MooreCo's not going to run itself.'

'But what about fun? What about pleasure?'

He lowered his face and his voice. 'Are you offering?'

She let that one go through to the keeper. 'Can you even remember what fun felt like?'

God, she was fearless. 'I have a very good imagination.'

The tart smile she threw him should not have been such a turn-on. But it was. The women he dated were either amenable or aggressive. Great socially or under the covers but never both. The kind of forceful he liked in the bedroom didn't fly too well at gatherings like this. And the obliging, easy-going ones tended to be that way about sex, too.

What he wouldn't give for a woman who struck a reliable, happy medium. Confident socially. Confident in bed. Confident at business. Confident about themselves. The image of Tash all trussed up in her glass-blowing gear—and then just all trussed up—blazed into his mind.

'Aiden?'

He forced himself back into the conversation. The echo of her words reached his eardrum. 'Tomorrow? Working. What else would I be doing on a Monday?'

She let his inattention go, and it pleased him on some unwanted level that she didn't pout or make a big deal out of it. 'Silly question, I guess. Can you make any time in your day?'

'What for.'

'A road trip.'

That didn't sound like *some* time. That sounded like a lot of time. 'Where to?'

'I schmoozed your room. Now it's payback time.'

'Payback?'

'A glimpse into how the other half live. Tomorrow is half-price day at the underwater observatory.'

He blinked at her. 'No. Tomorrow is a work day.'

'You work every day.'

She had a point. But he wasn't about to ditch MooreCo to go sightseeing. He'd only just got his father back on task. The echo of Jardine's *insidious* crossed his mind. 'How about we go on the weekend and I'll shout you the ticket price?'

'That would be flagrant condescension.'

This had all the hallmarks of a set-up, but damned if he was going to let her think he wasn't up to it. He could work while he played thanks to the smartphone in his pocket. 'All right. Half-priced aquarium it is.'

'Underwater observatory.'

'Whatever.'

'No. An aquarium is perfectly lit and artificially stocked. What we'll be looking at is nature as it happens. You never know what you're going to see.'

He knew he was going to see her, and that was all that mattered. And that was a vaguely disquieting thought. He hadn't blown off work for a woman for a decade. If you didn't count a hot-and-heavy interlude with a catwalk model a few years back, and that had been so brief he'd barely been missed at the office.

But he'd sure got a lot of work done that afternoon. Sex always energised him. No matter how much he put into it. Not that anything physical was on the agenda for tomorrow; this was purely a psychological exercise. One good mind against another.

Weirdly, just as stimulating.

Though he wouldn't be hitting the office pumped up and ready to take on the world, afterwards. More was the pity.

'Better make it after lunch.'

CHAPTER SIX

SERIOUSLY? ALL THAT beauty out there and he was going to stare at his phone the whole time.

'I can see you,' Tash murmured. 'In the windows.'

Aiden lifted his eyes after a short pause, just long enough to finish reading his latest email. Glass panels surrounded them, keeping them dry and alive in this 360-degree submarine observatory. Curious fish bobbed around them, occasionally nosing the glass as if trying to work out why they couldn't cross into the human world.

'You're working,' he pointed out. 'Why can't I?'

'Because the whole point of this is to show me that you can take as good as you give. I was hoping your competitive spirit would have kicked in by now.'

He glanced compulsively back down at his phone and didn't quite catch himself in time.

'How many deals have you negotiated since we got to the observatory?'

The look he gave her would have made a lesser woman quail. 'I don't negotiate deals by email…'

'But?'

A long breath huffed out of him. 'But I've approved three.'

'Your guests are going to be so bemused when I come to dinner on Friday night and sit in the corner sketching.'

'It's not the same.' He smiled.

'It's exactly the same.'

He regarded her and then switched his phone off. 'Satisfied?'

'Not until it's in your pocket.'

He actually hesitated.

'Seriously, Aiden…' Tash laughed. 'I would have thought half a day's wait for your attention would keep your clients on their toes. Isn't that straight from your playbook?'

'It's not about them.'

'What's it about?'

He shrugged. 'Managing my workload.'

She turned back to her sketching very purposefully. 'Mmm-hmm.'

He fidgeted slightly in her peripheral vision. God, she loved silence. All the more because it was one of his favourite tools.

'Okay, Ms Corporate Coach, what do you think it's about?'

She flattened her pencil on her sketchpad and turned back to him. Since he'd asked so nicely. 'I think it's about controlling, not managing.'

'Not the first time I've been called a control freak.'

'There's nothing freaky about it. I'm sure it's very necessary in your role. But surely part of the skill of wielding control effectively is to stop it controlling you.'

He turned and stared at her. She ignored him and went back to her sketching. 'You're twitching to turn your phone back on right now,' she murmured under her breath. 'Admit it.'

The heat of his regard burned into the side of her tilted face. But then he simply swapped his phone to his left hand and held it out to her. It was impossible not to smile, yet it was only half smugness. The other half was genuine pleasure that he'd seen the truth of her words and not made an issue out of it.

She took the phone from him, slid it straight into her hand-bag and quietly went back to her sketching.

He stood. Paced up to the glass. Turned and looked at the whole space. Made much of examining the engineering. Then finally he returned to the comfortable leather bench by her side.

'Now what are you doing?' she asked.

'If I can't work I'll watch you work.'

Hmm. That's not distracting at all. She stabbed her pencil in the direction of all the water. 'Watch the fish.'

'I am watching the fish,' he said, not taking his eyes off what her fingers were doing. 'I'm seeing them as you see them.'

'I'm pretty sure we see them the same way.'

'Our eyes might but our brains don't.'

She turned away from her sketching. 'What do you see?'

He looked out to the dozens of grey bodies drifting around the observatory, then back at her occasionally flashing with silver from the sunlight far above. 'Lunch.'

Tsk. 'Heathen. Wait just a few more minutes; this thing happens on the half-hour...'

'What thing?'

She found his eyes. He really was bad with delayed grati-fication. Well, she wasn't about to enable him. 'A surprise thing. A delightful thing.'

'Delightful? What are you—Mary Poppins?'

'I enjoy nice things.'

He snorted. 'All women like nice things.'

'Nice *moments*. I'm not that fussed by possessions.'

'You grabbed my two-hundred-and-fifty-dollar smart-phone with quite a bit of glee just now.'

She turned to him. 'Aiden, if this is genuinely difficult for you I will happily give you your phone back.'

Really, what could he say without looking pathetic? Or desperate. Nothing at all.

'Nah. I'm good.'

The smile wouldn't be denied. 'Excellent,' she said through it. 'Give it a chance. If the sea life isn't spectacular enough for you now…'

Sure enough, the lights around them started to dim until the whole space was lit only by the fluorescence of the emergency exit sign to their far left. The natural light streaming down from the ocean's surface far above formed an eerie shaft of brilliance in the dark of the water. Then, as a slow reveal, a series of black lights mounted to the entire outer of the spherical observation bubble glowed into life, illuminating everything in the immediate surround in ultra-violet.

Those same drab, dark grey fish suddenly morphed into new creatures. One deep purple, one a deep blue, another almost crimson. Glittering, sparkling. All against the deep teal of the UV-lit depths.

Aiden caught his breath.

'Amazing, huh?'

'It's beautiful,' he whispered into the darkness and it was more intimate than if they were alone together in a bedroom. 'Is this how they see each other?'

'I like to think so. Who else is it for if not each other?'

She felt the exact moment that he turned to look at her. 'Is that how you see them?'

'I always see the potential before the actual.' Did space itself shrink under black light? Her tight breath certainly thought so.

'Some people might call that fanciful.'

'Some might. But there's a hidden side to the dourest creature. You just have to catch it in the right light.'

His gaze fell on a starfish, clinging to one of the pylons that held the jetty above them up off the ocean floor. Moments ago, he'd not even noticed it, she'd wager. But under new light, it was a rich orange rather than a dull brown to match the crusted timber of the pylon.

'Is that what you were drawing? There on the left?'

The left side of her notepad was filled with little sucker feet. She returned to one to give it some imaginary detail in the ethereal light. 'I'm going through a foot phase. Last time I visited, he was climbing the glass. I think I stayed for about six hours. Until he eventually moved on.' Every edge, every crease, every subtle shift of weight in those super-glue suckers. Imagining the whole time how it was going to translate in glass.

They fell to silence and Aiden stood and roamed quietly around the observation bubble that was empty of anyone but them. The more he looked, the more he saw and his curiosity gave Tash minutes of silence until, eventually, the automatic timer dimmed the external UV and raised the interior lights back to a dim glow. Back to reality.

She sighed.

'Why wouldn't they leave that on the whole time?' Aiden murmured, returning to her side.

'Because then it wouldn't be special. People might think that's what it really looked like below the surface. I like to imagine their world as vibrant and brilliant rather than dull and grey, but I know that the vibrancy is not for me.'

'So why confuse us with two different perceptions?'

'It's so spectacular their way. I think it's healthy for us to know there's a whole part of the spectrum that we don't experience. Keeps us humble.'

'Is that what you try to create? In your artwork?'

Was it? She did tend to see things in an extrasensory way while being creative. And she tried to portray that in her work. 'I don't have a problem with perceiving something differently in different environments. So maybe my work does the same thing, yes.'

She'd never thought of it that way before. Were her pieces doing for people what the black light did down here?

'Are we still talking about fish?'

Her eyes lifted to his. 'People too. Humans are particularly context-dependent.'

'How do you perceive me?'

Her snort ricocheted around the little glass room.

'Let me rephrase,' he modified on a glare. 'How do you perceive me differently in different contexts?'

She made him wait while she pretended to think about it. But she'd had her fill of thinking about Aiden so the comments came very naturally. 'In your professional context you're arrogant and decisive, impatient. Brilliant, of course, but with a tendency towards ruthlessness if there's something you want.' He didn't look entirely displeased by that description, which she perhaps should have anticipated. 'Socially you're good value, and a good contributor. You're generous with your money and time and mostly at ease—'

'You haven't seen me at Maxima yet.'

'That's more work than social. Anything there will be strategic.'

He gave her that point.

'Around your mother you're protective, tense, yet about as vulnerable as I've ever seen you. And around your father you're very much the son: respectful but frustrated.'

'Frustrated?'

'Like you just want him to get the heck out of the way so you can run MooreCo.'

He frowned at that. 'That's not how I feel.'

'Your body language says otherwise.'

'I love my father.'

'I believe you.' But then she'd yet to see him in a truly social situation with his dad. Their meetings to date were loaded with subtext. Until today. 'The two aren't mutually exclusive.'

He stepped closer. 'What about when I'm with you?'

'Like I said, you're good value—'

'Not socially. With *you*. When we're alone.' He leaned in as a young child sounded on the steps high above them. 'How do you perceive me now?' he murmured.

'Like a shark.' She blurted the first thing that came to her. 'Circling. Assessing. Flashing those teeth just enough to remind me they're there. Never taking your eyes off me. Relentless. Every move strategically planned.'

He gave her a grin full of those teeth now. 'Yet, you're not swimming away.'

'Sharks are as exciting as they are scary,' she breathed. 'All that danger. All that power and promise. Is he or isn't he all bluff?'

His lips hovered just a breath from hers. 'He definitely isn't.'

'You're very confident,' she murmured.

That gave him pause. 'Why do I get the sense that's not the word you wanted to use? You don't like confidence?'

'I do. Very much. But I don't automatically trust it.'

'Explain.'

'Confidence is captivating when it's earned. But it's exhausting when it's fabricated.' Kyle's was all bluster as it turned out. When the chips were down—when it mattered—he quailed. And a blusterer abhorred assurance in others.

Or maybe it was just in her.

Aiden's grin turned Cheshire. 'You don't think my confidence is justified?'

'It could all be for show.' But it wasn't. She knew it.

'Like yours, you mean?'

'You think I lack confidence?'

'Don't you?'

She considered her next move for a moment. 'Actually, I'm tempering it.'

That wiped the polished veneer off his gaze for the first time all day and Tash got the sense that he was really *seeing* her for a moment. 'Why?'

But that was a story she couldn't half tell. So best not to start. 'Not everyone likes self-assurance in practice as much as in principle.'

'Men, you mean?'

She wasn't about to answer that.

'So you just…what? Turn it off?'

'Down moderate it.' Her father had taught her, cruelly, the value he placed on modesty and her inability to contain it infuriated him. So she'd had to learn fast.

He grunted. 'I spend my days moderating. Maybe we're more alike than I suspected.'

'I thought I reminded you of your father.'

'Him too. You sure you're not a changeling stolen from my family?'

A ripple of gooseflesh ran down her back like an undersea tremor but she was saved from commenting by the arrival of a young mother and the toddler they'd heard earlier at the bottom of the spiral stairs.

Aiden withdrew with obvious regret, saying, 'Are you done with your drawings?'

'You trying to get me alone?' she murmured, totally on board with that plan.

He slipped his hand around hers—all warm and promising—and hauled her to her feet. 'I want to get you somewhere you can let all that confidence off the leash.'

'So, not entirely misplaced, then.' Aiden gasped, flopping onto his back next to her, chest heaving and skin damp. 'All that confidence.'

Tash turned her head to face him—the only part of her capable of movement after such an intense workout.

'You're a strange man, Aiden Moore.'

'Because I like paddle boats?'

Tash plucked her sea-soaked trousers away from her bent legs. She'd had to wade out to her hire-a-boat. 'Because you chose paddle boats as your duel weapon.'

'I used to come here on family holidays and race my cousins. It's a tradition in my family.'

Her heart did a tiny flip-flop at the thought of being considered part of his family. But that was dangerous thinking. 'Huh. So you stacked the deck.'

'Totally. I had to cover my butt in case you were the paddle queen of the West.'

'I *was* the paddle queen of the West.'

'I still won.'

'Your boat didn't have a hole in it. And your legs are like tree trunks.'

They went over it one more pointless time, how only a poor worker blamed her tools. And, again, the argument ended in laughter.

'Thank you for taking my phone,' he said, sobering, staring up at the two puffy clouds populating the blue sky.

She let her head flop sideways on the earth, towards him. He was lying much closer to her than she'd realised. 'You're welcome. How are you doing without it?'

'Better than I've felt in ages.'

That momentary flash of vulnerability deserved a reward. 'Well, thank *you* for the paddle-boat race. It's nice being able to give something one hundred per cent.'

'Yet you still lost.'

'Barely.' She reached over and thumped him, aiming for his stomach but encountering only hard, trained muscle under wet shirt. It felt as good as it looked.

Sigh.

'Seriously,' he said, 'why would you not give it your full effort, ordinarily?'

There was no judgement there, just curiosity. 'People don't like being shown up, as a rule.'

His groan was more of a curse. 'Do you know how long it's been since someone gave me a run for my money in any capacity? Bring it on.'

'Maybe no one wants to cross the rich guy?'

'You cross me daily.'

'I don't care about the money. Or the power. Or the sexy, expensive suits. But other people do. Maybe your cousins just *let you win* at paddle boats when you were young.'

His gasp turned into a chuckle. 'Wash your mouth out.'

The nearby water lapped the shore and washed against their beached paddle boats in dull *whumps* that exactly matched the steady thrum of her blood.

'Was it your father that taught you to downplay your assets?'

Every part of her tensed up. So much for the relaxation of the afternoon.

Aiden pressed, ignoring her flashing neon body language. 'I know it wasn't your mother. Not from the way you've spoken of her. Or was it Jardine?'

Pfft. 'I wouldn't give Kyle the satisfaction.'

He leaned up on one elbow and held her eyes. 'So your father, then.'

Trust didn't just materialise. It took risk. 'When I was seven I started to express my independence, like all kids.' His steady gaze was encouraging. 'Dad found it amusing for about five minutes.'

Aiden frowned. 'He punished you for testing the boundaries?'

'I think he punished me for being too much like her.'

The words bubbled up from her subconscious for the first time. 'He thrashed me a few times but realised pretty quick it wasn't effective. It just made me more determined to stand my ground. And that just inflamed him more.' She took a breath. 'We lived pretty much in a permanent state of conflict, the two of us, and he disciplined me with whatever he could without getting arrested by the Child Protection Authority: denying me permission for school excursions, withholding pocket money, refusing to sign my school notes so I'd get in trouble.'

Yeah, Eric Sinclair loved other people to do his dirty work.

'So what changed? If you were seven that was right before…'

'He found my off switch.'

Aiden frowned. And he hesitated for an age before risking, 'What was it?'

She picked at the grass on the bank of the shore. 'Mum. When I was bad, he hurt her instead of me.'

Blue eyes widened and flooded first with relief—that her father hadn't touched her, presumably—but then the reality of Eric's insidiousness dawned on him and they filled with the same expression she'd seen on his face when he'd locked them in the coatroom. Fury.

'Pretty soon he was hurting her preventatively, if he even got a whiff of attitude from me. It was like negative conditioning.'

Aiden just stared, unable to make words.

'As long as I was subservient and respectful and didn't show off or try to antagonise him, he left her alone. But if he got the slightest suggestion I was defying him…' She twisted her fingers around in the grass and pulled a dirt-packed clump free. 'It was quite effective.'

Aiden gently unfolded her fingers and let the dirt fall free, then wrapped them in his own warm strong ones. 'What changed?'

'She told me much later she'd spent all year trying to figure out what she was doing to cause his rages. But she knew me, she saw me dying inside and she started watching him. Finally she realised what was happening.' Tash lifted her eyes. 'And so she called your father.'

Aiden froze. 'That's why they got back in touch after all that time?'

'He was the only one she knew could help.'

It took three swallows before he could speak clearly. 'And did he?'

She shuddered in a breath, glad to be rid of those days. 'Within a month we were in our own place and my father's hand was forced by how public it all was. Saving face was everything to him. He let her go. But not before trashing her name with everyone we knew.'

His eyes blazed. 'Did they even sleep together at all? Or did he just want your father to think that?'

The question was clear. *Did he destroy my family to save yours?*

'In her diary she talks about how ashamed she was to lie with him given the marks of abuse on her body, how all she could remember was how he used to look at her when she was young and beautiful.' She squeezed the fingers still curled around hers. 'But he made her feel beautiful one last time.'

Aiden frowned.

'As soon as he'd set the wheels in motion he went back to your mother. To you. I think he might have paid my father a visit, too. Warned him off.'

He fell to silence, and she let him process. As he did she poked around in her heart for the usual shame she felt when she thought about those awful days, but there was nothing there. As if revealing it had allowed it to flutter free. Adele

Sinclair had spent the next decade trying to undo the damage her husband had done, trying to patch up Tash's fractured little soul. Yet she was thirty before she realised none of those days were really about *her* at all.

He hurt her mother to punish Tash.

And he punished Tash because that hurt her mother much more than any bruises ever would.

Win-win.

Aiden's words came after a very long time. 'Do you hate him?'

'I will never love him. Or like him. But reading her diaries has helped me understand him. He was so weak. Such a victim. Even back at uni. I was the only one he could dominate.'

'And then you started showing your natural strength.'

'I didn't always feel strong.'

He sat up, taking both her hands in his. 'Never dumb yourself down, Tash. Not for anyone.'

She could have kept it light. Put them back on more familiar footing. 'Sometimes it's just easier.'

He nodded. 'Correction, then. Promise me you'll never dumb yourself down for me.'

He said that just as if they'd be spending a lot of time together. But the echo of such a serious statement—such a serious conversation—hung awkwardly between them. Until Aiden threw out a life preserver.

'So…what did you think I dragged you out of the observatory for, if not a lusty bout of paddle-boating?'

She grabbed the subject-change willingly. 'Something a whole lot less public.' But every bit as lusty.

'You came very willingly.'

There was a hot question in his gaze. A question she wasn't in a position to answer. 'There was a child there. I thought it would be more appropriate to move the conversation—' and the undercurrent '—elsewhere.'

He matched her smile. 'Good call.'

'Sadly, now we're exhausted.'

'I rally very quickly,' he assured her, leaning closer.

Oh, that she could believe. 'I promised your assistant I'd have you back at your office by four p.m. All those messages, remember?'

'Screw that. Simone will reschedule. I can even put on one of my *sexy* suits for you.' The ridiculous eyebrow waggle mended one of the fissures in her heart. Inexplicably.

Her laugh flung up high, then settled softly back down where they lay like a gossamer parachute. 'My work ethic is sound even if you're embracing your new phone-free status. I have a prototype piece to start work on tonight.'

The teasing dropped immediately and his eyes grew keen. 'The starfish?'

'Yes. I'm determined to capture those little tube feet just right.'

'Maybe not everything can be recreated in glass?'

She pulled herself up to a sitting position. 'Now it's your turn to wash out your mouth.'

He didn't want to let her go. It was evident in the deep blue depths of his eyes. But he pulled himself into a sit and smiled sadly. 'I have a favour to ask.'

'Wow. One lusty bout of paddle-boat racing and you think you can ask favours.'

'I want to watch.'

Everything in Tash's chest tightened up with a twisted kind of anticipation. But experience had taught her not to assume. 'Care to rephrase?'

'Your work. I want to watch you make the starfish.'

That was even more personal than what she'd thought he meant. Momentary panic robbed her of brain cells. 'Why?'

'I want to see the whole process.'

Again… 'Why?'

'Because it's interesting. And because it's your work.'

A small fist formed high in her gut, where her throat started. 'I usually don't work with an audience....'

Intent blue locked on her. 'Would you make an exception?'

The only person she'd ever blown glass for was her mother. It was something special between them, so that she could understand her daughter's passion. Maybe that was all Aiden wanted, too. She took a deep breath.

'Sure.' Though the permission was nowhere near as casual as that. 'It'll only be a test piece. I'll have to spend some time on it to get it right.'

'Test piece is fine.'

She narrowed her eyes as something dawned on her. He looked as awkward as she felt. 'You look very uncomfortable.'

'I don't do supplication.'

Her laugh exploded out. 'No. I can see that. How does it feel?'

He took his time answering, and then a word formed after his chest rose and fell heavily, just once. 'Odd.'

'Well, that's okay, then. As long as you realise how special this opportunity is.'

'Oh, I'm getting that loud and clear.'

Was he talking about more than just a glass-blowing demonstration? It was tempting to imagine.

'Thursday?' Because, secretly, there was no way she was letting him see her first feeble efforts. If she pushed herself, she could get somewhat proficient with the sea star by Thursday.

Preserving her dignity had become strangely meaningful around Aiden.

'See you then.'

CHAPTER SEVEN

A CHANGELING STOLEN from our family...

Aiden's words swirled around and through the troubling undercurrent from his father's startling pronouncement just days before. That he and her mother had been together at university. The moment he'd uttered the casual words in the observatory this afternoon, something had shifted and clicked in her subconscious. Like the barrels of a lock clunking into place.

Tash stared at the books scattered around her on the pretty rug on her lounge room floor. Yet there was nothing about it in her mother's diaries. Nathaniel suggested that was born of fear. It made sense. Adele Sinclair had feared many things about her husband; he absolutely was the sort to violate her most private thoughts in feeding his own ravenous paranoia. That would have been the lesser of many, many evils.

She shook her head and murmured, 'Why did you stay with him so long, Mum?'

Because she had made her bed, probably. Or maybe because she didn't think she would do better after she'd watched the love of her life walk away with someone else. From her mother's diaries it was clear that Eric Sinclair was no prize in their youth—never quite as bright, quick-witted or vibrant as the rest of their group of friends—but he'd apparently seemed harmless enough...then. In the years after they all went their separate ways his true colours emerged—or maybe they were drawn out of him by his fear and suspicion—and perhaps her mother stayed with him out of a deep-seated belief that she'd somehow *earned* her lot. Eric had resisted every subtle attempt his wife had made to change the dynamic in their relationship and he'd flat out refused her attempts to seek counselling and her threats to leave to *force* things to be better.

His irrational fear made so much more sense if Nathaniel and Adele had actually been sleeping together.

Tash reached for the palest of the diaries. The oldest. She'd pored over these multiple times; she knew what was there. Or not there. She knew there was no mention of any kind of intimacy between her mother and Nathaniel in their university days, but maybe she was missing something. Something between the lines.

Or between the pages....

She left blank pages in the diary where I would be, Nathaniel had said.

She flicked through the earliest pages in the book. Tales of going to the movies with Laura, or class with Eric, or lunch at the student cafeteria with Nathaniel. But nothing more meaningful. A few pages wailing about some tough exams and—

There!

A blank page. After her first-year exams. Positioned so it just looked like the passing of time. And *there*—another. On a mid-semester break early in second year to a sleepy little town with Laura. At least it had appeared to be just the two of them, but there was a gently humorous tale of her and Laura in the back seat of the car killing time with a word game.

So if Laura was in the back seat with Adele, who was driving?

No mention. Just another blank page two days into their trip. *Did* Nathaniel occupy the blank pages of her mother's diaries just as he'd said? And if he did, what was she being so careful to leave out? He wasn't completely absent; Tash supposed that would have been as telling as full disclosure when Eric knew the group of friends spent so much time together. So what had they done that warranted blank pages?

It wasn't hard to guess.

Her mother and Nathaniel had been lovers. Years before that *one time.* And then something pulled them apart long enough for Laura to get her hooks into the man she, apparently, had a thing for all along and she got pregnant by Nathaniel.

He and her mother had reunited, according to Nathaniel, but when he'd discovered Laura was pregnant with his child, he'd made the hard choice and stuck by the woman he didn't love.

Which left Eric the last single man standing. Conveniently poised to pick up the pieces of a shattered Adele. Lucky for Tash or she might not exist at this moment. She'd come along not long after Aiden had. Almost as if her mother couldn't bear to watch the man she loved be father to someone else's child when she was—

An icy chill worked its way through Tash's arteries.

She'd come along not long after Aiden had. And he'd come along pretty much straight away thanks to Laura and Nathaniel's irresponsible hook-up.

A flicker-show played out behind Tash's eyes. Of the tilt of Nathaniel's head when he laughed, so like her own. The two of them cheering the same football team on and her turning to smile into eyes the same colour as her own. Their similar taste in food and in humour. His obsessive focus on her and the way he was letting his business slide to spend time with her.

A changeling stolen from our family…

The chill turned to a thick, stagnant goo that made beating agony for Tash's straining heart.

What if there was a reason she and Nathaniel had connected so instantly? Were so alike? What if something other than heartbreak came of those few weeks that her mother and Nathaniel were back together? Before he discovered he was a father.

Her heart hammered. What if Adele was pregnant, too, when they broke up? That would explain why her mother would have stayed with a man like Eric. And it would explain why Tash had nothing in common with Eric Sinclair. And—absolutely—why he'd have hated her enough to treat her the way he did.

Because maybe he *wasn't* her real father. And maybe he knew it. And maybe the reason her daddy had hated her so much was because of whose genes she carried, not because of who *she* was.

Blind hope welled, warm and soothing through the thick dread. What if Nathaniel Moore was her real father? A man that she could respect. A man that she could love so very easily. A man worthy of the title. A raft of tingles settled through her body and it was almost the angelic touch of her mother from on high, soft and benevolent and comforting...

And all-confirming.

A slight tremble started up deep in her muscles. How different might her life have been if she'd had Nathaniel as a father instead of Eric? A father who encouraged and praised her successes rather than trying to break her. A father who moved heaven and earth to keep their family together instead of throwing it away in a poisonous, vengeful and public outburst.

She blinked back tears.

God, how much better might she have been being raised a Moore, like Aiden, instead of a—

The blue diary slipped from her suddenly nerveless fingers. *Like Aiden.*

If she was a Moore then that meant Aiden was—

Nausea swilled in and replaced the breathless excitement of moments before as she replayed the memory at the football game when Nathaniel had urged her, so intently, not to get involved with Aiden.

Promise me...

A sickening kind of dread took root deep in her soul. The longer she sat there, the more awfully, horribly right it felt. Her stomach muscles locked up hard on the implications.

Aiden was her half-brother.

There was no question about *his* heritage.

She was losing hours each day imagining herself with him, thinking about what it might be like to have him in her life on a more permanent basis.

But she'd cast him more as a lover than a—

Self-loathing, raw and all too familiar, washed through her and she battled the duelling desires. To be a Moore: Nathaniel Moore's daughter, to have a decent father finally, someone she could relate to and connect with. And respect.

But to be Aiden's *sister*...

All the saliva in her mouth decamped.

How could that possibly be? Surely her body would know, even if her mind didn't?

She saw herself twisted back in his arms amongst the expensive coats, his tongue challenging hers. She remembered the rush of excitement and expectation as he'd slipped strong arms around her. She heard herself flirting wildly, putting a toe into the waters of the sexual attraction that raged between them.

And she pressed her palm to her suddenly roiling belly.

Shame flooded through her, but she could live with that. Kyle had made her out to be little better than a tramp at the end of their relationship—over-sexed and under-barefooted—and she'd managed to swallow the humiliation of that very public breakup and keep on surviving.

She could do it again. This time in private.

But rejecting Aiden now, after the promise she'd made him this afternoon.... If she cancelled Thursday on him, he'd demand an explanation. And rightly so. Except she just wasn't free to explain. Nathaniel was out of the country this week with Laura, trying hard to mitigate the damage he'd caused—a very different thing from trying to save his marriage, Tash suspected—so she couldn't call and drop a grenade into that careful work.

So that meant she had two choices—cancel or go ahead with the glass-blowing demo.

Could she keep him at bay for the time he was with her? Heat and danger were her friends in the hot shop. It was work for her; she could behave professionally. And he wasn't about to force himself on her, right?

Surely, they could pass an hour in each other's company without doing anything inappropriate.

Surely.

Aiden jogged down the old, paved, port road towards Tash's studio. City council had established this part of town as an arts precinct decades before, back when artists were the obvious choice to sequester away in substandard buildings. They got tenants to keep an already seedy part of town from worsening and they also got points for supporting the very vocal art community.

Double win.

Maybe someone in council lacked foresight though, because you'd think they'd have put limited zoning on the waterfront precinct in case the social dynamic ever changed and they wanted to use the land for something else. It did change, and now rich people were buying up the old wool stores and converting them into creative, heritage-style accommodations left and right of the remaining artists. Squeezing them out incrementally. But the council couldn't evict the arty set without causing office-losing scandal.

Tash didn't lack foresight when she traded a pile of her best works for her quarter of the then derelict building. She had a great studio in what was fast becoming a great part of town. The artists and the wealthy mainly enjoyed a symbiotic relationship: the presence of the cashed-up residents made sure cafés and buses came to their part of town and that the precinct bustled even at night where it used to be a dark, port wasteland. And the artists loaned the area a whole bunch of cool-factor credibility.

'Knock-knock.'

Aiden paused at the last door in the row, a heavy sliding timber thing that flaked enough to tell anyone passing that it was occupied by an artist. In case the hot air pumping out of it wasn't clue enough.

Tash appeared in the opening a moment later, dressed in her usual glass-blowing gear—battered, closed-in boots, overalls and a T-shirt. Its sleeves were the only thing that was different from the first time he'd seen her all those weeks ago. That and the tiny leap of pleasure she failed to disguise before she got her expression under control and flooded it with caution.

Sigh. So they were back to caution. That didn't bode well.

'Sorry I'm late,' he said. Wouldn't it be great if that were the reason for her wary expression?

'I thought you might have changed your mind.'

Was that *hope* hiding behind her brown eyes? 'Are you kidding? After working so hard to get you to let me come along in the first place?'

It was easy to joke but it really wasn't all that funny. He was halfway through negotiations before he realised he didn't know *why* he wanted to come so badly. It wasn't just because he wanted to see the developing starfish—though that was what he'd told her. And it wasn't because he wanted to see her again—though he very much did after he realised it could otherwise be a whole working week before he saw her again.

The closest he could get to his own version of truth— from somewhere way down deep—was because it was the one thing she'd told him he couldn't have. Last time he'd stood here in her doorway. She'd seemed so shocked at the idea of revealing her craft. Her self. As if he'd asked her to strip naked and dance for him. And so it had intrigued him.

Actually, he thought she might have danced naked before she agreed to this.

And now he was imagining her naked. And she was staring at him as if he were deficient.

Awesome.

'Well, here you are,' she said, grudgingly. 'Do you want to see the MooreCo pieces?'

Not really—he just wanted to stand here with her a moment longer acting like a total sap. 'Sure. Lead on.'

She turned and he enjoyed the bonus view of her sexy hip-sway ahead of him. It helped force his mind back into more familiar, physical territory. He focused on the sensation.

'This is the shoal taking shape....'

Three dozen tiny, silver-stained fish hung suspended from the studio roof, cleverly bonded together with invisible glass welds so that as the biggest pieces changed direction in the light ocean breeze the whole shoal seemed to follow, with fishy, military precision.

He could well imagine them glinting and bouncing prisms around MooreCo's glass entry gallery. And their clients staring up at them from underneath. To replicate that view he crouched and examined the whole effect from below. Somehow, she'd managed to make looking at them from below feel like looking down at them from above. Like being under and above the water at once.

'It's extraordinary, Tash.' The compliment was out before he thought it through. He usually liked to reserve his hand a little longer. Until it counted.

Apparently not today.

'I'm contemplating another three dozen. It looks big here but they'll be lost in your foyer.'

'I can't wait to see it installed.'

She struggled to disguise her smile. On one hand, it pleased him to have pleased her, but it disappointed him that she didn't want to show him that. She wouldn't even give him a hint of her pleasure. He thought something had changed between them after the paddle-boating.

Or maybe this was the universe giving him an out. Because he really shouldn't be worried if a woman wasn't emotionally forthcoming. What the hell use were emotions to him?

'This is only the base element,' she continued. 'These are some of the hero pieces....'

The more she showed him, the harder it was for her not to reveal her pretty pink glow at his praise. Pretty soon, making her blush was all he could focus on. She fought it—inexplicably—but she was losing.

And *that* was definitely familiar territory. He loved a well-fought battle...as long as it came with a resigned surrender at the end. And not on his part. It was much safer to focus on the tantalising tingles than on the other feelings bubbling away below the surface.

The ones whispering at him to come here today. In case bending her to his will in this way might be catching.

Because that spoke of a desperation he wasn't about to acknowledge.

She carried on with her impromptu tour of the glass pieces littering her studio.

He leaned on a workbench after they'd examined the final piece. 'This is really going to blow our clients away. They'll be late to our meetings because they're standing down in the foyer, lost in your undersea world.'

Again with the pleasure. Until she dipped her head.

Why did she keep fighting it? Why not just go with it?

Every other woman he'd known just went with it. Some faster than others, admittedly, but ultimately they acquiesced. Persistence. He'd been raised with it on two fronts. A father who believed that reward only came from effort, and a mother who'd taught him, through example, the value of dogged determination. Whenever there was something she wanted, she just stayed the course and remained unmoved and—usually—things ended up going her way. She worked on the principle that if you ignored 'no' often enough eventually it became 'yes'.

'So, has our lesson started?' he nudged, figuring that if the studio was going to be full of tense heat between them they might as well melt glass with it.

She looked him up and down. 'You're dressed okay.'

His wardrobe didn't have a lot of grunge in it but he'd managed to pull together an old-looking sweater, jeans and boots. She didn't need to know how much he'd paid to get that look in the first place.

'How come I have to have long sleeves when you don't?'

She lifted one critical brow. 'I've been doing this all my life. You're going to have sparks flying everywhere.'

'Doesn't that happen every time we get together?'

Her expression flattened. 'Hilarious. You want to learn or not?'

'Wow. Tough room.'

'I need to know you're concentrating before I let you near a vat of what is effectively molten lava.'

He forced his brows down. 'I'm listening. Honestly.'

She thrust a face shield at him and slid regular goggles on herself. 'This will stop your retinas from ulcerating,' she murmured, leading him to the kiln that pumped intense heat back at him. At the last minute, she also tossed him a pair of enormous fire-retardant gloves. 'And your skin from melting.'

'Is this really necessary?' he asked, feeling very much like a catcher in a baseball game.

She turned and glared at him. 'Do you want to watch or not?'

Did she seriously think that a few layers were going to protect her? He held the ridiculous gloves up either side of him and she continued.

Since he was a silver-lining kind of person he cheerfully told himself that the face shield might mean he couldn't smell her the way he wanted, but, in better news, it meant he could check her out without her knowing. He took full advantage of that as Tash slid the door open on the gaping maw of the furnace with hands covered in her own fire-retardant gloves. Then she turned to him.

'Pass me that blowpipe.' She nodded at a four-foot tube laid out on her workbench next to a medieval torture rack of tools. She took the pipe from him and raised it over her head, dipping it squarely into the middle of the orange glow within the furnace and turning it steadily, as if she were twisting up a forkful of spaghetti. After a hypnotic twist-a-thon, she backed up, withdrawing a blazing, deadly ball on the end of her pipe, turning, turning constantly. Her tanned shoulders flexed at the weight exchange as she lowered it down onto a waiting brace.

'The bolus is two thousand degrees,' she said, over the roar of the open furnace, turning it steadily. 'To make it into a vessel I have to introduce an air pocket inside. The air does part of the work. Right now my hand's job is just to keep the glass hot and moving.'

She did that, carefully and methodically. One hundred per cent focus. She squeezed a saturated sponge over the middle of the blow tube with her free hand, sending steam billowing up and around them both. It left a filmy sheen of moisture across her bare skin, droplets clinging to every hair on her body.

'That's so I can put my lips to the tube safely.'

Wait… 'You're going to suck that thing?'

She snorted. 'That's a fast way to kill yourself. No, I'm going to blow it. But I can't start until the shape is better.'

She reached for one of the torture-rack tools, a thick, burned wad of drenched newspaper. At least it once had been; it was mostly charcoal now. With nothing but her bare hands, she slapped the saturated newspaper to the underside of the molten mass and cupped it, shaping and polishing the glowing glass ball until he practically forgot she had newspaper in her hand at all. It was as if she were stroking the glass into compliance with her bare touch, persuading it to be what she wanted it to be. Massaging it with her courage and mastery.

His entire body responded, imaging her artist's hands polishing the shape of his muscles, massaging his flesh into compliance. Persuading him with her proficient touch.

He gritted his teeth against the sensation.

You just want what you can't have.

Damned right he did. But he wasn't a total creep. He wanted her to want him just as badly. She *couldn't* be totally indifferent to him, not when he was so very aware of her.

Could she?

He distracted himself with conversation. 'Don't you have better tools?'

'If you walked into a hot shop two millennia ago you'd see very similar tools. Sometimes the old ways are just the best.'

The shifting facets in the glowing, molten mass hypnotised him as she worked it around and around until it looked as if she were polishing a ball of toffee. Aiden stepped up hard behind her and laid a gloved hand on her shoulder so she knew he was there.

The blowpipe lurched as she fumbled a turn.

'What would happen if you didn't keep it moving?' he asked.

'Um…' She rounded her shoulders and got the momentum under control again. 'It would start losing form the moment the inertia stops.'

'Would it drop off?'

'Keep distracting me and we'll find out.'

She was right. Manipulating a kilo of volcanic eruption was not the time to be peppering her with questions. He stopped talking and concentrated on watching over the top of her head.

She twirled for a few minutes longer and then lifted the whole thing higher, pivoted it sideways onto on its brace and placed the end of the pipe to her lips. He didn't see her shoulders rise or her ample chest expanding with breath, but he saw the bolus expand a little. Just a little. Just enough.

Looked as if it was going to be a fat little sea star.

It was like watching a bagpipe player. Steady and controlled. And watching her lips working the end of the pipe so expertly gave him a personal heat that had nothing to do with the roasting warmth coming off the three furnaces in the room.

Pervert.

He forced his attention off Tash and onto the shape beginning to form on the end of the tube. She swung the whole thing sideways and onto a pair of braces with a seat in between them. With two thousand degrees practically sitting in her lap she kept the thing moving, horizontally, on the braces and started working with some of the tools. A cupped block that gave the blob a pear-shaped bottom—ah, his favourite shape—and a pair of nasty-looking pincers that trimmed and poked and shaped and cut as the whole thing endlessly spun.

Twirl, snip, twirl, snip. Every cut liberated more of the creature within the glass and she tapped the edges of each leg to open some space between them. They spread joyously outwards with the force of the spinning.

His body twitched again.

God, there was something so sexy about her proficiency. And her focus. And the sheen of sweat on her body amid the roasting heat swilling all around them. It made it near impossible to concentrate on what her hands were doing.

He moved behind her again and leaned down until his eyes were at the same level as hers. Conveniently, that meant curling his torso around her somewhat.

The turning and snipping faltered. 'What are you doing?' she choked, low and concerned, twisting towards him just slightly.

'I want your eye level. I want to see it how you see it.'

He wanted to *feel* what she was feeling—if he couldn't *be* felt. But the first thing he wanted was to not remain separate from her for a moment longer while this sensual display was going on.

'It's like there's actually a mental connection between you and the glass and your hands are just there to preserve the illusion.'

Her back cranked straighter and her shoulders set. 'You think I'm just willing the glass into shape?'

'Right now, I think you could talk it into doing anything just to please you.'

Tash stood violently and scooped the blowpipe and nascent starfish up with her, dislodging Aiden's clinging presence as she went. His words carried a payload of subtext and none of it was appropriate given what she knew.

Thought she knew.

But, oh, my God, if she was right…

She plunged the starfish back into the reheating drum to boost its temperature and to buy herself a few moments away from him. She was used to the furnace's scorching heat, but its extremes kept him safely back.

'Can you please pass me one of the glass straws on the work table?' she asked back over her shoulder. All business.

Colour—that was what this piece needed. And space—that was what *she* needed. Adding colour to the molten piece required lots of twisting and turning and Aiden simply couldn't stand that close while she did that or she'd take his eye out with the end of her pipe.

Tash pulled the starfish out of the drum and transferred the emerging shape onto a glass rod for easier handling, and then she fired up the blowtorch and took the orange colour stick from Aiden's waiting hands. She exaggerated every movement so that he wouldn't have an opportunity to step that close again.

Lord, bad enough having him here, in her studio, watching her work, without him bringing a whole lot of *tsss* into what was already a hot enough space. Just had to stay focused.

As he'd noted, she was very determined.

He watched her in silence as she dribbled melted colour along each leg under the sear of the brace-mounted torch repeatedly, until all five legs had organic colour streaking down them. She pulled the lot away from the torch and waited the few seconds for the glass to cool enough to see the natural colours emerging.

It was so hard not to glow as bright as the sea star at the awe in Aiden's gasp. 'Cool, huh?' she said. 'Furnace-born.'

Steadfastly ignoring his closeness, she set about adding dozens of blobs to the underside of each leg and then went over the lot again, pressing an indent into each little sucker. Not perfect yet, but she was getting there.

Aiden began circling her as she worked, watching from all angles. Wherever he moved, she felt his regard despite his mask; the intensity of his stare, every bit as scorching as the heat she worked with. He reminded her of the shark again....

Circling.

Waiting.

Finally, the sea star was finished. She killed the blowtorch and the sudden silence was startling. She dropped her goggles and Aiden flipped his visor up. As she laid the starfish on the edge of her brace its legs curled and sank in a slow, descending wave exactly like the real thing—as though it really were alive—until two legs hung over the edge of the brace as it would hang over a shelf. Or a fish tank. Or a bookcase.

Just like the one she'd watched at the observatory bending around the sharp angles of the timber pier.

It wasn't the best that she'd made, but it was the best she was going to do today. The intensity of Aiden's stare, the intimacy of him watching her work...if ending that came at the price of a half-arsed starfish, then so be it. She apologised to the spirit within the glass as she gloved it carefully into the kneeling oven where it would slowly cool over the next twenty-four hours to preserve the integrity of the glass. Then she slid the heavy door closed.

And her best excuse for not facing Aiden evaporated.

'Your arms must be screaming,' he murmured, coming closer now that all the heat was safely behind asbestos doors. At least the heat from the furnace. The friction between the two of them was still creating its own blazing warmth.

'They're used to it.' She backed away a step for each one he took towards her, busying herself with removing her gloves and setting her tools back to rights. 'It's my back where I tend to feel it.'

Idiot. She'd spoken just for something to say—surely, while they were talking she couldn't be busy thinking about anything else—but he took that as encouragement and crossed to her more quickly than she could avoid.

'Here,' he said, spinning her around and tossing his safety gloves. 'Let me do something about that.'

No. No, no, no… She tried to twist out from under his strong hands as they kneaded down into her aching muscles but they were too powerful. And warm. And way too good. How often had she wished for someone to do this at the end of a long day in the hot shop? Or even a short one. His fingers probed and kneaded the worst of the developing bunches, rhythmically pressing into her and then easing off again, using the same kind of rhythm that she seduced the glass with.

Seduced…

Tash twisted away without any hope of it being subtle. 'Aiden—'

He raised his hands beside his shoulders in as non-threatening a manner as a man of his size and presence could possibly achieve. 'Tash…' he mocked.

'This is not going to happen.' It just couldn't. And wouldn't.

'You're attracted to me.'

'I'm—' *So dead.* 'No, I'm not.'

'Liar.'

Yes, more than she'd ever lied in her life. He was making her into one. '*This*—' her finger ping-ponged between his chest and hers '—is not going to happen.'

'Why not?'

Frustration roared through her. At being put in this position. 'Because I don't want it.'

'Your body disagrees, it seems.' His eyes narrowed. 'What am I missing?'

She pressed her lips together. Anything she said could be used against her in the court of Aiden.

'Am I not good-looking enough for you? Not rich enough?'

She threw him a glare. 'I'm not interested in your money or how pretty you are.' She used the word intentionally to distract him from his line of questioning. 'Give me some credit.'

'I believe you. And that intrigues me. I've never met anyone who puts so little value on the things I have to offer.'

'I'm just a challenge to you. The novelty will wear off in no time.'

His eyes darkened. 'I wish that was true. Because I'd understand that.'

Her breath tripped over itself and backed up in her throat. 'What don't you understand?'

He stepped closer. 'This hold you have over me. I'm not in the habit of begging.'

'You haven't begged.'

'Feels like I have.'

'Why, because I didn't crumble at the first sexy smile?' Damn. She hadn't meant to admit that.

If nothing else, he was a gentleman—when it counted. He didn't call her on her slip. But the intensity in his gaze doubled. 'I'm intrigued by you. I respect you. I even admire you.'

He said the words like they were anathema. 'Are those not qualities you're accustomed to in your...dates?'

His stare grew bleak. 'Not particularly. But they have pretty faces. And great bodies. And they're very...sympathetic to my way of doing things.'

His eyes grazed her.

'Maybe it's that simple, then,' she murmured, scrabbling around for a legitimate answer that didn't mean betraying anyone's trust. 'You've grown spoiled. And bored. Perhaps you're just hungering for a challenge?'

Those blue eyes narrowed. And the step he took towards her officially pushed her up against the wall of her studio.

He placed a braced fist on either side of her. 'That would explain it.'

Her hands came up to rest on his chest and his eyes flicked
down, full of speculation.

Until she pushed against him and all she could think about
was how gorgeously hard his chest was. 'Unfortunately,' she
said as she slid out from his imprisonment, 'I'm not all that
sympathetic to your cause. Certainly not enough to oblige
you.'

He shook his head. 'You will.'

The certainty made her bristle. 'Actually, I won't.'

'Why won't you?'

'Can't I just not want to?'

'If I thought you genuinely didn't want to I'd turn and walk
out right now. You do want to.'

'You're very fond of telling me what I should be thinking.'

'I just think I know you better than you do.'

'No. You're just hearing what you want to hear.' She
twisted away from him, picked up the still-hot blowpipe and
wielded it across her chest. Like a weapon. 'Now, if you don't
mind I have a lot of work to do today and I've already lost the
morning catering to the whims of my commissioning client.'

His left eye twitched but he didn't argue.

'Fair enough. I'll leave you to it.' He pulled the open visor
off his head. Sweaty hat-hair only made him look infuriat-
ingly more handsome. 'But we'll resume this conversation
tomorrow after Maxima.'

Oh, crap... *The dinner.*

A function she couldn't possibly attend anymore. Not
knowing what she now knew. Not knowing how terrible at
deterring his touches she was, how much her own body would
sabotage her best intentions. How could she sit beside him
as he slid those bedroom eyes her way and not feel what she
didn't dare feel?

Or if he touched her.

Or—her stomach knotted—tried to kiss her again.

Based on the steam in his expression right now he would do those things unless she explained. But she couldn't explain; that was for his father to do.

By the way, Aiden, you have a half-sister and she's been working with us these past weeks. Oh, and—PS—you've had your tongue in her mouth.

Surprise!

If she cancelled, she'd need a rock-solid excuse or he'd see right through it. And if she went, then the night would be full of knowing glances, the two of them against the world. Sitting pressed together. Smiling. Being delightful.

Just she and her—

Even her mind choked on the word.

—brother.

CHAPTER EIGHT

'GET DRESSED.'

The first thing Tash thought when she opened her cottage door to find Aiden leaning there, all concerned and gorgeous, was how darned edible he looked in a dinner suit. The second thing she thought was what had happened to all her self-control—and her dignity—that she couldn't even last two seconds without feeling something she shouldn't.

'I'm *sick*, Aiden,' she overcompensated.

'You're a terrible liar.'

'I told you on the phone—'

'Yeah, I know you did. That way you could hide the fact that you're pink and healthy and the least sick person I've seen all week.'

'So someone tells you they're sick and your first reaction is to go to their house and give them grief?'

He held a translucent plastic bag high. It sagged with the weight of something inside. 'No. My first reaction is to go to their house with chicken broth.'

Tash stared. He'd brought her soup.

A whole bunch more feelings she'd promised herself not to allow came rushing to the fore. She almost wished she *were* sick so that she could accept kindness from him. Instead of tossing it back in his face with her lies, which she had to do.

She crossed her arms.

'Thank you, Aiden.' He glared.

'Oh, please. You just needed an excuse to check up on me.'

'I needed you to feel better.'

Even he looked surprised at the word that slipped across his lips. *Need.* Tash forced her resolve to hold. 'Uh-huh. And that's why the first words from your mouth were "get dressed"?'

'You opened the door looking so bloody gorgeous and *not sick*. That's why I told you to get dressed. Which I notice you still aren't doing.'

'That's because I'm not going with you to dinner.'

'Why not? You gave me your word.'

Lying just sat so uncomfortably on her. She was sure it showed. 'I don't feel well. What if I'm viral? I'll give it to everyone there.'

'Instead of just me.'

'Hey, you came knocking on *my* door, remember?'

'You don't sound much like a sick person, either.'

'What do you want? A temperature reading?' Nice one. Plant the idea. He was suspicious enough to pull out a thermometer, too.

His eyes narrowed and she could practically *see* the cogs turning in his sharp mind. 'Okay, I'll come in, then. A nice night in, behind closed doors. Just you and me.'

No. That was not an option. No matter how fantastic it sounded. Because if he came into her house there was no way soup would be the only thing steaming up the place. The arms wrapped around her torso tightened. The hug helped a little, even if it was her own. Her face must have spoken volumes.

'What's going on, Tash?' He leaned on her doorframe. 'I thought you were up for this.'

'That's a little direct, isn't it?' Even for him.

'I'm talking about dinner.'

'Oh. I just—' *Oh.* 'Why don't you just go yourself?' Away. As far from her as possible would be good.

'I am going, of course. But I wasn't expecting to be dateless.'

Was that his problem? A face-saving thing? 'I'm sure you have any number of women on standby for occasions just like this one.'

'Occasions where my present date is lying through her beautiful teeth?'

She wanted to be angry but how could she? She *was* lying. 'Can't I just ask you to trust me that I have a good reason not to go?'

His eyes roamed over her face and finally settled on her eyes, curious and probing. 'Is it the dinner or the after-dinner that has you all worked up?'

'Aren't they a package?'

'No. One is not conditional on the other.'

She narrowed her eyes. 'So we could just have dinner?'

Dinner was doable. Friends had dinner all the time. Siblings had dinner all the time, too.

'We can totally just have dinner. Is that what this is about?'

This is about me not trusting myself for five minutes in your company. But she could do dinner. Dinner was just eating and talking, right? And then he'd leave her alone. Their scoresheet would be square.

She spun away, towards her bedroom. 'Give me ten minutes.'

Aiden watched the light spring of Tash's steps and then closed the front door behind him and placed the pointless soup on the nearest flat surface. Then he yanked it up again and looked for something a bit sturdier, a bit less polished timber-y. His mother's meticulous upbringing coming to the fore. She wasn't much on mess.

He crossed to the kitchen bench and set the soup there.

Then he turned and looked around Tash's house, studying the hotchpotch of items pinned to her fridge door as he went. Bills, takeaway menus, a gorgeous photo of what could only be a younger Tash with a sparkly-eyed woman. Her mother.

Her little cottage was full of modest, mass-produced furniture that would have been bland if not for the liberal addition of throws and rugs and a disparate collection of bright wall-mounted artwork. There was no particular style or artist; it was just crazy. Like the woman herself—complex, contradictory.

Confusing.

Hadn't they been on the same page on Monday? On the same page and even in the same book, and he didn't often find someone who had the same book he did. He'd been as clear as he could be, and his heart—which didn't make a habit of speeding up for just anyone—had actually lurched when she'd smiled at him and followed him so eagerly out of the underwater observatory. She'd thought she knew what they were leaving for, and she'd been comfortable with what she thought.

He'd seen it.

Yet here she was baulking—and lying, though about as miserable an attempt as anyone he'd ever met—to get out of whatever obligation she felt about what was planned for après dinner.

He eyed the one old piece of furniture in the room, an over-stuffed chair covered in an Aztec-patterned throw. That was more his size. He just about groaned as he sank down into its welcome comfort. It was a chair made for lounging in front of a game, or a long night of conversation or—he looked at the sturdy armrests—something else. All he needed was a glass of red and Tash and he was good for the evening.

Except that she'd looked almost panicked at the thought

of the two of them here alone. Ludicrous after what they'd virtually committed to earlier in the week, but there it was.

Maybe that was what was behind this fake illness.

Nerves.

Under normal circumstances, he wouldn't have had much time for indulging the modest blushes of his date, but this was different. This was Tash. He found himself prepared to indulge any of her quirks if it meant she'd let him near her. Let him touch her. So a few blushes were a no brainer. He'd pull back a little, reduce the haste and increase the flirt. Romance her. Women liked that. And Lord knew he savoured the agony of anticipation. It would make eventual success so much sweeter.

He'd once been described as 'relentless and persistent' in a protracted negotiation, but it was those qualities that eventually won the day. He literally outlasted and outgunned everyone else. The same qualities would help him now. He understood nerves—actually, he *didn't*, but he understood them in someone else—and he understood reticence. No one liked to surrender, especially not someone as spirited as Tash.

And that was pretty much what it was, wasn't it? Surrender.

He tuned in to the sounds of shuffling behind a half-closed door as Tash dressed for a dinner she didn't want to go to.

Relentless it was, then. And Tash would be his for the taking.

He almost—*almost*—regretted that. Because taken was taken and then what would sustain him if not the thrill of the chase? He knew himself well enough to know what to expect then.

Not a problem for tonight. Tonight was about the onset of the campaign.

Operation Romance.

CHAPTER NINE

HONESTLY, IF HE touched her one more time she was going to explode. And not in a good way.

Tash was certain that Aiden hadn't been this…hands-on… the other times he'd been with her, but it was hard to stay certain when every brush clouded her memory, every light pressure from those strong fingers muddled her mind. Or, worse, the times he *didn't* touch her, but came within infuriating millimetres and then all she could think about was whether he was going to make contact again.

Dreading that moment.

Wanting that moment.

It had taken her about twenty-five seconds behind her bedroom door to come up with a plan to get through the evening. A great mental filing system that would give her some way of managing the feelings that had started swilling through her blood as soon as she opened the door to see him leaning there, waving the ridiculous bag of soup.

Two mental folders: one marked 'brother' and one marked 'other'.

All the qualities that she could appreciate and enjoy about Aiden in a safe, appropriate way went in the folder marked 'brother'. Admiration for his professional aptitude, appreciation of his dry sense of humour, fascination with how he worked individuals and a whole room at the same time…

They were all perfectly wholesome things to appreciate about a sibling.

But all those less-than-wholesome feelings—the ripple of goose flesh at his touch, the tightening of her chest at his glance, the catch of her breath when he smiled, the screaming desire to get closer to him, the awful, awful *want*...

Those things went in the file marked 'other'. Not to be opened for fifty years.

It worked for about an hour.

The touching had started on the front stairs of her veranda—a gentle, scorching hand at her lower back as he directed her to his car. Then the brush of his body as he needlessly reached across her to fix her seat belt in place. Then his knuckles—curled around the gear stick of his expensive car—that somehow managed to brush the tight fabric of her skirt every time they shifted gear.

So that by the time they arrived at the restaurant, the 'other' folder was already bulging.

Then came the conversation—so witty and attentive and damned *interested* in whatever she was saying. Her Achilles heel after a father like Eric—who just wasn't interested, ever—and a boyfriend like Kyle, who struggled to fully attend to anything that didn't involve him. Those things were okay to go in the 'brother' folder, but the deep, golden glow of appreciation that started to form certainly wasn't. It was too dangerous.

She shook the 'other' folder to make some room and she shoved that in deep.

Distracting herself with exchanges with the dinner guests was a great strategy, except that she then became disturbingly conscious of his eyes on her when she was speaking with his colleagues. A cautious glance at first, then curious to see how she handled herself, then quietly pleased. And

pleasing him had her shaking that 'other' folder again to settle the contents lower.

She rolled tight shoulders. 'Must you stare at me so relent-
lessly?' she muttered sideways at him.

Something in what she said made his eyes crease and twinkle. 'Sorry, I'm just enjoying watching you ignoring me.'

That brought her glance back to his and she realised it
had been a long time since she'd let them make contact. 'I'm
schmoozing with your colleagues,' she said under her breath.
'Isn't that what I'm here for?'

He grew serious yet flirty at the same time. How was that
possible?

'It is. I'm not complaining.'

No. He was just locking those bedroom eyes on her and
making the 'other' folder impossible to squeeze the lid shut
on. She glanced around for a distraction but everyone else in
the room was otherwise engaged.

No rescue there.

'Why don't we sit?' Aiden indicated a vacant double-seater
in the lounge part of the restaurant.

It wasn't tiny, but a three-seater would have been more to
her liking. She sank into one side, as far over as she could
go, and cupped her drink. When Aiden sat, the entire sus-
pension of the sofa seemed to change, and she immediately
felt the slight lean of her body towards his.

As if she needed gravity's interference. She forced herself upright.

'Can I ask you about your mother?' he asked.

That brought her focus quickly back to his. 'Here?'

'You don't have to be on the job all night. I thought you
might enjoy talking about her.'

Oh. That was sweet. Her mother was so central to the difficulties between them; she was the one person they could

almost never talk about. But licence was almost crippling. 'We talk about her all the time.'

'No. We talk about *them*. What was she like? Specifically.'

It was easy to smile. Answering would have been easy, too, but Aiden wasn't asking lightly. Part of her was vaguely disturbed that he was asking at all; it seemed like strangely intimate territory for them, given what a careful line she wanted to tread. But another part of her hungered to have a normal conversation with him. Just like a regular couple—

She kicked herself mentally.

—of siblings.

'She was like me. Optimistic, perfectionist, imperfect but accepting of her own flaws and doing the best she could.'

'She must have been proud of the woman you grew into.'

Her whole body softened at the memories of the pride in her mother's eyes the first time she sold a piece. 'She was, mostly. She loved my work.'

'Mostly?'

'She wasn't thrilled with my...relationship choices.' And how she would have turned in her grave as she and someone as risky as Aiden started to get closer. 'But she recognised that I had to learn through experience. Like she did.'

It was the closest they'd come to talking about her mother and his father. As close as they'd get tonight.

'Are we talking about Jardine?'

'Mum never liked him.'

'No one likes him. Except him.'

She sat up straighter. 'He wasn't always like he is now.'

'You're defending him?'

Tash frowned. 'I think I'm defending me. Because I chose to be with him, so it reflects on me. He wasn't an ass then.'

'You just turned him into one?'

'Not intentionally.' She laughed. 'But I definitely think our relationship wasn't good for him.'

That caused his eyes to narrow a fraction. 'Why not?'

She hesitated. Just because she'd rationalised their breakup to herself didn't make her right. Her hair tickled her cheeks as she shook her head. 'I don't want you to think I'm a narcissist.'

'Why would I think that?'

She took a breath. Went for it. 'I think he was threatened by me.'

That didn't even surprise him. He nodded. 'By your success?'

'That, and…other things.'

Aiden frowned.

Oh, God, how had they arrived here? Weren't they talking about her mother just a moment ago? A warm, fuzzy, safe topic?

'We weren't all that compatible.' Tash leaned heavily enough on the last word to break it.

Again, with the blank stare. Until suddenly it wasn't blank at all. Blue eyes widened. 'Right! *Compatible.*' His lips split to reveal even white teeth. 'So Jardine is a lousy lay? That's priceless.'

'Why would you assume it's Kyle?'

'Because it's you—' the warm glow rushed in again until she batted it away with the entire crowded folder marked 'other' '—and because he told me you were a dynamo in the sack.'

The glow all but shattered, it froze so fast. 'He what?'

'Don't get angry. It was all bluster.'

'What the hell were the two of you doing having a conversation about my sexual performance in the first place?'

His hands rose in front of him as if he could physically lower the volume with which her words had erupted from her lips. He glanced around to ensure they hadn't been overheard. 'It was an introductory monologue more than a conversation and it told me more about Jardine than it did about you.'

'Except that I'm a *dynamo*.'

He slouched back against the sofa back. 'Actually "cracker" was the word he used. You should be flattered.'

'Well, I'm not.' She could totally imagine the tone with which he'd said it. It was too close to the old hurts at Kyle's hands. The implication that she was somehow aberrant.

Broken.

But she could hardly cast stones since she'd just volunteered how beige Kyle was in bed. 'I think it's time for a subject change.'

The smile didn't leave Aiden's eyes, but a curious spark formed there. Thankfully, he let it go. 'We were talking about your mother. She didn't like Kyle,' he reminded her.

'She thought he put me down to make himself feel a bigger man.'

Aiden's lips pressed tight. 'I concur with her assessment. It surprises me that you would have put up with that. You don't strike me as the type to let anyone get the better of you.'

She shrugged. 'I'm slow to learn but I get there eventually. I watched my father do the same thing to my mother and then I went out and found a man just like him.' She shook her head. 'She was delighted when I broke it off with Kyle.'

'Why did you, finally?'

'I grew up. Expected more.' Hoped for more, anyway.

His eyes took on a molten sheen. He leaned closer. 'What do you expect from a man?'

Someone who would treat her like an equal. A man who got satisfaction from watching her be the best she could be, not by trying to make her who he wanted her to be. A man who treated her as if she had value outside what she could bring him. And a man who would not blanch if she stepped out of the bathroom in something risqué.

A grown-up, in other words.

But, no. Those were not thoughts she could express aloud.

She'd shared quite enough for one evening. Especially with this man. He was just as likely to take anything she said as a job description.

And, regardless of whether or not he fitted the criteria, there was no way he was now suitable for the job.

'I expect a man who wouldn't leave his date thirsty and empty-handed,' she hedged, looking pointedly at her fingers.

Aiden smiled. 'Don't move.'

She took three long breaths in and exhaled just as slowly. She wasn't thirsty and she didn't want a drink. What she wanted was the few precious moments his departure in the direction of the restaurant's bar bought her.

'Brother' and *'other'* she repeated in her head like a mantra.

She just had to keep her filing system going. And keep him at arm's length.

She wiped her damp palms on a restaurant napkin and curled it into a ball in her fist. Perhaps the best way to force some distance between them was to give him a return dose of the Spanish Inquisition. She had a question about him for every one he had for her. There were still lots of blanks about Aiden Moore that she'd like to see filled in. In a perfect world.

Which this wasn't.

In this flawed world, she was going to have to confront Nathaniel with her suspicions and he was going to tell Aiden that they shared genetic material. And that would be that. They'd be relegated to the polite exchange of cards at Christmas and nods across crowded parties. Because there was no way the bastard child of Nathaniel Moore would be accepted into the perfect Moore family.

Which was probably just as well, because if tonight was any indication then the only thing that was going to convince her body that Aiden was now hands-off was distance. And lots of it.

Even now, she had to concentrate to keep her heartbeat regular as he headed back across the room towards her. His suit looked even better on him from a distance. Fitted and flattering. All shoulders and lean waist. He moved like a thoroughbred.

'When is your father back?' she asked the moment Aiden returned, to keep the topic from swinging back to where they'd left it. All the relaxation fled from Aiden's body.

'His flight landed this afternoon. Back at work on Monday,' he said, sitting stiffly.

'How was their trip?'

His lips flat lined and her heart squeezed to see him swallow the pain. 'Not terribly beneficial.'

'Things are no better between them?'

'This wasn't a disagreement about finances or what colour to paint the living room, Tash. He went behind her back in seeing the daughter of a woman he'd once had an affair with and that was just too close to what he did once before.'

She softened her words to minimise the impact. 'Do you think it would have made a difference if he'd been up front with her?'

That brilliant mind turned over—and over—behind his eyes, and his response was more sigh than sentence. 'No. The hurt is in the act.' His brows dropped. 'But it's amplified by the cover-up.'

Would Laura feel any differently if she discovered it was his *daughter* he was secretly seeing? Maybe she might find it easier to forgive that? And maybe sea stars would fly.

'Better that they deal with the underlying issues, though, right?'

His eyes pierced her. 'What underlying issues?'

She regarded him steadily, welcoming the emotional gulf opening up between them. Yes, that was what they needed. Emotional distance. 'All families have underlying issues. As upsetting as this was for your mother, chances are there's other stuff going on that's really at the bottom of all of this.'

Hint hint...

'My father's poor decision-making is what's at the bottom of this.'

'Perhaps.'

His hiss was a little too loud for this refined restaurant. 'Are you a card-carrying member of the mutual admiration society, Tash?'

It was only the defensiveness in his voice that stopped hers from rising. He was particularly touchy about his mother. But it came from a very fundamental place. 'I just think you're very quick to blame him.'

'And you're very quick to defend him. And your own mother. Which only leaves one person by implication and she's the only innocent one of the lot.'

Laura Moore, innocent? The woman who stole her best friend's man at the first opportunity? Tash picked her words as carefully as if she were collecting berries from a cactus field. 'I'm not blaming your mother. I'm just suggesting that this issue might be the trigger, but it's not necessarily what the troubles between them are all about.'

'Who says there are troubles?'

She lifted one brow. 'Aiden. He had an affair.' *With his first love.* 'There must be troubles.'

'That was twenty years ago.'

'My mother died still loving him.'

'That's sad for her.'

The speed of his comeback was disturbing. And telling. But, no, she wasn't going to let him do this any longer. She needed him to pull his head out of the sand and start putting the puzzle together, and if she couldn't do it for him without breaching Nathaniel's trust then she'd have to lay out some serious breadcrumbs.

'He left her a message on her cell phone just a few months ago for what should have been her fiftieth birthday. So clearly she was still very much on his mind.'

That stopped him flat. His mind was fast enough to realise what that meant. He shook his head. 'He gave Mum his word he'd never see her again.'

'He honoured that. He didn't even go to her funeral.' Her voice cracked just slightly on that and Aiden curled his fingers around hers. She extracted them just a moment later by changing her still-full drink into the other hand. 'Since we're talking about mothers, tell me about yours. What is it about her that you love so much?'

His face grew blank. 'She's my mother.'

'You defend her so fiercely. That's very telling.'

'She's my mother,' he repeated, slower for the cognitively challenged. But then he deigned to elaborate. 'She was always there for me when my father was working. Taking me to school, making my lunches, salving my wounds, mixing with my friends' mothers, which helped me to fit in, volunteering in class.'

Something inside her squeezed. 'You didn't fit in at school? Did you struggle making friends?'

'On the contrary.' She thought that was going to be it, but then he surprised her with a rare moment of candour. 'But I struggled keeping them.'

She didn't find that hard to picture. He would have been charismatic even as a boy, but his high expectations when it came to others must have meant constant disappointment in the friend department.

'I was seven when the whole Moore v. Porter thing began, so I grew up knowing something bad happened, and it happened because of my father.' His eyes beseeched her. 'But it happened *to* my mother, you know?'

Laura—always the victim…despite getting her man, and a

beautiful son, and the luxurious lifestyle and everything that brought with it. But Tash forced herself to be charitable. 'It's right that you love her so much—'

'Thanks for the permission.'

'—but you're also an adult, so you should be able to look at both of them with adult eyes.'

The eyes in question narrowed. 'What is it that you think I'm not seeing?'

Uh-oh. One breadcrumb too many. 'Just…there's always more to the story.'

He stared so long and so hard she wondered if things were about to turn dangerous. But then his brows folded—just a hint—and the cogs started turning behind his eyes. 'I'll keep that in mind. Right now, I wouldn't mind hearing more of the story we were just discussing. Your story.'

Instantly her body tightened up as her mind shut down.

'My story is not all that exciting.'

'Only child, estranged from asshole dad, dumps jerk boyfriend and loses beloved mother in the space of a couple of years. So who does Natasha Sinclair turn to when things get bad?'

Tash pressed back into the sofa back. 'She turns inward. Finds the strength in herself.'

'That's very Zen of you.'

'It's also true.' She chuckled. 'Though I will admit to asking myself what Mum would do in situations I can't handle.'

He shifted only slightly but it seemed to bring him—and his mesmerising lips—much closer. 'I can't imagine there's anything you can't handle.'

Dangerously close. But she worked around the danger as best she could. 'You might be surprised. Situations where I only have two choices and both of them are bad.'

'Bad for whom?'

'For the people involved. Bad for me.'

'And what do you do then?'

'I just navigate my way through it.'

'You don't ever want to just offload on someone? Share the burdens of life?'

Oh, my God…did she ever. She used to do that with her mum. 'That would be a bad reason to commence a relationship. Just to have someone to decompress with.'

His lips twisted. 'There are worse reasons.'

'What do you know about sharing?' she asked, her curiosity well and truly piqued by the strangeness of his expression. 'You're the most island-like of men that I know.'

'We were talking about you.'

'We might as well have been talking about you; we're quite similar,' she mused.

Without warning, he reached out and caressed a single lock of her hair with his index finger. Tash forced herself not to flinch. 'We are. I've noticed that. Not in the detail, but in the essential things.'

There's a reason we're so similar, she wanted to scream. Instead, she leaned forward and placed her glass on the small table in front of their sofa, subtly dislodging his touch. Or at least effectively. 'I have my aunt Karen. And friends.'

'You have friends?'

Her laugh was immediate. 'Of course I do. Did you imagine I just inflate a few minutes before you walk in the room? I have a lot of art friends, and a couple of school friends I'm still close to.'

'Why don't you ever talk about them?'

'Because we don't talk about ordinary things like friends. We only talk about safe things.' Or dangerous things.

'We talked tonight.'

Yes, and the timing was exquisite irony. 'Even that had an agenda.'

'What agenda?'

'You're buttering me up. Making up for bringing me out this evening.'

'From your deathbed?'

'Okay, I possibly wasn't as sick as I made out, but this has hardly been casual conversation. Are you trying to lull me into a false sense of security?'

His eyes grew serious. 'I'm trying to get to know you, Tash.'

'In Braille?' He had to know all that touching was getting heavy-handed.

A tiny splotch of red appeared halfway up his tanned throat. 'Was it that bad?'

'It's not *bad*.' Though it couldn't be good, now. 'It's just obvious.'

'I confess I'm not usually in this position.' The words were grudging and Tash got the sense that they'd never crossed his lips before. 'Having to work at keeping the conversation going. The women I date usually take care of the chat. Or they just don't bother.'

Her chest squeezed. 'Is this a date?'

'I don't know what this is. It's a mystery.'

It grew impossible to remember the difference between the two folders. 'A pleasing mystery or a count-the-minutes-until-it's-over mystery?' she breathed, hypnotised by the way his eyes turned smoky.

'Do you see me looking at my watch?'

'Consider me an education, then. Maybe this is how the real people do it.'

'As opposed to the fake people?'

'You're not fake, you just don't move on the same plane as everyone else. Or by the same rules.'

'And you don't like that?'

She couldn't afford to. 'I do like that, actually. But I don't trust it.'

'You mean you don't trust *me*.'

'I don't trust anyone.'

'Why not?'

'Experience. But I trust you more than most, so that's something.'

'You trusted me the other day, lying on the edge of the water.'

It was impossible not to be honest with him. Despite the 'other' folder. That day was one of the nicest she'd had in ages. 'I saw the real you that day.'

'Did you like what you saw?'

It was there, sheltering right at the back of his eyes behind all the arrogance.

Uncertainty.

But she wasn't about to kick a man on his way to being down. Besides, hope had a place in both folders. And she was the first to acknowledge that even the perpetually positive had their demons. 'You are an amazing man, Aiden Moore. Handsome and rich and available.' *Until the next sure thing came along.* 'I'd be a fool not to recognise it.'

His eyes narrowed.

'But I like you best when you're not trying so hard. When I don't feel like part of the latest angle you're playing. Or, worse, part of some kind of set-up I don't yet understand.'

His long, silent stare graduated into a slow, appreciative nod. 'I'm amazed Jardine came away able to function at all. I would have expected that kind of insight to neuter a man like him.'

Her breath twisted into a painful ball in her chest. But he saw the flare of her nostrils and hurried to continue. 'Don't get me wrong. That's very definitely his failing, not yours. You've said nothing that isn't true—to my shame—and you said it very carefully. But it's not an easy thing being so transparent when you're more accustomed to obsequiousness.'

Tash curled her fingers into her lap. 'If I had such great insight then I should know what this play is.' But she didn't. What was he doing now? 'I can't read you.'

'Maybe because I'm being genuine. I *was* playing you this evening. I wanted to stroke you into submission, ease the nerves I assumed you were feeling.'

'Feeling about what?'

'About us. Tonight. About where we were going. But that was just wishful thinking on my part. We weren't going there at all, were we?'

She stared at him and gave two answers. One for each folder.

'No. But that's not to say I haven't enjoyed your company or our conversation.' That was for the potential brother she didn't want to wound. 'And it's not to say I mightn't have chosen differently earlier in the week.' And that was because she had to be true to herself. Although she protected herself by being safely cryptic.

'You want the bad news?' Aiden said after a long, awkward silence. Tash shrugged. 'This candour isn't making me want you any less.'

He couldn't want her. It was that simple. If—no, when!—he found out why, he'd look back at all these moments with humiliated fury. But he didn't have to remember her making it worse. Or making a scene.

She flattened her skirt and stood decisively. 'Apparently unattainability is part of my charm.'

He joined her on his feet. 'You think you're charming? That's sweet.'

It was still flirting, but everything had shifted gear these past few minutes. Into safer territory. As if the shark were increasing the diameter of its circles. Giving her room to breathe. Respectful, kind room.

'You know what else is sweet?' he murmured, guiding her to rejoin the other guests.

She cast him a curious look.

'You think this is over, too.'

This *was* over. It had to be. Otherwise the hurt was going to be too profound.

Tash glanced at her watch. Ten o'clock. She spun on him. 'You said your father got back today?'

'Back at work Monday.'

'We need to see him.'

That stopped him in his tracks. 'What?'

'We need to speak with your father. Now.'

'Why?'

'When we speak to him, you'll understand. This has gone on long enough.' She gathered her handbag closer to her—like armour—shaking but determined. 'Can you call him?'

'Are you okay, Tash? You've lost all your colour. Please don't tell me you were sick all along....'

'I'm fine.'

'Maybe I should take you home—'

'Call your father, Aiden. Get him to meet us at MooreCo.' The offices would be abandoned this time on a Friday night. They'd have total privacy.

He reached for his phone. 'Tash. What's going on?'

'I'll explain when we get there.' She took his arm a smidge more forcefully than she meant and steered him towards the door. 'Come on.'

Time to end this.

CHAPTER TEN

'I'M WHAT?'

Aiden's incredulous rasp cut across the top of Nathaniel's astonished gasp. 'Tash—'

'Half-brother, really,' she rushed, holding Aiden's blue eyes. It was hard to tell which man was the palest.

'Natasha—' Nathaniel croaked.

She turned to him. 'I'm sorry if this makes things more difficult for you, Nathaniel. But he had to know.'

Nathaniel's eyes dropped and he murmured, 'Oh, God...'

'Do you have any idea what it was like for me, growing up with him?' she begged, unable to hold it in any longer. 'Believing my own father hated me?' Yet that thought was painfully validating. She'd never believed that a true father could possibly loathe his own offspring. It had to be biologically impossible. 'And all along...'

She didn't need to finish. She needed to stop talking, let the men process.

Aiden's horrified stare moved between the two of them, but his accusations finally landed on his father. 'Your affair started before I was even born?'

Tash's breath puffed out of her in an angry hiss. 'Seriously? That's what you're taking from this?'

I'm your sister!

'It wasn't an affair then,' Nathaniel defended, his focus entirely on Aiden.

'Semantics,' Aiden barked.

Nathaniel's mouth flattened in a way that was so like his son's. 'No. Not when you're casting judgement as you are. Your mother and I had parted when I got back together with Adele.'

'After you got Mum pregnant?'

'Yes, as it turns out.'

'And then you got Porter pregnant, too?' Aiden cut in.

Nathaniel paused, and then turned to Tash, his eyes full of grief. 'No.'

'Yes!'

He curled a creased hand around her wrist and just held it. As if his skin over her pulse would help lessen the impact of what he was saying. 'No, Tash. I am not your father.'

Grief such as she hadn't felt since losing her mother welled up and voiced in her croak. 'Yes…you are.'

He didn't deny it again, he just slid his fingers lower, to thread through hers.

'You were together,' she wobbled. 'You slept with Laura to get back at Mum. You were angry at her.'

Aiden's gasp was audible. 'Is that true?' He came around to Tash's other side so he could see his father's face.

Nathaniel's eyes fell shut. 'It's true. Adele and I had fought and I went with Laura to get back at her. To make a point.'

Aiden's entire body froze up.

'But then you were with her again,' Tash urged. 'After Laura.'

'Yes, but we never…' Nathaniel took a long deep breath. 'We were never together, Tash. Physically.'

Aiden snorted.

Nathaniel rounded on him. 'Well might you scoff, Aiden. With the choices you make and the women you seek out, it wouldn't occur to you that two people could be desperately in love and never consummate it.'

'Bull.'

'Not everyone lives their life quite as fast as you do, son.' Then he turned away again, dismissing his own flesh, and focused on Tash. 'Your mother was wild and crazy in some ways, but she was traditional in one way that really counted.'

'You never slept together?' Tash croaked.

'It's why we broke up in the first place.'

Tash lifted her lashes. Her eyes burned with unshed tears. 'Because she wouldn't sleep with you?'

Shame etched into his handsome features. 'I was young. Stupid. And I made a beeline for the first person I knew would. To hurt Adele as much as I was hurting.'

'You son of a bitch.' The insult spewed from Aiden and Nathaniel spun on him again.

'You know what, son? I've lived with your judgement for twenty years. From the moment you got old enough to form an opinion, you've held one of me—a bad one—without knowing any of the facts. I've let that ride *because* you didn't have the facts and because I could see how much validation you got from being your mother's champion and how much of *her* world revolved around your good opinion. But I've more than done my time. I walked away from the woman I loved to do the right thing by your mother when I got her pregnant. I stood by her even knowing that she—'

The sudden silence drew Tash's eyes up again.

'Even knowing what?'

Nathaniel's lips pressed impossibly harder. 'Even knowing that I'd never see Adele again.'

'Why did you?'

'Because whatever I chose I was going to ruin someone's life. It might as well have been my own.'

Aiden blanched as pale as the ivory trim of his expensive tie. He flopped into the nearest chair. 'Right.'

'No,' Nathaniel sighed, seeing immediately which way Aiden's mind was going. 'I never blamed you and I never felt that way about you. I had a *son*, the only consolation in an otherwise miserable period. But choosing your mother over Adele had nothing to do with my feelings for her and everything to do with penance for what a bastard I'd been, pressuring Adele for more than she was ready for.'

'Does Laura know?' Tash whispered, her first pang of sympathy for her mother's rival.

'She knew in her heart at the time. And she knew for sure after…' His eyes found the horizon out of the window. 'But I'd never fully committed to her until the truth was exposed.'

'Why didn't you go with Mum when she was finally free?'

His hands rose to his side and then fell, defeated. 'Because I'd committed to Laura. And I realised I'd kept her in stasis for eight years. I couldn't then abandon her.'

'A bit late for chivalry, wasn't it?' Aiden snorted, and his father locked eyes with him.

'I chose your mother, Aiden. Freely. Twice. But I will not lie to you that I loved her the way I loved Tash's mother. Adele Porter was—and will always be—my heart.'

Nathaniel's voice cracked and Tash's tears spilled over. It took them both a moment to get their emotion under control.

'Think it through, Tash,' Nathaniel said gently, stroking her hair. 'Adele would have told you, if she thought you were mine. Before she died. Wouldn't she?'

The sense of that filtered through her confusion. Yeah. She would have. She had a long, lingering death to share the most important information in the world. A detail like that would certainly have qualified.

But she wasn't ready to nod. Not just yet. She was still grieving.

'I would be the proudest man on earth to say I was the father to two such amazing children and I would have given anything to know that my child was growing in Adele's body. And to have saved you the misery of your childhood with Eric.' He bent to engage her lowered eyes. 'But I give you my absolute word, we never had sex and so you cannot be mine.'

There really was no doubt in his tone. No room for misunderstanding. But still she hoped in a tiny voice, 'But we're so similar.'

'We are. I've noticed it too. I wonder whether it's your mother's traits you have and maybe she picked some of them up from me all those years ago.'

'I have your eyes.' Desperation was such a terrible optimist.

His laugh was gentle. 'You have *brown* eyes, Tash. Along with half the planet. Including your aunt Karen, if I remember rightly.'

She made a desperate, final-ditch plea. 'You warned me off Aiden...'

'Because he's so damaged—'

'Hey!' Aiden's head snapped up from where he was lost in the plush carpet at their feet.

'I would give my life for yours, son, but you're the product of my dysfunctional relationship with your mother. You learned your values about love and trust from a very imperfect example. I see the legacy of that every single day.'

Aiden's nostrils flared, but respect kept him silent.

'I so wanted to be your daughter,' Tash whispered.

He turned back to her. Pulled her to him, right up into his shoulder, and murmured, 'I know.'

'But I was torn,' she whispered against his ear. 'Because of Aiden.'

His arms tightened. 'Please be careful, Tash.'

She let his words sink in. She thought back to her own

family, how much damage her parents' dysfunctional relationship had done. But how much more might have been done if they had stayed together. And Aiden had grown up in that environment. Long, impressionable years. Empathy washed through her.

She pulled back. 'Thank you for validating her,' she murmured.

'I wish it could have been more.'

Aiden pushed to his feet. 'I need to…some air. I'm going home.'

'You're my ride,' she stammered, needing escape but needing to not be alone just yet. And more than a little bit worried for Aiden. This was all a massive shock to him, once again.

'I'll work with Max to cover your appointments,' Nathaniel volunteered, concerned brown eyes on his son. 'Take a few days off.'

Aiden spun back and if he was going to say something sharper, he changed his mind. 'Thank you,' he simply murmured instead.

'You're welcome.'

God, so painfully polite. She thought back to all those altercations with her cold, cutting father the few times she'd had to see him as an adult. Moments rather like this one.

'Are you okay?' she asked Aiden as they waited for the elevator, wanting to touch him but not daring.

He didn't even look at her. 'My head feels like it's going to explode.'

'It's a lot to take in.'

'I'm not sure who I feel more betrayed by—him or you.'

She turned to him. 'How could I tell you? It had to be him.'

'You've known all week. This is why you were so weird about the party.'

'I suspected.'

'You thought I was your *brother*. What the hell were you doing coming out with me at all?'

'You came to my house.'

'You should have just told me to hit the road.'

'I'm not very skilled in that kind of brush-off, strange as it might seem to you. I handled it as best I could under the circumstances.'

Surely, he couldn't fail to remember the many different ways she'd kept him at arm's length.

'Must have been highly entertaining for you to watch me hitting on my own sister.'

That would have stung if she'd thought for a moment he meant it. 'It was awful. I wanted to tell you, I wanted to share the information and the anxiety and have someone I could talk to about it. I thought I had a whole other family.' Her voice tightened. 'I was so excited.'

And yet dreading it at the same time because of what it meant for them.

His eyes slid down to hers. Softened. 'But you don't.'

Her heart sank. 'No. I'm back to being alone.'

Aiden considered his words. 'I saw the way my father just was with you. Whatever happens I don't think you'll be alone. If he could have fathered you I know he would have.'

Tash concentrated on the changing elevator numbers above them, blinking back moisture. Had they always moved this slowly?

'You're lucky, you know,' she eventually said. 'To have him.'

'Really? A workaholic adulterer incapable of loving the mother of his child?'

Pain seeped from his words. 'I'm not saying it's not a tragedy. But he's a good man, no matter what he's done in the past. He saved my mother's life. And mine, probably. And he did the right thing by Laura. Twice.'

'It's good to see that you have such a strong streak for forgiveness. You might even be able to see past *my* apparently numerous imperfections.'

'He loves you, Aiden. He's just worried for you.'

His dark head shook.

'We wouldn't be human if we didn't have flaws, Aiden.'

'Really?' He rounded on her. 'What are yours?'

Tash shrugged. 'I say what I think way too readily. I believe in the best in others even after I've experienced their worst.'

'Is that a polite way of saying you're gullible?'

'I mean for a girl who had my upbringing I'm surprisingly fast to trust.'

His snort echoed around the large, empty parking floor as they stepped out into it. 'You must be joking.'

'What?'

'It took me weeks to earn your trust. I consider it somewhat of a milestone the day I did.'

'What day was that?'

'The paddle boats. So it was a short honeymoon.'

'Perhaps some people just shouldn't be trusted.'

His tight lips split into a wolfish smile. 'Oh, honey… Truer words have never been spoken.'

They fell to silence for the bulk of the journey back to her cottage, his eyes grazing her periodically.

'You realise what today means?' he finally said, pulling into her street.

She dragged her eyes back from faraway thoughts. 'That I'm not the bastard child of a good man.' She was just the good child of a bastard.

His eyes shimmered for a half-breath, compassionate and understanding, but then he pulled up outside her gate, turned sideways on his luxury leather seat and faced her fully. 'Today means we're not related. Today means there's no reason we can't be together. Unless you have another hurdle queued up for me.'

'I didn't set this one up, intentionally.'

'It was convenient though, wasn't it? To keep me at a safe distance. What will keep you safe now?'

She stared at him. 'That's the thing, Aiden. I do feel safe with you.'

'You did say you were too quick to trust.'

The laugh burst out of her, reluctant and grudging. 'Your idea of flirting is kind of screwy.'

He slid an arm across behind her seat. 'This isn't flirting, honey. It's foreplay.'

And that was working, too. The whole bad-boy-with-prom-ise-in-his-eye thing had her pulse racing and her palms damp-ening. And it was impossible to forget that she'd got one secret wish even while being denied the other.

Aiden was not her brother. No shared DNA.

She practically tumbled out of the car and up her short garden path. Aiden followed her up the couple of steps to her house. At the door, she unlocked it and then turned to face him. 'Thank you for the ride.'

He lifted one brow. 'I'm coming in.'

Her breath tightened up in her chest. 'I thought you wanted some thinking space.'

'Change of plans. I have no interest in thinking about any of it. Not right now.'

'You can't just avoid it.'

'Yeah, I can.' He pressed her back against the door and whispered against her lips just before his touched hers. 'Watch me.'

His lips descending towards hers were like a homecom-ing. She'd wanted this—and loathed herself because of it. Her body clearly knew the truth even as her mind couldn't accept it. But now there *was* nothing standing in the way of the kiss she wasn't even trying to run from.

Her lungs inflated just as he sealed her mouth with his, the soft, firm, heavenly pressure causing a riot in her nerve endings. The warmth of his skin against hers, the tickle of his breath and the pressure of his arms as they circled behind her. The firm press of hard body against soft.

And the insane explosion of the chemistry that zinged between them. It surged through her system, triumphant at finally being able to express itself, and pooled in her lower half, robbing her legs of strength. She twisted her arms up around the neck she had no good reason not to twist around, and kissed the lips that she had no good reason not to kiss.

And she was lost—the moment she tasted him.

The moment she felt his tongue and lips lapping against her own, exploring and teasing. Her body rejoiced at being back in his arms again; this man she'd believed she'd never be able to look in the eye, let alone kiss.

Her head actually spun with all the blood rushing to it and away again.

'Inside,' he mumbled against her lips.

His arm at her waist released her long enough to fumble around behind her lower back, before tightening again and supporting her as the door swung inwards.

She stumbled back into her own living room, shunted by the steam engine that was Aiden, and he kicked the door shut behind them. Every part of her wanted to launch at him, to press him back against the wall and climb all over him. But old fear held her back, and she waited to see what his next move would be. But not for long. As soon as the door clicked into place he forked his long fingers into her hair, pulling it back from the feverish face he framed between his palms. He stared into her eyes, one thumb sliding over to make sure her lips didn't get lonely as he spoke. 'I've wanted this since we met.'

'So, not just physical, then?' she breathed, amazed that a coherent thought could form, let alone a facetious one. Then she bit into the soft pad of his thumb—unable to ignore it any longer—and he pressed the advantage, sliding it into her mouth and out again as his lips returned.

'Minx.' He kissed her, long, hard and drugged. 'If it was just physical it would have been much easier to ignore.'

The implication provoked her but she wasn't about to indulge it. 'You don't strike me as a man accustomed to self-deprivation.'

Yep. Because this was the right time for conversation. But if she didn't ease back on the throttle this was going to go a little bit too fast and a little bit too furious. And—though she'd longed for something faster and more furious than Kyle and though the promise of Aiden's strength spiced her blood—she wanted to savour every moment. In case they were the only moments she ever got.

He tugged on her hair enough to expose the long line of her throat and he murmured into her skin, 'Just one of my many depravations.'

She laughed gently at the wordplay. 'Oh, really? What are some others?'

He smiled against her flesh and moved his lips to her ear, hot and seductive. 'We have all night for those.'

And then his hands left her hair and made their way down her body, stroking and exciting her nerve endings as they went. Every man she'd ever been with had had a heavy touch—demanding, rushed, or clumsy. But Aiden traced the lines of her body as if it were one of her own artworks, discovering her, savouring. Then he took her hands and pinned them behind her body, which he pressed against hard, holding her captive.

The contrast between his feather-light touch and his sheer command boiled her blood even more. She'd had a taste of his strength in the coatroom, and she'd liked it. And she'd wanted to match it. But it wouldn't be the first time she'd misread someone's intent. It was too easy to remember Kyle's shock when she'd stepped up to the sensual challenge *he'd* posed and then quailed when she'd taken the cue.

Literally quailed. He'd scrabbled backwards from her in his expensive, overly stuffed bed, flushed and uncomfortable, and been sure to dominate any encounter the two of them ever had after that. Not in a good way. In an afraid-of-your-own shadow kind of way. And that was *not* sexy. It had made her feel dirty and ashamed for rising so enthusiastically to meet Kyle's sexual bravado that had turned out to be all show.

As if she needed any help with shame.

But Aiden wasn't Kyle. Far from it. The signals he was sending seemed crystal in their clearness and unshakeable in intent. And he'd spoken before of liking a woman who was bold.

Lord knew she hungered to be bold.

Dare she take this chance? Was that the kind of bold he was really looking for? Someone who took the initiative?

She forced strength into the arms pinned behind her back and circled them up above her head and then back down in front of her. Aiden immediately eased his weight back, letting her escape, but as she brought them back down she shoved him clean in the middle of his chest.

Hard.

He regained his footing against the door, panting, watching her intently. She stood, chest heaving, desperately trying to read his closed expression, and then she did exactly what she'd wanted to since he first stood in the doorway to her workshop, judging her. She pursued him to the wall, pushed him back against it with a thud and tore his shirt open, buttons pinging everywhere.

Outing herself in as graphic a fashion as she could possibly have *not* wanted to do.

It was the inwards suck of breath that drew her eyes up to his. She hoped it would be surprise and not shock, not dismay. Definitely not anxiety. But she didn't expect to see the roasting glow of unfettered desire as he challenged, 'You owe me a shirt.'

No judgement. No distaste. Just...*want*.

The push of his strong shoulder muscles against the wall was enough to propel them both into the centre of the room, towards the sofa that divided the open space into two parts. As the back of Tash's thighs hit the upholstered rear of the sofa, she braced herself on its top and met the furious kiss that Aiden meted out.

Met it and matched it.

She curled her fingers into the destroyed remains of his shirt and pulled him towards her, bending backwards over the furniture. One masculine hand stabilised next to her hip and the other fisted in her hair, and he resisted long enough to stare hotly into her eyes.

'You want to drive?' he questioned softly.

Her heart hammered so hard it was almost pain, but she embraced even that.

This was it. The defining moment she'd always hoped for. A good man—a beautiful man—giving her control and giving her licence. Creating a safe environment in which to test her limits and offering himself up as her crash test dummy. She had thought that moment just a minute ago was the big risk: turning the tables and revealing this aspect of herself to Aiden, but articulating it—*taking* the control he was offering—was so much more terrifying.

Because she wanted it so much. And because it meant she wasn't broken after all.

She just hadn't yet found her equal.

Astute Aiden read her hesitation. 'I'll look after you,' he vowed, his molten gaze committed.

And he would. She knew it instinctively. Because that was the man he was. All those qualities that split the seams of the bulging 'brother' folder hadn't diminished now that he was officially an 'other'. His intelligence, his compassion and focus and interest in anything new and challenging, his spirit and his loyalty and values. All the things that had wheedled in under her skin and made him so hard to walk away from. They were highlighted—amplified—by the desire now pumping off him in waves, but they weren't overruled.

Aiden Moore would look after her until the day he died if he let himself. Look at his concern for his mother. He was a keeper.

It was why she'd fallen for him.

She stared up into the simmering pools of igneous blue as everything fell into place with an inevitable *thunk*. That was why she felt so connected to him. That was why the threat of having to walk away had hurt so much. That was why she felt safe enough in his arms to expose her deepest secret.

She loved him.

He stroked a loose lock of hair back from her face as if sensing her turmoil, not pushing, but not retreating. Just… waiting.

She took a deep breath. And poured all her trust into her smile.

And reached for him.

CHAPTER ELEVEN

HAD THERE EVER been anything quite as beautiful as this moment? Tash spread gloriously naked across her bed. Unconscious. Inelegant. Vulnerable.

All things she would hate most.

And mine.

The word just kept floating back across Aiden's consciousness no matter how hard he worked to push it away. He loved to make someone his. To brand them. To win them even against their better judgement because they just couldn't help themselves. A besting.

But, no, this wasn't that kind of 'mine'.

This was a whole other beast. A rabid, jealous, protective kind of 'mine'. The kind of mine that made him want to tiptoe out of here, hunt down Eric Sinclair and slice his belly three ways before morning for hurting her so badly. Or get him arrested and let the other incarcerated filth have at him.

Or even deck his own father for *not* being hers as well. Simply because she'd wanted it so very much and some part of him had suddenly decided that protecting Tash and meeting her needs was now his job. Which was ridiculous. *She'd* deck *him* for even thinking it.

That was not what they were about.

He backed away from the doorway and returned to the kitchen to see if the coffee was ready yet. He'd sought refuge in the kitchen because he didn't trust himself to lie half sprawled under her and not reach for her again. And she'd earned a rest, God knew.

His beautiful, wild Tash.

No, not *his*. He'd never had a stronger urge to make that clear to the stars peppering the sky. What they'd just done, what they'd just been to each other was a partnership. Two equals. And that was new for him.

And more than a little bit unsettling.

His father had called him 'damaged'—charming!—but while his past relationships were about expediency, they were also with decent women. Women who wanted a similar, brief, no-strings exchange. Not quite as special or unique as Tash, granted, but it wasn't as if he'd picked them up on some street corner.

Sex and power were so intertwined. And he liked to control the power, ergo he controlled the sex. When it happened, where it happened, who it happened with. He might have ceded some of that control to Tash tonight but he'd taken it back by the end of the night, until she begged for his touch. He always did. The physical aspects, the emotional aspects. All tightly marshalled. That was how he liked it. And time was the greatest co-driver a man could have. The shorter the relationship, the more control he wielded.

Amen.

And you know what…? Daddy dearest really wasn't in a position to criticise his relationship choices given how he'd treated the two most significant women in his life.

Pot. Kettle. Black.

Speaking of which…Aiden flipped the switch on the now fully percolated coffee and splashed a healthy amount plain into one of Tash's mugs. He'd accepted he wasn't going to sleep again tonight—his mind was way too busy even as his body wanted him to tumble into satiated slumber—so coffee it was. Black. Strong. And lots of it.

It did only a partial job of purging the guilt he still felt for being so weak.

Ironic that someone who embraced the challenge of corporate conflict so heartily should struggle as he did with personal conflict. But deep-and-meaningful discussions weren't really done in his family. In his case, he'd also refined the art of finding something—or someone—to convincingly steal focus. And since he'd hit puberty that something was sexual.

Like tonight.

He should have been at home, unable to sleep, working his way through the emotional minefield that was his messed-up family, not here, making Tash into a human displacement activity.

Using her.

The guilt nibbled again. This wasn't a small deal for her. He'd seen how she struggled to open up with him and let her raw sensuality out. And he knew she didn't sleep around casually. And—just in case he was missing the point—the universe rammed it home just half an hour ago when her beautiful, exhausted eyes had fluttered open and locked on his for seconds and then fluttered shut again. In that unguarded moment, she'd completely failed to disguise a blazing kind of intensity saturating the chocolate pools.

A kind of half-asleep worship.

He'd practically scrabbled out from under her, the big thumping muscle in his chest near exploding. Because it had almost looked like—

No, he wouldn't go there. Going there had consequences.

He sipped the scalding coffee as his eyes trailed over the explosion of bright, happy photographs stuck to Tash's fridge, trying to piece together a timeline of her happiest moments. Moments of joy. Moments of love. He got another flash of those chocolate eyes blazing into his with such…sleepy optimism. He drank a gulp so hot his eyes literally watered, and it banished all other thought effectively away.

He'd faced this moment of realisation many times in the past. It was part of his process. It was also why he never brought anyone back to his place. If you're in your own place you can't leave. And he left the moment things turned sticky. The moment he got the slightest sense that the woman he was with was getting entangled.

Or, in this case, *he* was.

The very fact it was happening against his better judgement meant it shouldn't happen at all. He stared at the biggest of the photographs on the refrigerator. Tash with her mother, somewhere beachy, both blissfully happy.

The Porter-Sinclair women.

The most unsuitable woman in the world for him if he also wanted to have any kind of relationship with his mother. Which he did. She'd been abandoned enough by men for one lifetime. He wasn't about to add to that.

His eyes drifted upwards to the top of the fridge and then froze as they encountered a translucent bluey-orange leg, complete with a series of delicate nubs beneath it, bent over the top edge of the white appliance. A chubby little sea star, with its perfect sucker feet and almost living appearance. He touched one of his fingers to one of its.

His starfish. The exact same one he'd watched her make yesterday. How was it even possible that so much could have changed in thirty-six hours? He'd been sure that this little guy would end up in the shards bucket on principle; she'd thrust it into that cooling kiln with such perfunctory disinterest. As if it was valueless to her.

Yet, here it was. Squirreled away in her house.

It dawned on him then that, for a woman who made her living working with glass, this little starfish was woefully outnumbered in her cottage. Which made its presence painfully significant. He took its slight weight in the palm of his hand and let those cool, hard legs hang off the edge of his hand into space. It was far from perfect—the legs were irregular and its colours not evenly distributed. Then again, Tash had made it under duress. But, overall, he found the flaws, partly hidden by the smooth beauty of the glass, rather appealing.

It reminded him of him.

Except he liked to think he did a much better job of disguising his flaws.

But then the reality sank in: women didn't collect things like that for no reason, at least not practical women like Tash. If she'd been planning on giving it to him, she would have done so earlier when he picked her up for dinner. So that meant she was keeping it as a memento—his chest tightened up hard—and that wasn't good news.

The keepsake put that honey-blast she'd fired at him from her beautiful chocolate pools into a whole new light. And the trust she'd shown in revealing her wild side, too. And just about every smile and glance she'd sent his way these past weeks. It meant they weren't the casual kind of looks, or smiles, or actions that you just walked away from. Responsibility surged in thick and awful as he stared down at the little fella in his hands. Then up at the fridge.

Yeah, the starfish was him, all right. And Tash had put it where she displayed her most precious memories.

Which meant it was time to leave.

And the sheer force of his desire not to meant that he absolutely had to.

Funny how a bed could feel empty even when it normally was. After just a few hours of cohabitation.

Tash stirred into wakefulness, skirting her fingers over the cool sheets beside her and forcing gritty eyes open. Five in the morning was not enough sleep at the best of times, never mind when several hours had been occupied with intense, exhausting physical activity. She trained her ears to her left, towards the en suite.

Nothing.

Frowning, she pushed her pleasantly aching muscles into a half-upright position.

'Aiden?' she murmured, holding back with forced positivity the chill that wanted so badly to settle.

He hadn't left. He hadn't.

He wouldn't do that to her.

She switched on the bedside lamp and glanced around, breath suspended, for a hastily scrawled note. Nothing. She flipped over on a groan and swung her feet to the floor, before sliding on her robe to further keep the chill at bay. Was no note good news or bad news? Did it mean he hadn't left or he *had* but didn't feel obliged to even tell her? Absence in a house this small was a rather self-evident thing, if you looked. And Aiden was a logical guy.

Just look! She scolded herself, wishing she was cool and collected enough not to need to; the sort of person who could have just rolled over in bed and gone back to sleep. Eight o'clock would have been a much better time to be having this crisis of confidence.

Light footfalls took her out into the living area.

Nothing. But her nose told her everything she needed to know.

'Needed the caffeine?' she murmured, stepping into the entry to the kitchen.

Aiden stood in front of her refrigerator, staring at the clutter pinned to it with cheerful magnets. Behind him through the window, the navy sky sat heavy as her heart. As he turned, Tash glanced at the coffee pot and saw the remnants of the high tide mark ringing the glass.

That had to be at least three refills given the size of the mug he'd borrowed. How long had he been out here staring at her fridge?

When her eyes returned to Aiden's, his were guarded. And intensely apologetic.

The chill officially won.

'Oh.'

It was all she could manage past the sudden gridlock in her throat. It seemed incredibly inevitable now and she wondered how she could possibly not have seen this coming last night. But here it was.

The moment.

'How are you feeling?' he murmured.

She didn't want him asking that. *How are you feeling?* implied he gave a toss. *How are you feeling?* suggested she'd done something she should have felt awkward about. *How are you feeling?* was a prelude to *Well, I should be going.*

'What happened, couldn't work the inside deadlock?' she asked, folding her arms across her chest.

His lips pressed together. 'I wasn't leaving.'

'Overdosing on caffeine instead seems a bit extreme.'

His smile didn't deserve to warm her. 'I wanted to wait until you woke up.'

But you are leaving? 'I'm awake now.'

'Why are you?'

Because you weren't there and the absence felt wrong. She might as well tattoo 'high maintenance' to her forehead. 'It's odd to have someone else in the house. I must have sensed you moving around.'

He didn't believe her and she didn't blame him.

'So…this is a world record,' she squeezed out, hideously brightly, 'even for me. Is there such a thing as a half-night stand?'

His eyes fell shut. 'Tash—'

'No, I get it. Now. I didn't really get it before, though. The way you looked at me earlier...'

Ugh. She *so* didn't want to be one of those women that said 'but I thought'. But she really *had* thought.

'I shouldn't have come here.' He shook his mussed-up head. 'We shouldn't have slept together.'

She blinked at him and tightened her arms one more notch. So maybe she was broken after all. She'd come on way too strong and freaked him out. Though she'd truly believed him un-freakable. He was Aiden Moore. A man with his reputation had to have encountered stranger than her.

'Nobody forced you,' she defended, and then got an instant visual of her slamming him against the wall and buttons flying around them both. 'Initially.'

'I care for you, Tash. And I knew this wasn't going further so I shouldn't have started it. It wasn't fair of me.'

She stared at him and heard echoes of Kyle and even her father. Making lame excuses. Taking responsibility in the patronising, masculine way that made it patently clear it was secretly all her fault. As if they were doing her some kind of favour. It was beneath a man like Aiden and she was offended *for* him as much as *by* him.

She nodded and turned to leave the kitchen, as dignified as she could manage, but at the last minute the social justice campaigner in her—the part that wasn't much troubled by dignity or lack of it—forced her to speak.

She spun back from the doorway. 'Sorry... *Why* isn't this going further exactly?'

'Tash, don't do this.'

Every part of her tightened.

'Hold you accountable for your actions?' Suddenly she very much wanted to hear what he had to say, precisely because it was unpleasant for him to say it. She shouldn't be the only one feeling the pressure here. 'All those lusty stares, the coatroom kiss, the paddle-boat day…I would have thought you have had plenty of opportunity to have a crisis of conscience.'

Come on, Aiden, say it. Even Kyle-the-gutless had managed to say it. *You came on too strong, Tash.* Just as she had with Kyle. Just as she had with her father the one time she tried—really tried, but failed—to find some common ground with him and begin patching their fatally flawed relationship.

Seemed like try-hard was just her thing.

'You looked like you were enjoying yourself,' she gritted. And he'd willingly given her control. Did he not expect her to actually take it?

'This isn't about tonight, Tash.'

Of course it was. She'd been here before. Stupid her for imagining this time would be different. 'Then what's it about?'

What did I do?

'I don't want—' He swore and turned away, but then thought better of it and turned back. 'I don't want to hurt you, Tash.'

'Too late.' Her chest rose and fell several times as she gathered the courage to say what needed to be said. 'You gave me control, Aiden. You wanted me to take it.'

Ironic that she should be speaking of control while her voice was demonstrating so little of it.

'I told you, this isn't about tonight. Tonight was amazing.'

Pfft…words. He tried to touch her arm but she shook him off. 'Then what is it about?'

He curled his fingers back into his body. His blue eyes roiled with indecision. 'You're not someone I can see…fitting into my family.' He cleared his throat. 'Long term.'

Her stomach clenched hard and ice washed through her veins. It was only slightly better than what she'd feared. Both were rejections of who she essentially was. Humiliation surged up fast behind the ice. 'I must have missed your proposal.'

That did bring his eyes back to hers. 'A few weeks isn't going to change that. So why waste your time?'

Huh. If she'd imagined him overwhelmed with desire, she must have been projecting. Madly. 'Or yours?' she pressed.

He tipped the remnants of his mug into the sink and tightened his lips. 'This isn't about me.'

'No. It's about your family, apparently. But let's be honest. You mean your mother.'

'I have six aunts and uncles and their respective partners, too. None of them are going to accept the daughter of Adele Porter in their backyards, let alone their family.'

Tash's eyes strayed to where he'd been looking at the fridge. To the central display of a photo of her with her mother. And her heart ached.

'No. Not while no one challenges their prejudice.'

He hissed his frustration. 'You're expecting me to go up against my family for you.'

Yes, of course. How *inconceivable*. Clearly, she was nothing to him. 'Then why not do it for your father?'

His eyes narrowed. 'Leave my father out of this.'

'Poor Nathaniel must have been living in a war zone all these years. Enemy territory. With a bunch of hysterics who can't put the past in the past.' The steam was building pressure now. Every affront and resentment she'd ever felt at the hands of people who were blind and judgemental and stupid poured out onto her kitchen floor and onto his family. 'He abandoned the woman he loved to do the right thing by Laura and give you a father. And yes, he gave in to a momentary impulse when you and I were young but he stayed with Laura for *twenty years*, Aiden. To do the right thing by her again. But that's not enough for any of you, is it?'

He stood straighter and loomed a warning over her. 'Tash—'

'What the hell do you people want from us? I'm sorry he didn't love her more. But that's not my fault any more than my heritage is.'

'I could ask the same, Tash.' He breathed down on her hot and passionate. 'What the hell do you want from me? Give me some credit for trying to do the right thing by *you*, here. It would be so easy for me to just carry on with you, hiding the truth and having a good time for the weeks it would take me to bore of you.'

Was it so inevitable?

'You're every bit the cracker Jardine claimed. Why wouldn't I just take what you were so eagerly offering and enjoy it?' She winced but it didn't slow him any. 'But I'm not; I'm being chivalrous—and, believe me, gallantry is not my natural habitat—and ending it now before it goes any further with a woman who can have no place in my future.'

His words ricocheted off the shiny surfaces in the kitchen, making them endure painfully longer than the original. Once they subsided, the only sound was the respective heaving of their chests and lungs. In Tash's case, muted by the tight wadding of agony that pressed in around her thoracic cavity like saturated gauze around an open wound. She reached for the starfish she'd made with him the day before and clutched it to her heart for courage.

Would it be this way for ever, for her? *Tash Sinclair—for a good time but not a long time.*

'You're right,' she squeezed out past the bracing hurt, rich with sarcasm. 'Thank you for putting me out of my misery.' Unspent tears clogged her throat but she was damned if she'd let him see how much he'd hurt her. She ran her hands repeatedly over the cool, smooth glass of the sea star. 'It's ironic, really, that for you to be a man worthy of me you *have* to walk out that door.' She shuddered in a breath. 'And if you stayed then I'd be settling.'

His eyelids fell shut again.

'I don't know why I expected more. Everyone warned me that I shouldn't trust you, your father included. Turns out you're no different from the Kyle Jardines or the Eric Sinclairs.'

It wasn't until the words were out that Tash realised she never planned on calling him her father again.

Aiden's lashes lifted to reveal blazing anger.

'He beat his wife and six-year-old child for having the strength and character he lacked. It must have killed him to have that deficiency reflected a dozen times a day. Kyle, as well. Too emotionally insecure to maintain a proper relationship. I was stupid to think that you would be different. You're just as emotionally stunted as they are. You just dress better.'

His nostrils flared. 'Careful, Tash…'

'Or what, Aiden?' She pushed the challenge past the fist lodged in her throat. 'Do you imagine that you can do anything to me that my father didn't? Or say anything to me that Kyle didn't? I am over feeling diminished at the hands of men. If you're not into me enough to throw a single pebble into the dysfunctional surface of your family pond then that's fine, but at least *own it*. Don't preach to me about what a great man you're being by saving me the discomfort of not being welcome in your home. Your family would be *lucky* to have me in it. Maybe I'd add some character and strength to your diminishing gene pool.'

The insult hung, potent and awful, between them.

'It wouldn't be a pebble, Tash. I would be lobbing a grenade.'

She turned and threw the sea star against her hallway wall. It exploded into a hundred orange glassy fragments. 'Then hurl it, Aiden! Like the man I believed I'd fallen in love with. A strong and exciting and worthy man. God, I am so tired of *boys*.'

His body sagged and his voice, when it came, was tortured. 'You don't love me.'

She straightened, her chest racked with tight agony. 'Please don't measure me by your own standards. And please see yourself out.'

She turned and walked as steady as her wobbly legs would take her, over the broken glass and back into the bedroom where he'd conveniently removed all evidence of his presence while she slept off the after-effects of their passionate hours together.

She closed the door behind her and leaned on it, resolutely forbidding her eyes from filling, breath suspended and ears acutely honed to the noises coming from the other side of the door until her lungs burned with the need for air. The sounds of Aiden rinsing his mug and placing it on her stainless-steel draining board. Unlocking the internal deadlocks. Closing the door quietly behind him.

She welcomed the numbness, her old friend, and knew it would get her by until she could deal with the complicated mess of emotions burbling up inside her. It was only after she was certain that she had the acoustic protection of several walls between them that she let herself suck in a long-overdue breath and then slid down the door onto the carpet. She pushed her hair away from her face and stared in total confusion as her hands came away wet.

The tears she hadn't wanted to shed. The tears she hadn't even felt sliding down her face. Just like the lacerations on her bare feet that leaked a rich, awful crimson onto her mother's carpet.

The tears and blood—like the heartbreak—that spilled freely in total defiance to her will.

CHAPTER TWELVE

Six weeks later

IF NATHANIEL NOTICED they'd reverted to clandestine, just-the-two-of-them meetings to catch up, he didn't let on to Tash. His conversation, as it always was, was easy and low pressure, and she got the sense that he enjoyed the freedom of agenda-free exchanges as much as she did. He'd mentioned Aiden only twice. The first time her wince couldn't have failed to get his attention and, the second time, his scrutiny was so intense as he casually dropped his son's name into the discussion Tash knew he must have been fishing.

But when she'd kept her face rigid and let the clang of the name-drop go unanswered, he'd sat back and then carefully not mentioned Aiden again.

For weeks.

'So how's the new place working out?' she asked, stirring her latte.

'It's fine. I never was much of an accumulator; most of what I took with me we could stack on this café table so the size is fine.'

'Do you need anything?'

His hand curled around hers. 'Bless you, Tash. No. Anything I need I can buy.'

Oh, that's right. Money. She shrugged. 'Do you need company, then?'

Tiny lines forked at the corner of his eyes. 'Are you offering?'

'You know I enjoy our time together.' Lord. Was she actually as desperate as she sounded?

'Shouldn't you spend that time with your friends?'

'I thought *we* were friends.'

The look he gave her was so…fatherly. 'I'd love to see you any time.'

'At least I'll know you're not burying yourself in your work.'

'It's tempting, but no,' he said. 'One workaholic in the family is sufficient.'

Tash's entire body tightened. 'Is Aiden pulling long hours?' she asked as casually as she could. Like the carefully orchestrated mentions in her mother's diary. She had to start doing it some time.

Nathaniel snorted. 'Long, intense. And dragging others with him. He's presently the menace of the entire firm.' He studied her closely. 'Would you know anything about that?'

She was as bad with feigning innocence as she was with lying. 'When did it start?' she hedged.

'The day he found out my history with your mother.'

Her chest tightened. 'Well, there you go, then.'

'I assumed it was that but when I tried to speak to him about it he brushed me off as though he had more important things to think about.'

Maybe it was a guilty conscience. Good. She hoped that her parting words might have had some impact. She shrugged. 'Who knows?'

'Actually, I thought you might know, given the changes in your behaviour started right at the same time.'

Her eyes shot up to his. 'What changes?'

'You're so flat now. All the vibrancy and the joy you had are absent.'

It was true. She could see it in her work.

Nathaniel carefully picked his way through a bundle of things he obviously wanted to say. 'Tash, I don't care whether we're blood relatives or not—you have become as close to me as a daughter and I want to keep it that way. I'm worried about you.'

Strange that the question of her parentage was no longer even on her radar. Nor, truth be told, Eric Sinclair's absence in her life. Something about her miserable encounter with Aiden a few weeks back had given her some much-needed perspective.

People treated you exactly as you let them.

Had it really taken her thirty years to work that out?

She'd accused Aiden's family of living in the past, but wasn't that exactly what she was doing with her father? She was who she was; the why of it really didn't matter anymore. She would only drive herself crazy worrying about things she just couldn't change.

She smiled up at Nathaniel. 'I'd be happy to be your hon-orary daughter. Except—'

'Aiden is a grown man.' Nathaniel guessed the direction of her thoughts. 'He doesn't have to like our friendship but he has to accept it.'

'He's very complicated,' she whispered. 'And very con-flicted.'

'I could have left Laura,' Nathaniel sighed, on a tangent. 'When you were young. It would have been the right time. But I saw the huge influence she was already having on Aiden and I knew that would go unchecked if I wasn't there to bal-ance it out.'

Air rushed into Tash's lungs. 'You stayed for Aiden's sake?'

'I am not perfect, but I could at least remediate the worst

of Laura's own issues. Ensure he grew up a good man. A sane man.'

'You did well,' Tash breathed. *You know, except for the whole arrogant, narcissistic, emotional-cripple thing.*

'I often wished I had even part of your mother's fortitude. When the time came to do the tough thing, she just did it. She didn't look back. Perhaps Aiden would have been less affected if he'd been raised away from his parents' issues.'

She leaned over and slid her fingers onto his. 'You might not have had much of a relationship with him at all, then. And imagine what that would be like.'

She didn't have to imagine it. For her it was a reality.

Nathaniel separated his fingers so hers could slip between them. Then he squeezed. 'Whenever I got in a bind I used to think, *What would Adele do?*'

It was so close to what she did, herself, it was hard not to smile. 'What do you think she would have done differently in our position?'

He stared at her a moment, thinking. 'She would have done exactly what she always did. *Act.* Concrete positive action to change her situation. Not just waited to see what others would do.'

For weeks, the only path Tash could see ahead of her was dark, musty and singular. Forging onwards, forcing herself to forget Aiden and patching up her life as best she could. Surviving.

But Nathaniel's words blew a hole in the side of that tunnel, revealing a whole other pathway running parallel. Bright and filled with fresh air and the smell of violets. Like her mother's moisturiser. Forking off to the left.

Lord knew she was ready for a fork in her life. A new direction. A new way of doing things. Because the old way sure wasn't working. Maybe it was time to do more than just survive.

She sat up straighter at the café table.

Maybe it was time to fight.

She pulled their joined hands up to her lips. 'Nathaniel,' she whispered as he blushed. 'Has anyone ever told you that you are a brilliant man?'

'Someone once did.' His eyes twinkled dangerously with emotion. 'I'm so very glad I'm finally able to repay the compliment.'

The dying strains of Big Ben's chimes echoed in what was obviously an expansive hallway beyond the ornate front door. Tash ran her fingers along the shapes carved into its timber and waited for a response. The distinctive *click-clack* of approaching heels on marble came just a moment later, but they stopped at the front door and then...nothing. She could practically feel the gaze burning down onto her through the security peephole and the weight of the silence afterwards.

Would Laura open the door when she saw who'd rung the bell?

Seconds ticked by.

Maybe not.

'I just need a few moments of your time, Mrs Moore,' she offered in an even voice, eyes neutrally forward. Non-threatening. Like approaching a stressed-out dog.

Still nothing. Then, finally, the reluctant click of a deadlock and the door swung inward. Though not wide open, Tash noticed.

'Mrs Moore, I'm—'

'I know who you are,' Laura Moore began. 'What do you want?'

The words should have been rude, if they weren't so terribly defensive. And old. It struck her then how much beyond her actual age Laura Moore seemed. She must have turned fifty this year, too. But she seemed two decades older.

'I was hoping I could have a word with you.'

'About?'

Here went nothing... 'About your son. Please.'

That was the last thing Laura was expecting, obviously. Surprise had her stepping back, leaving a Tash-width aperture in the expensive doorway. She squeezed through into the ornate foyer and followed Laura into the house. Beyond the foyer, a luxurious home unfolded. Above them, at the top of a wide staircase, yet more rooms and landings sprawled. Tash's entire cottage could have fitted in Laura Moore's enormous kitchen, alone.

The phone rang and Laura excused herself to get it, murmured quietly and briefly into the handset, and then turned back to Tash, sliding it back into its cradle. 'What can I do for you, Miss Porter?'

'Sinclair.'

She didn't acknowledge the correction. 'I never expected to see you here.'

'No. I can imagine.' Tash glanced at four tall, leather stools peeking out from below the marble overhang of the expansive kitchen counters. 'Shall we sit?'

Laura didn't move. 'Will it take that long?'

Okay, defensive and now officially rude. 'I guess not.' She shifted her feet wider. 'I wanted to ask you about those days at uni with my mother and Nathaniel.'

She stiffened horribly. 'I thought you wanted to talk about Aiden.'

She stuck to her guns. 'It's related. Are you aware he now knows that Nathaniel and my mother were together before he married you?'

Judging by the way her colour bleached just slightly, no, she didn't.

'Aiden wouldn't have said anything to hurt me. He's very kind in that way.'

Kind or maybe just well trained in issues-avoidance.

Laura's lips pressed into a straight, rucked line. 'I assume I have you to thank for that?'

'Indirectly.' She took a deep breath. 'I thought I might have been Nathaniel's biological daughter.'

Two things happened then; the bleaching intensified and the most curious glint hardened in Laura's eyes. Like vindication. But it was wholly internal. Her voice, when it came, actually trembled. 'And…are you?'

'I am not.'

'Ah.'

That was a curious response. 'Did you expect me to be?'

Laura considered that for moments. 'It would have explained so much.'

'That's what I thought.'

'So you are Eric's?'

That threw her. 'As far as I'm aware.' Though she'd still give anything not to be, just on genetic grounds alone.

'Did that please you?'

Tash worked hard to keep the sarcasm out of her voice. Things were tense enough between them. 'No. Not at all.'

Laura nodded. 'I can imagine. Eric was a difficult young man. I can't imagine he improved with age.'

Out of nowhere, a new question burned on her tongue. 'Why were you friends with him?'

It seemed to throw Laura, too. But she shifted sideways and leaned against her expensive kitchen counter. 'Eric was just always…there. We formed a little group on orientation day and never really parted until—' she stumbled and changed tack '—until I withdrew from my studies. He was peripheral to the three of us and never seemed to understand that.'

Or maybe he had…only too well.

'You didn't like him?'

'I didn't trust him, particularly. None of us did.'

Rightly, as it turned out. But the opening was too good to pass up. 'Why would my mother marry him?'

Maybe it was the parent in Laura—unable to let another woman's child go unanswered on something so fundamental. Or maybe she'd just been telling herself this for so long. Consternation flitted across her face before she responded, 'Because he asked. And because she wanted to make a statement.'

It would be easy to imagine the latter, but not the former. 'I can't believe she would marry someone like that just because he asked.'

Laura's face pinched. 'She was…adrift. And he was available and eager. Your mother didn't like to be out of the centre of things.'

Tash bit her tongue. She had a purpose coming here today, and proving Aiden right by riling up his mother was not it. Besides, once again, Laura's words were laced with bitterness, not vindictiveness.

'Do you know why he was like that? Eric Sinclair?'

For the first time, Laura's eyes seemed to soften. 'He came from a broken family. Not very nice, if I remember rightly.'

Tash came from a not very nice broken situation, too, but she hoped she was nothing like him.

'And he loved your mother completely. He always did like shiny things.'

'He can't have loved her. Look how he treated her.' She wondered how much Laura knew about the punishment meted out to her mother before she found the strength to leave him.

'You weren't there, Natasha. You never saw how much he adored her, hovering like a bee to her daisy. But she never gave him the time of day.' That hard glint returned. 'Not until…'

'Until Nathaniel left her.' *For you.* 'So he should have

been the happiest man on the planet. Shouldn't he?' Something was off here.

'Can you imagine what it's like—' Laura gritted out '—to be the second choice of the person you love? That wouldn't have sat well with a fragile ego like Eric's. Even if he was getting what he wanted.'

Or with a damaged woman like Laura, Tash suddenly realised. How had she missed the obvious parallels in the two old friends?

'To have reminders thrust in your face every day,' Laura went on, warming up to her topic. 'Even in the things they didn't say. To have your own child named for another man.'

An ice covering formed on the confusion pooling in her gut. 'I'm named for Nathaniel?'

Those blue eyes, so like Aiden's yet so very different, hardened impossibly further. 'He always believed so.'

He who? Eric? Or Nathaniel?

She tried to imagine life with Aiden while he was secretly in love with someone else. And then she tried to imagine it wasn't a secret. How that would eat at you over time. The sudden realisation didn't make her like her father any better, but it did help explain his great slide into antipathy. 'But Mum was always very careful not to rub it in his face,' Tash defended. 'She didn't even use his name in her diaries.'

'Infinitely worse!' Laura barked. 'As though his name was something to be cherished and kept close. Or as if that made it even the slightest bit possible to forget what had gone before.'

Oh, they were definitely talking in code here. She absorbed Laura's words. 'Yes. I can see that. It must have been difficult.'

'Don't patronise me. Or him. Until you've lived it you can't understand.'

She stared at the older woman, her face wrought with a

lifetime of sorrow, and whispered, 'You still love Nathaniel, though. Even now?'

Fierceness filled her eyes. 'I will die loving that man.'

Just like her mother. 'Which is why you don't like me.'

'I don't have an opinion either way about you,' Laura spat her lie. 'Your mother and her offspring are of no consequence to me.'

Tash leaned in. 'You were friends,' she urged and Laura's face pinched. 'Her diaries are full of the great times you had together before it all went wrong. What happened?'

'My father happened,' a deep voice said from behind her. 'Isn't it always a man at the root of every female complaint?'

'Darling…' Laura's face and entire demeanour changed on seeing her son. Even her body language somehow grew more…frail. More vulnerable.

Viper.

'What are you doing here?' Laura purred.

Aiden threw her a frustrated, blank look. 'You pressed the panic alarm. We spoke by phone a few minutes ago. I came because I thought it was an emergency.' He turned his glare onto Tash, punishing her for wasting his time. As if *she'd* pressed some duress button. 'Instead I find the two of you in a cosy tête-à-tête.'

A thousand miles from cosy. Tash squared her shoulders against the hot surge that seeing him birthed, and faced his scorn. 'I decided that if your family's inability to accept me was all that was stopping us being together then I'd see if there wasn't something I could do about that.'

Behind her, Laura gasped.

Aiden's brows dipped. 'Proactive, as always—'

For Aiden, that was a very mild response. Would she get off that lightly?

'—and deluded, as always.'

Right. *Good to see you, too.*

'You got here very quickly,' Tash commented, all suspicion.

'It's Saturday. I was working at home.'

A silver thread stretched out between them, binding them together. 'Your father said you were pulling long hours,' she whispered.

'Aiden lives in the next street,' Laura announced apropos of nothing. 'Family's always been important to him.' It was a gush but it wasn't for her benefit. In fact, it reeked of a reminder. Or maybe an instruction.

Aiden looked as if he found it about as distasteful as Tash did.

'Tea, darling?' Laura cooed to Aiden. 'Natasha, are you sure I can't persuade you?'

Oh, please. But growing up the daughter of Eric Sinclair had at least taught her what to do with passive aggression. Play the game.

'Well, perhaps if it's a party...' She threw out a tight smile.

'Don't let me interrupt your conversation,' Aiden challenged, locking eyes with hers. They said, *What the hell are you doing here?*

Tash swallowed the ache and lifted her chin. *I'm fighting for what I want.* 'How much did you hear?'

'You were asking about your mother and mine, what happened to their friendship.'

Not an answer. Which meant he could have heard everything, or nothing.

Laura waved an elegantly manicured but papery hand. It reminded Tash, suddenly, of something that might flop out of a sarcophagus. She placed the kettle back onto its electric base and set it to boil. 'Oh, you know how it is. Those years of your life are so dynamic. Friendships come and go.'

'Mother's first diary is full of her sadness as your friend-ship waned.' If she wanted to do this in front of a witness, fine.

Laura turned bitter eyes in her direction, not quite as gracious or befuddled as she'd gifted Aiden with. She thought it was secret, but Tash saw Aiden see it in the mirrored splash-back behind the induction cooktop. 'Adele always was good at turning it on and off as required.'

'Was it only about Nathaniel? The troubles between you?'

'My goodness, you certainly inherited her sense of enti-tlement!' Laura blustered, all wit and sarcasm. 'As if some-one as *delightful* and *fabulous* as Adele should automatically be loved by all.' She slapped her hands on the counter. 'She was as flawed as the next person. She and Eric deserved each other in my opinion.'

'Mum…' Aiden murmured, dangerous and low.

Nausea threatened deep in Tash's throat. 'Really? She de-served overnights in hospital and being beaten with a phone-book so the bruises would be less distinct? She deserved the coroner's investigation when she died because of the number of old injuries on her body?'

Laura's hands froze in the midst of dropping a gourmet teabag into each of three designer cups. But she pulled herself together enough to finish the job. But not enough to stop her hands from trembling visibly. She tucked them out of view as soon as she could and turned to pour the kettle. She lifted it as though it weighed a ton and then replaced it succinctly onto its base when her unsteady hands couldn't keep it still.

Finally, she half turned back to Tash and whispered, 'He beat her?'

Tash nodded and Laura echoed it, though slower and jerk-ier. Aiden crossed behind his mother and poured the cups for her, placing a supporting hand on her shoulder. That little bit of solidarity only undid her more. She slid her own up to thread through her son's fingers.

'I didn't know it was that bad,' she whispered, all pretence vanished.

Tash clenched her teeth. 'But you knew it was happening?'

'It was Eric.' She shuddered in a breath. 'I discovered Nathaniel's expenditure. The legal costs. That little house. I forced him to explain. But he never said why she had to get out, just that she had. I assumed…'

She couldn't finish and Tash knew what that meant. Laura had assumed it was a prelude to Nathaniel taking back up with Adele.

'He saved both our lives that day.'

Laura nodded. 'He would have done anything for her.'

'Mum—'

'No, Aiden. Enough.' She turned haunted eyes up to him. 'I'm so tired of all of this. Time that it all came out.'

'Without Dad here?'

'He knows all of it. He's always known.'

'Known what?'

She turned to Tash. 'Adele shouldn't have valued my advice, Natasha. It was selfish advice.'

'What do you mean?'

'She confided in me, about Nathaniel pressuring her to… consummate their relationship. And he confided in me as well, his fears that her not wanting to be intimate meant she didn't care for him the way he did for her.' Her laugh was dark. 'It was so easy to turn their minds. To convince *him* he was right and to convince *her* that holding out would be good for their relationship.'

'They trusted you.'

'Of course they did.'

'What are you saying, Mum?'

She spun on her son. 'I wanted them apart. I wanted an end to the endless soap opera that was Adele and Nathaniel's great love affair and I wanted to turn the friendship that I had with him into more.'

'You broke them up,' Tash whispered.

'Oh, don't say it as though I defaced some holy relic,' she hissed. 'I seized my chance. My future. I knew what I wanted and I went for it. I won't pity Adele for waiting for the world to give her things. She already had beauty and intelligence and—' She bit back the rest.

'And Nathaniel?'

'To the victor go the spoils. That's how it works. Well, I was the victor.'

'Until you weren't,' Tash whispered. 'He went back to her.'

'And then returned to me.'

Intense pity suffused Aiden's face. His hand squeezed on Laura's shoulder and his eyes fell shut.

'He just needed time. He just needed an opportunity to love me.'

Aiden turned her slowly and stared down on her. 'Was I that opportunity?'

Her whole body trembled now. 'He was a good man,' she urged up into Aiden's face. 'He just needed a good reason to come back to me. To get out from under her influence.'

And a pregnancy was a very good reason indeed.

'You trapped Nathaniel,' Tash whispered. And destroyed a whole bunch of lives in one fell swoop.

Aiden's hand slipped from her mother's shoulder and he turned and braced himself on the opposite counter.

'It wasn't a trap,' she urged. The earnest proclamation of the condemned. 'It was a *reason*.'

Tash stared; saw the fragile, broken women that must have lived under the gloss and glamour. Perpetually. Even back then.

'I've blamed him for so many years,' Aiden whispered. 'I was convinced he'd done you great wrong.'

'He did do me wrong,' she begged. 'He *slept* with her.'

'He was desperate,' Tash murmured. 'He discovered my father's brutality and he wanted to save her, but she wouldn't let him leave you. So he staged it so that Eric would find out.'

Laura spun on her, fire in her eyes below the tears. 'No. She would have taken him in a heartbeat.'

'It's true. It's in her diary and Nathaniel told me, too. She wanted him to go back to his family.'

Panic filled her face. 'No!'

'Why "no", Laura? Does it upset you to think maybe she was a good person after all? That the woman you cheated out of her love didn't deserve what you did to her? That you abandoned your friend and set her up to be with a man who abused her horribly?'

Her thin lips opened and closed wordlessly. She turned and begged Aiden with her panicked gaze. 'Why is she here?'

'I'm here because I want the truth.' Tash moved around to put herself directly in Laura's line of vision and she locked onto her eyes. 'I'm here because I know what I want and I'm going for it. *I'm* seizing my chance just like you did.'

'You want Aiden,' she nearly shrieked.

'I absolutely do.'

Behind her, Aiden straightened and then walked past them both, out of the kitchen and through a sliding door to the pool deck.

Laura turned on her with triumph. 'Looks like the feeling is not mutual.'

Every part of her tightened. 'That might be true, but I'm only going to accept that from him. Hasn't there been enough lies and deception in this family?'

'It's not bad enough that *she* got Nathaniel's heart, now I have to give you Aiden's?'

The sneer finally got to her. Tash struck back. 'Maybe the hearts of the Moore men have always belonged in my family? Maybe this is just the universe putting things to rights?'

'No!' Laura's wail was pain incarnate. And broken.

Pity swamped through Tash for a woman who was so crippled by fear that she'd let it run her whole life. 'I don't want it exclusively, Laura,' she urged. 'I could never love a man who didn't cherish his family.' She glanced up at where Aiden paced, furious, along the decking surrounding the opulent swimming pool and then back at his bitter, fearful mother. 'But I want my chance. And I'm taking it.'

Mascara-streaked eyes widened and stared, and then dropped to where her fingers twisted in front of her. 'You're just like her, you know,' she murmured, disarmed.

'Like Mum?'

'Adele had a very strong sense of what was right and wrong. I knew that. Despite everything.'

'You knew she wouldn't fight for Nathaniel.'

Breath wheezed out of her. 'I counted on it. I'm so sorry that you lost her so young. There but for the grace of God....'

Tash was nearly overcome by the strength of the hatred coursing through her. For what this weak woman had done to her mother's life. But she forced it to morph and change. Into pity. And acceptance. She'd meant it when she said she was tired of living in the past.

'Thank you.'

'We were true friends. At the start. I hope that Adele knew that.'

'She knew.'

And then no more words would come. Laura just nodded and turned back to finish making the tea that nobody wanted. Tash stepped back, turned her eyes to the pool deck and started walking. But as she reached the door a croaky voice reached her.

'I made him into the man he is, you know…' Tash stopped, looked back at Laura. Was she still going to stake her claim on her son? But a broken heart shone through in her red-rimmed eyes as she lifted them. 'This man that can't trust love.'

Tash nodded and looked around this beautiful, empty, soul-less home. 'Why would he?'

And then she pulled on the door.

'Aiden?'

He stopped where he stood, his back still to her. 'Did you suspect?'

'I had no idea. I just wanted to talk to her, try to understand where you're coming from. Try and change it.'

He nodded. 'Do you think Dad knows she got pregnant on purpose?'

'I think so. He always seemed on the verge of saying more. But he never did.'

'Still doing the right thing by her.'

Her chest lifted and then slowly deflated. 'Yeah.'

'Do you think there's any future for them?' he asked, monotone.

No. Not according to Nathaniel. 'Perhaps it's time he put himself first?'

Aiden turned, found her eyes. Found her soul. 'He's earned it.'

She stepped closer and curled a hand around his wrist.

'I've misjudged him so much,' he whispered.

'He understands.'

'You're very certain.'

'You're his son. The only person in his life that he's free to love unconditionally. He's not going to give up on that lightly.'

'He loves you, too.'

Tash smiled. 'For who I remind him of.'

'And for who you are. He told me.' Clouded eyes held hers.

'He's made discussing you in my presence a sport.' His eyes flicked to the house. 'When she told me on the phone you were here…I thought you'd come to force my hand.'

'You looked pretty mad when you walked in.'

'Your persistence riled me even as your courage shamed me.'

'No…'

'You confronted my family, knowing how they felt about yours. Knowing how she would be. Why did you do that?'

'Because all my life I've ceded power to other people. My father. Kyle. Even you to some extent. It was time I took control into my own hands.'

'By fronting the lion's den?'

'Wounded lions always lash out.'

'You don't judge her?'

'What she told us is going to take a lot of getting past. But she's lived with her own judgement all these years; I don't think mine would add much value.'

His eyes narrowed. 'That's very generous.'

'It's not generous, it's just smart.' At his blank look, she elaborated. 'If I want to be in your life.'

'Tash—'

'I know what you said. I just don't believe you. This can't be just about your family.'

'You believed it enough to come here.'

The tension in her shoulders made shrugging a strain. 'I'm covering all my bases.'

'And now?'

She took a deep breath. 'You were right when you said I could never fit comfortably in your family. I couldn't. But what you failed to understand is that I'm prepared to live uncomfortably in it. For you.'

His gaze intensified. His throat lurched. 'That's no way to live. Look at my father.'

'It wouldn't be my first preference.'

'I thought you were done ceding power to others?'

'Don't get me wrong. I'm not saying I wouldn't move heaven and earth to change it. I'm saying you're worth the discomfort.'

His eyes slated sideways. 'I thought I was no more *worthy* than I am strong or exciting. Or manly.'

'I'm not perfect either. I wanted you bleeding the way I was.'

'Oh, I've bled, Tash. You have no idea.'

'Why? If I meant so little to you.'

He paced to the corner of the pool, then retraced his steps. 'So much of who I am is based on who I thought he was,' Aiden muttered. 'I saw and heard more than everyone believed back then. I knew what he'd done. *Thought* I knew,' he corrected himself. 'And on some level I think I took my cues about relationships there. How vulnerable you are to hurt when you give yourself—your heart—to someone else.'

'It's not like that for everyone.'

'I wonder if your mother ever said that to my father?'

'And *I* wonder how much might have been different if they'd been honest with each other from the start. Not made all those assumptions.'

'Do you think it would have changed his decision when he found out Mum was pregnant?'

'No. Because he was and still is a man who owned his actions. But I don't think he would have gone with her in the first place.'

'Then you and I wouldn't exist. We never would have met.'

Was that what he wanted, deep down? Would it be easier, for both of them, if she'd never opened her mother's diaries? Never opened the door to her curiosity? Perhaps. But easier was not necessarily better.

She peered up at him. 'Meeting you was a turning point

for me. *Being* with you. I don't like how it came out but I wouldn't wish it undone for anything.'

A small bird flitted down into the garden and made a show of bouncing between perfectly manicured shrubs. Tash fixated on it.

Aiden cleared his throat. 'I need you to know something, Tash. I didn't know, going in, how I was going to feel on the other side of us sleeping together.'

At least he hadn't said *having* sex. But it was a long mile from *making love*, which was how she'd viewed it. When she wasn't thinking of it as *changing her forever.*

'I was numb coming out of the meeting with my father. The only thing that could pierce that was you. Your presence and your touch. I craved it.' His eyes dropped. 'I used it, to distract myself from the reality of everything I'd learned. I used you. And I hate that.'

'I'm not all that crazy about it, either,' she muttered.

'My experience of relationships has been limited,' he admitted.

She gaped. 'I read the newspapers, Aiden. I have an Internet connection.'

'I'm not talking about quantity. I'm talking about scope. I've had hundreds of the same kind of relationship. Fast, limited. Safe. I'm sure the papers don't cover that.' He plunged his hands into his pockets. 'You were a totally new experience for me. Someone who challenged me. Someone who bested me. Someone who was quite prepared to be disrespectful of me.'

He roamed back and forth across the deck. Tash stood frozen.

'And then we stood in your apartment on the verge of being together and I saw how nervous you were to really be free with me, and I burned with such intensity I was overwhelmed.'

Doubt washed through her. The old distrust. 'Out of your hundreds of experiences?'

'I'm not talking about my raging desire to *take* you. I'm talking about the force of my desire to take *care* of you. To protect you, even with me, and with anyone else you would ever meet. I wanted to liberate you from the doubt that jerk Jardine instilled in you and beat your stinking father to death with my bare hands for how he treated you. I woke up next to you and never, ever wanted to wake up next to anyone else. Ever. You were so brave and so wild and so perfect and that…terrified me.'

A thick clog of tears mustered high in her chest.

'And then you smashed the starfish—*my* starfish—and I realised that's what I'd done to you. Broken this fragile, beautiful thing into pieces. Maybe never to go back together. With my own cowardice.'

'You're not a coward, Aiden—'

'You called it, Tash. I wasn't prepared to go up against my family for you. My mother. Our whole life has been about maintaining the status quo, keeping her happy. She raised me to be the man she wanted my father to be. Compliant and loving and all-worshipping. In fact, she's pretty much conditioned the people around her to be like that too.'

'Aiden, don't—'

He shook his head. 'I would have happily beaten a man to death for you but I wouldn't risk bringing you home for dinner. What kind of a man does that?'

'An imperfect man. A human man.'

His snort turned ugly. 'A child.'

'You *were* a child when these patterns were set. As controlled by your mother as I was by my father.'

'She's so manipulative. I'm only just seeing it.'

'She's also your mother. You don't get two of those. And all of those things she did for you as a child are still valid.'

He turned his confusion up to her. 'You have more reason than anyone to hate what she's done.'

She tipped her face to the sky. 'Enough with the hate between our families. If I can accept it, then so can you. Her legacy nearly hurt us both but it didn't. We stopped it. We're both standing here. We can't change the past, only the present.' She moved directly in front of him. 'So, Aiden Moore, what are you going to do with the present? That's what counts.'

His nostrils flared wildly. 'I barely know what to do.'

'Me neither.'

'I have no right to expect anything from you. After what I did.'

'No. You can't expect. But you can hope. And you can ask.' She stepped up and circled her arms around his neck. 'And I can deliver.'

His hands curled around behind her as if they were independent of his body. 'You'd do that?'

'Yes, I would. In fact, I think it's time for a new commission for MooreCo.'

He tipped his head. 'You haven't finished the first one yet.'

'This one is going to be something special. Something with unlimited facets and so much glorious potential. My best work yet.'

'What is it?'

'I'm going to smelt us a life together. And you're going to help me. Sharpen my tools with your insight, fuel the furnace with your passion and keep me safe from the flames with your love. We'll display it in our first home together.'

He bent and pressed his lips to the soft place behind her ear. 'Love,' he murmured. 'Is that what this is? This total inability to sleep, this horrible, churning stomach when I think about that night? This feverish sweat when I remember our one night together?'

One night. That was all her mother ever had with Nathaniel. And, for the first time, she understood how one night might have fuelled a passion that lasted twenty more years.

She curled her arms even higher and breathed into his skin. 'Yeah, stupid. That's love.'

'I thought maybe I was getting your flu.'

'You look too good for someone with the flu.'

'You never know.'

'I should take your temperature.' And she did, with her lips, long, hard and hot. 'Wow, you are kind of warm,' she breathed. 'Maybe I should bring you soup.'

'Only if you have it with me. In bed.'

He kissed her again and her head swam with the closeness. It was so much more than proximity. This closeness went cell deep and bonded them on a level Tash had never imagined was possible. This closeness was the same she got in her hot shop, melding two pieces of glass together with a blowtorch. You never melded two of the same pieces of glass because then you just had glass. But bond two very different pieces together and you had something new. Something surprising and risky and beautiful.

You had a work of art.

'If this is love,' Aiden whispered into her lips, 'I don't ever want to get better.'

'Your mother?' Tash gasped as she surfaced for air.

'She'll have to learn to live with it.'

Light surged through her body and it carried the same gooseflesh, the same tingling rightness that she'd once associated with endorsement from her mother's spirit. 'And your father?' she asked, for Adele.

'I have a lot to make up to him for. But he'll want to give you away at our wedding. And then accept you into the Moore family.'

She pushed against that rock-hard, beautiful chest, mouth agape. 'We're having a wedding?'

'At some point. Not this week. I need to see how the original MooreCo piece works out. See if you're the right artist for our life together. You might not be.'

'Aiden Moore, you conceited—'

But that was as far as she got because those beautiful, conceited lips stole her words—and her breath—completely away.

* * * * *

BLIND DATE RIVALS

BY
NINA HARRINGTON

Nina Harrington grew up in rural Northumberland, England and decided at the age of eleven that she was going to be a librarian—because then she could read *all* of the books in the public library whenever she wanted! Since then she has been a shop assistant, community pharmacist, technical writer, university lecturer, volcano walker and industrial scientist, before taking a career break to realise her dream of being a fiction writer. When she is not creating stories which make her readers smile, her hobbies are cooking, eating, enjoying good wine—and talking, for which she has had specialist training.

and perched on the very edge of the hard seat

CHAPTER ONE

'WELL, good afternoon. Have I reached the offices of one Sara Jane Fenchurch? The same Sara Jane Fenchurch who is shortlisted to be the next local Businesswoman of the Year? I have *Orchid Growers Monthly* waiting on line two for an exclusive interview. Could that be you, Miss Fenchurch? Hiding behind the smuggest grin in the potting shed?'

Sara sat back in the chair she had rescued from a skip two weeks earlier and twirled her pen between two fingers like a cheerleader. Her best friend, Helen, waltzed into the cramped office on crazily high heels, whisked dirt from an old dining room chair with a perfectly manicured hand and perched elegantly on the edge of the hard seat.

'Oh?' Sara replied, wide-eyed in pretend amazement, and pressed the fingertips of her left hand to her chest. 'Could that be little old me?' And then she fluttered her eyelashes dramatically towards a framed newspaper cutting which dominated the plain wall of the log cabin which had been a potting shed but was now her garden office. A photographer from the local free newspaper had caught her grinning like a loon and looking as stunned as a rabbit caught in car headlights as the organiser congratulated her for being on the shortlist. 'Why, yes, I believe it is. Fancy that. Maybe this year I will win it? That would be nice. Not to say useful. Cottage Orchids needs as much publicity as it can get, thank you.'

Helen snorted derisively and brushed away a trail of cobweb from the skirt of her otherwise immaculate burgundy bouclé suit. 'Of course you'll win and your orchids will be positively flying out of the door. Although…' and Helen raised her eyebrows and tilted her head to one side as she looked at Sara from head to toe before tutting loudly '…you are going to need a serious makeover, young lady, if you want to impress those judges. We can start by getting rid of that hideous pen.'

Helen tried to snatch Sara's favourite pen from between her friend's fingers, but Sara was too quick for her and lifted it out of reach behind her head.

'There is nothing wrong with my pen,' Sara replied indignantly. 'Leave it alone.'

'It's green and sparkly with a bendy plastic flower stuck on the top. Not very professional, is it?'

'It came free with a bag of orchid compost and I like it and it writes,' Sara replied. 'Professional pens are for girls who have money to spend on luxuries. Not girls who need to save every penny to invest in their orchid houses.'

Helen sighed out loud and shook her head. 'A green flowery pen. What would the Dragon have said?' Then she grinned across at Sara, pressed the back of her hand to her forehead and went on in a thin, high, whiny voice of horror, 'How inelegant, my dears. *The shame.*'

Sara laughed out loud, pushed the pointy end of her green pen behind her ear so that the yellow flower bobbed up and down at Helen, and leant her elbows on top of the pile of papers stacked several inches thick on the pine kitchen table which served as her office desk. The headmistress at the private boarding school where Sara had first met Helen had been a former actress and was famous for seizing on every opportunity for an over the top dramatic performance. Helen had always been able to mimic her perfectly.

'Maybe you are right, but at least one of us didn't let her down on the elegance front.' Then Sara brightened and looked at Helen through narrowed eyes. 'You look far too chirpy for a girl who is celebrating being a year older. In fact, if I didn't know you better I would have said you were scheming about something. Let me guess. You've changed your mind about celebrating your birthday here in the quaint little English village I call home and are planning to fly off to some exotic paradise with your be-loved Caspar instead?'

'Are you kidding? I've loved this place since the very first time your lovely nana took pity on me during the school holidays.' Then Helen smiled and gave Sara that certain innocent look that made Sara's eyebrows lift. 'Actually, this time it's more along the lines of what I can do for you!'

Helen leant forward and flashed her expensive dentistry for a second in a wide grin. 'It took some doing, but Caspar finally managed to persuade his friend Leo to leave London early so that he can come along to my birthday party at the hotel tonight! Isn't that wonderful news?'

Sara shook her head very slowly from side to side. 'Oh, no. You are not doing this to me. Not again. Just because I'm single does not mean that you have to try and set me up with every single, divorced or otherwise unattached man within a hundred mile radius.'

Helen sighed in exasperation. 'But he is perfect for you. Just think of it as a small thank you for offering to do the wedding flowers! Besides, Caspar doesn't have many close friends and at this rate Leo Grainger is going to be the only single usher at my wedding! Come on, I hate the idea that I'm the first of us to be getting married and you don't even have a boyfriend who I can torment. Who knows? You might actually like him and enjoy yourself?'

Sara picked up a bulging document folder from her desk and let it fall back with a thud, causing the withered elastic band that was holding it together to give up and twang into shreds. 'It's a good thing that your wedding isn't for another four weeks! Seriously, Helen, I'm swamped with paperwork and there is so much still to do I'm dizzy. *And* I have to be up on time tomorrow to meet the Events Manager at the Manor. There is no room in my life for dating. And you might recall that my last boyfriend was not a huge success.'

Helen waved her fingers in the air and coughed. 'That was three years ago and I thought we promised to never talk about that loser again. Don't waste one second even thinking about how he let you down.'

Sara pushed her lips together. 'Let me down? Is that what you call breaking up with me and running off to Australia with his office junior? No, Gorgeous. I love you and you have been my best friend since the first time we shared homesick stories aged eight, but no boyfriends. Thank you all the same but I am sure that Caspar's friend will have a great time at the party without me boring him to tears with talk of orchid fertiliser.'

Helen glanced around the wooden walls, shivered and sniffed dramatically and dropped her voice down to a pleading whisper. 'Fair point. Except, you know this could be the last time we go out partying together as single girls, don't you? In only a few weeks' time, I am going to be Mrs Caspar Kaplinski. I shall *try* to understand that you are so busy in your own life that you can't spare a *few* hours to help your old friend celebrate her last birthday as a single girl. Although it is going to be quite a struggle. I…I don't know if I can go through with it knowing that my one and only bridesmaid is going to be sitting in her tiny hovel all evening. Lonely and rejected while we are all enjoying ourselves…'

Her voice tailed off with a dramatic over the top fake sob, and she pressed a real silk handkerchief to the inner corner of each eye.

'That. Is emotional blackmail. And my cottage is not a hovel. Yesterday you called it a bijou gem!'

'Absolutely!' Helen replied with a wide grin, already on her feet and heading for the door. 'So, it's decided then. Cinders, you shall not stay home with only your elderly cat for company. Not this Saturday night. I shall slip through the back gate to collect you at eight with the props and stuff. Leo will take one look at you and be totally smitten, you wait and see. This is one party you're going to remember. Ciao.'

'Props? Helen! Wait!'

Sara stared at the space where her best friend had been sitting. How did Helen do it? A costume party *and* a blind date? Sara pressed her eyes tight shut and slumped back in her chair. *Oh, no.* She had a horrible feeling that she was going to regret this.

'Leo, my old mate,' Caspar bellowed down Leo's car telephone system, 'where are you? Helen is starting to panic that you've run away in terror at the thought of meeting your blind date this evening. You have to help me out here.'

'Me? Run away from a gorgeous lady? Perish the thought.' Then there was a pause before Leo asked, 'She isn't another of Helen's old school friends, is she?'

The less than reassuring silence on the other end of the telephone confirmed his worst fears. 'Ah, well,' Caspar answered. 'This one is different! Sara might be a country girl but she is very sweet.'

'A country girl?' Leo laughed. 'You do remember you are talking to a city boy? London born and bred. I don't do country. I have no idea why Helen thinks I'm in desperate need of female company. Perhaps she has a secret yearning to change direction and set up shop as a matchmaker?'

'That's my girl!' Caspar snorted. 'Always looking out for her friends. Anyway. Any idea what time you might be arriving? I need to get your costume ready.'

Leo checked his car navigation display. 'Apparently I should be with you in about ten minutes. In fact I've just turned into Kingsmede and seen the sign for the hotel. Kingsmede Manor, here I come.' And then he paused, distracted for a moment by another car. 'Did you just use the word costume? *Caspar?*'

'Brilliant! Ring me when you're settled. I owe you a drink.'

And, with that, Caspar's voice closed off, leaving Leo to the luxury of the hum of the powerful engine as the car made its way down the country lanes of the sleepy English countryside on a warm Saturday evening.

A blind date! And of course Caspar had only informed him about that small detail when he was already halfway to the middle of nowhere! Helen had a heart of gold but the last thing he wanted at this precise moment in his life was a blind date, or any date at all for that matter. He already had more than enough on his plate at the moment.

Of course he would be polite, and he was grateful for the rare chance to enjoy himself with Caspar and celebrate Helen's birthday but the rest of this weekend was going to be work!

He felt guilty about not telling Caspar the truth but his aunt Arabella had made it clear that she did not want anyone to know that she had hired Grainger Consulting to work on a very special project. Her company had bought Kingsmede Manor three years ago and invested heavily to restore it.

Now she was determined to leverage the asset and maximise the returns to justify that investment.

The latest idea from the management team was to buy the land next to the hotel and build a luxury spa extension. But Arabella wanted a second opinion—*his opinion*—before they gave the spa idea the final go-ahead.

Normally he would have sent one of his team along to do the work, but not this time. He owed his aunt more than he could ever repay. And for that he was willing to take time away from the London office and do the work himself as a personal favour, when he could least afford to. His workload over the past few months had been hectic.

Worse. He had a deadline. And it was tight. He had to come up with something very, very special in five days. The entire board of directors of Rizzi Hotels would be meeting at Kingsmede Manor over lunch on Friday for their annual general meeting.

Nothing so unusual about that.

Companies paid Grainger Consulting to make the hard decisions about what they needed to do to survive in hard times, and he had built his reputation on doing precisely that. But this time it was personal.

Leo's fingers wrapped tight around the steering wheel.

The Rizzi Hotel chain owned some of the most prestigious boutique hotels around the world, but it was still a family business, with one domineering and driven man at the top—his own grandfather. Paolo Leonardo Rizzi. The man he despised for his uncaring ruthlessness. The man who expected his orders to be obeyed by everyone, and especially by his own family.

There was no room for sentiment or consideration of the human costs to the hotels they bought out in Paolo Rizzi's world.

Of course Arabella knew that he would create something outstanding to present to the family on Friday. Clever, shrewd and powerful, his aunt was giving him the chance to settle the score with the grandfather who had so fundamentally rejected his own daughter and her family.

And Leo was determined to prove just how big a mistake that had been.

All he had to do was to create a stunning proposal on how to make Kingsmede Manor Hotel more profitable, and keep the project secret for the next few days. *Nothing to it.*

Leo Grainger eased his foot off the accelerator and turned slowly into the long paved drive that led to the hotel. Each side of the drive was lined with full-size beech trees with branches so high and wide that they joined in the middle to create a tunnel of soft green leaves, shading the drivers from the June sunshine. At eight in the evening, the shadows and sunlight created a dazzling display on the windscreen of his sports car.

These tree-lined avenues had been created centuries ago to impress guests arriving at the house for the first time in horse-drawn carriages. According to the dossier his aunt had sent over, Kingsmede Manor had been a private house until only three years earlier and had actually remained in the same family since the time it was built.

That had to be a useful selling point. Overseas visitors adored English heritage—especially when it was as eccentric as this.

Coming out of the shadows and into the low sunlight of the summer evening, Leo squinted through the windscreen and took his first sight of the house. The drive in front of the house turned into a wide circle around a central fountain where a swan frolicked in the cascading spray.

A brief smile flashed across his lips. *Impressive.* No wonder his aunt had snapped the house up the minute it came onto the market. She had impeccable taste.

Minutes later, Leo threw open the car door, swung his body out of the bucket seat and stepped out onto the cobblestone car park. His favourite designer black boots emerged first, followed by the rest of him, all six foot two of gym-toned muscle, sharp reflexes and an uncanny instinct for what made a commercial business a success... or at least that was what the financial press liked to say.

In his high-profile work with international clients, superficial aspects such as his designer clothing were simply parts of a business image he had spent years perfecting. His clients expected prestige and results and that was what they got. It was as simple as that. They did not care that he had started his working life washing dishes in the kitchens of his aunt's boutique London hotel. Why should they? He was paid to make a difference to their business. Nothing else mattered. This was business, not personal.

And now it was time to do the same for Kingsmede Manor.

Leo strolled around to the back of the car and lifted out his leather weekend bag. His only hope was that there would be a marked absence of those boring white orchids that every hotel in the world seemed to have at the moment. Perhaps this time he was going to get a pleasant surprise?

It was almost nine that evening when Sara finally tottered in her evening sandals through the familiar white marble hall with its twisted double staircase and grinned up at the huge scarlet banner which hung suspended from the ornate plasterwork arch above her head.

The words 'Hollywood Night' had been printed in enormous gold letters across the banner. Trust Helen to choose a movie theme for her birthday party. And subtle did not come into it.

Shaking her head with a low chuckle, Sara could not resist checking on the pair of stunning orchid plants which she had delivered only two days earlier as a special order.

This variety of Phalaenopsis was a triumph. At the heart of each of the huge ivory blossoms was a crimson tongue speckled with gold dust. Of course she did not expect the guests and staff at the hotel to appreciate how much work went into create such perfect flower spikes from each plant, but they did look amazing. She had suggested other colour combinations, of course, but the Events Manager had insisted on the ivory blossoms. They were a lovely match for the antique console table which stood along the length of the hall below the huge gold framed mirror which had once belonged to her grandmother.

It had been heartbreaking for her to watch so many of her favourite pieces of treasured antique furniture being sold off in auction to strangers, but her mother had been right for once. Huge heavy pieces of furniture and enormous gilt mirrors belonged in a house large enough to appreciate them and not in some minimalist apartment or tiny cottage. And of course they had needed the proceeds of the sale so very badly.

At least the luxury hotel chain who had bought Kingsmede Manor had the good sense to snap up as many of the lovely original pieces as they could while they still had the chance.

At that moment the front doors opened to a gaggle of laughing guests who swept into the hall, bringing a breeze of evening air to waft through the orchid spikes. Sara did not recognise anyone in the group—but that was hardly surprising. Helen's jewellery design business was based in London and it had been three years since they had shared a flat together. Their lives had changed so much since then it was little wonder that they had different friends and such different lives.

For a moment Sara looked past the orchid blossoms and caught her reflection in the mirror. Her hand instantly went to her hair and flicked back her short fringe. There had been a time when she had been one of those laughing, happy city girls, with their smart high heels and expensive grooming habits, who could afford wonderful hairdressers. Now she was simply grateful that the pixie style was back in fashion.

Sara checked her watch. She was late. Correction, make that *very late*. Perhaps her blind date was already here and waiting for her? Frightened of being stood up? And probably as scared as she was.

She lifted her chin and fixed a smile on her lips as she wandered into what had been her grandmother's drawing room and stood on tiptoe to see if she could spot Helen.

At five feet nothing, Helen had always been petite enough to make Sara feel like a gangly beanstalk. That was one reason why Sara had chosen medium black sandals to accompany her simple black shift dress—one of the many treasures her grandmother had left behind in the dressing-up box! Helen had supplied the pearl necklaces and huge black sunglasses but she had turned down the plastic tiara. Not with her current hairstyle. The long black evening gloves and cigarette-holder were the only other props she needed to become Audrey for the evening.

Then she spotted someone waving to her from across the room.

Sara worked her way through the crowd of costumed strangers, trying to reach Helen's table which was just in front of the wide patio doors that led out onto the terrace. A warm breeze from the garden wafted into the packed room. Perfect.

'Thank goodness you are here,' Helen called against the background noise. 'We need to come up with a plan to make sure that we win the karaoke contest later on, and you're the only person I know who can sing vaguely in tune.'

Helen was dressed as Dorothy in *The Wizard of Oz* and looked absolutely charming, from her simple gingham pinafore dress to her red glittery shoes and a tiny little basket with a stuffed toy dog inside.

'Oh, thanks a lot, Dotty,' Sara replied with a laugh and bent down quickly to kiss her friend, while trying to avoid kissing away the bright spot of red on Helen's cheek which she had helped apply. 'Sorry I'm so late. I think the mice have been in the orchid house again and Pasha refused to move from his comfy cat bed without a fight.'

Sara stretched out her left arm and turned it from side to side. 'Can you still see the scratch marks? I've taken two antihistamines and tried to cover them up with several layers of make-up and long gloves. What do you think?'

Helen waved her fingers in the air. 'Forget about all of that. I need you to focus, sweetie. Focus. I have just decided that our table will win the most points so you have to be on top form.' She nodded and tapped her finger against her nose, which was slightly redder than normal, and Sara wondered how many glasses of champagne Helen had sampled in the past hour.

But, before Sara could answer, a tall slim man in a pinstriped suit with huge shoulders, black and white brogues, a fedora and black eye mask sidled up towards them, tipped his hat to an even more jaunty angle, lifted Helen's hand, bent over sharply from the waist and kissed the inside of her wrist. 'Hiya, Gorgeous,' he said in a very fake American gangster accent, 'are you ready to be my moll tonight? You and your little dog too.'

'Good evening, Caspar,' Sara said with a smile. 'You are looking terribly elegant.'

The black silk mask was hoisted up with a sigh of exasperation.

'Come on. What gave me away?' Caspar asked.

Sara pointed to his wrist. 'I'm afraid designer watches like that were not so very common in the organised crime community.'

He looked casually down and snorted. 'Serves me right for accepting gifts from every jewellery designer I promise to marry,' he answered, grinning down at Helen, who raised her eyebrows in recognition.

'Anyway—look at you! All dressed up for a Saturday night and looking very handsome.'

'Helen dragged me here.' Sara nodded. 'Apparently this is the poor girl's last chance to have some fun before she leaves the world of young, free and single.'

Caspar was already looking over Helen's head towards the bar, and nodded to the wine waiter who was carrying trays of chilled champagne glasses with what looked like dry ice streaming out of them.

'I consider it my solemn duty to help my future bride achieve all her goals. Be right back with the drinks, ladies. Prepare to try the famous Kaplinski movie night cocktails.'

And with that he swaggered off across the polished floorboards with his shoulder pads leading the way.

Sara sighed and sat back in her chair. 'That man is almost good enough for you. Almost. And how is the birthday girl?'

Helen slapped her a little too vigorously on the back. 'Fan. Tastic. I need to catch up with the catering manager, and find out where your date has got to, but I will be right back. Stay put.'

'You are not going to leave me here on my own?' Sara could not hide the desperation in her voice.

'Of course not,' Helen replied, giving her one of her looks. 'Mingle, darling. Mingle. See you in five!'

Sara shook her head with a grin as Helen skipped her way through the crowd, then stopped to chat to a sword carrying pirate who had started a play fight with a young man waving a light sabre.

With a low chuckle, Sara lifted her evening bag higher onto her shoulder, sashayed out into the room and accepted a cool glass of champagne from a formally dressed waiter who winked at her as he presented his silver tray. She winked back. The young couple who ran the village post office were always grateful for extra work at the hotel and she could see his wife on the other side of the room reorganising the buffet display.

Fantastic! Now she had two more people to chat to.

She was just about to turn away when a slim man in a very stylish black suit, wearing white gloves and a flowing cape with huge red lapels, strolled into the room as though it was the deck of a luxurious yacht. He held his body in a stiff and mannered way—aloof and imposing. He was dark and so classically handsome that Sara could only gaze in awe. The gene fairy had certainly waved her magic wand over this boy.

All in all, he looked every inch the poster boy for the modern city executive he no doubt was. Polished and slick as steel. Confident in his abilities and accustomed to taking charge in any situation. A true captain of industry.

Sara gave a low sniff at the memory of all the boys she had dated over the years who had been clones of the man she was looking at. She had been there, done that and had been disappointed time and again when it turned out that they were far too interested in dating someone who they could introduce to their family as the only daughter of Lady Fenchurch rather than find out who she was as a person.

Being at the end of a long line of aristocratic landowners certainly had its disadvantages. Especially when she did not have any rights to a title of her own.

Then Caspar instantly greeted him warmly and pointed him over towards the bar, except that as he turned away she caught a fleeting look on Count Dracula's face which she identified with only too well. It only lasted a fraction of a second but it spelt out that he felt lonely and foolish and out of place. Almost as though he had been dragged there and dressed up against his will.

Leo Grainger glanced around the room, then stared in horror as Caspar passed him a very odd-looking steaming drink. 'You do know that you are the one and only person on this planet who could drag me to Helen's birthday party dressed like this? I just thought you ought to know that. For the record.'

'What are friends for?' Caspar replied, waving his Kaplinski cocktail in the air. 'Think nothing of it. And no, I had nothing whatsoever to do with Helen setting you up with her old school friend. Sorry, pal, but she who must be obeyed has decreed it so. Anyway, it is the least I could do after you offered us the free use of the hotel.'

Leo tipped his head and raised his glass towards Caspar's. 'It was my pleasure. There are some compensations for being related to the owner. I was happy to help. And Helen looks as lovely as ever.'

'That she does,' Caspar replied, slapping Leo on the back one handed and almost making him spill his drink. 'Why don't you make a start on the food? And while you're checking out the buffet I'll check on my future bride. The lovely Helen has some sort of surprise entertainment up her sleeve to finish off the evening and I want to be prepared. Back in a minute.'

And with that the gangster rolled across the room, swaggering his shoulders dramatically from side to side.

Leo blinked several times, shook his head, took one sip of the cocktail, almost choked and quickly picked up a glass of sparkling water from a passing waiter with a smile and grateful thanks. If that was the effect a Kaplinski cocktail had on an otherwise fairly normal lawyer like Caspar, he would pass. For this job, he was prepared to remain sober and very alert. And risk the canapés.

Only as he peered across the room towards the buffet table he was struck by something rather remarkable. One of the elegant party guests was talking to the waitress who was juggling empty platters and plates. And not just idle chatting in a condescending way but really laughing and sharing a joke so that when she started jiggling along and shaking her slim and very attractive hips in time with the lively music playing in the background, his own feet starting tapping with them.

For the first time in days an ironic smile creased the corner of Leo's mouth. He had so many vivid memories about the rude and arrogant guests and diners he had served during his days as a general waiter and dogsbody in his aunt's hotel. They had been tough times when he had been glad of the work but it had been hard going and he had never truly got used to being ignored or verbally abused—it had been part of the training at the University of Life.

One thing he had learned was that a guest who actually took the time to connect with the serving staff and treat them as human beings was a rare creature. The crowds cleared a little and he could just make out that the tall brunette with the short hair was even lovelier than he had expected.

She was wearing a classic little black dress and black evening gloves. Pearls, of course. Elegant. Cool, but she still came over as somehow comfortable. That was it. She looked comfortable inside her own skin. She was not beautiful or sleek but somehow real with a natural prettiness and totally relaxed body language that she was not ashamed of.

The fact that her long slim legs tapered into lovely shapely ankles was an added bonus. This was no country bumpkin—this was an elegant and classy city girl who had been trapped here in the back of beyond like himself.

Perhaps he had found someone to talk to at this party after all.

CHAPTER TWO

SARA walked slowly along the buffet table, loading up her plate with bite-sized mouthfuls of the most delicious food. The hotel chef was amazing and, after three glasses of the Kaplinski cocktail whilst waiting for Helen, who was still mingling, she was in need of something more solid to add to her stomach. Her snatched lunchtime sandwich was a distant memory, and she wasn't entirely sure she had finished that. Okay, she was having a slight problem using the serving tongs while wearing long evening gloves which were slightly too large for her, but hunger had won out in the end and her reward was a plate heaped up with goodies.

The gloves were going to have to come off during the actual eating process—but some things were worth the sacrifice. And at this rate it would not take long for her to scoff the lot.

She had just paused at the mini pizza platter when the strains of a familiar musical theme song belted out above the background chatter. Her hand trembled as a tsunami of emotion and sentimental angst swept over her. All it took were a few lines of lyrics and the sound of a studio orchestra...and she unravelled.

It had always been the same. Sounds and music were associated for ever in her mind with specific people and places and events, and there was nothing she could do about it—that was the way her mind worked. All she had to do was hear the opening bars of a tune and she was right back in that moment.

Pity that it had to be now.

It had been a long busy week and the last thing she wanted was to walk into a party with a soundtrack playing music from one of her grandmother's favourite musicals. Just the memory of her grandmother holding her hand as they danced around this room, both singing at the top of their voices and having so much fun, was enough to get Sara feeling tearful.

She had so little left of her wonderful grandmother that even these memories seemed too precious to share in public.

No, she told herself sternly. She was not going to weep. This was Helen's birthday party! And she still had her grandmother's orchid houses—and they had meant more to her than anything else in this fine house. The fact that her grandmother had bequeathed them to her with the cottage was worth any amount of ridicule from her mother. She had trusted her to take care of them as their new custodian and that was precisely what she was doing.

So she had every reason to smile and pretend that everything was fine and she was just dandy! After everything Helen had done for her, she was not going to let her down. No way. Not going to happen. And so far her blind date had not appeared so she had this time to herself.

She needed a drink to ease the burning pain in her throat. That was all.

Sara quickly loaded up her plate with savoury bites, then paused in front of a superb dessert trolley. And right on top was a black satin-lined tray of chocolates which had been shaped into small award statuettes. Except that

the few remaining chocolates had been crushed by other
guests in their rush to gobble them up and from where
she was standing looked more like body halves, with a
luscious creamy-white centre. *Perfect.*

She had just scooped up some chocolate legs onto a
silver spoon when there was a clatter and a loud beeping
noise and Helen's distinctive voice called out from the
centre of the room. Sara turned around just in time to see
her friend stand on a chair holding a microphone in one
hand and waving her basket in her other hand with such
gusto that poor little stuffed Toto was joggling about and
threatening to jump out at any minute.

'Hello, everyone. Me here. Thanks for coming. Just
to let you know that there are five more minutes before
the karaoke starts, so finish off your drinks and food
and get ready to sing your heart out. Yes. That's right.
Hollywood musicals. I just *know* it is going to be the best
fun. Thanks.'

With that, Caspar strolled up and wrapped his arm
around Helen's waist to lift her off the chair and back
to the table, both of them laughing and so very happy.
And, despite the fact that she wished her friends every joy,
Sara felt her heart break as she watched Helen and Caspar
clinging together. Was she ever going to find someone
she wanted to be with who could return her love without
seeing her as little more than an aristocratic trophy girl?

Sara was so distracted that it took her a second to realise that the other partygoers were making a sudden rush
towards her and what was left on the buffet table. Drat.
She would have to work fast to stock up before the hordes
descended. Good thing she was at the dessert end of the
queue. And with that she turned back to the trolley.

Only her way was blocked by the man in the cape. And
as she moved forward and he turned towards her, her hand

banged into his arm and some of Sara's chocolate legs went flying onto the floor, narrowly missing his suit.

'Oh, I am so sorry,' she said, suddenly aware that she had not even realised that he was standing there as she reached across. 'How clumsy of me.'

Sara looked straight across into a pair of blue-grey eyes, the brightness backlit by the gentle light from a crystal chandelier over the buffet table. Their eyes locked for a moment, and something inside her flipped over. Several times.

This vampire was probably the best-looking man she had seen in a very long time. He had a long oval face with a strong chin and cheekbones which could have been carved by a Renaissance sculptor, backed up by light Mediterranean colouring.

The only things that stopped her from melting into a pool at his feet were the deep frown lines between his heavy dark brown eyebrows. Perhaps he was as worried about the karaoke as she was?

Sara blinked several times. On the other hand, perhaps mixing allergy tablets with strange cocktails was not such a good idea and she should skip that question? But there was definitely something in the way he looked at her which had her skin standing to attention and her entire body waving *hello, handsome*!

'My fault entirely,' he replied 'Ah. Now it makes perfect sense. I came between a woman and her next chocolate fix. I now consider myself fortunate to have survived.'

He bent down and picked up what was left of the chocolate leg, which was now covered with a thick layer of whatever was on the fine parquet flooring from the feet of the guests. Only he squeezed it a little too hard, and the chocolate burst to release a gooey white chocolatey sticky mess over his white vampire costume gloves.

Sara held out a couple of napkins at arm's length. 'Don't get the chocolate on your gloves—you'll never get the stain out!'

Leo nodded wisely, tried to wipe the fragments of melted dark chocolate from the white fabric, gave up, then picked up a fresh piece of broken chocolate from the tray with his fingertips and bit into it. 'Might as well make the most of having messy fingers and be reckless. White fondant icing and bitter dark choc. Um…not too bad at all.'

Leo lifted the box from the display like a waiter and wafted them in front of Sara's nose.

'Miss Golightly, please allow me to replace your crushed confectionary in exchange for a nibble. And try saying that after one of Caspar's cocktails without getting slapped.'

Sara laughed out loud, making him raise his head, and he gave her a warm smile, which was slightly set off by the chocolate on his teeth—but warm nevertheless, with a certain twinkle in his eye which was infectious enough to make it impossible for her to refuse.

'Only if you can spare one, dear Count? How kind, thank you.'

Sara turned her head and nodded over her shoulder. 'All ready for your party piece? I have to warn you, Helen is relentless. Nobody will escape.'

He looked from side to side and leant closer, giving her a free whiff of a stunning body wash. 'Ze Prince of Darkness does not do diz party piece. No, no. It ees no elegant.'

'Can't sing for toffee?' Sara asked in a light voice, eyebrows raised.

His reply was a small shrug and a flip of one hand. 'So many talents.' Then he dropped his head and said through the corner of his mouth, 'Every dog in the village would start howling at the moon if I started singing. Tone deaf. Tried before. Crashed and burned. Not going to embarrass myself again.'

Sara was about to reply when a large gentleman in a huge gorilla suit joggled her arm en route to the buffet table, almost causing her to lose her dinner plate, and she had to snatch it away from catastrophe.

'I have a suggestion,' Sara whispered in her very best conspiratorial voice.

She glanced from side to side around the room. The way onto the patio was blocked by the karaoke machine and Helen and her workmates, who were setting up some fiendish plan to persuade them all to sing. Drat! That was one exit down. *Time to get creative.*

'What would you say if I told you that I knew a secret exit onto the garden and we could escape the karaoke machine and eat our dinner in peace?'

Dracula's reply was to take a surprisingly firm hold around her waist, which made her gasp, and a firmer grip on his dinner plate before he whispered, 'I would tell you that I will follow you to the ends of the earth, my precious beauty. But make it fast. Caspar is on the prowl, looking for victims. And he has found a plastic machine gun.'

'Okay, now I am intrigued,' her fellow escapee whispered as they casually strolled along the wide terrace which ran around the full length of the hotel.

The sound of clinking glasses, tunes from the classic musicals, really bad singing and lively chatter floated out into the summer evening through the open patio doors from the drawing room. Helen's party was in full swing but they had escaped and enjoyed their dinner in luxurious calm—and without the hindrance of evening gloves.

'How on earth did you know about that secret staircase leading down from the hall to the back door?'

Sara looked up at him and her lips curled into a smirk before she replied, 'Oh, I know every hidden passage and room and secret stair in that hotel. But of course you wouldn't know... I'm a local girl. In fact—' and at this she paused '—you might say I am *very* local.'

Then she took pity on his confusion, smiled and leant forward before adding, as casually as she could, 'I grew up in that house. Kingsmede Manor used to be my home.'

She stopped suddenly, dropped her shoulders back and pointed towards the upper floor of the building. 'Do you see the arched window with the stained glass? The room just at the corner on the left-hand side with the tiny balcony? That was my bedroom. I could lie in bed at night and watch the stars and the trees through the big picture window. It was magical!'

'Now I'm really confused,' he replied. 'Are you telling me that your family used to own this house?'

'That's right,' she answered with a shrug. 'I am officially the last in the line of a family of Victorian eccentrics who built this house many generations ago. My grandmother passed away three years ago and left the whole place to my mother.'

Sara tilted her head and was grateful for the darkness in their corner of the garden so that he could not see the glint in her eyes. Talking about those sad times still hurt. 'Mum didn't want to live here—there were huge debts to clear and I'm sure you can imagine how expensive this house would be to run as a holiday home.' Sara waved one hand, then let it fall as she turned back to face him. 'And now it is this lovely hotel.'

'Wow,' he replied, with a look of something close to

awe in his face. 'Are you serious? Did you really grow up in this amazing place?'

'Oh, yes,' she answered with a tiny shrug. 'I was sent to boarding school at the age of eight but this was the place I came back to every school holiday. We didn't have much money to spend on luxuries but it was paradise for a child.'

She stopped talking and stood still for a moment, her eyes scanning the whole front of the building. 'I have wonderful memories of my life here.' She turned back to him with a smile and raised her eyebrows to ask with a lift in her voice, 'How about you? What is your old castle like back in Transylvania?'

'Oh, the usual problems of living in a dungeon,' he replied with a sniff. 'You just cannot get the staff these days. Draughty. Cold. There is a lot to be said for central heating.'

'Oh, I so agree,' Sara said with a nod. 'The modern vampire needs his central heating.'

'Even so,' Dracula said, leaning against a wrought-iron balustrade at the edge of the terrace and peering out across the grounds in front of the house, 'I envy you growing up here.'

Sara moved closer so that she could stand next to him with her arms stretched out on the metal railing. The cherry trees in front of the house had been strung with white party lights so the front entrance looked like a picture from a children's fairy tale. A pergola filled with climbing white roses and multicoloured clematis in pinks and purples had been built on the western side of the house to capture the last rays of the setting sun and as Sara and the vampire looked out onto the lawns a light breeze lifted the perfume and surrounded them with warmth and fragrance.

It was a magical evening and Sara felt her shoulders relax for the first time in many days. A new moon appeared in the night sky, which was clear and already twinkling with the first stars.

She was suddenly very glad that she had accepted Helen's invitation to the party.

This was why she'd never found peace when she'd lived in London. It had never come close to this special place in her life.

She leant in contented silence and grasped the balustrade with both hands and inhaled the warm air and the warm atmosphere drifting out from the party, which was going on quite well without them. She was also aware of how very close she was standing next to this man she had only just met. Close enough that she could hear his breathing and the way his cloak rustled in the slight breeze, silk on silk.

This was new! It had been a long time since she had spent the evening alone with a handsome man. Especially one content to enjoy the view in silence. He seemed happy to allow her to do all the talking but she was relaxed enough in his presence to chatter on about nothing in particular.

Of course he knew very little about her and they could enjoy the type of conversation that could only happen between strangers, unfettered by past history.

Perhaps she should start talking about orchids and fertiliser and the poor man would run away for help? As it was, she knew Helen would soon send out a search party to track her down so that she could be introduced to her blind date whether she liked it or not.

A twinge of guilt made Sara wince. Caspar's friend was probably inside, feeling most neglected and rejected. She should go in and face the music in more ways than one.

Soon.

She would go in soon.

She could stand here for another few minutes and enjoy herself before going back to the party and throwing herself into Helen's celebrations. She was not going to spend her best friend's party hiding in the garden feeling sorry for herself or mourning the life she had once known. Especially when she had such a good listener as a companion.

'I don't come here very often,' she whispered, even though there was only the two of them on the terrace. 'My cottage is just across the lane so I can see the house every day if I want. But this garden is for hotel guests now, not previous residents. This is a rare treat.'

'That's because you love this place so much and you miss it,' he replied in a gentle voice and chuckled at her gasp of surprise. 'Yes. It is fairly obvious. Especially...'

'Especially?' Sara asked in a shaky breath. She was not used to opening up to a complete stranger in this way and it startled her, and yet was strangely reassuring. *Weird.*

'I was going to say, especially considering that your family sent you away to boarding school when you were only eight years old.' He blew out hard and blinked. 'Eight! That's hard for me to get my head around. You must have been so miserable.'

Miserable? How did she even begin to explain to a stranger the misery of leaving her home in the middle of the most traumatic time of her life? Abandoned by her mother, who didn't know what to do with her. Worse, by the father she adored, who thought he was doing the right thing by leaving them to start a new life in South America when the life of luxury he'd thought he had married into when he'd chosen a girl with an aristocratic title and a country estate had completely failed to materialise.

Her whole world had shifted under her feet and was still shifting now. Even after three years of living in her tiny cottage, there were some days when she had to remind herself that she had a home that no one could take away from her. She might be unloved but she would never again be homeless and rootless. She had sold everything she had and burnt her bridges to make the orchid nursery a reality—but it was hers.

Sara blinked hard. The blur of constant activity which she used to fill each day created a very effective distraction, but even talking about those sad times brought memories percolating up into her consciousness. Memories she had to put back in their place where they belonged.

Selling the house and most of the contents had been the price her mother had to pay for the chance for them both to be independent. But it had still been incredibly painful.

Instinctively, she felt the man in the black costume looking at her, watching her, one elbow on the metal railing, waiting for her to give him an answer to this question.

She turned slightly towards him and noticed for the first time, in the light from the party room and the twinkling stars in the trees, that his eyes were not grey but a shade of blue like the ocean at dusk. And at that moment those eyes were staring very intently at her.

On another day and another time she might even have said that he was more gorgeous than merely handsome. He was certainly striking and wore the cape and costume as though it had been made for him.

Allure of this quality did not come cheap.

It was a shame that she had sworn off dating for at

least a year or two until she had a new greenhouse up and running. Until then, she could keep her loneliness to herself and wear her happy face to the world, even if it was a struggle sometimes.

'Oh,' she said, 'they had their reasons. And it wasn't all bad. I knew that I would always have this home to come back to in the holidays. My grandmother had such fun here. She loved this old house, especially the gardens.'

'The gardens?' he asked and his hand swept out towards the long stretches of simple grass lawns. 'What was so special about the gardens? They seem pretty normal to me.'

'Oh,' she breathed, and a great grin creased her face. 'The gardens then were nothing like they are today. They were…extraordinary. Unique. People used to come for miles just to see the gardens of this house.' Sara turned back to face the lawns and gestured past the cherry trees towards the beech hedges and the long drive to the lane. 'It's only a few minutes' walk to Kingsmede village from here and the gardens were somehow part of the community. She used to hold the most remarkable parties here. The local village fete, of course. Then there were weddings, birthday parties and all kinds of local and family events.'

She flicked a smile at Dracula, who was still watching her, almost as though he was studying her. 'I can remember my grandmother's eightieth birthday party as though it was yesterday. We started in the afternoon with most of the village turning up for afternoon tea, and then moved on to dinner with a live band with dancing and singing. Then there were fireworks. Lots of fireworks.'

Sara shook her head but when she spoke her voice trailed away. 'It was a magical night. The end of an era, I suppose.' Then she looked up into the sky at the new moon and felt the sting of tears in the corners of her eyes as the memory of the event swirled through her. She was so captivated by the intense memory of her grandmother dancing in her ballgown and jewels, and the music and the fairy lights and trees, that when Dracula shifted next to her on the railing, she suddenly came crashing down to earth with the harsh reality that those moments and those parties were long gone like the gardens that used to be here.

'Oh, I'm so sorry,' she said through a tight, sore throat. 'Here I am, rambling on about people you don't know and a world which has already long gone. How embarrassing! I don't usually go on about the house like this. The hotel company own it now and there's nothing I can do about that. But thank you for listening.'

Dracula inclined his head towards her. 'I got the feeling that you needed to talk. Apparently I was right. And you weren't boring, not in the least.'

He took a step closer in the fading light and in the harsh shadows his cheekbones were sharp angles and his chin strong and resolute. His body was tall and slim but anything but boyish.

Just the opposite. The masculine strength and power positively beamed out from every pore and grabbed her. It was in the way he held his body, the way his head inclined just that tiny fraction of an inch as he looked at her as though she was the most fascinating woman he had ever met, and oh, yes, the laser focus of those intelligent blue-grey eyes had a lot to do with it as well.

He was so close that she could touch him if she wanted to. In the calm tranquillity of their pergola she could practically feel the softness of his breath on her skin as he gazed intently into her eyes. Loud laughter and bright music was playing somewhere in the house but all of her senses were totally focused on this man who had outspokenly captivated her.

She couldn't move.

She did not want to move.

And then he did something extraordinary. He leant forward so that their bodies were almost touching and she sucked in a breath, terrified, exhilarated and excited. Was he going to kiss her? But, with a faint smile, he lifted his chin, his eyes broke away from hers and he reached out to the climbing rose behind her head and stepped back a second later with a perfect full white rose.

She stared, wide-eyed, as he swept his thumb and forefinger down the stem with his naked hand.

'A lovely rose for a lovely lady. No thorns allowed. May I?'

Completely at a loss as to what he was asking permission to do, Sara simply nodded and smiled as he stretched out his hand, lifted her left wrist towards him and carefully pressed the rose stem under the jewelled strap of her watch.

'I never had more than a window box growing up, so I am totally clueless when it comes to flowers,' he murmured in a smooth warm voice. 'But I hope you will accept this small token as a pitiful excuse for a wrist corsage.'

She smiled and bit her lower lip, and was instantly grateful for the cover of darkness to cover up her blushes. 'It's lovely. Thank you.'

'Excellent,' he replied and stepped back and extended both arms, his cloak flapping behind him. 'Well, that only leaves one more special request to complete the evening.' He twirled his right hand in the air and gave a dramatic short bow from the waist. 'May I have the pleasure of this dance, young lady? I shall try not to step on your toes or spread chocolate on the back of your dress.'

'Well,' Sara replied with a sigh and looked from side to side on the deserted terrace, 'my dance card is already quite full, but I suppose I could spare you a few minutes.'

Instantly she found his right hand resting lightly at her waist, and her right hand resting lightly inside his fingers. 'They're playing our song.' He smiled and drew her closer towards him so that the front of his black jacket was just touching her chest.

Stunned by being pressed against him by a firm hand in the small of her back, Sara blinked hard, swallowed down a gulp of shock and paid attention. 'We have a song?' she asked, then looked up from his shoes to find him smiling deep into her eyes.

'Of course.' He grinned and stepped forward with his right foot, then shifted onto his left, carrying her with him onto the wider part of the terrace. 'Just listen,' he whispered into her ear, and moved gracefully from side to side.

It was a waltz. A dreamy concoction from a long gone world of Viennese dancing in crystal ballrooms, captured for ever on celluloid and movie soundtrack albums so that she could listen to those soaring strings in a country garden in England, through the open patio doors of a party. And it took her breath away.

Sara was so entranced that it took her a second to realise that her feet were moving instinctively into the waltz positions she had been taught at school all those years ago.

'I know what you're thinking,' her dance partner whispered and she opened her eyes to find him smiling down at her. 'Is the Danube really blue? And are there woods in Vienna?'

'Ah. Caught me out,' she tutted back, suddenly grateful that he did not know what she had actually been thinking, which had a lot more to do with just how close their bodies were pressed together.

'I do have one question,' he said in a low voice. 'Don't you find it difficult to go back into the house as just a normal guest?'

'Yes, I do,' she answered as truthfully as she could. 'But I couldn't miss the chance to catch up with Helen for a few hours. We lead such busy lives these days.'

And then Sara tilted her head and looked up at the tall man whose eyes had rarely left hers for the whole time that they had been out on the terrace.

'And how about you? How do you know Caspar? I noticed you chatting when you came in and, no offence, but you don't look like a lawyer.'

The corner of his mouth turned up into a small smile which even in this light seemed to illuminate his face and soften the harsh contours, making it even more handsome than it was before.

'None taken,' he replied and pursed his lips. 'Caspar used to date my younger sister. And I think it's time for a twirl.' He stepped back as the music soared to a crescendo and lifted his left arm high above her head, just far enough so that Sara could turn around in probably the worst twirl under the sun, but they were both laughing at the end of it.

Judging by the applause and cheers that burst forth from the party, they had not been the only ones who had tried to match the music with some dancing.

Instantly the music shifted to a loud song from a children's cartoon sung by dancing kitchen utensils and her vampire looked at her and shrugged.

'I agree,' Sara murmured and shook her head. 'I think that's my signal to sit the next dance out. But thank you, kind sir. And now it is my turn for a question. Isn't that a little awkward?' she asked as his hands released her and she felt in desperate need of a distraction to fill the growing space between them. 'Seeing Caspar with Helen? You do know that they adore each other?'

He raised an eyebrow and chuckled as he leant back against the railing. 'I certainly hope so since I have been invited to their wedding. But no, it isn't a problem. In fact I'm pleased for him. It was years ago, my sister is happily married and quite pregnant and Caspar has found someone who loves him. Good luck to them both.'

Then he turned sideways. 'You dance beautifully. And in fact I should be thanking you for helping me to make a lucky escape.'

He chuckled loudly and thrust both hands deep into the trouser pockets of his tuxedo trousers. 'The lovely Helen had set me up on a blind date! Can you believe it? I am sure her old school friend is absolutely charming but there is no way that I intend to date a country girl who needs Helen's help to find an escort for the evening. Thank you but no. I don't do country. Never have, never will.'

Sara very slowly and carefully moved closer to the handrail that she could gaze out over the lawns without looking at the vampire. Was it possible? Was this the famous Leo that Helen was trying to set her up with? Caspar's friend?

She almost groaned out loud. Of course! Who else would it be?

Sara's cheeks burned with humiliation and embarrassment. How could she have been so stupid? She was never going to live this one down.

Now what did she do? Tell the truth? Try and laugh it off and save them both the embarrassment? What were the alternatives? After all, she already knew that he would be an usher at Helen and Caspar's wedding, so there was no escaping him. But right now at this minute he had no idea that she was the country bumpkin in question.

She glanced up at him and instant regret fluttered through her.

Just when she was enjoying this man's company, there was a sting in the tail. He was handsome, generous and a good listener. Those were good credentials for any date. Helen certainly did good work except for one tiny thing. This man had no intention of going out on a blind date with her, just as she had no intention of going out with him.

Suddenly all the enjoyment of her waltz in the moonlight seemed to drift away into the air like smoke in the wind. Every spark of energy and enthusiasm was extinguished, leaving behind a sad and pathetic girl whose friends took pity on her.

Dracula was right. She had become the country girl he so clearly despised, just as her mother had predicted she would. Clumsy, gauche, uncultured and unattractive. Destined for a life alone because no decent man would look twice at her. She could just hear her mother's voice, drenched with disgust and disappointment, on the day after the funeral when her ex-boyfriend had dumped her and taken off back to London as fast as his sports car could take him.

Well, it looks like you were right, Mum.

Suddenly the enormity of everything that was happening in her life seemed to crash down on her, and Sara shivered in her sleeveless shift dress. There was no way that she could go back into the party now.

It was time to go home. And back to the insular life she had created for herself and all of the harsh realities that lay there—and definitely without this man who had treated her as an equal for an hour. He looked so handsome and clearly successful, while she was a walking advert for a mess.

'Feeling cold?' Dracula asked and, without waiting for a reply, he reached behind his shoulders and slipped off the scarlet-lined cape and draped it in a single swirl of his wrists around her neck so that it fell almost to her bracelets in a cocoon of body-warmed fabric. Sara inhaled the perfume of the man's body and, despite her best efforts to resist, pulled the fabric closer around her so that his warmth penetrated her goose-fleshed arms and the shivering died away.

'Thank you,' she murmured but still could not look him in the eye. 'If you'll excuse me, I think I'll head home for the evening. It has been a long busy week. I'll make sure that Caspar returns the cape to you before you leave. Thank you for your company.'

'Hey, wait a moment, Cinderella,' he replied as she lifted her head and tried to walk casually back to the side gate which led to her cottage. 'Did you say that you were staying across the lane? Please allow me to see you home. It is the very least I can do, seeing as you gave me such a lucky escape.'

And, before she could accept or decline, Dracula stepped in place beside her and they strolled side by side across the lawns and away from the house in silence. Her throat burning with humiliation, her eyes stinging. Incapable of speech.

CHAPTER THREE

SOMEWHERE in her bedroom a full symphony orchestra was playing what should have been a soothing overture to a lovely ballet. Except, to Sara's ears, the instruments sounded as though they had been tuned in a sawmill.

She stirred and tugged the duvet farther towards her chin, then yawned loudly. The first thing on her to-do list that morning would be to retune the radio to a popular music channel.

She tried to snuggle back to sleep, but there was something uncomfortable on her pillow.

She reached up until her fingers closed around a string of pearls.

Oh, no! She must have slept in them all night. There would probably be bobble-shaped marks all over her neck and chin.

Never mind. It was early. She still had plenty of time to recover from last night and get smartened up before her meeting at the hotel.

Last night! Ah, the party. That would explain why she felt so weary. She ran her tongue over her parched lips. Juice. She needed juice. Then tea would be good.

Her eyes flickered slowly open and both hands lifted the duvet as she glanced down.

Helen Lewis had a lot to answer for. It had been years

since she had been so tired that she had crawled into bed in her underwear. Sara glanced around her bedroom and, sure enough, her black dress lay across the armchair at the foot of her bed.

Sara was still mentally shaking her head when an Abyssinian ball of fur and mischief launched itself onto the duvet and sashayed up, until Sara could scratch between his ears.

'Oh, Pasha, you know that you are not allowed in here.'

She laughed as the rich golden brown cat purred with pleasure, then started nudging her face, the cute red nose pushing against her neck so he could play with the pearls that she was still wearing.

'Ready for breakfast? Good. I'll head for the shower and repair the damage before anyone sees me.'

Sara pushed back the covers and swung her legs over the edge of the bed. It took a second or two before her world stopped spinning, but at least she was on her feet and ready to get to work. She had a lot to do today and not much time to do it in.

She was still feeling dreamy and slightly dazed when her toes crushed down onto something round and hard on the soft handmade rug that had come with the cottage when she inherited it...

She dared not look down.

Oh, please, not something else her cat had brought in.

Sure enough, Pasha came sidling up to her and started rubbing himself up and down her legs.

'Pasha, if you have been in the kitchen bin again, you are in so much trouble!'

Her grandmother's old cat had a knack for finding something from the floor to play with. Loose screws, plant ties, paperclips—they all ended up being scooped out and played with. And Helen had brought bags of treasures with her when they played dress up before the party.

Sara knew from personal experience that all jewellery and shiny small items had to be locked securely away unless she wanted them to be redistributed around the cottage as cat toys.

'Okay. Let's find out what you've brought me this time!'

Sara moved her foot and glanced down at the floor.

And stopped breathing.

It was a button. A large black button with a silver scroll on it. The sort of button that might be used on a coat. Or a black evening cloak. The kind of cloak a vampire count might wrap around a girl's shoulders late in the evening. For example.

Eloise Sara Jane Marchant Fenchurch de Lambert had many doubts in life, but one thing was certain.

That button had not come from any garment she owned.

Suddenly she felt dizzy and collapsed back on her bed, trying to ignore Pasha, who was headbutting her legs.

Breathe deeply. That was the secret. Inhale, and then exhale slowly. Slowly.

She clasped both hands to the top of her head.

Think. Think. Last night. What was the last thing she could remember from last night? Her eyes clenched shut.

The party. Dracula. Sharing her buffet dinner…with Dracula. Escaping onto the terrace and walking around the garden and talking and dancing…with Dracula. Then Dracula turned into Caspar's friend Leo instead of a bat and offered to walk her home. Then? Nothing specific. Her cottage. He opened the front door for her. Lights.

Her eyes opened just in time to see Pasha playing with the button between his paws.

Of course! She had been wearing his heavy cloak on their short walk from the hotel, but she had slipped it off as soon as she was inside and handed it back. The button must have come loose and Pasha had brought it in.

A great whoosh of relief came out of Sara's mouth and her shoulders dropped six inches.

Sara reached forward and snatched the button away from her cat before it was completely clawed to pieces.

'Sorry, Pasha. I need to give this back to Caspar so he can return it to his vampire friend.'

Shaking her head, Sara pushed herself off the bed and across the corridor to her plain white-tiled bathroom. This was going to be a two coffee morning if she had any chance at all of impressing the Events Manager at the hotel. It had not been easy to arrange a meeting on a weekend, but this was her one chance to convince him that Kingsmede Manor should choose Cottage Orchids for all their flower displays.

Of course she had made light of her business plans in front of Helen—her friend was getting married in a few weeks and she didn't want to worry her with finances, but a regular contract with the hotel would make a difference to her investment plans. She had so many exciting ideas for the next twelve months! It would be wonderful if she could transform at least some of them into reality.

No pressure then. Oh, no.

The Venetian glass mirror with its silver surround had been her grandmother's—and one of the few precious things her mother had allowed her to bring from the old house, only because the hotel did not want it. There was a chip in the frame where the mirror had once fallen off the wall when the plaster had got too wet to take the weight, but Sara didn't mind.

She brushed her hair out and peered at the glass. Not too bad considering she had slept in her make-up. The red lipstick was gone, probably onto the pillowcase. Time to hit the shower; she needed to be sharp this morning and it was already... Oh, what time was it?

And then Sara made the mistake of looking for her wristwatch. Which she had left on the basin the evening before. Same as always.

Only it wasn't there.

Her watch had been lifted away from the basin and any potential splashes onto a higher shelf. And in its place next to the soap dish was a solid white metal ring with a solitaire diamond in the centre.

Her fingers were shaking as she reached out and lifted the ring onto her finger. It was huge, just fitting her thumb. It was a man's ring.

She slowly turned around and looked left, half dreading what she might see.

The dressing gown she had left on the side of the bath the night before when she was rushing to get changed for the party was hanging up behind the bathroom door. And her fluffy hand towel was hanging from the towel rail so that the lavender embroidered design on the bottom was straight and parallel to the floor.

This was very nice, except that when she used the hand towel it usually ended up being tossed over the side of the bath or the basin. In fact, it was a standing joke that if you wanted to find a towel in Sara's house you had to look anywhere but on the towel rail.

Someone had hung up her dressing gown and used her hand towel. And that someone was not Helen, who was so used to Sara's quirky habits that she had long since given up clearing up in her wake.

The only thing that had not been moved in her bathroom was the indoor drying rack across the top of the bath. Her smartest lace bras and panties were still stretched out to dry, complete with frayed edges, re-sewn straps and labels which had been washed so many times that the print had worn away.

And then she saw what had been staring her in the face the whole time.

Her toilet seat was up and standing to attention.

Two seconds later, the scream that came from Sara's mouth drove Pasha through the bathroom and under the bed.

'Leo, you idiot! When was the last time you saw it?'

Leo Grainger groaned and pinched the bridge of his nose between his thumb and forefinger. There were very few people in this world who knew him well enough to call him an idiot to his face, but Caspar was one of them, and this time he could well be right.

'I know I was wearing it before I put the white gloves on to go out to the party, and then in the hotel bathroom when I took it off to wash my hands. After that. No clue.'

'The bathroom?' Caspar shrugged and stared at his friend in amazement. 'Who takes their ring off when they wash their hands?'

'I do. Always have. You know that ring is one of the few things I have left from my dad, so I take care of it. Okay?'

'Okay, okay.' Caspar raised both hands in submission and helped himself to more toast. 'What about after the party? I noticed you escaped the karaoke by taking off with Sara Fenchurch. Any chance you lost it in the gardens…? What? What did I say?'

Leo dropped his head to the table and knocked it twice on the breakfast tablecloth before groaning and sitting back with his eyes closed, grateful for the fact that Caspar had come to Leo's hotel room for room service breakfast.

'Sara? As in blind date Sara? That was the girl in the black dress and gloves?'

Caspar waved his buttered toast in Leo's direction. 'Sure. I saw you chatting at the buffet and the next thing I knew you were out on the terrace and…' The truth slowly dawned on Caspar and he sighed out loud. 'You did know that the girl you were feeding chocolates to was…'

Leo shook his head from side to side and closed his eyes.

'Ah. Right. So Helen hadn't introduced you after all.'

And then Caspar cheered up and leant across and thumped Leo on the arm.

'Does my lady love do good work or does she not? I told you that Sara was a great girl! Helen will be ecstatic. She adores Sara and apparently the girl went through a rough time before we met but, hey, good on you both. What? What?'

Leo stared cold-eyed across the table at Caspar. 'Do you think that Sara knew who I was? Before the party?'

'Of course,' Caspar replied, rolling his eyes and reaching for the marmalade. 'Helen always gives her friends a full colour dossier on any bloke she wants them to hook up with.'

'So Sara didn't know who I was before we met?'

Caspar shrugged. 'She would probably never have spoken to you if she had. I got the impression Sara was just as impressed with the idea of being set up on a blind date as you were. Why? Does that make a difference?'

'It might. It's amazing what a Kaplinski cocktail and a heavy dose of moonlight and nostalgia can do. She got upset and I ended up walking her back to her place across the lane.'

There was silence for a few seconds, before Caspar lowered his voice to reply. 'Walked her home…?'

Leo nodded once.

Caspar glanced towards the door before going on. 'Anything I should know before Helen arrives? Because these girls tell each other everything. And I mean everything.' He blinked several times.

'I escorted her to the door, saw her inside, then went to the bathroom before I left,' he replied in a low voice. 'She was already asleep by the time I came out.'

Caspar sighed in relief and rubbed his hands together. 'That's better. Now we're getting somewhere. All you have to do is call Sara and ask if she found a man's ring in her bathroom this morning. Simple. Right? Leo? Why are you shaking your head at me like that? You know who she is and where she lives.'

Leo made eye contact with Caspar and squeezed his eyes together. Tight. And winced. 'Oh, yes. Right after I tell her that I slipped her dress off and tucked her in last night. That is going to go down well, especially when I have to stand next to her and smile at your wedding at some point in the near future.'

'You undressed her?' There was amazement in Caspar's voice, even a touch of awe and horror. 'Oh, that is so not good. Did you know that Helen and Sara used to call themselves the two Musketeers at school? Upset one, upset both of them.'

'Thanks! I'm looking for some useful advice here.

I need my father's ring back before I meet up with my aunt and the rest of the clan on Friday, and you need to keep the lovely Helen from drowning me in the fountain outside.'

'I'm thinking, I'm thinking.' Caspar started drumming his fingers on the table. 'We need to come up with something so wonderful that Sara and Helen will forget any embarrassment and love you for ever.' Then his fingers stilled on a small crystal vase containing three cut pink orchid blossoms. 'Of course. Flowers. Helen is worried about the state of Sara's business.'

Caspar leant over the table and grinned. 'Leo, my friend? How would you like to become the lovely Sara's knight in shining armour and get your father's ring back at the same time? Time to put some of those Rizzi family connections to good use, my man.'

Sara Fenchurch pretended to look for something in her briefcase until everyone else had left the hotel reception area before gingerly stepping out and walking calmly to the Events Manager's office, smiling as she went and hoping nobody could see her shaking.

She was two minutes early for her appointment. Two minutes to somehow calm her racing pulse and steady her nerves just long enough to convince the Events Manager, Mr Evans, that he should choose her plant nursery for all of his weddings and special occasions. This could be a terrific new order.

If only she could get past her nerves about asking for work. She always hated this part of running her business. Helen said it was the whole idea that she was relying on another person to decide whether to choose her nursery, or not. And she was spot on.

Sara had already spent far too many years doing what

other people expected her to do, how they wanted her to do it and generally performing like a trained seal in a circus. Doing whatever she had to for their approval.

Until three years ago, she had lived her life according to other people's rules. That life had ended on the day she had started making decisions on her own. Good or bad. Safe or reckless. She was responsible for making her own way in the world now.

The orchid business had given her back some of the self-confidence she had lost, then had added more than she'd ever had before. It had taken most of her savings but it was working, and she was making enough to live on. Now she was ready to move up and on and take her passion to the next level.

This was her business and she was a businesswoman and she needed customers like this hotel.

Head up, shoulders back. *She was going in.*

Except that just as she stretched out her hand to knock, the fine panelled door was flung open and she almost rapped her knuckles on the nose of the man she had come to see.

'Well, good morning to you, Miss Fenchurch. And right on time,' he gushed and shook her hand with so much enthusiasm that his trendy wraparound spectacles joggled on the end of his nose. 'Tony Evans. Delighted to see you again so soon. I do so admire punctuality. May I offer you some tea or coffee? And do come in. I would like to get started as soon as possible.'

She managed a smile by biting the inside of her mouth to conceal her astonishment at the warm welcome. 'Thank you, Mr Evans, but I'm fine, thanks.'

By some miracle, her legs still worked as she followed the Events Manager into the palatial office which had once been the butler's room and sat neatly down, stiff backed and silent, until he had collapsed his substantial girth into the huge leather chair on the other side of the desk.

'You know what makes this hotel special, Sara?' he asked, pointing out of the window across the beautiful gardens. 'And I hope you don't mind me calling you Sara, but I just know that we are going to get on famously.'

He did not wait for a reply before going on. 'The small details. Our guests want something special and luxurious and that is what we aim to give them. And they want our suppliers to be local. Low carbon footprint and all of that. And we can't get much more local than your plant nursery, can we?'

Before she could answer, Tony Evans whipped his chair around and clasped his neatly manicured hands in front of her.

'I want you to be one of those suppliers, Sara. I've been looking at that portfolio of arrangements you sent me and I like what I've seen. I know quality when I see it. You've got potential, young lady. And I'm willing to take a risk on you.'

Sara sucked in a discreet breath. *This was it*. After three years of working seven days a week, someone was going to take a chance on her, based on the plants she had grown with her own hands. And, best of all—*most precious of all*—she had done this on her own.

Nobody had pulled strings to get her into a job or a step ahead in the line by using her aristocratic connections.

This was all her own work, and her heart leapt so fast she almost cried.

'A risk, Mr Evans?' her voice squeaked in reply.

'This hotel has events scheduled for every weekend until Valentine's Day next year. Right now, we have two florists working on cut flower arrangements for every room in the hotel as well as special events. I need you to prove to me that I can cut the carbon footprint and provide consistent high quality within budget by choosing you to do the same job.'

He passed a blue folder across the desk to Sara, who could only stare at it, stunned, as he stabbed his forefinger onto the cover several times.

'Inside this wallet are the plans for the biggest corporate weekend of the year. I want to see how you would handle an event this size before I sign any contracts.'

Sara glanced at the first page of the dossier and breathed out very, very, slowly. 'This is a big project but I will try to work through some proposals and get back to you in a few weeks. If that is okay…Mr Evans?'

He paused, then startled her by leaning back in his chair and crossing his arms.

'Our client is on a tight schedule. He has already asked for a detailed cost breakdown and I promised that it would be with him by next Friday at the latest.'

Sara sat in silence for a few seconds before replying in a squeak. 'That's wonderful and so exciting, but do you really mean *next* Friday? As in five days from now?'

Tony Evans nodded in silence, arms still crossed.

Sara swallowed hard before replying. 'I appreciate your vote of confidence, but I really would like more time to…'

'Our current florists are very keen to continue supplying this hotel,' he interrupted, 'and indeed all of the other hotels in the group, so it would be terrific if you could show us the benefits of choosing a local supplier instead of a large company. Don't you agree?'

Sara blinked and tried not to jump onto her chair and punch her fist in the air. Other hotels? Oh, yes. She could supply the other hotels in the group. No trouble at all.

'Of course I have every confidence that you will come up with something spectacular. Leo Grainger tells me that you are the best in the business and I couldn't have a better recommendation than that.'

Sara's eyes flicked open and she stared at Tony Evans in disbelief.

'Leo?' she asked incredulously and cleared her throat. 'Leo Grainger recommended my orchids?'

'He did indeed,' Tony replied and tapped the side of his nose, 'and in glowing terms. That is quite something from a man with his reputation.' And then he paused and frowned at her. 'I confess I was a little concerned about how you are going to manage with your relocation. Finding land to rent around the village is not going to be easy. But I am sure you will let us know your new contact details.'

In an instant all thoughts of Leo Grainger were swept away and Sara sprang back into full focus. 'Relocation?' she replied with a broken smile. 'I'm sorry but there must be some misunderstanding. I have no plans to relocate.'

The smile dropped from Tony's face and he pushed his chin out. 'Ah. You should have received the letter from our managing agents saying that the lands you rent from us will no longer be available from later this year. Part of our redevelopment plan. Big part.'

The air crackled as Sara tried to pull herself together long enough to ask what on earth he was talking about, when the telephone started ringing. 'I'm so sorry but I shall have to take this,' he said with obvious relief in his voice. 'Shall I expect to see your proposals for the event in time for me to agree to them before Friday, Sara? Excellent. Have a great day.'

Sara was just about to turn away, when she looked back

over one shoulder and casually asked, 'Leo Grainger. How exactly do you know him?'

'Oh, apparently Leo is related to the owners. Works as some sort of business consultant,' Tony Evans replied with a shrug, his hand over the telephone mouthpiece. 'Okay, Sara? Friday?'

Seconds later, Sara stood in the corridor feeling as though the cream-and-gold carpet has been whipped out from under her feet.

Leo Grainger was a business consultant who had been in her bedroom, seen her underwear and straightened her towels.

Worse. He was related to the famous Rizzi family of hoteliers who had bought the Manor.

No wonder he had actually thanked her for saving him from a terrible blind date—her!

But then he had recommended her business to the hotel team.

What was going on? Did he feel sorry for her?

With a groan, her fingers tightened around the handle of her briefcase and she remembered the file Tony Evans had just given her.

Suddenly she didn't know whether to kiss Leo in grovelling thanks for opening the door to this amazing opportunity, or kick him hard in the shins for making her feel so worthless and pathetic as a woman.

She closed her eyes and took a breath.

She *should* be grateful that Leo had recommended her work to the hotel—it was a nice thing for him to do.

Except somehow she felt deflated and disappointed.

This was totally crazy! She *should* be enthusiastic. It was just that for a precious few seconds she had thought that she had earned this opportunity because of her own hard work. Instead of which, the decision had been influenced by connections to the powerful people who demanded respect and got it.

But what choice did she have? This was a terrific opportunity which she was going to seize with both hands.

Sara sighed and started to walk towards the curving staircase that led to the guest bedrooms. Helen and Caspar would be heading back to London soon for Sunday lunch with Caspar's parents. This was the ideal time to give Helen Leo's ring, which she had found in her bathroom, and try to laugh off her embarrassment about the blind date.

Or perhaps the famous Leo was feeling a little guilty about his parting comments? Helen and Caspar would have already grilled him over breakfast about how the blind date had gone. If he didn't know who she was last evening, he certainly would know by now.

And she had his ring.

Then Sara stopped at the foot of the staircase and thought for a second.

No. If Leo Grainger the famous business consultant wanted his ring back, he was going to have to come and ask her for it. That way, she could thank him in person for his recommendation and clear the air, for Helen's sake as well as her own.

It would be humiliating, but she could face him and get the embarrassment over and done with. Whatever Leo's reasons for helping her.

In the meantime, she had to call the letting agent. And fast. She didn't want any more of her clients being worried with silly rumours about her moving the orchid nursery. What a ridiculous idea!

That land had been the old kitchen gardens of this house and her grandmother had only sold it to pay for the roof repairs on condition that she could keep her orchid houses in a tiny corner next to the gardener's cottage.

There was no way that the farmer would sell the land to the hotel. Was there?

CHAPTER FOUR

LEO GRAINGER raised his right hand and waved as Caspar and Helen drove slowly away from the hotel and back to their happy London life, leaving him standing in the car park feeling rather like a teenager left at boarding school watching his parents drive away, while he was left alone in a land where he didn't totally understand the local rules and customs.

The feeling was so ridiculous that he shrugged away a moment of disquiet inside his black cashmere jacket before lifting his chin and strolling out onto the stone terrace.

His aunt Arabella had seen something unique and special about Kingsmede Manor, and he certainly trusted her judgement. She had impeccable taste with a superb eye for detail and for spotting the potential of a property, a skill she had built up over a lifetime spent in the hotel trade at every level around the world.

His footsteps slowed and he paused for a minute to admire the imposing stone house in the bright sunlight on a Sunday morning in rural England. Yesterday evening the hotel had been in shadow from the twinkly bulbs scattered amongst the trees and the electric light streaming out from the windows, but this morning it seemed to have more of its own personality.

His mother had grown up in a house like this in Italy—he had seen photographs of the palazzo his grandfather had built after years of creating one of the most successful hotel chains in Europe.

It was magnificent in every respect. Opulent and imposing. The whole building designed with the express purpose to impress and impose a vision of the owner and the power and wealth required to build it, without a hint of the sacrifices the family had made to achieve that wealth.

The rest of the world considered his grandfather to be a successful and brilliant businessman—but that came at a price.

And his mother had paid the price of his fury when she had married for love and not prestige. A price he and his sister were still paying, twelve years after his parents' death, right down to the real reason why he had stolen days away from his team and the frantic lifestyle he had created for himself to come to Kingsmede in the first place.

There could only be one driving goal as far as Leo was concerned.

He was here to do a job and part of that job was honouring his aunt's risk and commitment when she had taken in her orphaned niece and nephew and even found them work in her hotel.

He owed it to her to repay that loyalty with the best work he could do. Of course she had already told him many times that his success in the business world was more than enough reward for any help she had given him.

But that was not how Leo Grainger worked. *Far from it.*

Arabella Rizzi had taught him the most important lesson he had ever learned in his life.

She had told him to respect loyalty and personal integrity more than anything else in this world. So far she had been proven right time and time again and Leo had no intention of changing the way he did business.

His loyalty to his parents went deeper than money or power or reputation—even deeper than his constant drive to maintain control. Grainger Consulting had built up a reputation for being totally objective, and that was precisely what he was going to be now. Objective and focused on the goal—nothing else mattered.

Leo turned away from the house and looked out across the lawns to the trees and open farmland that spread out in all directions around the property.

Sunlit and calm, it was an idyllic setting, if unadventurous.

But what would it be like in winter? On a grey autumn day when the cold wet wind howled across these open fields?

Perhaps the Rizzi team were right? Perhaps an indoor spa extension was the ideal attribute for this small hotel in the middle of the countryside, which could attract visitors winter and summer alike. It certainly needed something to give it an edge.

What could Kingsmede Manor offer him, for example? What was so special about this place that would make him want to choose to come here in the first place and then return time after time? His mission was to find that unique feature which would sell the hotel and keep on selling it.

And the only remarkable thing about Kingsmede Manor that he had seen so far was its previous resident— Sara Fenchurch.

But he had to work fast. His aunt would be flying back to London on Wednesday in time to travel to the Manor and prepare for the meeting on Friday lunchtime. She had asked him to present his recommendations to the whole family. Her family. The Rizzi family. The family who had disowned his mother.

This report was going to have to be spectacular.

He was going to show Paolo Rizzi that he had made the mistake of his life when he had disowned his own daughter and her children.

It was time to show the old man that his grandson was a total professional and that Arabella Rizzi had made the right decision all of those years ago. And Kingsmede Manor was going to be the stage for the big event.

And he was going to be wearing the wedding ring his beloved mother had placed on his father's hand. Oh, yes.

Which brought him right back to the first task of the day.

Leo lifted his head and slid his sunglasses onto his nose.

Time to face the music and find out if Sara Fenchurch had found his father's ring in her bathroom that morning. And eat some humble pie—*his least favourite dish.*

Drat Caspar for setting him up for a blind date in the first place.

Sara had been an astonishing delight until he had opened his big mouth and put his foot in it. Surprising and intriguing and more than just attractive. She had a certain unique quality about her that Leo could not put his finger on and he was kicking himself for being so insensitive.

She certainly would not be hard to find.

The previous evening he had only moonlight and a few fairy lights to guide his way, but this morning he could see that the small wooden gate they'd slipped through the night before was in fact part of a tall red brick wall which formed the boundary to one side of the hotel.

Drawing the gate forward, he stepped through and was immediately on a small lane facing a long low cottage with a red tile roof, square mullioned windows and a low beech hedge providing a barrier to the lane. It was the kind of cottage which would have had a thatched roof when it was built. Flowers spilled out of window boxes, softening the black and white framework and timbered construction.

In the other direction the lane stopped abruptly at a long wooden gate leading to a long orchard. He recognised apples and pears and cherry trees heavy with large red fruits ready to be picked.

But what really caught his attention were the buildings that lay beyond the fruit trees. He had not been able to see them the previous evening but now, rearing up at the end of the cottage garden and extending the full length of the orchard he saw three remarkable ornate glass structures. The closest comparison he could make was to the elaborate hotel palm houses and conservatories he had seen in warmer countries.

Instead of steel structures with thousands of glass panes, these no doubt Victorian designs were white painted wood with ornately carved roof decorations resembling church spires and mediaeval cloisters. These were not greenhouses—these were architectural works of art which called out to his passion for fine design and craftsmanship.

He loved them.

Slightly stunned, Leo strolled across the lane to the gate leading to the painted wooden front entrance of the cottage only a few yards away, complete with pink roses around the door. The picture could have come from a postcard of a classic English scene.

In front of the cottage was a small flower garden about

the same size as his car. What it lacked in space it made up for in the exuberance of plants and flowers of every different hue and colour, size and shape which burst out of the small area, creating a riot of pinks and yellows, purples and blues. It was a startling combination and so different in every way from the formal landscaping of the hotel grounds that he could not help but smile. Perhaps this was the precise effect that Sara wanted to create?

Leo stretched out to press the doorbell just as he noticed that a piece of pink fluorescent paper had been taped onto the door. Someone had written in large letters: *'Direct sales to the public. Buy your orchids straight from the greenhouse. Turn right for Cottage Orchids.'*

The notice had not been there last night!

Caspar had told him that Sara grew orchids, but he was not expecting her to grow them at the bottom of her garden! Surely orchids were imported from tropical countries and she would simply have a wholesale warehouse?

Following the instructions, Leo strolled around the corner, followed the length of the cottage wall and directly in front of him was the first of the ornate conservatory greenhouses with a totally charming wooden chalet guarding the entrance. A white hand-painted sign on the wall of the log cabin told him that he had reached Cottage Orchids, Kingsmede Manor. The door was locked but in front of him was the entrance to the greenhouses and as he peered through the glass he saw a hint of movement inside. The door was slightly ajar and, with a small tap on the frame, Leo opened the door and slipped inside the most remarkable room he had ever been in.

Stretched out in long rows were waist-high wooden racks covered with plants, not in a random pattern, but in strict order by colour and size. Directly in front of him and along one side of the building were pale colours. White, ivory, cream and every shade of gold and yellow. As he stepped closer he realised that all of the plants in this room had the same kind of leaf and flower. The flower shapes and types of blossom were all the same, no matter what colour they were.

So this was a specialist nursery! Niche marketing. Clever. Someone had done their homework. He liked that.

A narrow footpath the width of one paving slab separated those plants from the middle row, where the colours were pinks, oranges and stunning apricots. Young plants, old plants, small plants and tall plants were arranged in strict order with scarcely space between them for the tiny transparent plastic plant pots holding their roots, which spilled out in green and grey tendrils over the surface of each container.

He looked over to the other side of the greenhouse to what must be a nursery area with baby plants in tiny pots as well as plants with stubby sticks sticking out from the compost. It seemed as though every inch of racking space was covered with orchid plants of one type or another.

A distinctive sound caught his ears. Somewhere a girl was singing along in snatches to a pop song with a very sweet voice.

Leo looked around the edge of the staging and shook his head, scarcely believing what he was looking at, and smiled across at Sara Fenchurch. It was the first time that he had smiled that day—but he had good reason.

Sara was nodding her head from side to side as she sang to herself. And it looked as if she was giving a plant a sponge bath.

It was probably the biggest orchid plant he had ever seen, with long thick green fleshy leaves. And she was sponging each leaf in turn underneath and on top. Her hands moved in slow languorous strokes, sensually caressing the leaves one after another with infinite care and with such loving attention that Leo's blood pounded just a little hotter.

At her feet a golden-coloured cat was stretched out so that the sun could warm his tummy on the bright sunlit floor. The cat's eyes were closed but as Leo stepped forward he raised his head just enough to look at him, yawned, stretched out a little longer, then went back to sleep again.

The radio was blasting out modern pop music, lively and fun, so that it was not surprising that Sara had not heard him come into the room, offering him the opportunity to observe her at close range.

Of course he could have interrupted her—but this was a totally self indulgent pleasure he wanted to stretch out for as long as he could. Especially when their next conversation might not be so cordial.

Sara was wearing a yellow T-shirt advertising a brand of orchid compost, green capri pants and spotty fabric plimsolls.

It was strange how this colourful and totally unlikely ensemble only seemed to make her lovely figure even more attractive.

This version of Sara was a revelation. Entrancing and natural.

As he watched in silence and appreciation, she gently lifted the orchid plant away onto a draining board and popped a collection of what looked to Leo like clear plastic food tubs into her sink. Her hands were in constant motion scrubbing and washing the tiny containers as she focused her total attention on the simple task.

An orange baseball cap covered her short brown hair and shaded her eyes from the light streaming in from the long window in front of the sink but he could see a sprinkle of freckles across her lightly tanned nose and cheeks.

The elegant woman he had met the previous evening was gone, replaced by a slim girl in working clothes who seemed to take great delight in scrubbing out plant pots on a hot Sunday morning. She did not need make-up or expensive clothing or accessories to look stunning—she was lovely just as she was.

The smart city girl in the slick black costume he had met last night he could deal with, but this version of Sara Fenchurch was far more unexpected.

Helen and Caspar were wealthy and successful, with lives in the fast lane of London society. That was the world where Leo had made his business—so who was this girl who chose to spend a hot Sunday morning washing plant pots? Was this her plant nursery? Was she an employee of some bigger company? He should have asked Caspar a lot more questions before they'd left this morning—background information was always useful for negotiations, and suddenly he felt out of place. This was Sara's territory—not his. The pretty girl in a T-shirt who looked absurdly cute might not be so generous when she remembered how he had slighted her the night before.

Either way, he was standing here in a black business suit and black shirt on a summer day, feeling completely overdressed, while she was comfortable and cool in her work clothes. He had rarely felt so out of his depth, or so attracted to a girl who was totally natural and comfortable in her own skin—and what skin!

That kind of combination would spell trouble if he stayed around long enough to get to know her better—she was dynamite with a slow burning fuse.

Leo was still trying to formulate some way of introducing himself without looking like a complete idiot when she turned around, saw him and dropped the pots back into the sink with a clatter and then a splosh when they hit the water.

'Good morning, Miss Fenchurch,' he announced calmly with a half smile on his face. 'I'm sorry if I startled you but there was no answer at the cabin.'

She looked up at him wide-eyed, then turned away and rested her hand against the sink. 'Not a problem, Mr Grainger. No problem at all. Are you interested in buying an orchid?' She gestured over one shoulder. 'As you can see, I have a wide selection in an assortment of colours.'

And then she looked up at him through her eyelashes and, as their eyes met, he knew that she was already two steps ahead of him. She knew who he was, why he was there and had absolutely no intention of letting him get away with anything.

He paused and nodded. 'Actually, I have come to apologise for ruining our pleasant evening—then I'm going to buy an orchid. Is that better?'

Sara twitched her lips and tilted her head slightly in his direction but turned back to her pots and kept on scrubbing and rinsing and scrubbing. Only when she had drained every single one of the pots did she slip off her rubber gloves and turn fully towards him with her back against the sink.

Leo braced himself. He deserved whatever was coming his way. Which was why when she did speak what she said knocked him more than he could have imagined.

'Is that why you recommended me to the hotel? To make up for your comments about the blind date you were so pleased to have escaped?'

He winced and gave her a brief nod. There was no point in denying it. 'Partly that,' he admitted, 'and I do apologise for insulting you in any way. I really did have no idea that you were the girl that Helen had asked me to meet.'

And then he took a breath. He had indulged himself far too long—time was money. Down to business. 'But there is something else. I believe I left my ring in your bathroom last night and I would like to have it back, please. That ring means a lot to me.'

'Of course. I understand,' she said and opened her mouth to say something else, then hesitated and seemed to change her mind and simply shook her head. 'And I do appreciate what you did for me. Thank you. It's a great opportunity and I have every intention of taking up the offer. I want you to know that the Manor can rely on me completely. Even if there is a *slight* delay while I make alternative arrangements. But I will do it. I will find a way of making it possible. It simply will take longer than I had expected. That's all.'

Leo was close enough to hear the trembling in her voice and he took a step forward, his hand resting gently on one edge of the wooden staging.

'A delay?' he asked and glanced around. 'The hotel manager was very interested and you certainly seem to have plenty of plants to sell. Assuming that these are your plants.'

She gave a half chuckle. 'Oh, yes. All mine. And there are two more greenhouses this size outside. I may have plants at the moment, but...' And then she swallowed and seemed to struggle with the words. Then she really did have problems talking and turned away from him and rested her hands on the edge of the sink so tightly that her knuckles were white but the stress was only too obvious in the tone of her voice.

'I heard the bad news about the hotel expansion plans

this morning,' she went on as though she were talking to some imaginary figure on the other side of the glass, then gave a half smile as the radio belted out a lively dance track. 'So I have been trying to cheer myself up. Without much success. At this precise moment I am…going through my options but, rest assured, the Rizzi Hotel group will have my proposals on Friday as promised.'

Leo covered the few steps that separated them so that he was standing next to her, looking into her face. She was blinking hard and clearly distressed about something.

'A luxury spa will create jobs for local people, and bring new investment into Kingsmede,' he replied in the low consolatory voice he had perfected for speeches where he had to spell out the hard facts. 'It could bring a lot more guests to the hotel, which means more opportunity for you to sell your flowers. I'm not sure how that equates to bad news.'

Instantly her shoulders dropped back and she turned her head around and looked straight into his eyes.

'In that case you clearly do not have even the remotest idea what this spa extension means to my business,' she said in a low calm voice, but her gaze stayed fixed, her eyes locked onto his.

Until now he had thought that her eyes were brown but in the warm sunlight he was so captivated by a pair of dark green eyes flecked with amber and milk chocolate flakes that he had to blink several times and break their connection so that he could focus on what had shaken her so very badly.

'Then tell me,' he replied with a slight nod in her direction, his upper body leaning slightly forward in encouragement.

Sara gave a brief nod. 'Okay. I will. Look around, Mr Grainger. What do you see?'

Leo glanced from side to side. 'A stunning glasshouse full of orchids?' Then he smiled back at her. 'And it's Leo. Please.'

Sara lifted her chin. 'Very well. Leo. You're right. It is stunning and I am lucky to have it. The floor we are standing on and this beautiful greenhouse came with the cottage.' Then she turned away from him again and looked out of the window before she continued. 'My grandmother also left me the other two greenhouses but they stand on a piece of land I rent from my neighbour.'

She waved her hand towards the high red brick wall to her right. 'All of this area as far as the wall used to be the kitchen gardens of the house. The high wall was the south-facing boundary of the gardens. My grandmother had to sell this land to pay to repair the roof about ten years ago and had always intended to buy it back again, but it never happened and she died before she could do anything about it.'

A long slow sigh was followed by a sharp intake of breath before she was ready to carry on, as though she had to prepare herself to say the words. 'I found out this morning that the organic farmer who bought the land all of those years ago has just received an offer from the hotel which will make it possible for him to retire. He can't afford to turn it down but was sworn to secrecy until the hotel was ready to go public. And now they have.'

Sara reached into the pocket of her trousers and pulled out a slim brown envelope. 'The official notice was waiting for me in the post.' Then she pressed her lips together and shrugged. 'You are probably used to seeing small businesses go to the wall for the sake of increased profits for the Rizzi Hotel chain but you'll excuse me if I take a more selfish view.'

Leo looked at her for a few seconds and recognised

that look on her face only too well. He had seen it on the faces of his clients too many times not to know what shock and dismay looked like. The last thing this girl needed was some foolish man asking about a ring left in her bathroom.

Then he gave himself a mental shake. Snap out of it! His dad's ring was the only thing that he was interested in. That was why he was here. *Wasn't it?*

Then his brain caught up with what she had said. And he almost winced in recognition that she was right about that, if nothing else. There were countless small suppliers and support staff that were casualties of the big company mergers and acquisitions he advised on every day of the week. But they were not his problem and never could be.

His clients paid him very well to give them an objective assessment of what needed to be done to increase company profitability. That was his speciality. Not sentimental consideration of the individual business owners who would have to go through what Sara was about to face. That was not his job.

Of course he never got to meet the many small businesses face to face or even know their names. Why should he? Unlike now, when the girl he had been dancing with the night before was fighting to hold back tears, with an uncertain future ahead of her. And all because of his aunt's drive to increase turnover at the Manor.

Suddenly the collar of his black fitted shirt felt tight on his neck, and he shuffled uncomfortably inside his summer-weight cashmere wool jacket. Sun was streaming into the hot and humid orchid house and he had rarely felt so awkward or out of his comfort zone. This was one spot where he did not have the clothing or the attitude to fit the environment. A hostile takeover of two international companies was nothing compared to actually being in the

same small space as someone who was reeling from the
impact of a chain of events set in motion by Rizzi management months earlier, someone who owned a business
his aunt would never have even heard of.

She dropped the envelope onto the draining board, not
caring that it would be soaked. 'I have been stupid and
naive. I am probably not making much sense this morning. This news is all still very new to me and I'm having
a problem working out where I go from here.'

Sara blinked several times and wiped a very grubby
finger under her eyes and gave him a half smile. 'I accept
your apology, and thank you for coming in person, but it
might be better if you left now.'

Then she lifted her head and gave him something close
to a scowl. 'From what Tony Evans told me, you are part
of the Rizzi family who have just bought me out,' she
whispered, her mouth tight and thin with suppressed feeling. 'I know that you are Caspar's friend but I have a great
deal to think about and would appreciate being left alone
to get on with sorting my business out. So thank you and
have a nice day. Life. Whatever.'

And, before Leo could reply or react, she grabbed the
nearest pale yellow orchid plant, which was about three
feet tall and bursting with huge blossoms, and thrust it at
his black jacket and shirt with such vigour that the only
thing that he could do was grab hold of it before it caused
serious damage.

He had only just clasped it against the front of his
jacket when she slipped behind him on the narrow walk-
way, giving him a waft of floral scent and bleach mixed
with warm girl, and grabbed hold of both of his shoulders
with hands which were probably grubbier than he was
used to, and physically turned him around to face the
entrance.

The next thing he knew, Leo was standing outside the greenhouse cuddling a yellow orchid in a transparent pot and not entirely sure how he'd got there.

CHAPTER FIVE

SARA stumbled down the centre of the greenhouse as best she could, her head dazed from all that had happened in her normally tranquil life in the past twenty-four hours.

She really could not handle any more surprises today—all she wanted to do was block out the effects of the shocking news she'd received and seeing Leo again in daylight, and liking him even more, with hard physical work.

There were people relying on her to deliver their orchids. That was what she had to focus on now—getting through one day at a time, and somehow, along the way, she would come up with a brilliant idea about how to get out of this mess.

Her hands stilled on the cool ceramic of the sink.

But of course there was no way out.

If the land was sold, then the hotel would want to use every square inch of the expensive real estate they had invested in. She could hardly blame the elderly farmer she had known most of her life for taking a chance to retire in comfort with his family when he was offered it.

And of course the hotel did not want only the kitchen gardens—oh, no, they wanted another ten acres of his land as well. For car parks.

Car parks! In a few months her cottage garden would be backing onto tarmac car parks.

Sara pushed away from the sink and walked slowly down to the side exit of the cool greenhouse, carefully drew open the door and walked the few steps towards the hotter and more humid tropical orchid house. She reached out a hand towards the door and then let it fall away, stepped back and looked around, content to simply enjoy this stunning place which she loved so much.

The high brick wall of the hotel which had once been her home was on one side, the curved walls designed to retain the heat of the fruit trees which were still trained against the surface. Apples and pears. Turkish figs. All so delicious when they were picked straight from the tree.

It had been her grandmother's idea to put the orchid houses on the opposite west-facing side of the kitchen garden so that she could control the light but still have the heat for most of the day, and this was where she had spent so many of her final years, just pottering around, enjoying the plants that she had treasured and created. A vegetable plot for one person did not make much sense, but orchids had been her passion. She'd even admitted over one too many glasses of sherry one Christmas that she sometimes preferred her orchids to people.

Orchids did not let her down, or run away, or desert their families when they needed them.

Oh, Nana!

Car parks. They would probably knock down the old walls to make a direct link to the main hotel building through this space, then onto the fields. Tearing away centuries of heritage at the same time.

What did they care about that? This was a business, after all. No room for sentimental nonsense about the past and the people who had created these buildings and cared for them with such love over the generations.

Her eyes fluttered closed and she sniffed away a rising

swell of panic. No. This was not the end. It could not be the end. Not after three years of relentless work.

She was so preoccupied with thoughts and concerns that the sound of footsteps at the door barely registered until she heard the greenhouse door creak open behind her.

Trying to fix a smile on her face, Sara turned back towards the entrance, then jumped, surprised to see Leo only a few feet away. Her shoulders slumped in startled surprise.

'Oh, please do not make this any more difficult than it already is,' she said to Leo, who was leaning casually against the door frame simply watching her in silence.

Last night, in his costume and under the moonlight, she could not have imagined that he could be more handsome or more attractive, but the soft sunlight infused his Mediterranean complexion with an entrancing glow that highlighted his natural tan and made the smile lines around his mouth and the corners of his eyes even more attractive.

He had a mouth designed for smiling. Those blue-grey eyes were so mesmerising that she could barely look at him without remembering the touch of his hand at her waist and how it felt to be swept along in the glorious waltz they had shared the previous evening.

For a few minutes she had felt like a normal girl out on a normal date with a normal guy and had actually dared to enjoy herself—until he had brought her crashing back down to earth by reminding her that she had been set up by Helen on a blind date. With the bloke who had no desire whatsoever of going out with his friend's school pal.

And she had been right back where she always was.

Last of the line when it came to being picked for anything.

She had been so humiliated even before she'd realised that he had seen her underwear and the turmoil inside her simple one-bedroomed cottage.

And now here he was, looking slick as a slick thing from slick land while she was... Who she was.

It was a shame that her poor treacherous body refused to ignore the fact that she was staring at the way the fine silky fabric of his fitted black shirt was stretched across a broad muscular chest—and liked it far too much for comfort.

She could not like him. She dare not like this strange alien creature who had just arrived from outer space to appear in her little world.

A slim tailored black suit and fitted black shirt was just about the most inappropriate clothing she could have chosen for any guest to come to a plant nursery and yet somehow he managed to look cool, contained and sophisticated. An elegant man used to an elegant lifestyle and elegant people in elegant surroundings. So what was he doing here with her?

Ah, of course—the ring! She had not given Leo his ring back! And from the determined look on his face he was not going to go without it. Leo Grainger could have invented the expression 'stiff upper lip'.

Pity that his plump lower lip was trying to smile and not succeeding. He must be hot under all of that black clothing in the warm sunshine but he didn't show it. The top two buttons of his black silk shirt were undone, revealing a hint of tanned chest and the possibility of chest hair. No doubt there was some beautiful fashion model-cum-personal assistant waiting for him back in London whose job it was to admire that broad muscular chest on a daily basis.

It was a tough job but someone had to do it, she supposed.

Perhaps she could go on a waiting list?

It was strange how the longer she felt him watching her, the warmer she became. A blush of heat burst up to her neck and she quickly turned away, back to the work in hand.

She was not allowed to stare at his chest or any other part of his anatomy, for that matter. Shame on her! Crushes of all kinds were for teenagers, not grown women, especially when she had only known him a few hours.

For all she knew, he could have found out the previous evening who she was from Caspar or Helen when he'd rejoined the party.

That must have come as a shock.

For a tiny fraction of a second she almost felt sorry for him, but then she remembered her humiliation and embarrassment and lifted her chin defiantly.

This was the man who was working for the hotel management who were going to evict her!

'Have you forgotten something?' she asked and blinked several times, content to watch his exasperated expression for a few seconds before the pale grey-blue eyes narrowed ever so slightly. 'Or have you come back to gloat about how your family are just about to put me out of business?'

Leo cleared his throat. 'Yes to the first question but no to the second. It's been a while since someone escorted me off their premises and I have to confess that I am not sure I like it.'

'Oh, I have every confidence that you will soon recover,' she said in a low voice and gave him a very brittle smile. 'I'm sure you appreciate that I am pretty busy trying to save what I can right now, so have a good trip back to London.'

She raised one hand and gestured over Leo's shoulder. 'And please close the door on your way out.'

'Not so fast. You seem to have all the answers,' Leo replied with a tilt of his head while the rest of him stayed stubbornly where it was, totally ignoring her. 'Except that you may not have all of the facts,' he added, folding his arms and looking down his long straight nose at her with a fierce sparkle in his eyes which was no doubt intended to pressurise business executives, and any female in sight, into total submission.

She should detest him for how effective it was, but instead she took the hit by locking her wobbly knees and breathing a little slower to calm her racing heart.

'Okay, I confess,' he said and pressed one hand flat against his chest. 'I did recommend your plant nursery to the hotel in the vain hope that it would act as a small form of apology, but I was happy to do so. I've known Caspar long enough to trust his judgement, even if it did mean putting my neck and my reputation on the block. And who is Tony Evans, by the way?'

Sara knew that she should leave this conversation alone and get back to work. All of her instincts started screaming and ringing alarm bells, warning her not to get involved by asking for more information, but she could not help it.

'Tony is the Events Manager at the hotel,' she answered meekly, only too aware that he was using this side question to deflect her from the true enormity of the problems. 'I went looking for more work there today and he mentioned that you had recommended my nursery and—' she paused and shrugged her shoulders '—he might have mentioned that you are related to the owners of the hotel. And apparently you are a mega business consultant.'

'Ah—' he nodded knowingly '—I only dealt with the hotel manager, not his team. And you added two and two together and came up with five? Is that about right? Well, at least some of that is correct. Yes, my aunt is one of the Rizzi family who bought this house three years ago from your family,' he said. 'But I actually have my own business consultancy—which has nothing to do with the Rizzi Hotel chain. Sorry to disappoint you but I am not on the hotel payroll.'

'Oh. So you don't work for Kingsmede Manor?'

Leo shook his head very slowly from side to side.

'And you didn't have anything to do with the decision to buy the old kitchen garden?'

His reply was a slight nod in her direction, combined with a killer smile. 'Nothing at all. That decision would have been taken months ago by senior management.'

'Oh. Okay. I always have had a vivid imagination,' she admitted with a tiny shoulder shrug. 'Especially when I feel sorry for myself. Which is not very often,' she hastened to add. 'It's just that I don't get out very often and every waking moment of the last three years has been spent building up these three greenhouses to the point where I can start to think about making improvements. This is my world and it means everything to me.' And then she shut up, realising that she was giving far too much away. 'And I'm rambling. Sorry—I don't usually tell my problems to a complete stranger.'

Her head dropped and she focused her eyes on the sunlight on the stone flagstones, which was why it came as a total shock when his forefinger pressed against her chin and tipped it up towards him.

'Hardly a stranger,' he said with a gentle smile. 'We

have our own song and everything. We even like the same chocolates. Besides—' and he dropped his hand and rested it lightly on her arm '—according to Helen, we are perfect for each other, and who am I to argue with such a higher force? Oh—and there is something you should know. I do not gloat. Ever.'

'You should gloat. Seriously. I have no idea why Helen thinks that we are in the least compatible. Apparently you are a famous business consultant—' and she gestured towards him with one hand, then flipped it over to point to her chest '—while I have a business which just started going downhill fast. Not a happy comparison. Let's just say that I suspected a heavy amount of guilt was involved in your decision to recommend me. Oh—and a burning desire to get your ring back.'

Sara could not help it. Her mouth twisted into a grin. 'No, I hadn't forgotten about it. I was going to bring it up to the hotel later,' and then she winced sharply as Leo moved his fingers over the scratches on her arm that Pasha had given her the evening before.

He gasped and looked down at the inside of her arm and the line of red scratch marks. 'What happened to you? Did you burn yourself? Or was it an attack of the killer mutant orchids?'

'Not at all.' Sara laughed. 'Did you see that giant lazy cat of mine? My boy might be an old man in cat years but he can still wield a mighty scratch.' And then she shrugged slightly. 'I'm allergic to cat hair so when Pasha scratches me I have to put up with an itchy red arm for a couple of days. I got away with it last night by taking a couple of allergy tablets, which was probably not a good idea combined with Caspar's special cocktail.'

Sara lifted her right hand to waist height palm side up, fluttered her fingers and then flipped it over and brought it sharply down towards her knees. 'I crashed out when I got back to the cottage, didn't I? I blame Caspar for the whole thing.'

Leo raised his eyebrows. 'You wouldn't be the only person.' And he looked at her with soft eyes. 'Why do you have a cat if you're allergic to cat hair? I can't quite understand the logic in that.'

'Pasha belonged to my grandmother and was thirteen years young when she passed away. Nobody else would take a cat that age and I promised my grandmother that I would give him a home. And that's it. I now have an elderly tomcat for a pet. He is good company, actually, even if he is hopeless when it comes to catching mice these days.'

Sara peered through the glass to Pasha, who was still stretched out in the sunshine with his tail flicking up now and again to indicate he was dreaming. But when she looked back towards Leo she was taken aback by the expression on his face.

'What is it?' she asked softly and their eyes met. For a fleeting second she felt as though he was looking at her as if he was seeing her for the first time. He had a look in those blue-grey eyes with that certain something that, in another time and another place, she could almost have said was interest.

Or was he more interested in her old cat and her sob story? Both of them pathetic and both of them on their way out, in one way or another.

Lovely. He must be so impressed!

'Don't you dare feel sorry for me,' she snorted before he had a chance to answer. 'I chose to give Pasha a home. I chose to invest everything I have in these orchid houses, even though I am only renting this piece of land. My decision, for better or worse—' and then she faltered '—no matter how dim that looks right now.'

'I didn't say a word,' he retorted and raised both hands in surrender, before dropping them back onto his hips.

'You don't have to. I know that I must seem totally pathetic. Gloat away.'

And then he did something which totally knocked the wind from her sails and the air from her lungs.

He pushed away from the greenhouse door, reached forward and took both of her hands in his so that her fingers were completely encased inside his palms.

She was so startled that she didn't have time to pull away before he was in her personal space and talking in a low intense voice and those stunning blue-grey eyes were focused totally on hers, making it absolutely impossible for her to look away.

'You are not pathetic,' he said in a clear, calm voice, as refreshing as a waft of cool air on a hot afternoon. 'And I do not feel sorry for you. On the contrary, I admire you for making a decision and sticking to it. You made a promise to someone you cared about and you did that knowing that it could cause you problems. That is something you should be proud of.'

He admired her? Was this some sort of joke?

Sara looked deeper into his eyes and saw only sincerity that brought a lump to her throat and the blood thumping in her chest.

'But you were looking at me as though I had two heads a minute ago,' she replied in a low voice which was a lot more unsteady than she would have liked.

'Let's just say that not many people surprise me these days,' he replied with a smile. 'I admire loyalty in anyone, especially if it costs them. Okay?' And then his voice softened to match his sweet smile. 'Okay?' he asked again.

Her shoulders seemed to drop ten inches just at the sound of his voice. Perhaps Leo should go into the massage business?

'Okay,' she replied with a tilt of her head, 'and thank you. I'm not used to being admired, so it has come as a bit of shock. Especially on top of the bad news about the land sale.'

Then she flung back her head and dared to chuckle as the irony of the situation hit her. She was holding hands with a dazzling, handsome man with eyes the colour of a winter sky while her plant nursery was just about to go to the wall.

'Do you know the funny thing? Cottage Orchids has actually been shortlisted for an award. Can you believe that? An award for my entrepreneurial skills.' Her right hand slid out from Leo's hand and traced the letters in the air above their heads. 'Local Businesswoman of the Year.' Then she dropped her hand onto her hip and gave him a tiny shrug. 'What a joke. I could use some serious business advice myself right now. If only I could afford to pay for...it.' Then she froze mid-sentence.

Leo was a mega business consultant.

She needed a business consultant.

And she needed one badly.

And he did have a point about Helen. Her friend would never have arranged a blind date unless she thought that she and Leo could get along.

But that would mean asking for help. And even the thought of asking this Adonis of a man to give his time and energy as a favour made her teeth go on edge and she cringed inside.

Worse—he was part of the Rizzi family! How could

she possibly trust him to give her impartial advice? No. It was impossible.

Especially when she still had his precious ring in her pocket.

Her mind raced. Oh, no, she could not do that! She could not hold his property to ransom. That would be totally wrong, not to say unethical. And he was Caspar's friend, after all.

Desperate times called for desperate measures. She had been out here working for two hours and the only ideas she had come up with to save her business were too long-term to be any use at all over the next few weeks before she had to pack up everything she could save.

His professional advice could make a difference and at that particular moment she needed all the help she could get.

All she had to do was forget the fact that he was a professional business guru who probably charged his clients the earth for the benefit of his advice, and swallow her pride and just ask him.

She could do this.

She could humiliate herself yet again.

She chewed at her lower lip, aware that he was looking at her with his eyebrows creased together, clearly bewildered at this strange woman who had been trying to get rid of him. Perhaps she could put it down to mood swings? That always confused boys.

'Look, Leo. It's like this.' She took a deep breath and blurted out her question before she could change her mind. 'I need a business consultant. You are a business consultant. It seems to me to point one way.'

Then she smiled sweetly at him, slipped her hand from his, reached into her trouser pocket and waved his ring between two fingers.

'I was going to give you your ring back this afternoon, but now I would like to offer you a trade. You can have your ring back in exchange for a few hours' work. Ten hours at most—even quicker if you really put your mind to my problems.'

She held up one hand when he started to bluster in protest. 'I know that your family own the hotel and I know that there is no way I can prevent the land from being sold. That ship has sailed. So I am not asking you to do anything that could harm your family.'

Then her hand dropped and she smiled through clenched teeth and looked up sheepishly into Leo's startled face. 'All I need is a second opinion about what I can do to make the best of this situation and save my business. Right now, I have no clue about the options I have and I am in great danger of losing everything. That's all I need—some advice about my options. It won't take long, and I would really appreciate it. So. What do you say? Want to make a trade? Your time for the ring. It's quite simple, really.'

Simple? Leo choked on the words that were bursting to the surface and stared open-mouthed at Sara, who was just standing there smiling at him in her prettiest, cheekiest, freckliest fashion as though she had just invited him for afternoon tea.

His situation was anything but *simple.*

He couldn't give this girl advice without compromising his position—but he also could not tell her that he was on assignment for his aunt.

He had given his word that he would keep this project a secret.

He had just told her that he was not an employee of the

hotel chain, and that was true—he was doing this work
for his aunt as a personal favour.

His aunt was the only one of his mother's Rizzi family
who had reached out to him and his sister and offered
practical help when their parents had died in a road accident. He owed her. And he would keep his reason for
staying on at the hotel to himself, even if it meant being
less than honest with Sara.

He had walked away from the Rizzi Hotel chain a long
time ago and had absolutely no intention of ever joining
the payroll. Not while his grandfather was in control.

And nothing—*nothing*—was going to come between
him and his mission here.

Not even a pretty girl who was so cheeky that she
somehow believed that he could simply drop everything
else in his life and give her his undivided personal attention in exchange for the return of his own property!

She had no idea what she was asking.

There was a waiting list of companies who were willing to pay top rates for this kind of advice, and it had
taken a lot of juggling to squeeze these few days away
from the office into his schedule. He had a mountain of
paperwork and emails and reports to finish back at the
hotel. There was no way he could take so much time away
from his core business and current projects to help Sara.

Of course, they were not friends of friends who
had struck rock bottom and were as intriguing as Sara
Fenchurch—but it was still a lot to ask.

So where did that leave him? *He had to have that ring
back. And fast.*

He raised an eyebrow. 'You want *me* to give *you* business advice in exchange for my own ring. Is that right?'

'Don't put it like that,' she said. 'It makes me sound as
though I might be…well…an opportunist. Instead of just

foolish and desperate. With an old cat to support,' she
added in a rush.

'Oh, well,' he replied. 'That makes all the difference.
How could I possibly forget about the cat?'

He lowered his head and glared at Sara down his nose
in a very half-hearted attempt to intimidate her. 'I could
always complain to Helen and Caspar that you are holding
my property to ransom. I think that they would take a
very dim view of that kind of behaviour.'

She sniffed and shook her head from side to side.
Then she raised her eyebrows and grinned cheekily. 'You
wouldn't. You like Caspar. And Helen is my best friend
in the whole world.'

Sara gave a short shrug. 'It would be such a shame if
Caspar's life was a misery because you could not spare a
few hours of your time to give some business advice to a
lady in distress. How could you be so ungallant?'

And then she sniffed and reached into her pocket for
her mobile phone. 'Why don't I give Helen a call now
and ask her to turn the car around because I've had bad
news about my business? Of course I haven't told her yet
because I didn't want to upset her so close to the wedding,
but seeing as I'm all alone and broke…'

Leo's hand came up and his fingers closed over the
open cell phone. 'You didn't tell Helen when you heard
your bad news this morning?'

She stuck her neck out and hissed in disbelief. 'Are
you kidding? She would have dropped everything and
stayed here to try and sort things out. I couldn't do that
to her. Not when her wedding is only four weeks away
and she is meeting Caspar's parents this afternoon to go
through the final plans. She has enough to worry about.
No—' and she stood back and dropped her voice '—I
have to work through the next steps on my own. When I

have something concrete to tell her, then yes, I will talk it through, but until then I would prefer to keep this to myself.'

She looked into his face for a second and frowned. 'You're giving me that two headed look again. Now what have I done?'

'More what you haven't done.' He lifted his head, sighed out loud, then nodded. 'Just how alone and broke are you? Because, coming from a girl who used to live in that house—' and he nodded over his shoulder towards the hotel '—you will forgive me if my idea of being broke is slightly different from yours.'

There was a sharp intake of breath and she stared at him wide-eyed. 'I don't believe it. You actually think that just because my grandmother left my mother a huge house that there was money in the family? Oh, dear. Another bubble for me to burst.'

Then she shook her head slowly from side to side. 'Huge debts we knew nothing about, followed by even bigger repair bills. Don't even talk about the tax. All of which means that I have no employees and no backup team. Cottage Orchids is what you see in front of you. There is me, the cat and a cheap delivery van. Everything I have earned has been ploughed back into the business. I have some savings, which had been intended to pay the rent, but that is it. That's why I have to resort to these sorts of tactics to persuade you to help me out. Otherwise, these glasshouses are going to *collapse* around me and I won't be able to do anything about it. I will lose everything.'

Lose everything. Leo bit the inside of his cheek. *Why did she have to use that particular expression?*

Grainger Consulting dealt with companies large enough to survive in one way or another even without his intervention, but to lose everything?

There was no way that Sara could know that she had just described his own personal nightmare made real, and the words rebounded inside his head.

He had fought long and hard to make sure that he would never, ever face the horror of losing everything again. He had checked his investment and property portfolio only that morning and, if he wanted to, he need never work again.

And it did not make one bit of difference. The fear was still there.

He inhaled slowly through his nose, anxious not to show Sara the impact of her innocent and totally open and honest statement. No complicated risk assessment needed here. She slouched casually against the glasshouse, looking at him with her hopeful lopsided grin as the sunlight brought out the freckles on her chin. Everything about this girl, who was pinning her hopes and dreams on him, of all people, screamed out to him that she knew as much about business management as he knew about orchid propagation. And she was asking him to help her. One to one.

He swallowed down something close to personal concern, and then sniffed it away. What a ridiculous notion. He did not do sentiment. He did objective analysis based on data.

Perhaps Sara did need someone like him to look at her options. But it would have to be done professionally. Advising a one woman plant business would be easy enough—if she was prepared to accept some hard facts.

There was a long pause before Leo lifted his chin.

'I'm beginning to get the picture. And you accept the fact that the Rizzi Hotel group is not going to walk away from buying the land? Nothing is going to change that fact.'

Her shoulders slumped and she seemed to falter and swallow down what he sincerely prayed was not the start of tears, before biting her lower lip and nodding once for emphasis before flicking back her head and glaring defiantly at him. 'Yes, I accept that my business is toast and I am going to be evicted. Can we move on now?'

'One more question. Have you ever had any kind of business or marketing advice at all?' he asked.

Her face seemed to relax a little at his first sign that he might actually be thinking about her proposal. 'No, but I can learn. Do you really think that will help me save my nursery?'

Not completely convinced that he was doing the right thing, even as he spoke, Leo reluctantly gave his terms. 'I can't promise you that—but I can talk you through some options. What you do with them has to be your decision, not mine. As you say, you have to choose the direction you want to go in. All I can do is give you a few maps to help you to decide.'

'Maps. I like the sound of that! Because I have to tell you, Leo, that at the moment I am feeling totally lost. I may need guidebooks as well.' She exhaled with a slow sigh. 'You might as well know that I hate asking anyone for help. Anyone. Which makes it extra hard for me to ask you to give me some advice. I wouldn't do it at all unless I was seriously desperate and it's important to me that you know that. Just so that we are clear.'

Leo fought back a smile. Perhaps they had a lot more in common than he had ever expected. To feel as if the whole world was against you and there was nowhere to go and nobody to help? Oh, yes, he knew what that felt like.

But, as he looked at Sara, the small beginnings of an idea crept into his mind.

He had one objective here at Kingsmede Manor and that was to find some way to give this hotel a competitive edge. And who better could there be to give him the inside story about the place than the girl who had lived there most of her life? She had twenty plus years of background and insider information about this hotel which he could use—if he could persuade her to tell him. While keeping his assignment a secret.

Yes, it would be a deception of sorts. But he couldn't afford to get sentimental and it was Sara who had suggested it. She stood to gain just as much as he did.

If he made sure that she never found out that he was there to help out the very family who were putting her business at risk.

Which was probably why the words came out of his mouth before his brain had properly engaged.

'I was planning to stay at the hotel for a day or two. I suppose I could give you a few hours of my time tomorrow morning. Just to take a look at your business strategy and work through some options. How does that sound?'

'A few hours?' she gasped in disbelief and waved her arms about. 'I am going to need more than a few hours! I have to save my entire family heritage here!'

'That's my offer,' he said, unmoved.

'What else can I offer you in exchange for some extra time?' she asked with a smile. 'Crash course in orchid cultivation? Budding for beginners? Or perhaps your lady friends could use an orchid in their lives? Girls love flowers and my special hybrids smell really wonderful. The girls will love you for ever.'

And that really did make him laugh out loud. 'Well, I might just take you up on your kind offer but not at the moment, thanks. However—' and he hesitated with a twinge of guilt as another far more pressing excuse for being with Sara kicked in '—there is something you could help me with. I am interested in Kingsmede Manor. Call it professional curiosity if you will, but the history behind a country house like this and the people who designed it and lived in it has always fascinated me.'

Now that was true. He *did* have a personal interest in the design aspects of the property.

'The Manor? You do realise that once you get me talking about the house you would never be able to shut me up? But yes, of course, if you're interested I've inherited a lot of material about the history of the house and you are welcome to look at it. But you do realise that an exclusive viewing of these historical documents will cost you a lot more than a few hours of your business time?'

'How about four hours a day for the next three days?' Leo replied and held back a laugh as Sara's mouth fell open in surprise. But then she pulled herself back together and held out her hand, clearly anxious to grab his offer before he had a chance to think about it and change his mind. 'Done. Do we have a deal?'

'Deal.' He nodded and they shook on it. Her hand was warm and small, but her handshake was solid. It was the handshake of someone who meant what they said, and the prospect of spending a lot more time in Sara's company suddenly seemed like the best decision that *he* had made all day.

'So how soon can you get changed?' she asked. 'I can be ready in about an hour. Oh, and one word of advice. Don't wear black. The compost gets everywhere.'

'Oh, no,' Leo replied in a slow languorous voice. 'I only come in one colour and that colour is black. And I start tomorrow morning. Take it or leave it.'

And he gave her that half smile that brought a bright flush to her cheeks for all of the ten seconds it took her to say, 'I'll take it. I will definitely take it.'

CHAPTER SIX

LEO swiped his thumb across the display on his personal organiser as he strolled across the stone patio outside Kingsmede Manor and checked down the list of emails which had come in from the project team leaders around the world during the night.

There was nothing that could not wait until later in the day.

Leo popped his organiser into his pocket, lifted his head and looked across the sunlit gardens and asked himself, yet again, why on earth he had cleared four hours from his schedule on a Monday morning to work for Cottage Orchids.

The first answer was too embarrassing to be ignored.

He had made a deal. A deal where he had actually agreed to spend hours of his valuable time in order to get his own ring back. *This was so totally pathetic that it was humiliating.*

Sara Fenchurch was a remarkable woman but he knew that she wouldn't have put up much of a fight if he had demanded the ring then and there and kept on demanding it back until she caved under the pressure.

Except that would have made him a bully, and he had a real problem with bullies. Always had. Probably always would. And he had no plans to become one himself. Despite the level of provocation.

He had worked late into the night and over his room service breakfast finishing a report for a top client who had demanded that Leo took personal responsibility for the final recommendations—and was willing to pay to make that happen. It was a difficult case involving the hostile takeover of several chains of family-run bakeries. Bakeries that used local suppliers who could soon find themselves in trouble when the company switched to one single supplier overseas.

And even as he typed up the final recommendation he could not help thinking about Sara and her situation. Now that. Was annoying.

Helen and Caspar's friend was in trouble because of a business decision made by the one member of the Rizzi family that he respected. That did not oblige him to help her—he knew that. And yet? There was something about Sara Fenchurch that made it impossible for him to walk away from her.

Helen or his sister would probably tell him that he was using the ring as an excuse to see her again. And even the suspicion that they could be right made his hackles rise.

She had somehow managed to squeeze under his radar and make him feel the kind of connection that he'd thought he had buried long ago.

And he had to block that out. Starting right now. Two tasks. Get in, give his advice. Ask for the inside information he needed. Then get out. *Simple.*

A few minutes later, after he had tried knocking on the door of her cottage, Leo gave up on that and headed back to the log cabin.

This time the door was slightly ajar and it looked as if Cottage Orchids might be open. He peered through the smeared and dusty window and, after a tentative knock brought no response, he turned the handle just as Sara strolled out of the nearest greenhouse with two children by her side. The boy was probably about eleven and he was clutching the hand of a little girl as he smiled at something Sara was saying.

Leo could not see what the girl looked like because her other arm was wrapped tightly around a single pot with an orchid plant in it which was so large that her head was totally obscured by the leaves. The flowers were tiny, bright orange with streamers of purple and red leaves coming out from each blossom. It was like a flower crossed with a bag of party streamers.

Sara smiled up at Leo with a tilt of her head. He noticed for the first time that, without her baseball cap, the corners of her eyes had fine white crease lines on smooth, gently tanned skin. She actually looked genuinely happy to see him.

And what made it worse was that he felt happy to see her!

Would she still be smiling if she knew how dishonest he was being? A cold, sick feeling of discomfort coiled around his gut at her misplaced trust and innocent welcoming smile.

'Good morning, Miss Fenchurch. New customers?' he asked.

'Actually, two of my best customers,' Sara replied, and then turned back to the boy. 'Now don't forget, Freddy. Tell your grandma that she only needs to water it once a week. Not once a day, like the one you gave her for Christmas.'

Freddy replied with vigorous nodding, then released his sister's hand and reached into his trouser pocket and pulled out a handful of coins.

'Oh, no. This is a replacement plant, remember? And I hope she likes it, but just bring it back if she doesn't. Now, go straight home. Bye for now. Bye.'

Leo stood next to Sara as they watched the unlikely pair stroll down the path towards the lane. The little girl had her thumb in her mouth, but wrinkled her nose at Leo and waved with her free hand before taking the boy's hand.

For one mad moment he was tempted to wrinkle his nose back at her.

'They only live in the first house down the lane,' Sara said. 'I've known the family all my life, but their grandma still doesn't know how to keep their orchids alive.'

Sara swung around on one heel. 'Good morning to you too, Mr Grainger. Ready to get to work? And, before you ask, no, I don't charge. They are my neighbours and the price list does not apply.'

She pointed in the direction of the cabin. 'I've made a start on finding the lease, but nothing so far. So I could use some help. Shall we go into the office?'

Leo replied with a tilt of his head and gestured for her to go ahead. She was wearing navy trousers today and a white blouse with little flowers embroidered on it. On any other woman it would look ridiculous and childlike and yet it somehow worked on Sara.

He enjoyed the view for a few seconds, and then stepped into the cabin behind her.

And stopped dead at the door, his brain scarcely able to take in what he was seeing.

In front of him was a scene of total disruption and what counted in his world as absolute chaos.

Two metal filing cabinets lay along one wall and on top of each were piled mountains of paperwork and folders and boxes, all bulging with sheets of paper and, as Leo walked forward, he could see most of them were invoices and receipts. More stuck out from the over-crammed drawers inside the cabinets.

The main part of the room was taken up by a long pine table—or at least he thought that it was pine, but it was difficult to make out the nature of the wood since every square inch of the surface was covered with bundles of paperwork, catalogues and unopened mail.

Peering over the top, he could see that a very ancient office chair was marooned in a sea of large sacks whose labels showed they had contained compost and fertiliser of various sorts.

That probably accounted for the very special odour in the room.

The last time he had smelt anything this bad was when the drains had been blocked for several days in his aunt's hotel and the waste disposal backed up. If Sara worked in here she must be accustomed to it, but it was making his eyes water.

'Have you been burgled?' He gagged and looked at Sara in disbelief as she rummaged around inside a large cardboard box overflowing with brown envelopes, then dropped it to the floor, revealing a very old wooden chair.

'Burgled? No,' she replied, her eyebrows squeezed together. And then she dropped her head back and shrugged. 'Oh, I see. Sorry. I suppose it has got a bit messy in here.'

He shook his head from side to side slowly in disbelief. 'This is not good, Sara. There is no way you can run an efficient business surrounded by this chaos.'

She sighed out loud and looked around as though seeing it for the first time. 'I know. There used to be a time when I knew where things were, even if they weren't filed away. But now?' Sara took a firm grip of the back of the chair. 'This is why I need help, Leo. The more I think about it, the more I realise just how much of a mess I am in. Thank goodness you turned up just in time.'

Several hours later, Sara stood next to her kitchen window and slipped Leo's ring onto her thumb, stretched out her hand and waggled it from side to side so that she could admire the sparkling diamond in all of its glory.

Helen had told her that he was single, but perhaps Leo had been married once and was widowed? Or maybe this was a treasured family heirloom only to be passed from father to son?

Whatever the reason, she had no right to keep it. Agreement or not, she should have returned it when she had the chance. But it was not too late—Leo *was* making an effort to sort through her documents and keep his side of their bargain.

Right on cue, there was a great crash and a deep groan from the direction of her log cabin office and Sara flinched with guilt. After forty minutes of frantic searching involving much grimacing and huffing and puffing, they had finally found the folder he needed on her lease, stuffed between a bundle of holiday brochures for orchid enthusiasts.

They had been in there for almost an hour when, after several attempts to work in the same room had resulted in document avalanches and an unfortunate incident with a sample of especially pungent organic fertiliser and Leo's lap, she had finally offered to make them some coffee and leave him in peace.

How had she let the paperwork and her office space deteriorate so badly?

She had planned to have a complete clean-up during

the long winter months, but somehow it had never happened. Crisis had followed crisis and, before she knew it, the demand for orchids for autumn weddings had become Christmas gift specials, then Valentine's Day and then back to the spring wedding season, and now she was busier than ever.

Normally, she felt happy and warm and comforted to be in her messy place, like a little nest she had made, but she had been so ashamed to show Leo her office that morning and to see it through his eyes.

She glanced though the kitchen window towards the cabin.

Yesterday he had refused to go away and had spent a good few hours of his precious Sunday reading and learning more about the plant ranges and the most popular lines.

He had even looked interested now and again. Either that or he had been more than just polite. Perhaps he wanted to get to know her better?

Silly girl! Why should a man like Leo be interested in her? That sort of thinking would lead to even more disappointment and pain. Her mother was right—she was never going to be good enough for any man to care about her without an aristocratic name to attract them. And the sooner she accepted that fact the better.

She pushed herself upright and blinked away tears of self-pity, then quickly slipped his ring from her thumb.

There was a rustle of activity at the kitchen door and Sara quickly wrapped the ring and popped it back into her purse.

A tall slim man dressed in black was standing at her kitchen door, brushing away the dust from his clothing with his fingers. Leo!

'Oh, hello. Do you need anything? The coffee will be ready in a few minutes.'

'I need somewhere to work. I am really sorry, Sara, but that…' He opened his mouth to describe her potting shed and seemed to give up, so she stepped in for him.

'Garden office?' she suggested and was rewarded with a scowl.

'Glorified garden shed. Is driving me mad. I don't know how you can work in there,' he added and gestured towards the door. 'No filing system, no chance of finding anything. It is impossible.'

Sara checked her watch. 'You've lasted well over an hour, which is about forty minutes longer than I expected, so well done for that. Take a seat and I'll be right with you.'

Leo crossed her living room in what seemed like two strides, looked around the kitchen for somewhere to sit that was not already occupied by piles of junk and leant against the wood-burning stove instead. Sara frantically tried to find a second clean mug, gave up and started the washing-up from her hasty breakfast, before she'd had to make the early morning deliveries to the local florists.

The kitchen had rarely looked so messy. The old pine dresser which ran the whole length of the wall was loaded up with all of the bits and pieces she would find homes for. One day. Except that day never arrived and suddenly every piece of junk mail, orchid catalogues, cat toys and stray pieces of string sprang out at her. It was a mess.

Well, at least she had cleared away the underwear from the bathroom. With a bit of luck, he would have forgotten all about that.

'I have instant coffee or builder's tea. Any preference?' she asked casually and was rewarded with a snort and a definite twist of one lip from the handsome man in black who had found a clear spot by moving one cat and several bundles of old newspapers and was now reclining gracefully on her rickety old wooden chair as though he was lounging on a cruise ship.

Her heart clenched. The last man who had sat in that chair had been her ex-boyfriend, and he had asked for a clean towel before he sat down so that he would not dirty his suit.

She instantly sniffed away a musty smell of *goodbye and good riddance to bad rubbish,* and replaced it with the lemon balm tang of *hello, Leo Grainger.*

'What? No cappuccino machine? Ah, the delights of country living. No false airs and graces here.' And then he grinned. 'Only teasing. Tea would be great, thank you. Strong as you like. Milk, no sugar.'

She cringed inside as she caught him staring at the old pine dresser with its simple wooden shelves. Her collection of unmatched blue and white plates and bunches of keys of all shapes and sizes hanging from cup hooks screamed out in all of their unkempt glory.

If he hated the office she could hardly wait to hear his reaction to her kitchen.

'This is a lovely room,' he said without a hint of irony.

Sara dropped the teaspoon she was drying in surprise and had to start again. 'Thanks,' she replied. 'Not perhaps the neatest kitchen in the world, but it has everything I need.'

She risked a glance at him as she got the tea ready. 'You really are the most contrary person, Mr Grainger. One minute you are complaining about the state of my office and the next you are enjoying my messy kitchen. It is most confusing.'

His face wrinkled up into a wide grin and Sara's heart gave an annoying blip in appreciation. He was handsome at the best of times but, at that moment, in his trademark immaculate black trousers and fitted shirt, he was positively the best-looking man she had ever met in her life. She had thought her ex-boyfriend handsome in an obvious, booted and city-suited slick way, but this was another level completely. The kind of charm and deep attraction that could easily lead a girl into deep waters if she did not take care. Pity that her poor tender heart did not want to take care, no matter what her head might say.

His body seemed to fill the space in the small, low ceilinged room, squeezing her into a small corner.

'Then my work is done.' He laughed and stretched his legs out even farther. 'This is your room where you relax and enjoy yourself. That—' and he pointed with one finger out of the open window towards the shed and the greenhouse only a few feet away '—is where you have to work and make a business for yourself.'

He sniffed and sat back, making the chair creak alarmingly. 'Big difference. And, as much as I appreciate your…let's say…Bohemian lifestyle, I don't think that it is helping your finances in any way.'

She passed him his tea and a plate loaded with buns and muffins. 'Please help yourself. I traded a small desk orchid for a supply of cakes first thing this morning and the village baker loved it so much she went a bit mad. And I don't have a huge freezer so…enjoy.'

'Bartering,' he whispered. 'Ah. That might explain a few things about the cash flow. That and the fact you actually give your plants away to the neighbours.'

'Do not mock,' Sara replied and sipped her tea. 'Bartering is quite a family tradition in our house, although—' and she smiled '—I suppose my grandmother did go over the top sometimes. Her accumulation of salvaged and bartered treasures was legendary. It used to drive my mum totally mad.'

Sara shuffled over to the dresser and picked up a wooden picture frame and handed it to Leo and watched in delight as his eyes widened. 'Yes, that is what it looks like. A two-woman bicycle. That's my mum on the right and grandmother on the left. Apparently, she traded a pewter teapot for a tandem bicycle so that they could cycle around the countryside in glorious splendour. She fell off the first time we tried and never rode it again. But that was her. Incorrigible.'

Leo held the photograph in silence for a few minutes, then passed it back to Sara with a quick nod. 'I never knew my maternal grandparents until a few years ago and my dad was an only child without any family to speak of. But it must have been fun living with those two ladies.'

She cocked her head and pursed her lips. 'Good times and bad. My mother hated moving back here after she got divorced. She hated the isolation and she truly hated the chaotic lifestyle my eccentric grandmother had created for herself. But she didn't have anywhere else to go and I needed a permanent home. It wasn't the best situation for either of them but it was either that or face a horrible custody battle with my dad.'

Sara smiled and cradled the mug of tea between her hands. 'And whenever the arguments got too bad, I always knew that I had somewhere calm and beautiful to escape to. The orchid houses. They were my sanctuary in the tough times and I suppose they still are now.'

She blinked away a burning in her eyes, then passed the plate back to Leo as she shuffled on her hard seat. 'Little wonder my mother has a stunning all-white modern flat in London with not one cluttered surface in sight. And that is just the way she likes it.'

Sara shook her head and shrugged at Leo, who was just finishing off his bun. 'And I have been blabbering far too long about myself. So tell me about your kitchen at home. Let me guess. Granite? Stainless steel? I want to know every detail of your designer dream.'

'Well, this is going to be fast,' he replied. 'Sorry to disappoint you, but I don't own a kitchen.'

She put down the muffin that was halfway to her lips. 'No kitchen?' she whispered in a shock.

'I don't need one,' he replied, picking up another piece of bun. 'At the moment I live in a hotel suite with full room service twenty-four hours a day. And I don't miss the washing-up one little bit.'

Leo bit into the delicious soft hot cross bun, savouring its sweet and spicy flavours. It had been so long since he had enjoyed good ordinary baked goods, although it was ironic that it should be in this cramped and crazy little kitchen, instead of the swish elegant hotels and restaurants that were part of his life of international travel.

'This is good,' he said between bites, and sipped down some of his tea. Scalding hot, just how he liked it. He was just about to take another bite when he realised that Sara had stopped talking for the first time that morning, and he looked up into her face.

What he saw there surprised and astonished him. She was looking at him—not glancing, smiling, but with a face full of sadness and pity—for him.

'What is it?' he asked. 'Is anything wrong?'

'You are living out of a hotel room,' she murmured, and her sad voice was almost breaking with emotion. Instinctively, she reached out towards him, placing a hand on top of his as though she was comforting him after some terrible grief.

Leo faltered, not knowing quite how to respond. He

had a complicated relationship with the hotel trade at the best of times, but he could hardly explain that to a girl he had only just met without exposing part of himself that he did not talk to anyone about.

The fact that she had recognised something deeper in what he had said was quite remarkable. It struck him that in his daily work he met so many people but felt no connection to them.

Yet here was this girl, living in this tiny cottage, who was trying to reach out to him and comforting him for a wrong that she knew nothing about.

The silence of the moment stretched out, broken only by the birdsong on the other side of the kitchen window and the faint hiss of the kettle as it cooled.

He became aware that her short hair was not brown at all, but in the light shining through the window was actually a mixture of shades of copper and auburn and dark oak. Her eyelashes were dark brown rather than black, and her eyes—the wide eyes, which were looking at him now with such kindness and compassion, were a lighter shade of green today, flecked with golden flakes. The perfect combination against her pale golden skin flushed with pink.

She looked as lovely and as totally natural as any woman he had ever met. There was no false pretence here—this was the real thing.

And it touched him in a place in his heart, which was painful and raw and unaccustomed to being exposed to the light. And he instantly felt guilty, but he couldn't tell Sara the real reason why he was at the hotel.

'I didn't explain myself very well,' he answered, but this time in a calm voice, so as not to alarm her. 'It is only a temporary arrangement. I am actually designing my own home with my team of architects, but it's not ready yet.'

He raised his free hand and wiggled his fingers. 'Three or four months is the latest estimate. In the meantime, I am travelling a great deal to close various international projects and the hotel life fits me very well.'

'Oh, that must be so exciting.' She breathed out long and slow. 'You had me worried there for a moment.' And as he watched her a warm smile flashed across her face. 'Call me an old softie, but being without a home is one of my nightmares.' She gave a dramatic shiver for effect. 'What a horrible thought. But you probably don't know what that feels like.'

It was as if a bucket of icy water had been thrown over his head and for a moment he wanted to shout how very, very wrong she was about that.

There had been weeks and months after his parents were killed when he and his sister had been shuffled from house to house, friend to friend, until his aunt had obtained custody, stepped in and gave them a home. He had not slept, terrified that they would both be taken into care. It had been a dramatic time which he had shielded from his sister. His first act of real deception. Since then he had become a master of it.

But how could he share the pain with this girl he had only met the evening before?

He did not know how to demonstrate his compassion as openly as she had just done—he simply did not have those skills and tools in his arsenal.

So he held back. Same as usual. And flicked on his casual professional smile. It had taken him years to perfect the ability to look interested but distant at the same time.

'To answer your question,' he replied, 'I still haven't

decided between granite and one of the new glass work-tops. That is still to come.'

Sliding his hand back away from Sara, and brushing away crumbs of sticky sugary baked goods from his fingers, Leo took another long sip of tea to disguise his discomfort, focused his total attention on his mug of hot tea and came up with the only thing he could think of that was relevant and would change the subject—fast.

'Right. Time to get to work, I think. I suggest we start with your financial records. Bank statements and your accounts. That should tell us exactly what the balance sheet is like and what financial options are open to you—or not.'

Sara nodded and jumped up. 'No problem. I have them all right here. All organised.'

Leo peered over the table as Sara rooted around inside the cupboards of her pine dresser, then looked on in stunned silence as she proudly presented three over-stuffed, totally chaotic shoe boxes of paperwork and popped them in front of him on the table.

'There used to be sticky labels on things but I think that they must have fallen off. Hope that's not going to be too much of a problem.'

'Sara,' he asked, trying not to panic, 'don't you have these records on a spreadsheet on your computer?'

'I don't have a computer.'

His hand wiped across his mouth for a second while he tried to process that statement and failed. 'Then how do you update your website?'

'Oh, that is all in next year's plan. No computer. No website. Why? Do you think that might be a problem?'

CHAPTER SEVEN

AN HOUR and a half later, the cakes and buns were crumbs in the bottom of the cake tin and Leo was struggling to stay focused on financial reports.

Sara's kitchen was so small that he had to squeeze along one wall and stand to one side to pull out a chair so that he could sit opposite her. After the third time he kicked her in the ankle when he stretched out his legs absentmindedly, she suggested that he move around to her side of the table so that they could sit next to each other and file papers into boxes as they went.

Of course he had readily agreed. To make the paper-work easier, of course.

Nothing to do with her bruised shins at all and everything to do with the fact that he did not need an excuse to be in physical contact with Sara Fenchurch.

He had thought the log cabin office was cramped but it was positively spacious compared to her kitchen/dining room, which was jam-packed with so much clutter it should have felt claustrophobic. Instead, it felt homely and lived in.

He was close enough to see the tiny scar above the bow of her upper lip, the beauty spot just below her left ear and the fading red marks on her arm where her cat had scratched her. She smelt of shampoo, earthy compost and feminine old-money class.

What was worse, every time she stretched across to pick something up, an image of Sara wearing the lingerie he had seen on their first night kept flashing in on Leo so fast and hot that it startled him.

As though he was a mind reader, Pasha, the fluffy old sun-warmed cat, chose that moment to jump onto Leo's lap—only he didn't quite make it and dug his long claws into Leo's trousers to get a grip, piercing his skin at the same time and making him yell as Pasha scrabbled for purchase.

'Oh, no! Bad Pasha. Very bad Pasha,' Sara said and instantly broke the quiet connection as she slid her chair back and calmly picked up the cat around the middle and lifted his paws away from Leo's leg, giving Leo a quick flash down the front of her T-shirt as she bent over.

Yes. He had been right. She was wearing the pink lace against her creamy smooth skin, and he almost groaned out loud. He was rooted to the spot, the pain in his leg forgotten.

'I am so sorry about that,' Sara said. 'We don't have many visitors and Pasha loves people. Pity the old boy can't jump so well any more. Come on, you... Outside! You have disgraced yourself!'

Sara lowered the scrabbling cat to the floor and gave him a gentle shove towards the open doors leading to the patio. Then she waggled her bottom back onto her chair and gave Leo a quick look sideways. 'You have been very quiet for much of the last hour. Should I be worried? Not that I'm complaining,' she hastened to add. 'I like quiet. Quiet suits me.'

He liked her body pressed lightly next to his side, he liked the way she bit her lower lip and hissed and groaned when she found an unopened bank statement she had dropped inside her shoe box filing system months earlier and promptly forgotten about. And he especially liked the way her hands moved when she talked, expressive, warm and completely and naturally open and unguarded. Even if her clothing was covered with cat hairs which she shed as she moved around.

She was completely different to any of the women whom he met in his life. And it totally disarmed him. All of the defence mechanisms he had built up, and the surface gloss and prestigious trappings of success did not mean one thing here. He found it bizarrely calm and reassuring that there were people like Sara Fenchurch still around. Shame that it also made his job, and his task at that moment, particularly difficult.

Focus. That was it. Back to the work at hand.

'Your finances are not looking good, Sara,' he replied in a soft voice and half turned in his hard seat so that he could face her.

'I think I liked quiet better, but yes, I know, and that's with three greenhouses. If I lose two of them?' She sighed and blew out long and slow. 'Any ideas you have would be very welcome now. Please.'

Leo looked into her wide concerned eyes in silence for a few seconds, his brow creased with concentration.

'There are a couple of less pleasant options involving finding a day job which are fairly obvious but I suggest we keep those as last resorts. Does that shudder mean yes? Good.'

Leo picked up one of the bundles of receipts.

'You don't have a website and, from what I can see on paper, you don't spend any money on telling people how wonderful your orchids are and where they can find you. Your main customers are local florists and garden centres plus a few hotels and restaurants, but all within about a twenty-mile radius of where we are sitting. Is that a reasonable assessment?'

Sara sat back and grinned, then tapped two fingers against her forehead in a quick salute. 'You got all that just from a few scraps of paper? I am impressed. And yes, you're right. All of my customers came by word of mouth really. One person tells another and I get a call.'

She started to bite her thumbnail, and then pushed her hands onto her lap.

'Marketing and promotion were on that list with the computer and the website. Looks like I have left it too late. Doesn't it?'

'Not necessarily,' Leo replied and leant forward just a little, his elbow resting on the table. 'What I am looking for is some way to make your orchid nursery stand out from all of the other plant nurseries in this area. Once you find that unique aspect, then you can start to create a whole new brand for yourself and really get started on the marketing. That is when you need your computer and your website. With a new name and a new professional image you can begin to charge higher prices for your plants.'

He slid back and gestured towards the kitchen window. 'More orders, more income, more land you can rent. How does that sound? Sara? You're shaking your head. I thought you wanted to hear some realistic suggestions.'

'I do. I really do, but frankly the whole branding thing scares me silly. It is exactly what I wanted to get away from when I left my job in London. And I don't want to change the name of my company. I like calling myself Cottage Orchids. It says a lot about me. That has to stay.'

'And where is this cottage? And what makes it special? I don't even have any hint where the plants are grown from that name or who is growing them. For all I know, your cottage could be a huge corrugated iron warehouse in central London.'

Sara gasped in horror and threw a paperclip at him which bounced off his chest. 'That is a horrible thing to say. What do you want me to call it? *Phalaenopsis-R-Us?* Or perhaps we should go for something like my grandmother's cunning idea? Just wait until you see this.'

There was a great shuffling of chairs and table but Sara was able to squeeze out, slide along to her dresser and, after a few seconds of a spectacular view of the back of her trousers and much pulling and pushing, she emerged with a piece of once white card with a title written in very flowery and curving script which Sara passed to Leo as she read it out from memory in the highest, whiniest, poshest voice Leo had ever heard. And he had heard plenty in his time, but this girl had it down perfectly.

'Lady Fenchurch's Kingsmede Manor Heritage Orchids.'

She sighed and went to refill the kettle. 'Can you imagine it? I would have coachloads of tourists turning up in the lane expecting to find a huge museum dedicated to my orchid hunting ancestors, a team of professional scientists cloning endangered orchid specimens in a sterile lab and several acres of tropical glasshouses. There should probably be a gourmet café and gift shop on the side with photos of my grandmother wearing her tiara.'

A snort was followed by a hollow laugh. 'I could charge admission! Until they actually realise that all I have left is one orchid house and this cottage to show for three generations of orchid-mad ancestors and they all demand their money back. I might have got away with it when I was living in the Manor, but in a few weeks…? No, Leo. The last thing I want is to pretend to be something I am not. Kingsmede Manor Heritage Orchids should be grown at Kingsmede Manor. End of story. And would you prefer coffee or tea?'

'Tea, please. And I love it.'

'Love what?' Sara replied, looking around the room until she realised that he was grinning and practically drooling at the piece of card she had just passed him.

The penny dropped. And so did her chin.

'Oh, you cannot be serious. Please, no. Not that. There has to be something else we can do, Leo,' Sara said. 'Think. There are three generations of my family who have worked to create these orchids. I might not be an orchid-hunter like they were, but I have to do something to carry on the tradition they started. If I don't, then everything they did would be lost, and I can't bear the thought of that happening.'

'Then try and see this name with new eyes. *It is inspired.* I'm serious. Don't you see it?'

Leo grabbed the card, his eyes shining with excitement as though he had just unearthed some ancient treasure from a muddy field. 'You need a brand that launches you head and shoulders above the competition—and it's right here, staring you in the face. All you have to do is combine your name with your family heritage in growing orchids. It would make all the difference.'

He grinned, trying to contain his enthusiasm. 'Why on earth didn't you tell me that you had a title? Any links to the nobility are a terrific selling feature. Believe me. You will not come up with anything better than this.'

One of her hands pressed hard onto the tabletop, palm down for support, while the teaspoon she was holding in the other hand waved widely in the air, splattering droplets of cold tea across the paperwork.

'A selling feature. Oh, that is just perfect. The entire

history of my mother's family comes down to how I can use my heritage as a *terrific selling feature*. How foolish of me not to think of that before.'

Her hand stilled and Leo could see the faint tremble in her fingers but, when she spoke, Sara's voice was intense, quiet and absolutely crystal-clear and resolute.

'I need to make something very clear. I don't have a title and I never have had a title. My grandmother was the daughter of an Earl but she left that world behind when she married a commoner. Sorry, Leo. She may have kept her courtesy title but any links to the peerage ended right there. If I have learnt anything in my life it is that having a title is a curse, not a blessing. That's why I won't do it. I won't lie. And I certainly will not use my grandmother's title to sell my orchids.'

And just like that Leo's heart contracted and he felt a powerful cord pulling him towards Sara from a place deep inside that he had forgotten was even there.

It was so sudden and so powerful that he almost moved backwards to counteract the strength of the invisible bond that was locking him into this girl. But the tension was so strong there was no way that he could break it by the force of his will.

This was no trivial frisson of physical attraction. This was something else. Something much, much bigger which bypassed his head and hit him hard in the heart and the gut. Fast and hard and brutal in its intensity, but so miraculously uplifting his heart soared.

And the feeling knocked him sideways and speechless.

Here was this girl he had only just met, opening her heart and spilling out her feelings and her loyalties onto this messy table, while he just sat there, his secrets buried so deep inside his chest for so many years that he had almost convinced himself that they no longer existed. Until moments like this one when he saw how his life could have been so very different if he had taken a different path all those years ago. A path where he did not have to deceive the world around him every day of his working life just as he deceived himself to get through the day.

He had kept his secrets and resentments and pain to himself for so long that they had become almost like a story rather than the truth. It made it easier that way.

Until someone like Sara came along and in a few minutes told him that his story was not unique. Far from it.

Sara's grandmother had sacrificed her inheritance for love, just as his mother had left her wealthy family behind to be with her soulmate. And the aftermath of those earthquake decisions were still rippling through the lives of their descendents.

They were so alike it terrified him.

He had not told Sara one word about his own past and yet he felt as though she knew him and what was going on inside his head even better than his own sister. His aunt saw driving ambition and the search for status and position. But Sara? Sara had the power to disarm him with a few simple words as she wrapped her small fingers around his heart and squeezed.

And the walls around his heart started to feel just a little less solid, as though tiny cracks had appeared and alarm bells were ringing, warning him to be careful.

There was still time to repair the damage and rebuild this flash outer mask the world saw when they looked at Leo Grainger.

He should walk away from this connection and from Sara, wish her well for the future and simply get on with his life. He could deny the attraction. Why not? He had given her an option for a business idea and kept his side of the bargain.

He could leave any time he wanted. Just get up and go back to the hotel and drive away.

Leaving her to lose everything she had worked for.

He looked up to see Sara trying to make tea, only as he watched this pretty girl, her hands were so jittery the teaspoon fell onto the flagstones and she was so overcome that it was all she could do to cling onto the worktop.

Instinctively and without conscious thought for the consequences, Leo squeezed out of his chair and crossed the few feet that separated them and pressed his chest against the back of her T-shirt, wrapping his arms around her waist and enclosing her in his embrace.

He wanted to kiss away her fears and pain so badly that he could already imagine what she would taste like from the perfume of her shampoo in her hair and the aroma of coffee and baking. Honest smells. Real. Homely. All Sara.

But that would be too much too soon—for both of them.

Instead he pressed his chin onto her shoulder in silence and pulled her a little tighter towards him in the circle of his arms, savouring the feeling of her warm cheek against the side of his face, waiting for her to say something—anything—but not wanting to break this bond which connected them by something as powerful as words.

Her chest rose and fell several times before he sensed the tension ease away from her shoulders. His reward came as she relaxed back just a fraction of an inch farther into his arms, as though she was willing him to take her weight.

And his heart sang. For one precious moment he allowed a tiny, small and oh, so precious bubble of something other people would call happiness to burst into existence and he sucked in a breath of shock and surprise and delight.

Sara instantly stiffened and clasped onto his hands, drawing them away from her waist so they could rest lightly on her hips.

Leo stepped back just far enough to allow some space between them so that she could turn and face him.

The palms of her hands pressed gently onto the front of his shirt and her heartbeat increased and was so loud he could almost hear it. Every instinct in his body was screaming that this was right, but she had still not raised her head.

She wasn't ready for that. Not yet. His hand lifted so that he could caress the back of her head, making him tremble at the intensity of the waves of delicious sensation at the ends of his fingers.

His voice was low and so close to her ear that it was more of a whisper. 'I understand why you don't want to use her name,' he said. 'Better than you can imagine.'

'How can you possibly understand?' she answered, her words muffled into his chest. 'You are part of the Rizzi family. You have everything you could possibly want in life.'

His hand slid down her back from her hairline and he could almost feel the mental and physical barriers coming down between them as he pulled back and lifted her chin so that he could look at her.

And what he saw in those green-and-gold eyes made the breath catch in his throat. The intensity. The confusion. The regret. It was all there.

The only thing this woman deserved was the truth.

'I understand you because my mother gave up a life of luxury and privilege to be with the man she loved.

Her own family disowned her for choosing my father over them, but she did not regret it for one minute. That's why I understand why you admire your grandmother so very much.'

Leo's fingers caressed the back of her head as she gasped in astonishment, her eyes locked onto his.

'And that is why I am going to help you honour her memory in any way I can,' he said, smiling.

'What do you mean?' she breathed, her eyes wide and her skin flushed. 'Honour her memory?'

'From what you've told me, your orchid houses are a living memory to everything she created here and the deep love she felt for this place. And that is too special to let go. Am I right?'

'Yes, of course. They are her orchids! I am simply carrying on the work she started and trying to repay all of the love she gave me over the years at the same time. And yes, she did love this place. And so do I.'

Leo slowly and gently slid his hands down her arms in wide slow circles, and watched her sigh of pleasure as he did so.

'Then we had better get back to work. Although I do have one more question before we get started. How do you hunt orchids?'

'You hunt them in the wild, of course,' she replied with a laugh and started waving her arms around. 'The craze for orchids started in the early eighteen-hundreds and reached its peak with the Victorians and Edwardians. Everyone simply had to have exotic orchids in their greenhouses to keep up with the fashion—it was a mad and exciting time. Explorers were sent all over the world to collect hundreds of species of orchids of every possible size and shape and colour and it was dangerous work.'

Sara paused for a second and pointed to a sepia print

on the wall of a fine-looking man with a handlebar moustache who was standing with his arms folded and wearing a stiff-looking tweed suit. 'Alfred Fenchurch almost died of yellow fever and got caught up in a revolution, but on top of that there were all kinds of other tropical diseases, wild animals, fierce tribes and natural disasters. Travelling in Central America or Papua New Guinea at the turn of the century was no joke.'

She slipped away from him just enough to turn the kettle on and Leo mourned the loss of that deep connection that he had not even realised was there until she moved out of the comfort of his arms.

'The Fenchurch family caught orchid fever and it has been in the blood ever since. Would you like to see some photographs of the house in its heyday?'

Sara swept past him and practically skipped across the small room, energised and excited, and more animated than Leo had seen her since the party. He could only look on in wonder as she rummaged around at the bottom of the dresser and pulled out a large hat box wrapped with string.

In an instant she had swept her bundles of finance papers to one side to create a space on the table with a lot more enthusiasm than she had for doing filing and admin, and Leo watched in amazement as the hat box sprang open like a children's toy and bundles of photographs and documents tied with ribbon and, in some cases, garden twine, cascaded out across the desk.

All he could do was sigh and shake his head. These old sepia prints, faded in places and torn in others, were obviously of great historical value—and here they were, all stuffed in a flimsy hat box with broken sides in a draughty kitchen which was filled with steam one minute and heat from the oven the next.

Did Sara not realise how very precious these family memories were?

His own mother had brought very few photographs of her Rizzi family with her when she had eloped to marry his father in secret, and he had no true sense of the heritage she had left behind apart from the stories and newspaper clippings she'd kept in an album at the bottom of her wardrobe.

He would have loved this kind of treasure trove to delve into and explore his past as a boy, but that was impossible. His aunt had answered many of his questions following his parents' death, but it was not the same as sitting on a bed with his mother as she pointed to the faces of her family in newspapers and magazines.

Perhaps that was why he simply grinned and dived into the box so that he could share Sara's simple joy and excitement and enthusiasm at the mere sight of these photographs. She passed him image after image, explaining who each person was and what they were doing in their tropical costumes and exotic settings. But, just as she passed him a photograph of her great-great-grandfather, he noticed a folded piece of chart paper tucked down the side of the hat box.

'Is that a map of their adventures?' he asked.

'Oh, no,' Sara replied and drew out the page and quickly unfolded it. 'This was one of the original designs of the tropical glasshouses. That was when there was real money in the family—' she laughed '—and they could afford to hire one of the most famous garden designers in Britain to create something very special to house the orchids. Back then, there were hundreds of plants from all over the world with a full-time staff to look after them.'

'May I?' he asked. 'I've always loved architectural designs.'

Beautiful calligraphy ran down the side of the page and Leo smiled in delight at the stunning pristine craftsmanship of the hand drawn plans dated over a hundred years ago. They were some of the most beautiful architectural designs he had ever seen, and he instantly recognised the name of the designer.

'This is amazing,' he whispered breathlessly, aware that Sara was sitting so close to him that the side of her body was pressed tight against his as they looked at the chart together. 'Were these glasshouses ever made?'

'The money ran out,' she said with a tut. 'The two Victorian glasshouses I use for my orchids were based on a smaller version of the plan, but of course this was only one part of a much greater design. The other evening on the terrace I was telling you about the wonderful gardens that used to be here when my grandmother was a girl. The orangery and main conservatory were still in place then and they must have been quite magnificent.'

'What happened to them? Were they damaged or destroyed?'

'My great-grandmother sold them after the war when times were hard. She was a widow on her own and she couldn't afford the staff to run them. There are a few photographs in the stack here if you'd like to look at them.'

Leo watched in delight as Sara drew out photographs, then more photographs of her family and their servants standing in front of beautiful ornate glass structures next to the house he knew as Kingsmede Manor Hotel. And, as she did so, the first glimmer of an idea flitted through his mind. An idea for something so remarkable and grand that it startled him by the sheer exuberant ambition of it.

What if he could convince his aunt to invest in restoring the gardens?

He had been looking for something unique which

would distinguish this hotel from all the other country hotels in the area—something which would attract new guests with different interests. Perhaps Sara Fenchurch had just given him something to work on? And it could just save her business at the same time.

It was incredibly frustrating that he could not share his ideas with her without giving away his aunt's secret but he would not raise her hopes until he had something more tangible. Then he would tell her everything. But in the meantime he needed to gather together all of the information she had.

Drat. There went another one of those bubbles of happiness again. This was starting to become habit-forming and it only happened when he was around Sara. Strange, that.

'Sara, this design is fantastic. I would love to see everything you have on the original plans for the garden design and glasshouses of the Manor. Will you help me?'

CHAPTER EIGHT

NORMALLY, at six-thirty on a Tuesday morning, Leo was in the gym of the stunning London hotel which he had chosen to make his home. It was convenient, warm and he could sneak back to his room in the private elevator, knowing that a delicious breakfast would be served at his convenience.

Kingsmede Manor had proved deficient on both counts. No gym and no room service at that time in the morning unless he wanted a stale roll and coffee.

There were compensations, of course. Starting with the fact that he was alone on a sunny morning and was about to spend some of the day with one of the most intriguing and remarkable people he had met for a long time, and who was probably stamping her foot at that very moment and wondering where on earth he had got to.

Sara had promised to show him some of the local area from the passenger seat of her delivery van while he took her through a few ideas for the business.

She would be driving.

He could hardly wait.

He shoved his hands deep into his trouser pockets and marched down the patio steps and in minutes was across the lane and just about to knock on her front door when there was a rat-tat of a car horn with a musical chime, and he turned and stared in disbelief at the remarkable example of decrepitude in automotive engineering which was rolling down the lane towards him.

The tiny delivery van had originally been white, but was now more of a dirty, rusty pale yellow, decorated with pictures of orchids of various colours and sizes which were scattered around the words 'Cottage Orchids'. It was so girly and unprofessional he could hardly believe it.

Wait a minute! Cottage Orchids! Oh, no—it couldn't be! But there could be no mistake. His eyes closed for a second when he realised the true horror of the situation he had got himself into.

Sure enough, the engine juddered to a halt, the driver's door clanked open and Sara stepped out and he did a double take.

She was wearing a smart outfit of navy trousers and navy T-shirt with 'Cottage Orchids' embroidered in gold letters on the shoulder. Her hair was swept back with a navy bandanna and she looked cute, attractive, gobsmacking lovely, and parts of his body did a little happy dance.

Pop music blared out from the radio, bright and cheerful, and in total contrast to the look on her face.

Sara stood back and crossed her arms, her feet squarely on the ground in a stance that screamed out that she was not best pleased.

'You are so late. It is not funny,' she said. 'I was going to give you three more minutes before heading off on my own. You do know I have five deliveries to make this morning? Which, as you pointed out yesterday, are actually quite important to my income.'

Leo looked deep into her eyes and replied in a serious voice, 'I like the outfit. Very classy. Now, about the delivery van...'

She shrugged, uncrossed her arms and patted the roof

of the once white vehicle, her mood instantly transformed
to one of pleasure. 'You noticed. I know—' she grinned
and wrinkled her nose in pleasure '—isn't she fantastic?
I had to paint the letters myself, of course, to get it just
right, but Mitzi has never let me down once. She knows I
love her.'

'Mitzi?'

'Mitzi my microvan, of course. She's electric and quiet.
Not the fastest little motor in the world but that's okay.
And she's so cheap to run. This is a good thing.'

Leo decided that it would be dangerous to his health to
mock Mitzi or offend her owner.

'If you give me directions to the first stop, I'll follow in
my own car—that will leave more room for you and your
plants inside…' And coughed twice before adding, 'The
lovely Mitzi.'

Sara's eyes narrowed, and she gave him a hard look for
a few moments, then she threw out her arms to both sides
and laughed until she had to bend over and grasp hold of
her knees to recover.

'Oh, I should have guessed it.' She laughed and wiped
away tears from her eyes. 'Leo Grainger, you are a car
snob. A full on, totally over the top car snob. I bet that you
even have those cute little driving gloves so you don't get
nasty sweat on your steering wheel. Am I right?'

'They were a Christmas present from my sister,' he
replied indignantly with a twist of his lip. 'And I am not
a car snob. I merely appreciate, let's say, the finer things
in life. And poor old Mitzi here has seen better days. I do
have some standards.'

Her reply was a gentle smile, followed by a short nod.
Then she reached into the van, took out the keys and
tossed them to him.

He caught the keys one-handed as if he had been waiting for them.

And they stood there, smiling at one another like a pair of idiots in the morning sunshine.

Three hours later, Leo collapsed down into Mitzi's driver's seat outside a very pretty florist shop in a village ten miles away from Kingsmede, turned on the engine and banged his head twice against the steering wheel, his arms hanging loosely on either side of his body as he waited for his blood pressure to reduce until he was calm enough to drive.

'Oh, it wasn't that bad,' said Sara, pulling off her gardening gloves. 'They loved you in the shop.'

'She offered me a job selling cut flowers!'

'I know! And the manager is usually so shy!' Sara paused and sniffed. 'But well done. You will be pleased to know that this was our very last stop so you can turn off the charm offensive and speed all the way back to the Manor.'

'Twenty miles an hour,' Leo sobbed dramatically. 'Our top speed has been twenty miles an hour! I feel so ashamed. Is there a taxi rank in this village?'

'Hey!' she replied and hit him on the arm with her delivery notes. 'The bus goes once a week so you are stuck with me or hitching a lift. But, as a special treat, I will let you sit in the passenger seat going home.' Then she flung open her door and was about to jump out of the van, when she surprised him by closing the door quickly and shuffling down in her seat.

'Try to look interested in this paperwork,' she hissed, and passed him a bundle of loose papers from the floor of the van before reaching under his seat for a green baseball cap, which she pulled down hard over her head.

'Er, Sara… What is going on, and why should I pretend to be interested in your order sheets?'

'Shush,' she hissed out of the corner of her mouth. 'Do you see the lady who is coming out of the grocers? Beige suit. Cream handbag.'

Leo glanced casually through the windscreen before nodding and staring intently at an invoice with a muddy shoeprint on it. 'Blonde, mid-fifties, make-up from the same era. Do you owe her money?'

'Much worse,' Sara hissed, bending across to stare at the papers. 'She has been trying to set me up with her son for the past eighteen months and the woman will not take no for an answer. For some bizarre reason she is convinced that her son will rocket up the promotion ladder if he has a lady with a classy family name on his arm. And at the moment I'm his best bet for a trophy girlfriend.'

Sara had barely got the words out of her mouth when there was a small tap on the passenger window and Leo waved gently at the lady that Sara was trying to avoid, who was giving him a filthy look through the glass.

Sara instantly rolled down the window and smiled politely. 'Good afternoon, Mrs Tadley. Isn't it a lovely day?'

'Oh, indeed,' she replied, staring intently at Leo as she spoke. 'How nice to see you, Lady Sara. I was hoping to catch up with you about our summer soirée. I do hope you can join us.' And then she looked over towards Leo and smiled through clenched teeth. 'And perhaps your new friend would like to join us?'

'Oh, my business adviser is only in town for a few days, Mrs Tadley,' Sara replied casually. 'And we are on a very tight schedule.'

'Business adviser? Oh, yes, how clever of you,' she replied, clearly relieved that Leo was not a love interest.

Then she lowered her voice and stuck her head into the van. 'I have heard about your problems with the hotel, Lady Sara. It must be terribly distressing. Do call me if there is anything my family can do to help.'

From where he was sitting, Leo could see Sara's fingers were clutched so tightly around the paperwork that her knuckles were turning white with the strain of the self-restraint.

'That is very kind of you, Mrs Tadley. Thank you. I will. Have a good afternoon.' And she gave a small finger wave and smiled sweetly as the window slid up, ending the conversation.

Leo blinked. Proud, stubborn and independent. With very good manners. This was a very different side to the girl he had met at the buffet table in the hotel on Saturday night and danced with under the moonlight.

And she totally took his breath away.

His admiration clicked to a higher level.

'Well, that was interesting,' he said, 'Lady Sara.'

'Actually—' she blinked '—my mother named me Eloise Sara Jane Marchant Fenchurch de Lambert but, seeing as you are my business adviser, Sara will do splendidly, my dear Leonardo.' And she twirled her hand in the air as though giving him a regal wave.

'Delighted to meet you, Eloise. And I don't believe that we have been formally introduced. Leonardo Reginald Costantino Rizzi Grainger at your service, madam.' And he bowed towards her with as much grace as the cramped cab would allow.

'Leonardo Reginald. Oh, my.' Sara clapped her hand over her mouth and pressed her lips together before she embarrassed herself.

'Parents do have a lot to answer for.' He shrugged

and looked nonchalantly out of the window at the small street.

'That they do,' she croaked out, 'Reggie.'

'At last! Something we can both agree on, Eloise.' And he returned her smile, lifting into the cutest dimple on the right side of his mouth.

It was not the smile of a slick city power broker but much more like a naughty boy who had been caught enjoying himself far too much.

'Eloise and Reggie's Floral Specialities. That does have a certain ring to it, doesn't it? Any chance you could be available a couple of mornings a week? I could pay you in orchids and bartered cakes. I predict a great future. What do you say?'

Leo found something fascinating on the roof of the cab and tapped one finger against his chin as though he was giving her proposal serious thought, then shook his head. 'I don't think that *particular* brand would do much to sell orchids. But thank you for the invitation. If I decide to change direction, I shall give you a call.'

'It's a deal, and you could be right,' Sara continued with a chuckle, checking in her door mirror that she was now safe. 'They all know perfectly well that I am not a Lady anything and never will be, but as far as the residents of Kingsmede are concerned I am my grandmother's heir and the rules of peerage do not apply. Not much good having a trophy girlfriend if you can't brag, is there?'

She shrugged and laughed out loud. 'It's a good thing I've given up on the dating scene, that's for sure. No more boyfriends for me. I can't tell you what a relief that is.'

'No more boyfriends?' Leo laughed dismissively. 'You can't mean that. I take it that the Kingsmede singles scene is a tad limited if Mrs Tadley is anything to go by.

And yes, I am driving us home. I can't take any more excitement this early in the day.'

Sara stared at him down her nose as Mitzi pulled away from the kerb, and then snorted, 'And what makes you think that I don't have a fascinating social life? It might not be up to London standards, but Pasha and I have a splendid time and there is always the occasional costume party at the hotel.'

She sat up a little straighter in the passenger seat as Leo coughed disbelievingly and waved at a couple of pedestrians. 'Do not mock. I am actually thinking of taking a short working holiday next spring. There are quite a few companies running holidays for orchid enthusiasts who need specialist guides and it would be brilliant to see what other folks are doing.'

She glanced over in his direction. Leo had his lips pressed firmly together and was staring hard at the road immediately in front of him.

'Now, don't look like that. These tours are very popular.'

He responded by tapping the steering wheel. 'Oh, I don't doubt it,' he said in a low voice. 'In fact, would you mind if I borrowed a few of your holiday brochures when we get back?'

Sara's mouth fell open with a thud, then closed again. 'You want to go on holiday with a team of orchid-mad gardeners touring glasshouses? I would like to see that.'

'Research. And here's another idea. Seeing as the local social scene is a little limited, I was wondering if I could persuade you to join me for dinner in the hotel this evening as my guest? Say about seven? You've been kind enough to feed me baked goods on a regular basis so please allow me to return the favour. What do you say?

Are you willing to risk the hotel cooking again? There would be just the two of us this time.'

'Dinner?' she replied in a low voice and stared out of the van window at the other cars, the fields—anywhere, in fact, that did not require her to look towards Leo.

'You may have heard of it. Meal. Usually taken in the evening involving hot food which is cooked by someone else. Can be fun. I have tried it myself many times and would heartily recommend it.'

Sara took a tighter hold on the paperwork and unfolded it as a distraction for her hands while her poor brain tried to process the fact that Leo Grainger had just asked her out to dinner. At the hotel. Just the two of them.

Somewhere in the back of her brain a choir was singing hallelujahs, blowing trumpets and holding up banners that read *Sara has a date with Leo, Sara has a date with Leo!* while the quieter contingent was sitting with their arms folded and shaking their heads.

She stole a glance sideways while he was distracted by a roundabout where the Kingsmede version of the rush hour was in full swing. Pension day.

Leo gorgeous-from-the-shoes-up Grainger had asked her out for a meal. Not a date. He had never mentioned that, far from it. But it was a meal and she would be his guest. In a hotel restaurant.

That sounded like a date, smelled like a date and she could almost taste the delicious totally unaffordable food that the hotel had become famous for. If she went as his date.

Most girls would jump at the chance to be in the same room as Leo, never mind be his dinner companion. She would be the envy of every other woman in the room.

But she was not like other girls. And she had already been down this road before one too many times.

It was ironic in some ways. She had just accused Mrs Tadley of seeing her as a trophy piece of arm candy— when that was exactly what she would be doing with Leo and what she had done with every other handsome and stylish man who had ever asked her out. She was the one who used to like trophy boyfriends.

She had used them and they had used her.

Weird that she had never realised that until this very moment.

She looked down at the creased and now totally screwed up receipts and her eyes slid over to the driver's seat. The crease was still crisp in Leo's black trousers, which were made of fabric so fine and soft she longed to touch it and stroke his leg.

Of course she wanted to spend the evening with Leo.

Of course she wanted to hear him laugh and find out how he ate his peas and what kind of food he liked best in the world.

Of course she wanted to have her heart broken yet again when he left her behind to go back to his high-flying life in London. He would be the trophy date to end all trophy dates, and would probably ruin her for anyone else for a long time. And then she would have to face him again at Helen and Caspar's wedding. *Oh, no.*

Going out to dinner with Leo would be so wonderful that it would be terrible.

Smoothing out the pages of her now crushed receipts with the palms of her hands in the vain hope of making them legible, Sara lifted her head and looked from side to side.

'Thanks for the invite but I'm already booked for dinner this evening. I would really love some of those fondant chocolates if they are on the menu, though. Would you mind leaving some at reception for me?'

'You're turning me down?' He gave her a confused glance before focusing on his driving. 'Should I change my cologne? I don't usually have this much trouble persuading ladies to dine with me.'

She smiled longingly at him. 'No, and please don't change a thing.'

'I refuse to be thwarted. Let's pretend that we are having our dinner conversation right now. Driving along in this van.'

'Pretend we are having dinner together? I wish you'd warned me. I would have changed into something a little less…well…navy.'

He raised his right hand for a second. 'You look enchanting. In fact I have not been able to take my eyes off you since you entered the room. Could I interest you in some chilled pink champagne while we look at the menu?'

'Oh, yes, please.' She wriggled, suddenly feeling much better, safe in the familiar comfort of Mitzi. 'French, of course.'

'Absolutely. So, while we are waiting for the starters to arrive, I'll make small talk about city life. You mentioned that you used to work in London, but I have no idea how you spent your time. What did you do? Where did you eat? I'm curious. Perhaps we know the same restaurants?'

'Ah, yes, my old city life. My mother still lives there, you know. Do you know Pimlico at all? Very chic. As for my job, I worked as a general dogsbody for my mother's friends who ran a company renting out luxury villas. They paid me very little to sort out the problems their guests were having all over the world. When I was in London I usually ate out with my former boyfriend who was far more interested in my family connections than in me. He had nice manners, nice clothes and my mother totally approved of him.'

'Ouch. To both. Please have another glass of virtual champagne.'

'Don't mind if I do. Thanks. Most delicious.'

Leo stopped the car and waved some pedestrians across the road before moving on. 'Do you get up to London much to see your mother?'

'Ah, that would be no. We had a major steaming argument three years ago and as a result I gave up my job in London to open an orchid nursery in rural Hampshire and she has never been back. We haven't spoken much since.'

'Three years! I find it hard to believe that you're still not talking after three years!' Leo said in a shocked voice. 'You have to be one of the easiest people to talk to that I have ever met. What happened?'

Sara looked at him in silence. And suddenly the good opinion of this man mattered a lot more to her than she would have thought possible. She simply could not face the idea that he thought badly of her. It had been so long since she had told anyone or even thought about those sad days that it would be a relief to explain her decision to someone who did not know her history.

'Do you really want to know? Then watch out. Here comes the main course. Roast beef. All dried up. Overcooked. Tough and stringy.'

Her hands busied themselves pulling at a loose thread in her peaked cap while she deliberately tried to avoid making eye contact with Leo. 'My grandmother had not been well for some time, but she insisted on living on her own at the Manor and we used to visit at weekends and make a fuss of her. Well, the crunch came when my grandmother had to go into hospital and needed someone to take care of her when she came out.'

Sara lifted up the cap and pointed it at the windscreen. 'The villa company owed me about four weeks' holiday but every time I asked for it there was always some crisis which needed my urgent attention or their world would stop. I finally pleaded for one week just to be here with my grandmother.'

She dropped the hat and fell back against her seat. 'Of course that didn't last very long. Three days into my holiday I had a pleading phone call telling me that there was an emergency in the Caribbean and I was the only person in the world who could sort it out. I refused to go so they called my mother, who told me quite clearly that I could not let her friends down, so she offered to take my place with my grandmother until I got back. And I was foolish enough to believe that she would actually do it.'

Sara closed her eyes and shook her head slowly from side to side. 'I should have known better.' She looked over at Leo. 'Do you know what the emergency was? The jacuzzi at the villa was not hot enough for the guests. And nobody else was capable of adjusting the temperature. I called the plumber. I watched the plumber adjust the temperature control. Then I came home. And what did I find? My grandmother, alone, cold and hungry. My mother had lasted a total of two days before driving back to London after falling out over some trivial thing.'

Sara started tugging at the hat in her lap. 'I will not repeat what I said to my mother because it was not very dignified or polite, but let's just say that she was totally shocked that a girl with my expensive education had such an extensive vocabulary of expletives, including some she had never heard before.'

There was a pause as she realised that she had just

pulled the visor off her hat by tugging at it too fiercely. 'It was the biggest row we've ever had. And at the end of it I was so furious that I told her that I had no intention of working for a pittance for one day longer while her friends lived in Switzerland in the lap of luxury. If she wanted to help them then she could do the work herself. She told me that I had always been an ungrateful child who would end up alone and unloved. I resigned over the telephone ten minutes later and I have never looked back. Not once. I don't miss the travel and I don't miss the problems.'

'But you miss your mother,' he said in a low voice. And in the relative silence of their small enclosed space his words seemed to echo into her brain and reverberate there for a second.

One side of her face twitched into a half smile. 'Sometimes. She certainly taught me that not every mother loves her own child all of the time. I just didn't know that it showed.'

'What happened to the boyfriend? The one who was only interested in your grandmother's title. Did he offer to come and help?'

Sara laughed and rolled her eyes. 'Oh, yes,' she replied. 'He turned up for my grandmother's funeral, then took one look at my cottage, compared it to Kingsmede Manor and decided that my new life in the country was not one he would enjoy. But he was very generous—he did offer to wait for me to come to my senses and come back to London. Two weeks later he ran off to Australia with the office junior he had taken to a conference and sent me a text accusing me of not giving enough priority to our relationship.'

Her shoulders shook off the memory with a dramatic shudder. 'Last time I heard, he was happily dating the daughter of a Scottish earl. And good luck to him and very good luck to her because she's going to need it. And I rather think that I have eaten far too much of the tough meaty part of the meal and not left any for you. Your turn.'

'My turn?'

'Oh, yes. I may be your guest at this splendid feast but I should be polite and try learn more about my dining companion. Especially now that he knows all about my fierce bad temper and unforgiving nature.'

'True. And under the circumstances it would be rude not to offer you some business advice. Although, after what you have just said about your bad temper, I suspect that my suggestion might not go down very well. Perhaps I should wait until you have eaten your dessert first to sweeten you up.'

Sara sucked in a breath and looked at him for a second. 'I don't like the sound of that,' she said, 'but okay. I did ask you to help me. Go ahead. Bring on the gateau but let me prepare myself first.'

She gritted her teeth and clutched onto the dashboard with both of her hands. 'Okay,' she said, 'I'm ready. Hit me with it. You have my full attention.'

'Don't look so scared! This is just one idea. I was on the phone to a venture capitalist friend of mine yesterday who is interested in unusual start-up companies—like yours!'

She practically leapt out of her seat but Leo gestured with the flat of his hand for her to sit back down again.

'Before you get excited, he will want to know that you can guarantee constant supply of top quality plants to the marketplace. Right now, I can only see one way to make sure that happens. You need to move the two old orchid houses.'

Sara felt as though all of the air had been sucked out of

the van, making her head spin, but she could not—dare not—move until she'd heard what Leo had to say.

Leo paused while he turned back onto the main road where the traffic was much heavier. 'I have been looking at land prices around Kingsmede and they are higher than I expected but, with the right business plan and a new marketing campaign, you could afford to rent the extra space you need on the other side of the village. Shall I give him a call? And now you have gone quiet. Tell me what you're thinking. Interested?'

Sara stared at Leo wide-eyed, scarcely believing what he had just said. They had been working together in the same kitchen and he had not understood one single thing about why she was there and why she had stayed in this cottage in Kingsmede when she could have moved anywhere in the world. And how could he? When she had not bothered to explain it to him. She sighed at her own stupidity.

Why should he understand when even her own mother did not understand fully?

'Take down my grandmother's orchid houses?' she replied. 'Have you any idea how difficult that would be? They are huge.'

Leo shuffled forward in the driver's seat, checked the road and then turned the van off onto the tarmac on the side of the road in silence. Switching off the engine, he twisted around in the narrow seat and stared hard into her face. 'I don't think that you have thought through the implications of what happens when the land is sold, Sara. That letter means what it says. The builders will need to clear the land before they start. Of course they will give you a chance to remove the greenhouses, but if you don't... They would be within their rights to demolish them.'

The blood seemed to drain from her face and she felt dizzy. 'Demolish,' she said in a weak voice. 'Could they do that?'

'Only if they had to,' he replied. 'But you have to be ready for that possibility.'

'I don't know if I'm up to this,' she whispered, her eyes fixed on the dusty floor of the van, which was littered with sweet papers, cat treats and random pieces of paper and other assorted rubbish. Which at that moment looked like a fair representation of how this week was turning out.

Leo reached across and took one of her hands in his. 'I don't expect you to do it on your own,' he said. 'There are great removal teams who could have you up and running in two or three days. The plants would never know the difference.'

He bent his head down so that he was looking up at her with a wide smile, warm and encouraging. And she was so glad that he was here holding her hand, helping her to get through this, that her throat tightened and she blinked away treacherous tears before squeezing his hand between her palms.

She was being so totally pathetic it was ridiculous! She was a grown woman.

'Laugh at me if you will, Leo, but Kingsmede Manor has been the one constant in my life for as long as I can remember and I just can't imagine growing orchids somewhere else. It's the only place I've ever felt loved and treasured and wanted. It's my safe place. That probably sounds ridiculous, but I mean it. Every word.

'I'm sorry,' she said, looking into those grey-blue eyes which were gazing at her with such compassion that she almost lost it. 'I know that you're trying to save my business and I appreciate that more than I can tell you. It's just that…everyone I have ever loved and cared about has gone and left me just when I needed them. I haven't seen my father since I was six, my mother is a ghost and then I lost my grandmother three years ago. That's why I came back to Kingsmede, because it belonged to my grandmother. And it would not be the same anywhere else. Does that make any sense to you at all?'

Leo looked into Sara's wide eyes, filled with concern, regret and love of the one place that she had made into her safe haven in this mad world, and his heart melted.

He stroked her short hair back over her ears, caressing the cropped layers as though they were made of the finest silk, his fingers moving from her temple in gentle circles while all the time all he wanted to do was gather her up into his arms and tell her that it was all going to be fine and that he could fix this for her.

That was his job after all, wasn't it? Fixing things for other people.

But he couldn't give her that comfort.

He had spent hours poring over the old designs for the Manor, sketching and drawing out elaborate schemes for wonderful glasshouses and a stunning conservatory, and enjoying every minute of it. Sara had searched everywhere for the more detailed schematics without success but he had already seen enough to visualise just how splendid the buildings could have been.

But the cold light of dawn brought with it the hard truth.

These designs were so elaborate that the cost of restoring the gardens would far outweigh the benefits to the hotel short-term. And he simply did not have any information to show that they would provide enough income during the winter to be worth the investment.

But it was more than that. If he proposed a garden restoration plan to the Rizzi Hotel group, it could put him at odds with the other plans he knew *would* work for the hotel. At odds with his aunt and his family at exactly the time when he was trying to impress them with how very clever he was.

Grand and fanciful concepts like garden restoration would expose him to the worst criticism of all from his grandfather—that he was being sentimental and putting people before the business.

No. That idea had to stay just that. An idea which would never be realised. He could not risk being humiliated by his grandfather. Not even for Sara.

While all the while this wonderful, courageous woman felt as though she had been abandoned by everyone she had cared for.

All he could do was open up his heart and share some of his own life in the vain hope that she would believe that there was someone in her life who knew how she was feeling and hurting. Then talk through real ideas which he knew would work for her.

'I do understand,' he said, 'more than you think. My parents passed away in a car accident when I was sixteen, but until then we used to live in a little house in the London suburbs. When you are a child you don't realise how hard it must have been for your parents, but my sister and I had a very happy childhood. I always knew that I was loved and wanted. We might not have had the latest electronic gizmo the other kids had, but they used to love to come to our house because it was always full of music and life and chatter.'

He smiled at Sara and tapped her on the end of her nose. 'Sometimes I have to drive through that part of town and I miss that old house. I was happy there.'

Sara gasped and slid her hand onto his wrist and held it there. 'I'm so sorry to hear about your parents,' she said. 'I can only imagine how awful it must have been for you. But I'm glad that you have such happy memories.' She smiled. 'Tell me about them. Tell me about your dad. What did he do?'

Leo took a breath. He had not been expecting that.

'My dad worked as an architect in a city firm, but his real passion was painting. I remember sneaking down-stairs in the middle of the night so that I could watch him working frantically to cover the canvas with paint. Landscapes. Portraits. He could do anything. His fingers were moving so fast that they seemed to blur, and he was so wrapped up in the world that he was creating that he usually didn't even notice that I was there. It was his obsession.'

Then Leo's voice drifted away into a soft whisper that resonated inside the van. 'And then a few hours later he would put away his paints and put on his business suit and take a bus and then the underground to work in an office block with fluorescent tubes above his head, drawing up plans for more office blocks and car parks. And he did that year after year because he had a family he loved. I admired him for that sacrifice and I still admire him today.'

'He must have been a remarkable man,' Sara whis-pered, holding Leo's hand tightly.

Leo smiled and nodded, grateful for the rare oppor-tunity to talk about the parents he had so adored and still missed on a daily basis and yet never spoke about to anyone, not even his sister or his aunt. 'They were both remarkable,' he replied.

He looked at her and his eyes sparkled with a fierce passion which was invigorating and almost frightening in its intensity. 'And that is why I am going to prove to my mother's family that she made the right decision when she chose to elope with my father. He was a terrific man and he loved her more than anything else in the world. Nobody disrespects him. Nobody. And that's why I need to show them that her son is worthy of that same respect.'

'What do you mean?' she asked in a low voice, calm and collected, trying to balance out the pressure and electrifying tension that crackled in the air between them.

'I've been invited to join my aunt for lunch at the Rizzi board meeting on Friday. She kept in touch with my mum from the day she walked out of the family home, and was there to take care of us after the accident. But she won't be there on her own—the whole family is coming up to Kingsmede Manor for the meeting, and that includes my grandfather, Paolo Rizzi. It is not going to be easy, but I am willing to take the first step to talk to him if he is prepared to listen in return.'

Leo's upper lip twitched. 'And I might just show off a little about how successful my business has become. Or maybe a lot, depending on the reception I receive. I suppose that makes me a lesser person but this is a special occasion.'

'Of course.' She nodded slowly. 'Now I am beginning to get the picture. And I almost—almost—' she held up one hand as Leo opened his mouth to protest '—feel sorry for old Paolo. He won't know what's hit him. Good luck for Friday.'

Then she smiled and her voice dropped an octave. 'When are you going back to London?'

'Tomorrow. I need to catch up on my workload, but I'll be coming back here on Thursday evening. Why?'

'Oh, I was just thinking that I might be available for dinner on Thursday evening, Reg. Seeing as it will be your last night in Kingsmede before the big meeting. If the invitation is still open.'

'It would be my pleasure,' he murmured and reached out and took her hands in his as he stared deep into those green eyes, so full of hope and care.

'I want you to think about what I've suggested. You would still have your cottage and the main greenhouse at the Manor. That doesn't change. But your other two glasshouses would on the other side of the village. Would that really be so bad? You would still be Kingsmede Manor Orchids. Okay?'

'Yes…' she breathed out in a rush. '…I suppose I would. I will think about it. Thank you, Leo.'

The delight and fire of energy and enthusiasm in Sara's eyes burnt so brightly that Leo sucked in a breath of cooling air. If it meant so much to Sara to even suggest that there was a chance then he could give her a sprig of hope.

'Hey. We are a team, remember—Eloise and Reggie's Floral Specialities. Bring it on, Sara. Let's do this. Let's show them what Kingsmede Manor could have been. Ready to get started? We have a business plan to write.'

CHAPTER NINE

Sara stepped out of the shower, wiped away the condensation from the surface of the bathroom mirror and stared at herself through the hazy mist.

She was exhausted and it showed in the dark shadows under her eyes and the paleness of her skin. The plans for Tony Evans were complete. But even with Leo's help it had taken her twice as long as she had expected to photograph the orchids she had allocated to specific rooms in the hotel. She had eventually crashed into bed at two on Wednesday morning.

Leo was still working at the kitchen table when her eyes started to close and her head had started dropping onto her chest. She had a vague memory of his warm arms wrapped around her waist as he lifted her up and carried her in his arms the few steps to her bedroom.

Bliss.

She had only meant to nap for an hour or so; when she woke Pasha was asleep on the bed and the morning was gone. And so was Leo.

She ran her hands through her short hair, pushing it back from her forehead, and wondered how she had managed without Leo all this time. She would never have achieved so much in the past few days without his help. She knew that, but of course it was more. A lot more.

Leo Grainger had come crashing deep into her life like a tsunami wiping away everything in its path and leaving behind a new world of... That was the difficult bit.

She felt so helpless.

Her hands clamped around the cool ceramic basin before she slapped cold water onto her face and patted it dry.

She should go back to the hot orchid house and check the humidity levels. The weather had changed from hot sunshine to the type of sticky cloudy day that threatened rain or even thunder. It was oppressive and so warm that she had slept without covers all night.

It was as though the whole world had changed from warm sunshine to cloud—not only the weather but in her heart.

How had she got herself into this position?

She had become so comfortable with her routine existence, but it had only taken one man like Leo Grainger to come wafting into her life in a vampire costume and it was as though the windows had been opened and a powerful light had illuminated a dark space, revealing what lay within.

And she did not like very much what she saw there.

Sara turned from side to side and looked at her naked body as objectively as she could in the misty mirror. On the surface she was the same girl she had always been. Tall, gawky, slim and without much cleavage to shout about.

It was as though time had turned back on itself and she was sixteen again, getting ready for her mother's birthday party. And knowing deep inside that she was never going to be pretty enough or glamorous and stylish enough to be the daughter her mother wanted and needed. Slick and shiny and well groomed were the kind of descriptions reserved for other girls.

How could a country duckling like her ever hope to be enough for a man like Leo Grainger? What had she got to offer him?

There was no future in their relationship, and it was ridiculous for her to even dream that there could be. Their lives were so very different in every way.

Did she really expect him to drive down to this village every weekend? And she could hardly go to London or fly out to some romantic hotel at a moment's notice without neglecting her customers and her nursery.

So where did that leave them?

Any idea that they had a future together was just a glorious illusion like the magical gardens described in the Victorian documents Leo had devoured with such pleasure the day before.

She felt Pasha purring and rubbing against her bare legs and she instantly reached down and lifted him up. Her grandmother's old cat didn't even struggle or try and scratch her once.

'This is the end of an era, Pasha,' she murmured into his warm dry fur. 'Things are going to be a lot different from now on. But we will be okay in the end.'

Except that, as Sara caught her reflection in the mirror, she could only see weary disappointment and finality in the sad eyes of the girl looking back at her.

And that shocked her more than she had thought possible.

Was this how it was going to be from now on? Not if she had anything to say about it.

'Well, Pasha, if this truly is the end of an era—' she smiled '—then let's make this a night to remember. Don't wait up. I might be quite late.'

* * *

Leo stared out over the hotel grounds in the late afternoon sunshine towards the fine filigree roof of the glasshouses on the other side of the lane. He knew that there was a small cottage there with a girl who made his heart sing and if he wanted he could walk over and be there in minutes.

But he wouldn't.

In a few short days Sara Fenchurch had become the only woman he liked to spend his time with. The person he needed to talk to first thing in the morning and last thing at night. They had spent hours chatting about nothing in particular and the time seemed to pass in seconds.

He liked Sara. He liked her a lot. And maybe, just maybe, he more than liked her. But that came with a price.

Tomorrow he would meet his aunt and the Rizzi family in what had been Sara's grandmother's dining room and give a presentation he had been thinking about for so long it had become a myth.

But instead of working every hour he could on the details he knew he would be challenged on, all he could think about was a pretty girl called Sara and the orchids she loved so passionately in this special world she had created for herself. A world so foreign to his normal life it could have been a distant country. And yet, driving back to Kingsmede that afternoon, he had felt almost excited about seeing the Manor again.

Which was ridiculous. He loved his life in London and the pulse and excitement of the city in his pristine, ordered workspace and home. She loved the cramped, hot and humid space between her rows of plants and a crazy, messy cottage.

The view of the Thames from his office on the fifteenth floor of the glass building in Docklands was worth every hour of relentless and unending conference work.

She loved the view of her flower beds from her kitchen window.

His triple layer electronic calendar was now completely full for the next five months and into the New Year. Her diary hung from a peg near the kitchen door and was just about to get a lot less crammed.

He should be excited about making the presentation tomorrow and relishing the thoughts of his triumph with the family. Instead of which he felt hollow and exhausted from the thought of leaving Kingsmede and Sara behind him.

He had changed.

She had changed his life.

She had given him so much—and what had he given her? His time, his opinions—but not the truth. He had not given her the truth. And she deserved better than that.

No matter what happened going forward, Sara deserved to hear the truth from him.

She would be hurt and probably angry to discover that he was a liar and a fraud. Other people had let her down in the past and now he was adding himself to the list.

Leo drew back the curtain and opened the bedroom window.

This was his last chance to spend time with Sara as the man she thought he was.

Time to make this evening something she could remember for the right reasons.

Sara tugged at the skirt of her fitted azure cocktail dress one more time before sucking in a breath, lifting her head and walking as calmly as she could into the reception area of Kingsmede Manor Hotel. Not as a delivery girl or wannabe orchid supplier, but as a bona fide member of the public here at the invitation of a very important guest of the hotel.

Tonight she was just a normal girl out on a date with a charming, handsome man who had invited her to be his dinner companion.

And just the thought of that gave her the jitters so badly that she almost slipped on the highly polished marble floor in her uncomfortable high heels which she had not worn for three years. It was a mystery how she had managed to wear shoes like this every day and blocked out the pain as the price of elegance. She truly was not the city girl she had once pretended to be. Not that she had ever been one at heart, she knew that now. Which made it even more incredible that Leo Grainger was even vaguely interested in her and wanted to spend his last evening alone with her.

Smiling to the receptionist who had given her a sly nod and wink of approval on the way in, Sara wrapped her fingers around her clutch bag as tight as she dared without destroying the poor thing to hide her nerves, and strolled casually over towards the hotel bar. She had only gone a few steps when the elevator doors opened and out emerged the man she had come to meet.

Leo was wearing a sky-blue shirt, highlighting his tanned skin and broad shoulders, and she had to fight back a sudden urge to throw herself at him and drag him into the elevator and shock the hotel staff. But of course she would never do that... She was still the Lady of the Manor as far as the locals were concerned. *Pity*.

'For once I am on time,' she said, her voice low and shaky. 'Nice shirt.'

Leo made a joke of glancing down at the shirt and flicking off an imaginary speck.

'Your timing is perfect,' he said in a voice of pure chocolate—hot mocha with extra marshmallows and whipped cream on top. 'And I thought you might appreciate a change from black. Just this once.'

'Then I am truly honoured,' she quipped with a tilt of her head. 'And you know it suits you.'

His reply was a slow laser-focused swivel of his eyes from her strappy summer sandals to the criss-cross of her one-shoulder cocktail dress. It was a look that would set any woman on fire and it was certainly working its magic on her.

She squirmed, and he knew that she was squirming, which made her even more self-conscious. This man was infuriating! His blue-grey eyes flashed with fire and light and her pulse grew hotter. At this rate she was going to need a shower before she ate dinner.

'You look sensational,' he whispered in a voice just loud enough that only she could hear it. 'And I missed your grand entrance. I don't suppose you could just pop outside and stride in again so I could enjoy seeing you in the wonderful dress. Just for me?'

She gave him a look which clearly answered his question. 'Ah, perhaps not. Maybe that is a good thing.' He grinned. 'I'm not entirely sure I could take it.' And he waggled his eyebrows up and down several times.

'Leo,' Sara said under her breath, and she looked from side to side to check that no one was listening to him, even though she was grinning with delight, 'behave yourself! This is a very respectable hotel.'

Leo instantly stood ramrod straight and saluted. 'Of course, my lady,' then gestured flamboyantly towards the elevator. 'Your carriage awaits, madam.'

Sara took tighter hold of the clutch bag as a nervous shiver ran across her back. 'Aren't we going to the bar for drinks before dinner?' she asked. *Or perhaps we are by-passing drinks and dinner completely and going straight to your bedroom? That would be nice.*

'For you, my lady, the public bar is not nearly good enough.' And then he smiled and presented her with the fingertips of his right hand as if he were handing her into a carriage, then seized upon her hand hungrily. 'It's right this way.' He tucked her hand tighter against his chest so that they were touching from thigh to shoulder as they glided into the beautifully polished elevator, which was just large enough for two.

She was so entranced by the delicious scent of this man she was pressed against that, when the elevator started on its upward journey, she jumped and flinched away from him, only to be pulled back by a firm hand against the middle of her back. Almost as if he was determined to keep her by his side for as long as possible.

With a lurching feeling of resignation and regret, Sara realised that this was the closest that she had been to this wonderful man since they had danced together and shared that wonderful moment on the terrace that Saturday evening, and was so taken back to that dance that she could almost hear their music playing in the background.

Then she blinked hard and stared in amazement at Leo.

'Is that a Viennese waltz that they are playing?' she asked in amazement. 'Elevator music has certainly improved around here.'

'I hope so,' he replied with a smile. 'It took all of my considerable charms to persuade the lovely receptionist to change the tape to one of my liking.'

He breathed the words into Sara's ear. 'It had to be our song. Nothing else will do.'

'Of course,' she said with twisted eyebrows, 'I totally agree,' and then her face relaxed. 'That was very thoughtful.'

'My pleasure.' He smiled and gave her one of those looks which were intended to entrance any female creature within one hundred miles' radius. He must have had advanced training. Because it was a total success.

Sara was still feeling bedraggled and dazed when the elevator doors slid open and she looked out onto what should be the third floor corridor to the guest rooms, if the elevator button was telling the truth. Then her brain connected with what she was looking at. That was crazy. There were no guest rooms on the third floor. The top of the house had always been the attic storage room and the servants' quarters—and her bedroom, of course, tucked away in the corner of the tower.

Her old bedroom. Oh, Leo.

A lump formed in her throat, so large she was in danger of never speaking again.

Leo slipped away from her side long enough to step outside the elevator, then turned back and stretched one hand towards her.

Sara looked out into the corridor over Leo's shoulder.

The electric lights had been turned off. And in their place were two rows of tall candelabras with a full complement of tall lit candles. The breeze from the elevator created a flickering wave of warm light that floated across the golden wooden floor towards them, warm with the aroma of beeswax and exotic perfume.

The candles were lighting their way down a narrow corridor and she instantly recognised where they were going, and it knocked her sideways that her suspicions had been confirmed.

This was the same piece of flooring that she had skipped

and jumped and run down for so many years towards her old bedroom—the bedroom she had chosen as a child from every other room in the house.

'Shall we?' he murmured, and smiled at her with eyes transformed by the flickering candlelight into deep blue pools, and as she placed her fingers into the palm of his hand and stepped out of the elevator, she knew she had just taken a big step. She felt it in her heart and she knew it in her mind.

This was a journey she could not walk away from when Leo left her to go back to his life in the city. If she took one more step she would be resigned to a life of longing and missing Leo every minute that they were apart. A life of endless regret and emptiness until she could touch him and hold him and speak to him again.

It was a miracle that she had the strength to take that one step forward and clutch onto his fingers as though they were a lifeline being held out to a drowning woman.

His left arm rested lightly at her waist and he drew her to him as they strolled slowly down the narrow corridor in silence. It was probably only ten steps, but it was a journey she wished would never end.

Here in this carefully controlled space with Leo by her side, she felt contained and separate from the world and all the pressures and problems that lay outside both of them. With Leo she felt safe and sheltered and protected by someone who cared enough to go to all of this trouble because he knew that it would give her pleasure.

He would be an amazing lover.

It had been such a long time since anyone had actually done something so selfless for her and her heart swelled at the simple joy of it.

And she loved him for it.

She loved Leo Grainger.

It should have come as a surprise but it didn't. She had felt the world shift over these past few days as though tectonic plates were changing the shape of the continent that lay beneath her feet and underpinned her entire small world. She would not have it any other way, not when it felt this wonderful.

They slowed outside the wooden door she had once known as the gates to the secret world she had created for herself. But this time it was Leo who turned the handle and swung the door into the room and she gasped in delight and amazement at what she saw inside.

In contrast to the dim candlelit corridor, her old bedroom was bright with late evening sunshine, which beamed through the stained glass panels at the top of the open full-length windows.

Birdsong from the trees directly opposite the window combined with the distinctive call of peacocks on the lawns and a happy chatter of guests on the floors below them to create a soundtrack she had forgotten and yet was instantly familiar.

She closed her eyes and took in the special aroma of old lavender sachets, wax polish and dusty old wooden flooring and fixtures. It was all there.

Blinking away tears of delight and pleasure at being in this place again, she was aware that Leo was standing by her side and he gave her a small tug at the waist.

Where her bed used to be was a long sofa and right in front of the window was a fine marquetry table laid out for dinner for two with the finest porcelain, silver cutlery and crystal glassware. A bottle of very fine champagne was chilling in a silver ice bucket. Waiting for her to enjoy.

'I don't know what to say,' she managed to squeak out, scarcely able to take in the beautiful room.

'Then don't say anything,' he whispered, standing behind her with his arms wrapped around her waist so that his chin rested on her shoulder and they could look out through the tall windows onto the trees, open countryside and her very own cottage and greenhouses below.

'I am just content that you like it.'

All that she could manage was a gentle nod of her head and she leant back against Leo's chest, allowing him to take her weight and revelling in the sensation of the strength of his arms around her and the warmth of his chest against her back.

'It's magical,' she finally managed to whisper in a hoarse voice. 'But how did you know that this was what I really wanted to see before everything changes?'

'Oh, that is quite simple,' he replied, the side of his head resting against hers. 'This is what I would have wanted if I had been in your position. Now, I think it's time for a beautiful lady to have some champagne and the finest food this hotel has to offer.'

She sniffed away a moment of intense embarrassment and pleasure. 'Yes, please, and seeing as you have gone to so much trouble, I might save some for you as well,' she murmured with a half smile, trying to be gentle and wanting so very desperately not to break the connection and the wonder of this moment.

And that really did make him chuckle, and his gentle laughter echoed around the room as she turned inside the circle of his arms and slowly lifted her hand so that she could stroke his cheek.

And then she kissed him. Her lips moved gently and smoothly across his so that, as his smile faded into surprised recognition, her fingers could move slowly to the back of his head, caressing his skin on the way. While all the time her lips were moving from the corner of his mouth over the warm and full bow of his lower lip and then taking possession of his entire mouth.

Leo's arms wrapped tightly around her back so that he was holding her completely against him, and this feeling of his hands on her dress, burning through the fine fabric against her skin, only added to the utter delight and heat of their heady kiss as he returned her passion step by step, touch by touch and sensual movement by movement.

She had never been kissed like this before in her life or shared and given herself so completely into the passion of the moment, but she so desperately wanted this man to know how she felt and the intensity of how much she wanted to be with him. She did not need champagne to fuel her intoxication—all that she truly needed was Leo and this moment in time. Everything else was extra and unnecessary.

Whatever happened in the future or even in the next day or two did not matter. All that mattered was that they were together and she could show him how much he had come to mean to her in only a few short but remarkable days when he had opened up the doors to show her what her new life could be like.

It was almost as if she was saying goodbye to this room, this house and the only way she could survive that was to have Leo by her side.

Nobody else in the world would do—ever again.

Breathless, panting with heat and the pressure of the blood pumping in her veins, Sara rested her forehead on Leo's chin, sensing his heart racing and his lungs drawing in cleansing breaths.

'Hello, beautiful lady,' he whispered, his eyes finding something totally fascinating in her hair, and holding her against him and caressing her with unbelievable gentleness and tenderness.

Sara revelled in the luxurious sensations that flooded through her body in slow languorous waves. Her senses seemed ultra tuned to every part of Leo. The soft fabric of his shirt against the warm skin that lay below, fragrant with expensive bath products blended with a subtle musk and aromatic perfume that was all his own.

She could feel powerful bands of muscle and sinew below the palms of her hands under his shirt. He was totally intoxicating.

'Can I see you again?' she murmured into his neck.

'Um?' he replied, but his mouth was too busy kissing her temple.

'I know that you are going back to London tomorrow, but I'd like to see you again. If you want to,' she blurted out in a rush, not wanting to break the connection but desperate for him to know how she felt. Suddenly the most important thing in the world was to make him hers.

'Look what you have done to me, Leo Grainger! I'm wearing dresses and heels and having romantic dinners. And I like it. I like it a lot. I need you in my life, Leo. Come back—tell me that you will come back and see me.'

His hand pressed her head deep into his chest and he embraced her with such love and tenderness, but she could hear the fast beat of his heart under her head, and his heavy breathing. And then the low sigh that was nothing to do with passion and deep feeling and everything to do with the bad news he was about to tell her.

Had she made a mistake? Had she totally misread him?

Sara lifted her head and looked at his face and her grin faded. It was as though the blood had been drained from his skin.

'What is it, Leo? What's wrong? If you don't want me, just tell me.'

Sara reached forward to stroke his face, but Leo closed his fingers around her wrist and slowly, slowly, started stroking the back of her hand with the pad of his thumb.

'Oh, I do want you, very much, but there is something I have to tell you and it's not going to be easy for you to hear. There's no easy way of saying this, but I need you to understand that I had no idea how important it was for you to stay and work in the grounds of your old home.'

He took a breath and exhaled slowly before speaking again in a lower voice. 'You already know that the hotel chain want to redevelop the old gardens and build a spa extension to the hotel. What you don't know is that the designs for the spa are much larger than you might think, Sara. I've seen the plans, and the building work is going to extend across all of your kitchen gardens.'

She stared into his forehead and suddenly the realisation of what he was about to say hit her and hit her hard.

'Oh, no. No, Leo. Please tell me that they won't be building right next to the only greenhouse I will have left. The orchids need as much light and ventilation as I can get.'

He raised his blanched face and exhaled slowly before replying.

'I am so sorry, Sara, but the architect's plans have already been approved at the outline stage. The investment needs to use all of the space they have available to get the return they need, and that means building right up to the bottom of your garden. There will be glass—you can be sure of that. The architect wants to build a conservatory link between the house and the spa.'

'But that means they will be building over the foundations for the Orangery and the beautiful knot garden! Once that is under cement there's no going back. Oh, Leo, how do you feel about that after you've seen those original designs? Is there no way of changing their minds at this stage? And what about the old kitchen wall?'

'It will need to be totally demolished to make room for the new conservatory link.'

Demolished. The image was so Technicolor real she couldn't believe it wasn't happening at that moment, and her head started spinning, dizzy with the revelation. The fruit trees and the old orchard would be gone, swept away.

'I'm sorry. But this is not the end.' He smiled at her, squeezing her hand and making her look at him. 'I have given you other options, remember? I kept my part of the bargain, and I can help you find new property to rent. You can still have Kingsmede Heritage Orchids on the other side of the village. You did agree that was a possibility. Didn't you?'

'Yes, I suppose I did, but I was hoping that there was still a chance.' Her voice faded away and she caught hold of Leo's arms for support. 'When did you find out that the plans had been approved?'

'This morning. But you have to understand, I couldn't tell you about any of these ideas until I had spoken to my aunt. I was sworn to secrecy, Sara. I'm so sorry it turned out like this.'

'Secrecy? I don't understand. Why were you sworn to secrecy?'

Leo took a firmer grasp of her hands and his tongue moistened his lower lip in a nervous gesture which made the blood run cold in her veins without his need to say another word.

'You already know that my aunt is Arabella Rizzi. What I couldn't tell you was that she asked me to take an objective look at Kingsmede Manor and come up with some ways of increasing the profitability of the hotel. That's why I stayed here after Helen's party last Saturday. I was here on a secret project for the Rizzi Hotel chain.'

CHAPTER TEN

'Oh, no, Leo. No. *You couldn't do that to me.*'

'I was telling you the truth. Aunt Arabella asked me to take a look at the hotel and come up with a few ideas on how to turn it around and make sure it had a future. But she insisted that my reason for being here should be kept a secret. That was why I couldn't tell you.'

'I don't believe it,' Sara replied in a thin, tired voice. 'You were working for the hotel chain the whole time you've been here.'

And then her eyes closed. 'Of course. How stupid of me. All that talk about how much you loved design and architecture—it was all a lie, wasn't it? A carefully constructed plan so that you could persuade a foolish country girl to tell you everything you needed to know about the hotel so that you could feed it back to the family.'

Leo shook his head very gently from side to side. 'No, this was not a paying job—this was a personal favour to someone who means a lot to me. And I wanted to tell you, many times, but I gave my word that I would keep the real reason for my being here a secret. I am so sorry.'

'Did you know? Did you know that I was the only person who had access to those garden designs before you talked to me at the party last Saturday? I need to know.'

She scanned his face, desperate for him to deny it and

fight back. But his full lips simply opened a little wider as though he was looking for words. But for once the lips she could kiss all day and never be satisfied were still.

'And I fell right into your trap, didn't I? I cannot believe that I actually showed you my own family photographs.' She looked up into his face and swallowed down hard. 'I have told you things about my family that only Helen and my mother know. Oh, Leo, I hope all this is worth it.'

Her lips were trembling so much Sara wondered that she could even form the words through the pain in her throat. Tears were streaming down her face.

'I thought you were better than that. I thought you were someone who knew their own worth and did not need validation from other people—it seems I was wrong about that too.'

He flung back his head and raised both hands in the air, breaking away from her and stepping back, his face twisted into disbelief and resentment.

'Do you really think that I am so shallow that I would seek you out and pretend that I didn't know who you were, just to see what juicy bits of information I could use to impress my aunt? Are you serious? Do you truly believe that I would use you like that?'

'Yes,' she whispered. 'That is exactly what I think. You want to walk into your family party and score as many points as you can in the prestige status game and don't you dare try to deny it because I can see it in your face.'

She grasped onto the back of the nearest chair because her legs were wobbling so badly she thought she might collapse. Suddenly she was finding it hard to breathe. Her heart was begging him to convince her that she could not be more wrong.

'Sara! That was unfair. The spa is the best commercial option to make the hotel viable. Just as moving a few miles away and starting up again is your best option. Perhaps you are the one who was not willing to take the risk and move out of your comfort zone and your safe little cottage and get on with changing your life!'

His voice was sad and hard and bitter—and her voice sounded worse.

They were arguing, and she felt sick.

'I did take a risk. Leo. I took a risk on you! I trusted you, and you lied to me and you used me to get the information needed to impress your family. Is this what it comes to, Leo? Because if this is your world, I want nothing to do with it. Or you.'

'Now what? You plan to walk home? Sara! I'll take you back to the cottage if that's what you want. Stop being such an idiot! You can't afford to let some sentimental attachment to the past or to people come between you and your business decision. Trust me. I know. You have to put that all behind you now and move on.'

'Trust you?' She stared at him, her mouth slightly open. 'Yes, I have been an idiot. I was stupid enough to believe that you actually cared about me and wanted to help, and now I know the truth. And I am right back to where I always am. Unloved and alone, just when I thought someone cared about me enough not to walk away. Well, don't worry about tomorrow. You truly are a Rizzi—and in the worst possible way. Your grandfather will be very proud of you. Why shouldn't he? You are just as ruthless as he is.'

But, instead of facing her and answering her accusations, Leo turned and walked away from her, flung the windows open wide and stormed the few steps out onto the balcony; his powerful muscular body that she had held against her, so tenderly warm only a few minutes earlier, now seemed as hard and as cold as the ancient stones.

And in an instant everything she had worked for over the past three years was blown away as dust and trampled underfoot.

All that sacrifice! All those exhausted, sleepless nights she had spent worrying about not having the money in time.

And for what?

Her grandmother was gone—her dream lost for ever. And now she was about to lose the nursery and her heritage.

And where did that leave her?

'Thank you for your offer of help,' she whispered, 'but I need to do this on my own. You are going back to your life. So don't worry about me,' she whispered. 'You have such a bright future with your important family and that's all that matters, isn't it? Proving that you are worthy of their approval? Well, good luck with that. I'm sure they will love you for putting business before some foolish sentimental nonsense about people and heritage. Pity. I thought you actually had the courage to stand up for yourself... And for me, but it looks like I was wrong about that—wrong about a lot of things.'

Suddenly she stepped back and reached into her bag for the tiny package she had wrapped so carefully in tissue and ribbon and left it on the table next to their untouched meal.

'Thank you for your help, Mr Grainger. This is yours now. And I wish I had never kept it.'

Sara soaked in one final dose of the vision of his enchanting body, picked up her bag, turned her back on him and tried to leave. Only her feet refused to move and she felt dizzy and exhausted.

She could stay.

She could surrender to the need and admiration for all

of the other wonderful and totally unexpected aspects that made Leo who he was. She could do that—and go right back to the girl she had been only a few days earlier when she went to the hotel to celebrate Helen's party.

So much had changed in her life since then. She should be grateful to Leo for helping her to change. Leo had made her stronger. And more determined than ever.

Simply the profile of him standing on the balcony in front of her with the sunset framing his head was a picture frozen in time that she knew would stay with her for ever. How ironic that it was her old bedroom in her old home. The old Sara would have jumped at him and apologised for being so silly.

No more.

'Goodbye, Leo. You got what you came for. I hope your meeting brings you happiness.'

He flinched once but did not turn and beg her forgiveness or ask her to stay. And she was not going to ask him.

She was tired of all the compromises she had made over the years to win the approval of people she cared about.

Which was why she silently took a grip on her clutch bag, gave him one final sideways glance, then turned her back on him and walked through the door and down the candlelit corridor towards the elevator which would carry her back to her life.

Some of the candles had blown out. Others were flickering in the breeze from the open door to her room.

If Leo Grainger truly needed her in his life then he was going to have to prove it was for the right reasons—or not at all.

CHAPTER ELEVEN

SARA yawned widely, jammed the telephone between her chin and her shoulder blade and started loading the collection of blush pink and cream orchids into protective sleeves inside the delivery crates she had dragged out of the rain into her potting shed office at some silly hour of the morning.

The sunny weather had changed during the long night into light showers. She had watched the droplets fall in the dawn light, refreshing the parched soil but not enough to top up her rainwater barrels.

'Did she say what shade of pink she was looking for?' Sara asked while struggling with a double-spiked plant. 'Hot pink or more of a pale pink?'

She stopped working, took control of the telephone and pressed her finger and thumb to the bridge of her nose. The florist was tearing her hair out at the number of times this bride's mother had changed her mind about the flowers only days before the ceremony. The orchids needed to be loaded into Mitzi and with the florist that morning or there would not be a bouquet or wedding flowers at all.

'Now calm down,' Sara said, trying not to panic or give in to the fact that she had only had two hours' sleep that night and most of that was in snatches of a few minutes at a time. 'I'm going to bring three shades of pink and plenty

of the ivory with the pink centres just in case she goes
back to the first idea and wants a single colour bouquet.
Be with you in twenty minutes and we can sort it all out
on Monday. No problem.'

No problem. Sara returned the phone to the charger,
closed her eyes and dropped her head onto the surface
of the desk, then realised that the pile of papers which
usually cushioned the blow was missing.

Drat Leo Grainger for forcing her to clear up and file
and sort and organize while they were searching for the
garden designs. At this rate she might actually be able to
find things and have desk space to work on.

Providing, of course, she had work to do at all. One
medium-sized greenhouse was not enough to supply florists and hotels all through the year. Especially with the
prospect of a huge spa building blocking out the natural
light and ventilation, to say nothing of the view out of her
kitchen window.

She sucked in a breath and sat back in her chair and let
her head fall back.

Leo. He would probably be having his breakfast in
the hotel now. No doubt planning his presentation which
would knock the socks off the family who had failed
him.

Oh, Leo. He had only been gone a few hours and she
already missed him so much it was like a physical pain
when she thought about it.

All during the long night she had half expected her
doorbell to ring and his familiar face to be there, asking
her to give him another chance.

Stupid girl. Just another way of punishing herself.

Her heart contracted at the mental picture she created
in her mind of his strong lithe body dressed in nothing
more than boxers, strolling around his hotel room like the

male lion he was named after. Master of all he surveyed, proud and powerful.

She could walk over to the hotel in five minutes and be right back in his arms again.

She had done it again—she had handed over responsibility for her future to another person—and she had fallen into the same trap and the same habits, just like before. She had given her love and her trust to someone who was capable of destroying her in the simple act of walking away, taking her hopes and her dreams with him as he went.

Her dad, her ex-boyfriend and now Leo Grainger.

What made it even worse was that she had spent the night tossing and turning and thinking through everything Leo had told her about herself. And he had been right about so many things that it infuriated her.

It was her decision to hand power over to other people in the vain hope that it would buy their love and approval. Hers. Nobody else's.

She had worked so hard to do what they asked her to do and in the end it had not been enough. She had seen the pattern too late to save herself from letting her grandmother down, and she would never forgive her mother for that.

Sara's eyes fluttered open and she blinked away her tiredness and tears. The newspaper clipping on the wall seemed to mock her. Businesswoman of the Year? What a joke.

She was a joke.

She had turned into a silly girl who was trying to prove a point by staying on in this cottage when she could have stayed in London and found another job. Two other companies had offered her work and she could have moved overseas and made a life for herself in the sunshine. Her

mother had even asked her to come and live with her after
the funeral so that they could spend some time together.
There was certainly enough room in her three bedroom
apartment in a smart part of London.

Sara shook her head at the thought of her mother and
her sharing the same all white kitchen and the oven which
still had the instruction booklet inside because her mother
had no plans to use it any time soon. Oh, no—her kitchen
appliances were for show and certainly not intended to be
soiled by food. Toast crumbs on her granite worktop were
punished with fierce glares and the liberal use of kitchen
paper.

Just like the artwork her mother collected which she
did not like but had been told to invest in. The only genuine things in the whole apartment were the antique floral
prints in her bedroom and the framed maps in the hall.
The rest was modern abstract prints and…

Sara's head shot up and she banged the heel of her right
hand several times against her forehead.

Of course! The entire hallway of her mother's apartment was decorated with architectural drawings and
maps—and most of them were of Kingsmede Manor.

That was where the missing part of the garden design
had to be. No doubt about it. She might have sold it to a
specialist dealer but there was a chance that she had kept
it. A small chance, but a chance all the same. The name
of the designer was something she could show off with
pride to her friends.

Sara glanced at her watch and gasped.

She had five hours to deliver the orchids to the florist, drive to London in her electric minivan, get to her
mother's flat, find the drawings and garden plans she
needed, persuade her mother to hand them over, then

somehow get the plans to Leo before he could make his final presentation at the hotel over lunch.

Her hand paused over the desk telephone, then pulled back as she swallowed down a moment of fear and excitement.

What was she doing?

Leo did not want the plans. He had already made up his mind. This was his big chance to impress the family who had disowned his mother by showing them what a big tough professional businessman he was.

Turning up out of the blue at the Rizzi family board meeting would only embarrass him—and, knowing her luck, she would probably barge in with all sails flying just when they were congratulating themselves on welcoming Leo back into the family business because of his totally objective methods.

And humiliate and embarrass herself in the process.

Wouldn't that be a proud and special moment?

But what was the alternative? Sit here and wait for the axe to fall and the sound of bulldozers tearing through the walled garden? Or try and do something to make them change their plans before it was too late?

And then there was Leo.

Both of them had said things yesterday which could not be unsaid, and she was sorry for that, but he had been at fault. Of course he would never break his word to his aunt. But it still hurt to know that he had been working as a spy the whole time and said nothing.

And yet he was sincere when he told her that he loved the garden designs. She had recognised his passion and his interest.

This could be her only chance to give Leo an option to show what he could do. And let the family take him for the talented man that he was and not just some clone of his grandfather.

Um. Who was she to talk? She had her own family issues to sort out.

Straight back, chin up, she took a deep breath and dialled the number for her mother's apartment. *Time to make the call she'd never thought she would.*

'Hi, Mum? Oh—did I wake you?'

Sara glanced at her watch. Just after 7:00 a.m. Ouch.

'Oh, yes, I'm fine. Sorry about that. I have to be up early for the florists. Anyway, I won't keep you long.' She gulped. 'Are you going to be at home this morning, Mum? I need your help with something and I'm afraid that it is very urgent.'

Leo relaxed his shoulders and looked across the antique coffee table at the smiling face of his aunt and the disinterested glare of his grandfather.

Paolo Leonardo Rizzi was a stern, silent, stocky man with short grey hair and an exquisite business suit who still held the power in the Rizzi family hotel business. Except at that moment he was looking rather uncomfortable and out of place as he wriggled around a little to find a dignified pose on one of the sumptuous but overstuffed sofas that Kingsmede Manor specialised in.

It had been Leo's aunt's idea to have a private meeting for just the three of them in her suite so that they would not be scowling at one other from opposite ends of an imposing boardroom table when they met after so many years.

So far, it had not been a total disaster.

His first meeting with this man who he had last seen at his parents' funeral when he was a boy had not been easy. Their initial handshake had been guarded, almost as though his grandfather thought that it was beneath his dignity as head of the family to give Leo his tacit approval. And of course Paolo Rizzi had noticed that Leo was wearing a fabulous diamond ring, a Rizzi family heirloom, but was far too proud to do anything but glance at it and then glare at Leo through narrowed eyes.

Well, if that had been a tactic to intimidate Leo—it had failed. Miserably.

A week ago Leo would have been infuriated by that slight, but now he accepted it for what it was. One person's opinion. He did not need Paolo Rizzi's approval, but he would like it. And that made all the difference.

His aunt had asked him to present his opinion—and that was what he was going to do. Leo inhaled slowly. This was a tough audience but he was used to that.

They did not need to know that he had worked most of the night pulling together research and background information to create two completely new designs.

Sara had been right.

He had tossed and turned for hours, going over and over in his mind what she had said to him: 'You are just as ruthless as he is,' before giving up and starting work on the plans that he wanted to present.

He had become the very person he despised. He had become his grandfather. So focused and driven by the need to succeed that he had lost his family and his ability to connect to real people like Sara. *And it had shocked him to the core.*

Shocked him so much that he decided to do something to prove that Leo Grainger was his father's son, not just Paolo Rizzi's grandson.

And now was the moment of truth. Time to find out if all of that hard work had been worth it and his family would appreciate his ideas.

His family. He could see some resemblance to his mother in his aunt, but his grandfather? Oh, yes, she was there. From the blue-grey eyes and strong handsome face to the broad shoulders and natural poise, this was probably what he was going to look like one day.

He could see where his mother had inherited her good looks from. And maybe the strength to stand alone and make her own path in the world. He could not have been prouder of his mother and the decision she'd taken to go against her imposing father.

And Sara. Sara was right here giving him that edge as well.

Perhaps that was why Leo sat back against the sofa cushions as though this was a friendly family gathering rather than a formal business meeting and was rewarded by a definite lift in his grandfather's eyebrows for a few seconds, until his aunt laughed at something Leo said and passed him more coffee before she spoke.

'I am so pleased that Leo was kind enough to take a few days out of his hectic schedule to give me a second opinion on the turnaround plans for Kingsmede Manor. I am really looking forward to hearing his ideas. So, over to you, Leo.'

'Thank you, Aunt Arabella. It was my pleasure. And my delight. Kingsmede Manor is a beautiful property with enormous potential.'

Leo passed two copies of the dossier of his plans across the coffee table. Only his grandfather sat in disinterested silence while his aunt dived in with chuckles of delight and amazement.

'I will leave you to read the detail about the two proposals on the table. The spa extension is a great idea but the design is too modern. After a few days at the hotel, I know one thing. It is the heritage and design history of the house which makes it unique. The Fenchurch family who built the Manor had stunning glasshouses, an orangery and a superb conservatory with the most amazing level of craftsmanship. We need to incorporate those elements in any spa design if we want to make this hotel so very special.'

He gestured towards the dossiers. 'You can see that I have added a conservatory-style link building between the main house and the spa and changed the spa layout to resemble more closely the original concepts.'

His aunt responded by waving the folder towards him with a nod. 'This is stunning, Leo. I cannot believe you came up with all of this work in a few days.'

'I can't claim all of the credit. At the turn of the century the owners hired a famous garden designer to landscape their grounds and create special glasshouses for the orchids they were passionate about. The designs in the second option came directly from that work. The orchid collection at Kingsmede Manor was so remarkable that they used to attract visitors from all over the country. Only a couple of the original orchid houses remain at the property but they are very special.'

'How special?' she replied, her eyebrows raised and eyes full of interest.

'Special enough for me to make some preliminary enquiries with orchid organisations around the world. The market potential for specialist holidays is huge—and that was only scratching the surface.'

His aunt shook her head and turned from page to page of photographs.

'I had no idea at all. Lady Fenchurch did not even mention this history of the Manor.'

'A huge pity. There is so much potential here. For example, I would also like to recommend that we commission the creation of a new orchid variety in honour of the hotel. The Kingsmede Manor Orchid would have elegance, class, heritage and style—but with a perfume that is totally irresistible. It would be unique and exclusive to the hotel and to this hotel chain and could create a powerful symbol for the brand.'

'An orchid? Well, that could certainly be very appealing to a niche clientele with discerning tastes.' His aunt smiled, but then a very masculine voice with a strong accent growled out from the other sofa.

'You must really care about this hotel very much to be so committed to the long-term future of this house and jeopardise your own reputation in the process? I thought Grainger Consulting were more professional than to engage in foolish sentimentality and connection to some vague idea of the past.'

Leo looked up at the most senior director on the Rizzi family board and one side of his mouth rose in a smile. 'I do love this house. I love everything about it, but most of all I admire the spirit of the place and those who have loved it and cared for it over the generations to make it the building it is today. I arrived here as a guest only a few days ago for the very first time, and since then I have fallen in love with it as any other guest will do. It is a unique place.'

He shuffled forward onto the edge of the sofa and leant towards Paolo Rizzi. 'I have spoken to one of the descendants of the late owner of the house and she has agreed to share the original designs for the gardens necessary to implement the restoration. If these plans go ahead this hotel will become one of the landmark boutique hotels in this part of England. What is more, a garden of this quality would attract gardeners and specialist groups to the hotel and create a perfect wedding setting and a luxury conference venue.'

Leo paused for dramatic effect before adding, 'Kingsmede Manor could be the gem in your hotel collection.'

Arabella inhaled deeply and gave a gentle nod. 'That is quite a claim. But I like the proposal, I like it a lot. Although I do have a question.'

Leo tilted his head towards his aunt even though he felt as though his grandfather's eyes were trying to burn a hole in the centre of his forehead.

'You said that *we* should commission an orchid. Was that simply a slip of the tongue or have I finally persuaded you to join the family business after all these years? Leo?'

He smiled back at her. 'Many years ago I took the decision to leave the hotel trade and go into direct business management.'

He shrugged casually, then strolled to the back of his aunt's sofa and rested one hand lightly on one of her shoulders and she immediately raised her hand and held his.

'It was a hard decision to make after all you have done for me. I would not be standing here now if it was not for the opportunity you gave me. And now I have another opportunity to do something remarkable for myself and this time it concerns my whole family.'

His grandfather lifted his head and frowned at Leo. 'What do you mean by that?' he said.

'Simply this. I do not want to spend the rest of my life trying to prove that I am worthy of being part of the Rizzi family. I know who I am and what I am capable of—but I think you already know that. What you don't know is that I have decided to sell my consultancy business and retrain as an architect. It was the only thing I wanted to do as a boy.'

He glanced from the puzzled expression of his grandfather to the stunned face of his aunt. 'These past few days at Kingsmede have shown me that I have a choice on how I live my life going forward—and who I spend my life with. It may take a while, but I would like to take the time to get to know my Rizzi family. If they want that.'

He smiled down at Arabella, who was looking up at him with tears in her eyes.

But, before anyone could answer, there was a strange clanking noise from outside the window and Leo glanced out to see a very familiar off-white electric delivery van called Mitzi clatter its way into the circular drive outside the Manor and stop directly behind his grandfather's Bentley.

The wheels had scarcely come to a halt before the driver's door was flung open and a short-haired girl in a bright yellow T-shirt and flower-patterned capri pants jumped out and ran to the back of the van.

Sara! What on earth was she doing here?

Leo shook his head and grinned. *The cavalry had arrived.*

'You are so like your mother I cannot tell you,' his aunt whispered with a glint in her eyes.

'Thank you. I take that as a very great compliment,' Leo replied.

'You should. She was a remarkable woman I was proud to call my daughter, and it looks like she had a son with a good head on his shoulders. Orchids.' His grandfather sniffed. 'Might work. And it is a lot more interesting than another boring swimming pool that nobody uses.'

And with one nod the decision was made. 'Let's do it. And you—' and he pointed one finger at Leo '—I could use an architect on the team. Come to see me when you're ready to start that training. This is a family business, so let's keep it that way.'

But, before he could say another word, the door to the suite burst open and a slim brunette staggered through with a huge picture in her arms. It was so large that her fingers could hardly stretch to grasp the ornate gilt edges and it was in great danger of falling at any second.

'I found it,' Sara gasped as Leo took the weight and lowered the map onto the table, then gave a wave around the room. 'Hi everybody.'

'So I see.' He grinned in reply, then gestured across the coffee table. 'Here is someone I would like you both to meet. My friend Sara Fenchurch used to live at Kingsmede Manor.' And then he paused long enough to take Sara's hand. 'Sara is also the woman I am in love with. Who just happens to run the orchid nursery just across the lane.'

'Ah-ha. So this change of plan was not entirely business-driven after all?'

'The plan stands on its own merits, Grandfather. But yes, it was Sara who first told me about the remarkable garden designs which could make this house a unique tourist attraction. It was my decision to do more research into the profitability of a niche market. My recommendation stands. It's the right choice.'

'He is in love with me,' she said in a stunned voice as she grinned back at Leo. 'Well, fancy that. I suppose I have to marry him now and make an honest man of him. Good thing I am totally in love with you too, Leo. And I know the perfect wedding location.'

'Wait a minute. Are you asking me to marry you? In front of all my family?' Leo said, his mouth half-open in shock.

Sara nodded. 'Best way. My mother will be here in

about an hour to make sure that you are the kind of man who is suitable for her daughter. Character references may be required. But, as far as I am concerned, you are the only man I could ever marry. The only man I want as my husband and the father of my children. And I am saying that in front of your family and proud to do so. Marry me, Leonardo Reginald. Marry me and make me the happiest woman alive!'

His answer was to gather her up into his arms, lifting her off her feet as they both laughed and squealed with happiness before Leo kissed her with such passion and love that they were both breathless and exhilarated when they came back down to earth.

There was a low growl from the sofa and Leo's grandfather heaved himself to his feet.

'I've seen and heard enough. Arabella, my dear. Let's find out if this hotel has any good champagne. I need a drink and it looks like this family has something to celebrate. It is about time.'

EPILOGUE

'AND for the second year running the award for Business-woman of the Year goes to...Sara Grainger of Kingsmede Heritage Orchids!'

The ballroom of the prestigious London hotel exploded into a riot of cheering and wild applause and hoots of laughter.

Someone planted a kiss in the vague direction of her cheek and Sara knew that she was being hugged by some-one fragrant—probably Arabella or her mother, but she was so bedazzled and dizzy from the flashing camera lights that she did not see who or where.

Blinking several times, Sara turned back to the table. Helen and Caspar, Leo and his aunt and her own mother were on their feet cheering and applauding and giddy with delight and love—so much love, she felt carried aloft to the podium and the smiling regional organiser who handed her the prestigious award.

'Many congratulations, Sara,' he said. 'The judges were extremely impressed by your remarkable work on the restoration of the Kingsmede Manor gardens. How does it feel to know that your family's heritage will live on in such a wonderful way?'

Sara looked out across the sea of faces until she found Leo, who was smiling back at her with such pride and happiness that she thought her heart would burst with love enough to last a lifetime.

'I have enjoyed every minute of this project,' she replied. 'Grainger Consulting has put together a wonderful team of architects and garden designers. But we could not have done any of the work without the wonderful support of the Rizzi family and so many friends who have invested in the future of this remarkable hotel that I used to call home. This award belongs to them and the whole team and I'm so grateful for their passion and their time and the opportunity they gave me. Thank you all for making my dream a reality.'

The applause was still echoing around her as she made her way down from the platform in her stunning designer eveningwear until she was back in the embrace of the man who had made everything possible and the two families he had brought together.

Her husband, the trainee architect and garden designer.

And at that moment, as she smiled back at the man she loved, she was a winner all over again and could ask for no greater reward.

* * * * *

MILLS & BOON®
By Request

RELIVE THE ROMANCE WITH THE BEST OF THE BEST

A sneak peek at next month's titles...

In stores from 11th August 2016:

- **Heir to His Legacy** – Chantelle Shaw, Cathy Williams & Lucy Monroe

- **A Pretend Proposal** – Jackie Braun, Ally Blake & Robyn Grady

In stores from 25th August 2016:

- **His Not-So-Blushing Bride** – Kat Cantrell, Anna DePalo & Fiona Brand

- **Her Happy-Ever-After Family** – Michelle Douglas, Barbara Hannay & Soraya Lane

---

MILLS & BOON®

The Regency Collection – Part 1

Let these roguish rakes sweep you off to the
Regency period in part 1 of our collection!

Order yours at **www.millsandboon.co.uk/regency1**